THE ARNASAID SERIES

THE

MacKenzies

OF

TRANNOCH

FIONA H. PRESTON

@iamselfpub
www.iamselfpublishing.com

For my Mum, who, to my everlasting sadness, did not get to read this book. She was my inspiration and friend, and always believed in me, in everything I tried to achieve, most especially my writing.

As the land breathes in and out the tide, so too lives shift, quietly lapping between evil and good.

Chapter One

Colonel Mason Smith MacKenzie presided over his family like a reincarnation of the last King of Scotland. He stood on a little hillock overlooking his ancient seat of power, the magnificent Trannoch, an anachronism of tradition and class rule. The house itself, complete with towers and too many rooms and windows for anyone to be bothered to count, was a huge castle-like residence five miles inland from the coast, sitting on an extensive chunk of land which spread out for miles around. Trannoch gave ostentatious a whole new meaning, and opulence was as much part of the daily diet as porridge and whisky. The Colonel prided himself on having one of the very few existing estate houses which had not yet opened its doors to the public. This was due to the fact that he was rich beyond measure. He was therefore afforded the luxury of turning up his nose and dismissing the idea of paying visitors, as being distasteful. Tradition was kept alive by the Colonel's bombastic and manipulative attitude, which ensured *all ye who enter here* felt they were stepping back a few hundred years into a bygone existence.

Lady Ailsa Hamilton-Dunbar was the antitheses of everything the Colonel held dear. She was a modern, 21st Century woman. Brought up by adoptive parents in London, she had experienced no such luxurious lifestyle, until she was 'found' by her birth father. Sir Angus had brought her to Storm Winds, the neighbouring, rivalling estate to Trannoch, and had bestowed her with her inheritance, a fortune and a title, before he died and left her to it. Ailsa had made the life-changing decision to make a go of running her estate, which clutched the cliffs and overlooked the sea. If she had been in any way starry-eyed about her future, living alongside the Colonel and his family soon swept any dreamy notions from her head.

The MacKenzies were a force to be reckoned with.

'Your tea Ailsa, and come away from that window! You'll be back to square one and ill again if you don't!' Miss Cochrane, or 'Cocky', had been the housekeeper at Storm Winds since the days of Ailsa's father Sir Angus' childhood. Now the housekeeper looked after the thirty five year old woman, heiress, Lady and owner of the vast estate. Cocky had witnessed Ailsa throwing herself into her new life with a vigour and goodwill that had endeared her to the older woman, who had never married nor had children of her own.

'Thanks, Cocky,' Ailsa said, as she turned from the stone balcony, leaving the long doors open so the wind could circulate and she could hear the sound of the sea. She climbed back into bed, smothering herself with the huge duvet, and sipping her tea she cupped the mug to bring her chilled hands to life.

'Dr MacKenzie called and said he would join you for breakfast in an hour. Would you like me to ask Jean to fry some kippers?'

'Yes, Cocky, that would be wonderful, thank you.' Max loved kippers, although she loathed them, much preferring salmon.

'I'll have Jean set out the smoked salmon too.' Miss Cochrane's taught smile and abrupt way of talking belied the fact that she had great affection for Ailsa, and had grown to love her like a daughter over the last year. Wild horses would not have dragged this fact from the tight-mouthed housekeeper.

'Cocky said she found you standing on the balcony freezing when she took you your tea. Are you absolutely mad? Don't you understand how ill you have been?' This was Max's affectionate greeting as he swept into the breakfast room at Storm Winds an hour later.

Ailsa watched him as he sat at the table, put his plate in front of him, and reached for the teapot.

'Erm, excuse me?' she pointed to her lips. He smiled, got up and gave her a hug and an affectionate kiss before sitting again.

'Anyway, I wasn't freezing, Cocky exaggerates. I love the early morning turn of the tide and the sun coming up – and, I haven't coughed for days.' She proceeded to go into a volley of coughs, tight and hard, until she sat back in her seat exhausted.

Max looked concerned and angry. 'You see! This is what I mean about not looking after yourself! You are recovering from pneumonia, and you can't even follow basic instructions to ensure you are not ill again. What do I need to do to make you understand?'

'Max, I'm fine,' was her too-bright response. 'I'm not an invalid. Please don't treat me like one. Anyway, how's things at Trannoch?'

Max looked at her in exasperation, then mellowed as he took in the faint shadows beneath her eyes and the thin figure which had shed more than a stone in weight over the last few months. 'Why don't we go to Italy, to the villa for a few weeks, to give you time to recover?'

'You know, nothing would make me feel better than going to Italy, but it's only March, and would still be quite cold there. Plus, I really don't want to leave at the moment. There is so much to organise here, I can't wait to get stuck in.' She buttered a thin slice of toast in the pretence that she was going to eat it, then laid it down and sipped her tea instead. 'I promise we'll go soon though,' she smiled apologetically.

He looked at her long and hard. 'Okay, but you are not to do any estate work for at least the next few weeks. Roddy and Stephen will do the land work as usual, and Gennina can cope in the office without you. And, you may not...' He got no further as she interrupted him vigorously.

'Now, wait a minute, "you may not," is not the kind of thing I will take from you or anyone else. Come on, Max! I'm not Aria!' she said, referring to his daughter. 'So, just button it, Doc; we are a couple! Remember that newish development? You and me? Equals?'

He grinned suddenly. 'Sorry,' he said sheepishly. He got up, put his arm around her shoulders and pecked her on the cheek. He was aware again of how painfully thin she felt.

He was such a caring, blundering, at times socially inept person, but she loved him, nonetheless. 'How long's it been?'

He looked surprised. 'How long has what been?'

'Us. How long's Us been?'

'You know, for a writer, your grammar is awful.' He tried to deflect the question by saying.

'Well?'

'Oh, about a year? No, you moved up here to Scotland and took over Storm Winds, let's say, almost a year and a half ago?'

She looked at him incredulously. 'No, you daft lump! I moved here just over a year ago, but I was talking about our relationship. That night on the headland, since then, when you tried to make a move on me.'

'Made a move! How dare you!' He grinned. 'You were the one making all the moves on me...'

'Right you two, that's enough!' Cocky laughed, as she scolded them like they were a couple of school kids.

Max, or Maxwell to give him his proper name, was the third son of Colonel Mason Smith MacKenzie, patriarch and ruler of the stately and magnificent Trannoch. Surly Noel was the eldest son, the handsome womaniser Malcolm next, and weak-minded, feeble Thomas the youngest. Ailsa had gone over the last year so many times, how her vulnerability at being thrown into managing her inheritance had placed her into the path of both Malcolm and Stephen Millburn, her part time estate Ghillie, both with disastrous results. Max was the local doctor. She had met him at her first dinner party at Trannoch . Max had been aloof and non-committal, and Ailsa thought that he was the most obtuse man she had met. All this had changed; however, when she realised Max was worth more than his three brothers put together, with his sincerity, and his caring disposition. He'd shown himself to be a really good father to his two children, Ryan and Aria, who had been left motherless when Max's wife Elaine had died around 6 years ago.

'Well, pour me some more tea, and tell me about Trannoch,' she smiled.

'Well, Malcolm is back. He returned last night and went straight to his rooms. He joined us for dinner but said very little to anyone. Olivia kept to her own quarters – it's quite obvious she can't bear to be anywhere near him.'

'Who could blame her? She must detest him for what he did. I wouldn't want to look at him either. I can't believe how the Colonel was able to get him off the hook.'

Max looked thoughtful. 'I don't think Dad had to do much persuading. Olivia was determined to get the best for her baby, and, before you say anything, I'm in no way judging her for that! A life at Trannoch, where the baby will be brought up in the lap of luxury and go to the best schools, obviously seems a much better prospect to her than being cast aside on her own.'

'Yes, I agree, but who wouldn't want the best for their baby in that position?'

'That's exactly what I was trying to say. Malcolm is a womaniser who deserves to be in jail, but that's not on Dad's "to-do" list for anytime soon.'

'I can't believe how he was able to brush aside not just the rape, but Olivia's attempt to murder Malcolm.'

'The Colonel can do anything he wants, Ailsa,' Max said dryly, buttering another slice of toast. 'You know that Malcolm in Switzerland and Germany for the last few months, supposedly letting the dust settle. And, of course, Hunter joined him there for a few weeks.'

Ailsa looked at him in shock at this astonishing fact, so quietly put over, about her hated birth mother.

'Hunter? What the hell was she joining Malcolm for? What has she got to do with anything?' Ailsa asked disbelievingly. That beautiful, treacherous woman who would stop at nothing to get what she wanted. Ailsa could not and would not accept that woman in her life.

'Ailsa, I think your mother, sorry, Hunter,' he added hurriedly, 'and Malcolm have been having an affair for some time.'

'Well, now that you mention it, I did have my suspicions. That night of the party, when Olivia set us all up, I was sure I saw them sneak off together.'

'Yes, it doesn't surprise me. Malcolm and Hunter are, unfortunately, two of a kind. I don't know if the Colonel suspects Malcolm is with Hunter. Dad has always loved her. He's allowing her to stay at Trannoch for this reason. He said he was "sorry for her".'

'I can't believe the way she acts.' Ailsa shook her head as she chewed the words. 'She will never be welcome here again. What about his kids? What about Melissa and David? They lost their mother last year, and now, in the wake of raping an Italian student, their father decides to carry on an affair with a woman old enough to be his own mother!'

Max looked serious. 'Well maybe not quite old enough to be his mother, but, I agree, it is not a pretty set up. But there is another side to this.'

'Of course there is...' Ailsa was dripping sarcasm. 'You're going to tell me next that the Colonel is having an affair with Olivia, Noel is trying to win back Clem, and Thomas is not the Colonel's youngest son.' She looked at his face and decided that maybe she had gone a little too far. Max sat back in his chair and looked at her with that appraising, searching gaze of his.

'You know, the best gauge I have for you getting better is when you wheel in the heavy sarcasm. But you'll never be quite as good as me on that front!'

Ailsa laughed and cuffed him gently on the shoulder. 'Sorry, that wasn't very nice.'

'Malcolm is very ill,' he suddenly and startlingly said. 'We don't know if he will last the year.'

Whatever Ailsa might have expected, it wasn't this. She put down her cup and she too sat back in her chair, soberly doing her own searching of his rugged features and the tiny permanent frown etched on his forehead.

'It's prostate cancer. A particularly aggressive kind. He's had some treatment, but one of the reasons he went to Switzerland was to look up an old doctor friend of his and get some advice. The prognosis was not good.'

'When did you know this?' Ailsa fixed him in a stare.

Max looked back at her in surprise. 'Well obviously, I've known for some time, around two months, before he went to Switzerland.'

'I just thought you might have mentioned it before now,' she said huffily. 'We're supposed to be together – a partnership... whatever you want to call it.'

'Ailsa you've been ill with pneumonia for the last six weeks. You were particularly bad; I haven't dealt with such a severe case in years. What would it have achieved? You hardly knew where you were half the time. I wasn't going to say, "Ailsa, wake up out of your delirium till I tell you something about Malcolm"...'

The thought of Max actually doing this made her giggle. 'Okay, but firstly you need to stop seeing me as a patient. We're an item, Max! You just referred to me as a "case". Secondly, please just involve me in things, and trust me. It's what people do in a relationship.'

'Is it?' he grinned. 'You mean when people are "an item"? I can't believe you would say that. It's like something my children would say, not the *Lady of Storm Winds*, like you.'

'Oh do shut up and get going or you'll be late for surgery!' She stood on considerably weakened legs to see him to the door. 'Well!' she thought, as she took tea and toast into her library, where a fire was already lit, and curled up in her armchair. This was her favourite room in the vast estate house which had so many rooms – very few of them used at the moment. She loved the slightly musty smell of the books, which reminded her of her childhood, her huge oak table where she did her writing, and the snug area around the fire where she now sat, two steps down from the main library.

She thought about her conversation with Max. 'It seems Max is right, and even the Colonel can't fix everything,' she contemplated.

Max's children, Ryan and Aria, or Ariadne to give her hated 'Sunday' name, were almost 14 and 10 years respectively, and were coming home from school for the weekend. Ailsa was feeling quite apprehensive about seeing them again as it would now be the second time since their Christmas holidays, and since her relationship began with Max. They knew of course; their father had picked them up from school and told them that he and Ailsa were together. But, true to Max's introspective streak, he told Ailsa little about the conversation, and less about what he thought they were feeling about the situation. From Max's slim account, she decided Aria was quite happy, but Ryan was upset and a bit obstructive. She had no idea what Ryan thought about her. He was more similar in personality and characteristics to his father than his sister; he kept his feelings to himself and was not outwardly sociable.

Ailsa was feeling much more like herself when Spring checked in with its fresh winds and showers, bright spring flowers and new trees budding. Storm Winds opened its windows wide to the new month, curtains flapping bravely in the salty breeze, and brooms and dusters scoured the rooms looking for winter-dusty corners.

As she had done since she came to Storm Winds, Ailsa had a routine of work which shaped her days. After breakfast, she took Bluebell and Rosie, her Yorkshire Terriers, for a walk along the headland. She then worked on her writing in the library for a few hours until lunchtime. After this, she worked in the estate offices on anything to do with their charity work or events management which needed her attention. Gennina, her trusty secretary or PA, as the bubbly blonde liked to call herself, guided her through the piles of paperwork which had to be signed or read or both. She had done little since her illness, and had been warned by Max to take it easy, so instead of the three or four hours spent in the office she began with an hour.

'Mornin' boss.' Stephen Millburn strode into the estate office, seeming to fill the room with his handsome frame and dark good looks. He was dressed in his usual jeans and mountaineering jacket, a necessity in the inclement Scottish weather. 'Feeling better?'

'Morning, Stephen. Yes, thank you,' Ailsa answered, and backed into her tiny office in order to hide the faint flush which crept up her cheeks. She was bemused and angry that she still had flutters whenever she saw Stephen, especially at times when she was unprepared to meet him. 'Why is this happening to me when I absolutely adore Max?' She took a large gulp of water from the tumbler on her desk.

A gentle tap sounded on the open door behind her.

'May I come in?'

'Of course, pull up a pew.' Her voice was as cheerful as usual. She hoped it was hiding how uneasy she felt, but she did manage to catch his eyes on her disappearing flush before he stood beside her desk.

'I just wondered if you knew that we usually begin preparations for our "Glorious 12th" shoots round about now. I know you were only here five minutes last year when we needed to start, so I thought I would ask.'

'Funnily enough, Gennina mentioned it yesterday,' she said, looking at her calendar. 'How many guests normally come on a shoot?'

'When Sir Angus was here, it was around thirty. Two or three to a room mainly. The East Wing looks like a lot of dormitories. It's a bit shabby.'

Ailsa had left the East Wing mostly unused, as she inhabited the West Wing which overlooked the sea. She had only got around to decorating some of the West Wing so far, and she realised that the East Wing may need some serious refreshment, if not overhauled altogether.

'Okay, would you like to discuss with Gennina what is needing done, and then come back to me?'

'I was thinking more of a four-way meeting, if you are available?' he said, and she felt irritation rising unaccountably as she reminded herself that Stephen was not the kind of guy to take instruction on what needed to be done, especially something he had organised successfully for years.

'Who's the fourth? Roddy?'

'Yes. I know he wasn't here when Sir Angus was alive, but I really feel that an open discussion about what is wanted and needed from the shoot works best. Roddy has some good ideas and is willing to work hard.'

'Okay, but not today. This is my first day back in circulation here, and I have lots of things to do. What about tomorrow, say around 2pm?'

'Perfect,' he said very slowly, then, with a tiny bow of his head, left the room.

Alberto Franelli was in his local bar in the small Italian village of Guelemoro, around nine kilometres from Sienna. It was a traditional village, complete with a small village square, and a church almost as big as a cathedral. Alberto was a simple man, who had worked hard to build the best life he could for his beloved wife and his beautiful daughter. He ate bread and cheese with his own tomatoes and olive oil, every lunchtime. He went to church every Sunday, and met his friends every Friday and Saturday. He was not a learned man. In the evenings, on the porch overlooking their few acres of land, he had played his guitar while his wife sang, or read her books. Olivia, his only daughter, had liked this minimal existence to a point, but her spirit had always been in the tops of the trees and the waves on the sand. Alberto had known he was biding his time, and that he wouldn't be able to keep her in Guelemoro. Every man in the village had an eye for his daughter. She was like a modern day Sophia Loren, with her beautiful dark eyes and full sensual lips. She was smart too. She got that from her mother's side. He was so proud when she had been the first of the large, extended Franelli family to go to University. She had gone to Sienna to study Art History, and everyone in Guelemoro had known how she was doing and how well she had passed her exams. Then, when she wanted to go to Scotland, Alberto threw up his hands in despair. He didn't even know where Scotland was. Olivia showed him on the map, and he was astounded it was so far away and so very cold and wet, apparently. He had heard about the country through the football matches he attended occasionally with his friends. AC Milan was Alberto's team and he was sure he had seen Scotland and Italy play a friendly game at one point. He already had his own building business, and this elevated state allowed him to treat his friends to an overnight in a comfortable hotel and tickets for the games.

Alberto was a man worth knowing.

Olivia had always written to her mother and father. Alberto was not good on the phone. He had a short fuse, and when he said the wrong thing, or was corrected, he became angry and incoherent. Olivia's mother had been ill for some months, unbeknown to her daughter. When she had written a long letter to her parents telling them about the 'attack' that took place the previous year, and how she was now expecting a baby, her mother was already in hospital. Her doting father selectively read the letter out to Olivia's mother. He skirted over the bad bits, which he knew she did not need to know. She had sadly passed away hours after this, without learning of the baby. However, being a devout Catholic, she would have been distraught in her last days had she known her first grandchild had been conceived in such a way. She passed peacefully and happily away thinking her own child had made the best life for herself, and that the Franelli line was intact.

Alberto's only solace from the letter was that Olivia seemed to have landed lucky on the money side of things. She had been taken in by a rich family, or rather, a woman, a 'Lady' somebody or other, who was looking after her.

This evening, he had a group of friends around him, toasting to his good fortune. He had sold his business, making more money from the transaction than he ever had in his life, and was going to Scotland to be with his daughter and expected grandchild. The details of the father of this grandchild were little more than sketchy, in fact he knew virtually nothing. His pals couldn't have cared less. His friends circled around Alberto, Francesco raising his glass and noisily clinking glasses with them all shouting, 'Alberto, our friend, Salute! Salute!' They all drained their glasses and clapped him on the back, shaking his hand and wishing him well. As they turned to the bar to fill their glasses, Alberto found himself outside the circle and, without a word, turned and walked from the bar.

He was going to Scotland, to find Olivia, and cheerfully kill the bastard who had forced himself upon his daughter.

Chapter Two

'Would Friday night be okay to ask the kids over for dinner?' Max asked. They were cuddled up on a huge sofa in Ailsa's favourite blue sitting room. The open curtains gave them a view of the sunset as they sat sipping their red wine. They were listening to one of Max's favourite requiems. Ailsa had never been a huge fan of classical music, but that was really because she hadn't been exposed to it. Max was planning to change her mind in this respect, and she had to admit she loved the strains of the Pie Jesu.

Ailsa hesitated just long enough for him to draw away from her and study her face. 'Ailsa?'

Ryan and Aria were home at Trannoch for a half-term week. Ailsa had seen them only once, on Sunday evening, when the Colonel gathered the family together for a traditional Sunday roast. Ailsa had an open invitation to this, but last Sunday had been the first time she had felt fit to socialise after her long illness. Aria had been her usual bright bubbly self, talking about the clubs and activities she was taking part in at school, but Ryan had been openly hostile to Ailsa, angering his father and grandfather considerably. Two people, however, were highly amused: the lofty, beautiful Carys, and Hunter.

'Don't speak to Ailsa like that, young man!' the Colonel, who was incapable of speaking quietly, shouted at his grandson. Ryan, who knew better than to answer his grandfather back, threw a strop and stomped away from the table. Max had followed suit, but returned after about ten minutes, with no Ryan in tow, and refused to say what had gone on.

'I hope you are not still dwelling on what happened with Ryan on Sunday?' Max stroked Ailsa's hair.

'No, because it was not what he said, it was the way he was answering me. I mean, I'm not like you or the Colonel. I don't expect anyone to be deferential – I hate that – or use my title. I actually still can't get used to that myself, and don't really want to either, but the MacKenzie kids have all been brought up in a very old-fashioned traditional way – I've heard them calling you and their grandfather "Sir" on occasion – I mean, God, that's almost unheard of in the 21st century.'

'Well, Ailsa, you've got to remember that we MacKenzies come from a different world to you. You are very modern, but we're not. Dad demanded that level of respect from us when we were all young, and I guess it has just evolved from there. I certainly have never asked them to call me Sir, but they live at school most of the time, and they probably see us in the same light as they do their teachers.'

Ailsa looked keenly at him. 'Don't you think that's sad? That your children are so institutionalised to the extent that they view their grandfather and their dad in the same way as their teachers?'

Max sighed, trying to explain. 'Ailsa it's not like that. They have been brought up differently, and taught to respect in a way that none of the youngsters are that I see in my surgery these days.'

'Yeah, well welcome to the real world! And that aside, Max, Ryan just doesn't like me. I don't know how to reach him.'

Max picked up the remote and put on some different music. He rubbed the bridge of his nose as if he had a headache. 'He liked you fine before we got together. He just needs time to adjust, that's all. Don't try too hard.'

Ailsa was silent for several minutes. 'Okay, well why don't I give Jean the night off and we can all congregate in the kitchen? You can all help me to make pizza and we can sit there rather than in the dining room to eat?'

Max brightened at this. 'Great idea!' And the evening passed very pleasantly until he called for Jim Hutton and was driven over to Trannoch. He stayed with Ailsa at Storm Winds often, but when the children were home from school the Colonel insisted on him staying at Trannoch. Ailsa had teased him about doing what his father told him, like he was a teenager rather than a grown man in his forties, but Max insisted he actually agreed with this edict. The last thing he wanted for his children was instability. They had seen enough of the behaviour of their aunts and uncles and even their grandfather, at Trannoch, to know that the bad behaviour of their elders wasn't necessarily acceptable for them. Max didn't want his children to be affected by this and to feel insecure. In addition, they were away at boarding school most of the time, and he didn't see them at all, apart from the occasional weekend visit and holidays. So when Ailsa had broached the subject over why she couldn't stay over at Trannoch sometimes, just so that they could be together, Max had laughed and said the Colonel would never hear of it unless she slept in a separate room. Therefore, he didn't even bother to ask him. Ailsa thought, with all the womanising and treachery going on right under his nose, the Colonel was such a controlling hypocrite it was unbelievable.

Clem MacKenzie had at least escaped Trannoch. She had been married to Noel, eldest of the MacKenzie brothers, and was one of Ailsa's best friends. Certainly, Ailsa had her London friends, Connie and Jan, who visited often, but Clem was her only real true friend in Scotland. They had both been through so much in the last year, but a huge misunderstanding and subsequent painful argument between the two, concerning Stephen Millburn, had threatened to end their friendship forever. Clem and Stephen had been a couple since the previous November. Clem lived in a small building which housed her tiny art gallery, with a studio flat beneath, in the nearby village of Arnasaid. Since getting together with the estate manager who worked across both estates, Clem had by degrees been asked back to Trannoch for dinner and some other occasions. The Colonel had seen fit to accept her back chiefly because he had finally accepted that her marriage to Noel was over, but more so because he thought of Stephen almost as another son, and wanted him to be happy. Stephen had his own rooms at Trannoch, living as part of the family.

Clem had asked her over for lunch, and Ailsa decided to walk the few miles across the headland from Storm Winds, so she could take Bluebell and Rosie with her. It was a beautiful day. It was windy, coming in blustering gusts, but the sun shone warmly for March. The ground underfoot sparkled in the sunshine one minute, then darkened as if the blinds had closed, so wildly flew the clouds across the sky. Primroses clustered round the damp edges of the cliffs and banks, and the sea raced to the land, crashing noisily in whirls of white. The Cuillin ridge on Skye, those impressive jagged mountains, lent a spectacular backdrop to the walks around the coast. She laughed to herself when she thought about the fact that she had heard of Skye while growing up but didn't even know it was a most beautiful Scottish island with its own dramatic mountain range. Now, she herself owned vast swathes of land and houses, had a long title bestowed on her as well as her own estate, and a huge fortune. She turned at the point in the path where she got a last glimpse of Storm Winds, and sighed with gratitude. She had so many plans for the house; she couldn't wait to get stuck in. She loved it, and she loved this kind of day, when the sounds and freshness filled her lungs with life and made her feel glad to be alive. She loved living in this part of the world.

'Hey! Come in! It's a blustery day! Did you walk?' Clem asked incredulously, as she eyed the muddy dogs.

'Yes, sorry about the mud.'

'Don't be daft. I just meant, to come all that way when you're still recovering!'

'You know what? I have come through "recovery" and I am now "recovered" and I'm getting a bit fed up with Max telling me off, as if I'm a child. So please don't you start!'

Clem grinned sympathetically. 'Yes, I can see that side of Max, and I admit I would be tempted to slap him! Still, can't argue, he is a very caring man, and the least loony of all the brothers,' she finished breezily.

Ailsa threw back her head with a laugh. 'He is, and he also has his very loving side which nobody I suppose but his children and I really notice.'

Clem handed her a glass of red wine. 'Hope it's not too early? Do you think that's why Ryan has the hump over you?'

Ailsa started at her friend's forthright question. Clem had of course been at Trannoch on Sunday and witnessed Ryan's behaviour. 'Maybe,' she assented. 'They've been motherless for more than five years now, and they were both nothing but friendly before Max and I got together. So yes, that's probably why. I'm having them over for pizza on Friday night – the plan is we're all going to help cook. I hope by involving them I can cut through Ryan's veneer. Oh, and I really need your fab pizza recipe.'

'No problem, and, talking of food, would you like to come through and eat off my shelf, grandly described as a "fold away table"?'

Ailsa laughed and followed her friend through to the tiny white kitchen with its view of Arnasaid harbour. Estate agents would describe it as a 'side view', but the property, which was up a cobbled side street, had a view all the same.

'It's only chicken salad with crusty new bread made by my own fair paws this morning! Top up?' and she splashed the wine into their glasses.

'You amaze me, Clem, how you can cook and bake – your cakes are fabulous too. You should do this for a living, but then we would be deprived of your wonderful paintings!'

'Well, funny you should say that!' Clem took a sip of wine. 'I've been secretly supplying cakes to the hotel and the cafes in Arnasaid Bheag and Dunlivietor, and they are selling better than my paintings. The problem with paintings is there is a good profit to be had, but I only sell, on average, one a month – and most of that is from my online business, not really enough to make a comfortable living. So, I've decided to turn my property into a tea shop – I say 'tea' rather than 'cafe', because I will specialise in afternoon teas with sandwiches made from my own bread, and cakes too.

I would also love to serve Prosecco and a few other local speciality wines and ciders, but need to apply for a licence for that. Unfortunately, that will take a wee bit of time. I am going to continue painting and hope to still sell them too. There should be enough room for around ten tables. What do you think of that?' Clem sat back and eyed her friend sceptically.

'I think it's an absolutely great idea, but how will you fit ten tables into your tiny gallery? *And* have the time to paint as well as bake and wait on tables?'

'Well, I won't of course. I'll hire in help for the waiting and I'll do most of the baking in the afternoon for the next day. As for the space, I'll keep the gallery as is, then I'll have the tea shop here, in the living room of this apartment. It's got a kitchen, and a separate toilet I can use for customers. The living room is bigger than the gallery.'

Ailsa stopped eating and looked at her in amazement. 'Sorry, but you said you'll keep the gallery as is, and use your own apartment for the tea shop? Where are you going to live then?'

Clem pointed her fork at her. 'Knew you would ask that, and the answer is that I will find a room in Arnasaid – just big enough for sleeping in, as I will spend the whole day here anyway. I think I believe in my ability enough, so it's really only a matter of whether I can drum up enough business or not. I can sleep on a sofa bed in the gallery until I find somewhere.'

'You must come and stay at Storm Winds!' Ailsa said suddenly. 'I have more than enough space, in fact, I am rattling around the place as it is!' Then, as she saw Clem open her mouth to protest, she went on, 'I absolutely insist, Clem! I had a little apartment made up with a kitchen and bathroom, in what used to be the servants' quarters, for my half-brother Joshua when he was here from Australia last year. Only Miss Cochrane sleeps in that part of the house now, and there is a separate side door near the apartment. Of course there are lots of bedrooms you can have if it's only a bed you want, but having your own little apartment might suit you better? It means you will be as private as you want, and come and go as you please. You are welcome to join me at meals or for a drink or whatever, when you like! Eileen doesn't live with us; she comes in daily. She lives in Arnasaid as you know. I'll have Cocky take a look at it and arrange for it to be cleaned out and ready for you,' and she sat back with a self-satisfied smile.

'I can't thank you enough!' was all the surprised Clem could muster.

Friday brought two things which Ailsa was not looking forward to. The first was the meeting which Stephen had suggested for the grouse shooting parties in August, and the second was the dinner arranged for Max and his children.

Max had popped over in the morning, between appointments at the surgery, and joined Ailsa in the library. It was a horrible day, with sleet and high winds, the sleet falling to ice on the untreated roads, making the drive from the main road up to Storm Winds treacherous.

Ailsa had started on her second book – part of a trilogy set in this very area in Scotland not long after the Jacobite uprising of 1745. Her first book was at the publisher awaiting a decision, but she had decided to begin the second while she waited. The fire was lit, and, as she was wont to do, Ailsa was working at the huge oak table surrounded by books and yet more books. Miss Cochrane brought in tea, a pile of hot buttered toast and chocolate cake and set them on the little table between the wing-backed chairs at each side of the bright cheerful fire.

Ailsa's appetite was much improved, so she ate heartily and had two pieces of Jean's amazing chocolate cake – her favourite.

'I love this library, Max. But, you know, it is so much better sharing it with someone else?' Ailsa was not normally romantic in any way, and she lifted her head to see him looking distracted. He was not listening to a word she said. 'Great!' she thought. When she looked at him for the third time in a row and discovered him looking at the fire with knitted brows, she said, 'Max, do you have something on your mind?'

He took a breath. 'Well... yes... I wanted to talk to you about something, in the interest of letting you know what is happening and not keeping things from you.'

He would never be a gossip, but this, she had to admit, was an interesting opening, and she put her plate down and studied him silently.

'Carys is pregnant,' he said quietly.

Ailsa reacted immediately. 'Carys? I don't believe it! I thought they couldn't have children?'

'Well, unless I am mistaken, no one actually told you that.'

'No, you're right. I guess I just thought as much, as they seemed to have it all, like the rest of the MacKenzies...' She caught his frown, which was deeper this time. 'Sorry, I didn't mean... anyway... I think I either heard a rumour or just surmised wrongly myself, I'm not exactly sure why I thought that.'

'Well anyway, she is pregnant...'

'Well, she certainly managed to hide that!' Ailsa unceremoniously interrupted him in her amazement. 'Having said that, she has such an amazing figure – and I say that grudgingly as another woman – that I would have thought she was too vain to ever want such a thing!'

Max nodded. 'I think that will be most of the family's thoughts on the matter. Dad will be over the moon though, to have another MacKenzie baby at Trannoch. Thomas is walking on the ceiling with excitement, and I am happy for him. Carys uses him like a lap dog, so it is great to see him looking so excited and on top of the world,' he surprised Ailsa by adding.

At two o'clock Ailsa crossed the courtyard to what had once been the stables and was now the estate office and storage space. She felt slightly nervous at having this meeting. Ailsa knew Stephen Millburn irritated her very easily.

The three of them sat in a row, with a chair in front left vacant, apparently for her. They acknowledged her when she came in; Stephen stood up, and she couldn't make out if he was making fun of her or if he was just being naturally polite. All were armed with writing pads and pens.

'Good afternoon!' she said, and sat down with a forced smile.

'Good afternoon!' they all chorused. Stephen was eyeing her with amusement twinkling in his dark eyes.

'Can you move your chairs a bit so that we are in a circle, and I don't feel left out on a limb?' she said, laughingly, and as one they rose and shuffled their seats. Roddy and Stephen were either side of her, and Gennina directly facing her.

Stephen very confidently started the meeting off. 'Okay, so we are here to discuss the grouse shoot on and around the twelfth and how the time and money can be maximised.' They all nodded in agreement. Stephen continued, 'I think one of the first things we need to do is to see what work and cleaning of accommodation for guests needs to be carried out, and...'

'Yes, good idea, and actually, I've already asked Miss Cochrane to take a look at the rooms and get back to me,' Ailsa said smilingly.

'Right... that's... great,' he answered slowly. 'So... this is one of the reasons we needed you to attend, Ailsa, so that you can keep us up to date with this sort of thing.' His sarcasm was not lost on her.

'Well, I took the bull by the horns.' Her expression was surprised, quickly changing to mutinous.

'Good. Okay, budget? Time frame for completion? Who will do the work?' He fired out the questions at her, his eyes beginning to glint with annoyance.

Ailsa saw that he was riled, and relaxed. 'Oh, I only asked her on Wednesday, and there are several rooms to look over – I'll let you know when she comes back to me.'

'Great, I'll update the project plan,' Gennina gushed, awkwardly trying to defuse the situation.

'Here's a copy.' Stephen almost threw it on her lap, and she in turn snatched it up to look at it.

'It looks great, Gennina, thank you,' Ailsa said, through pursed lips.

'Oh, it wasn't me who drew it up, it was Stephen. I only update it,' and, to Ailsa's annoyance he sat back in his seat and stretched out his legs, with a huge grin on his face – waiting for the compliment and apology.

None came.

That evening, Ailsa made sure she had prepared for the get together. Clem had given her the pizza recipe, which was inordinately simple, but the technique was the key for the base. She set out the ingredients on a large chopping board, and rather than asking Jim Hutton, her handyman, to select some wine from the cellar as she normally did, she picked the wine herself. She had a bath and pulled on a pair of her favourite jeans and a white shirt with a necklace of coral bought from a gift shop in Arnasaid. When Max and the children arrived, she tried to act as normally as possible, though inwardly she was quaking. Ailsa had put on a popular radio channel playing all the current hits, and the kitchen, though huge, felt warm and inviting, with the range lit and the lights dimmed just enough to see clearly to cook.

'Well! I wondered if you would help me to make pizza?' she asked invitingly, as Max opened the bottle of red wine. 'Your Auntie Clem gave me the recipe, but I've never actually tried it myself.'

'Oh yeah! I would LOVE to make pizza!' This was from Aria of course, who, dressed in white jeans and a pink floating top looked childlike and lovely. Ailsa gave her a chopping board and pulled a pinny over her clothes before she glanced surreptitiously at Ryan. He looked straight at her, then pulled his brows into a frown.

'Have you got any burgers?'

'No, sorry Ryan, but don't you think it will be fun to make our own pizzas?' Ailsa suddenly realised she had asked the wrong question.

'No, not really. I'm not really into cooking,' he said, with one eye on his father, waiting expectantly for the reaction.

'Fine!' Ailsa said, breezily. 'Could you get some bottles of juice from the fridge for you both? I got some J2Os for you – I think they're orange and blackcurrant.'

As expected, Aria piped up, 'I LOVE J2Os! We only ever have nasty diluted juice at school. Thank you, Ailsa!'

'Have you not got any Irn Bru?' Ryan asked sullenly, scowling at her. 'I love Irn Bru.'

'Ryan, that's enough. Ailsa has very kindly got these drinks, which I suggested you would like, as you drank them and appeared to like them last Sunday. Now stop being rude and open two.' Max turned away and poured wine for himself and Ailsa. Ryan, however, continued to snipe at Ailsa with little comments which made her feel that he was definitely on a bit of a mission.

She followed the recipe to the letter, and they had great fun making the bases using their clenched fists and swirling the dough on top in a circular motion, making the right size of pizza. Ryan, it has to be owned, did not really enter into the spirit of the cooking. When he was making his base, he threw it around as the others did, to make the shape, but somehow the base landed on the floor. He burst out laughing, as did Aria, who innocently thought it was an accident, but Max was furious, and moved towards his son, determinedly.

Ailsa put her hand on his arm gently as she said, 'No matter, you can just make another base from scratch! Here's the flour and water,' and she pushed it over to Ryan, who wore a thunderous expression. With his father looking like that, he had no choice but to make another base, which he did with extremely bad grace.

Aria asked if she could use the pizza cutter to slice the pizzas when they came out of the oven, and, with watchful eye, Ailsa agreed. Ryan sat silently sipping his juice.

'Would you like to watch a film in the little sitting room at the back?' Ailsa asked. The pizza had been demolished, the dishes had all been cleared away, and, most importantly, the counter tops had been scrubbed in readiness for the return of Ailsa's trusted cook, Jean Morton. Jean would very firmly voice her displeasure if her kitchen had not been restored to its natural order.

'Oh my God, that was hard,' Ailsa said, as she pushed her back into Max's side, with his arm around her waist and their hands clasped round their glasses of wine.

'I could smack Ryan for his bloody cheek,' Max said, in a disgusted voice. Ailsa laughed, partly with amusement, partly with relief that Ryan was in the room at the other end of the hall and could not hear them.

'Max darling, he's thirteen years old, nearly fourteen! You can't smack a thirteen-year-old. Anyway, we managed it without too much of a problem, I hope. The pizza was made, and we all ate it, even Ryan.'

'Hmph... I won't allow him to behave like that with you, Ailsa. That is not the way I brought him up.' Max was wounded.

'Don't worry, I can handle him,' she said, more confidently than she felt.

'I had a staff meeting today in the estate office,' she said, without thinking, and by way of changing the subject.

Max rubbed his eyes. 'Oh? And what did you meet about?'

'Well, Stephen Millburn came to me on Wednesday and wanted to tell me what they had always done before and proposed an open staff meeting about the grouse shoot in August. I'm happy to have the shoot. We have the rooms to accommodate these parties in the East Wing, but it's his attitude which irks me. He is so sure of himself that it does get my goat.'

'Yes, he is. I guess that is what makes him a good estate manager here, and at Trannoch. So, what did you decide?'

'Oh lots of ideas to market the shoot so that we can optimise income. Also, Stephen had an idea to use some of the birds to send to a local cook to test recipes and give to homeless or needy people in Fort William and Glasgow. The birds would otherwise not be used. He says it's almost like a good ending can come of something which, I'm afraid, I really don't believe in. I don't think it's right to kill birds for sport.'

Max stared at her with a glimmer of new respect. 'But that is the country way. You can make a lot of money from housing and hosting shoots for the season.'

'I know, but that doesn't mean I have to like it.'

Max left around half past eleven. He installed his children in Jim Hutton's car, and gave Ailsa a long lingering kiss in the shadows before he made his way back to Trannoch. They were met by Denbeath, the ever-faithful butler as they quietly made their way through the side entrance of the great house, but Max dismissed him saying, 'Thank you Denbeath, we won't need anything.'

The two children were already moving towards the stair when Max caught Aria's arm and gently kissed her forehead. 'Off you go up, darling. I will be there very shortly to tuck you in.' She skipped happily up the stairs, as her father turned to his son. 'In here, Ryan!' he said to the surprised boy, as he opened the door to a small room, turned on the light and closed the door quietly. He perched on the arm of a small settee, studying his son with a mixture of annoyance and impatience.

Ryan looked uncomfortable, shifting from one foot to the other, characteristically sniffing and running his fingers through his hair until it stood on end.

Max's words were to the point. 'Ailsa means a lot to me, I hope you know, and although I will never love anyone as much as I love you and Aria, I am with Ailsa now and you should respect that. Ryan, you were sullen and rude and really not very nice to her, and for this, you will have your phone and iPad taken away for two days – I want the phone and iPad on my desk in my study tonight before you go to bed.' He said all this in a voice which was taught with temper, held at bay with some difficulty.

'Dad, I wasn't cheeky!' Ryan said defiantly.

'You were. You were also rude and difficult, but if you really want to discuss the way you talked and exactly what you said and why, then I will be happy to talk to you before breakfast tomorrow. It's much too late this evening. Otherwise you know what's to happen, and please, don't be so horrible to Ailsa again. Off you go.'

When Ailsa turned back towards her home, Miss Cochrane was standing in the hallway.

'Hey, Cocky, I thought you would have gone to bed ages ago! I hope we didn't disturb you?'

'On the contrary, I happened to be returning to the house after visiting my sister when a man met me on the front step and insisted on seeing you. At this time, I knew you were in the kitchen with Dr MacKenzie and the children. I advised him to come back tomorrow, and he gave me his business card, requesting I pass it on to you.'

'Alberto Franelli, builder,' Ailsa read. 'So? Why did you feel you needed to tell me about this at this time of night?'

'Because I think he is Olivia's father. I think he has come to find her.'

Chapter Three

Joyce Whitelaw was a plain, matronly looking woman in her middle age. She had not had an easy life. She had never married, nor had she had any children of her own. She had opened a nursery in Fort William several years ago, and it had been mildly successful. She was moderately good with children, and being moderately good at anything was good in her own eyes, as she knew she excelled at nothing. The past crime to which her name was linked was sufficiently distant in the past to enable her to move on, and she had built up quite a little enterprise of a handful of children, from rich families, who had made up her nursery. However, she had soon got bored. The tedium of break time, story time, outdoor time and teatime, soon took its toll. Even the crafts which she was compelled to go through with little hands which couldn't even write their names became a chore. She felt she had to take over the making of items the children took home, ensuring they were of a standard that the parents were deceived into thinking their little darlings had produced: lovely painted Easter eggs, Christmas cards, and all manner of items suitable to attach to a fridge in a penthouse flat and provide a talking point for party guests.

So Joyce had grown lax. The maiming of a child wasn't really her fault. A family from abroad had come to Scotland. The father, taking up a highly paid executive post, had placed the child within Joyce's nursery. His child had one day found the kettle unattended while the nursery assistant was otherwise engaged, or at least that was what Joyce had ultimately stated. The child was burned severely, up her right arm, as she stretched to pick up the shiny kettle from the countertop to make tea for Teddy. The assistant was subsequently and conveniently blamed, and Joyce's nursery was shut down.

She had decided to go to Italy for a holiday. She couldn't have cared less about the accident other than it left her with no income, but she would not let a little thing like this get in the way of her ambitions.

Joyce was on the lookout for a new opportunity.

Max strode into his study at six thirty the next morning. The sun was attempting to shine through ominous black clouds. The land around Trannoch was dull and heavy in misty greyness. His study was his favourite room in the house, his haven, and part of the suite of rooms which he and his two children called their own. The high sash windows overlooked the land to the side of the house, facing due west. Just above the tops of the forest surrounding the estate he could make out the East Wing of Storm Winds. Beyond this, he even got a glimpse of the silver ribbon of sea which seemed much farther than six miles away. One wall was shelved to the ceiling and packed with books. Most were medical journals and scientific books, but a whole shelf was devoted to his favourite novels which ranged from thrillers to autobiographies. His desk was one he had picked up in an antique market, made of oak and polished within an inch of its life. It had an old-fashioned inkstand and an antique phone from the 1950s which he had bought from the same market. There was plenty of antique furniture in the many rooms at Trannoch, and the Colonel had suggested a beautiful French seventeenth century desk for his study, but Max was adamant that he preferred the shabby well-worn desk he bought for less than a hundred pounds. The fire was always lit when he worked here for any length of time, and the two much-loved oxblood leather chesterfields, covered with assorted comfortable cushions, sat either side of the hearth. Although the room was huge, like most of the rooms in Trannoch, which was about three times the size of Storm Winds, this room still managed to feel cosy and lived-in. When Ailsa came over, they generally escaped to the study rather than the more formal sitting rooms downstairs.

He picked up the cup of tea which had been placed as usual on the coaster on his desk and leafed through a few papers to read through before breakfast. It was then that he remembered Ryan and noticed that his son's phone and iPad weren't on his desk. Now Max did not particularly pride himself on his parenting skills, but he thought at least that he was always fair. It had not crossed his mind that his instruction would be ignored. He felt the anger rise like a flush from his chest to his face, and his mood plummet.

To Max's surprise, Ryan was not in his bedroom when he looked in a few minutes later. His iPad was on the bedside table, but Ryan, and his phone, were nowhere to be seen.

'You were late back last night!' the Colonel bellowed, as Max quietly came into the breakfast room shortly after. The Colonel had a habit of sitting in his library until long after midnight, getting updates from Denbeath on who was out and who still had to come in. He would not, however, admit this to anyone but Denbeath.

'Mmm... Aria, have you seen your brother?' Aria looked up from her boiled egg in surprise.

'No, Daddy. Is he not in his room?'

David and Melissa, Malcolm's children, looked blankly at their uncle when he asked them the same question. They shook their heads – they hadn't seen their cousin this morning either. Melody, the lovely sophisticated oldest cousin and daughter of Noel and Clem, looked up from her phone, where she was reading an email from her Uni boyfriend, but she too shook her head.

'I was just going to say that there is no point in changing our breakfast time for the benefit of you children, if you can't even manage to get here on time!' the Colonel said, in an exasperated voice. 'Well if he turns up now, he'll have to eat what's here. I'm not asking the staff to make him fresh eggs. It's damned impolite...'

Max ignored his father rambling on. Inwardly, Max was fretting over his handling of the conversation with Ryan. Had he been too strict? No, he hadn't. Ryan was a cheeky young pup at times, and he was not going to tolerate rudeness to others from either of his children. He filled his plate with eggs and bacon and placed on top a few slices of toast, then escaped from the breakfast room back to his study to do a bit of work before surgery began.

As he booted up his laptop, he noticed a bulge in a pile of papers on the left-hand side of his desk which had definitely not been there earlier. He lifted them to discover the iPad and phone.

'You *what*?' Ailsa looked at Max askance.

'I looked into his messages on his phone,' Max said calmly.

'But that's like reading someone's diary, Max. For goodness sake, surely you don't think it's as serious as to warrant that!'

'I think it might just be. I was really angry with him, and I saw his iPad at his bedside, before I went down to breakfast, but no phone. He definitely had just put them there.'

'So?' Ailsa was bewildered. 'He probably fell asleep last night and forgot to put them on your desk, then went out to phone one of his friends, before it was confiscated.'

'Well, that's just it. I thought he might be contacting two boys from Arnasaid, and my suspicions were right. He is hanging about with John Miller and Michael Dougal again, when he was expressly forbidden to see them.'

Ailsa tried not to laugh. 'Max, darling, who says "expressly forbidden" nowadays? And why did you *expressly forbid* him to see them in the first place?'

'Well if you're going to make fun of me...' he said huffily.

Her tone softened as she looked at his wounded expression. 'Don't be daft, Max. I think you are a brilliant dad, but maybe you just need to loosen up a bit. I think you could just have asked him outright rather than looking in his phone.' Max fell silent as he tried to take on this new concept. 'Maybe if he felt he had your trust he would be more receptive?'

'Well, he hasn't shown himself to be very trustworthy lately, but maybe you're right. What I found out, though, he would never have admitted to,' he finished cryptically.

Ailsa got up, 'Okay, well I'll get us another wine, and you can tell me what he's been up to.'

They had met in 'The Wee Dram' after Max's work as they had begun to do once a week since Ailsa had felt well again. It was the only pub in Arnasaid, apart from the hotel bar, but even when busy, it still managed to successfully hide its occupants with its high-backed black settles and shady corners. Max's pet hate was his patients approaching him and asking his advice about various ailments when they saw him out and about, rather than making an appointment to see him. Because of this, he had rarely socialised in Arnasaid before he and Ailsa got together. In fact, he rarely socialised at all, except with members of the family and Ailsa. He loved her ability to talk and be friendly to all she met. This was something that Max had never quite accomplished – that none of the MacKenzies had accomplished for that matter. They had been brought up in a family which, by reason of social standing and status, had been naturally separated from the mainstream inhabitants of the North West. It helped that the MacKenzies were steeped in tradition, and hugely wealthy. They were considered, especially by the older generation, to be pinnacles of society across the county. Ailsa's father, Sir Angus, had been the rightful authoritarian figurehead by virtue of his Knighthood, but had not possessed the qualities of personality necessary to propel himself forward. The Colonel, however, *demanded* authority. Max and his brothers had all gone to boarding school then University, Oxford for Max. As doctor, Max was the only one of his brothers who worked in the community, and his patients would, without exception, admit he was a brilliant GP, but moan equally about his poor social manner. Max kept work and home life completely apart.

She brought the wine back to the table and noticed that Max was looking pensive, the way he did when he reverted into himself. She pretended not to notice.

'Ok, so what?' she said, carrying on the conversation.

'You know, it doesn't really matter.' He was like a petulant schoolboy, himself, as he responded.

She thought for a minute, then tried another tack. 'Well, I'm not a parent, but think of me more as an arbitrator, a referee or something like that. I may just be able to help?'

He took a sip of his wine and smiled. 'Sorry, I just find all this quite hard to handle.'

'No harm in that. Everyone says it's the hardest job in the world! So, firstly, how did you manage to get into his phone? Is it not password protected?'

Max smiled reluctantly. 'Yes, but, unfortunately – for him, my son is about as imaginative as I am, and it's his date of birth. I got in first try.'

'So, what did his texts say?'

Max shifted in his seat, took a sip of wine and sat back. 'His wee pals John and Michael are a bad influence. I caught them last year at Trannoch, up behind the stable yard, drinking and smoking. I, of course, have no jurisdiction over the other two. I went to their houses and their parents did everything but laugh at me, especially John's. They even had the audacity to say, "boys will be boys". At least Michael's parents offered to pay for the drink they had stolen from Dad's drinks cabinet. I grounded Ryan for the four remaining weeks of the summer holidays, and told him he had had a lucky escape, because if it had been Dad that had caught them...' He shook his head at the possible scenario, as words failed him.

'It gets worse!' Ailsa said, with real concern in her voice. 'So, what did the texts actually say?'

'He had sent several texts with meeting places and times and talking about how much money they would need for the *stuff*.'

Ailsa blanched at this. 'You don't mean you think he is using?'

'Yep. I see it often Ailsa, and Ryan is displaying all the signs. Erratic behaviour, mood swings, temper, rudeness; none of which are like him normally.'

'Well, that could be said about any teenager I have ever met, including myself when I was one.'

'Quite, but you weren't using drugs... were you?'

'Of course not, you ape,' she said, then turned serious. 'It might be alcohol again, but then alcohol causes just as many problems, Max.'

'I know that! I'm a doctor, for God's sake!' and, as a few heads were turning at Max's raised voice, he subsided and spoke more quietly. 'Ryan will be fourteen in a few months' time. He is still a child. The other two are fifteen and sixteen, and much more streetwise and savvy than him. They are meeting tomorrow night at seven o'clock behind Mufty's barn just up the brae from Clem's house.'

'Sounds like something out of an adventure book!'

'Ailsa, be serious.'

'Okay, what do you want to do then?'

'I want to be there and catch them at it.'

Ailsa came home to Storm Winds by herself after the pub, and was met at the door again by Miss Cochrane.

'Deja vu!' laughed Ailsa. 'We need to stop meeting like this, Cocky!' and then she spotted a red holdall lying in the hall.

'Mr Franelli is waiting for you in the blue sitting room.' Cocky pulled herself up to her full height, with an indignant look on her face. 'He came about an hour ago and wouldn't leave until he could see you.'

Ailsa sighed, 'Okay, could you bring us tea, please?'

'He's drinking whisky,' Cocky snorted at what she considered to be the sheer cheek of the visitor, asking for this when she had offered tea.

'Okay, well if you don't mind, I'll have a glass of red then.'

'Lady Hamilton-Dunbar!' The short fat Italian rose with difficulty from the deep couch, almost bowing as he took her hand.

'Mr Franelli!' she said, as sweetly as she could muster, 'and please call me Ailsa.'

'Oh no! Is no possible! You the great Lady!' he gushed, in stilted English.

'Well, not so much of the great,' Ailsa said with a smile, but the sarcasm was lost on him. She motioned for him to sit back on the couch as she sat opposite.

'What can I do for you, Mr Franelli?' She decided that she would be as formal as he wanted her to be.

'I here for Olivia, my daughter. I find her. I take her home.'

'Oh, okay.' Ailsa chose her words carefully. 'When was the last time you saw your daughter?'

'For two years no. She write me. Her Mamma, she die, I come to tell Olivia and make a new home. She has baby, I know, she write bad man 'take' her. I find him and kill him.' Ailsa could just about keep up with this disjointed language, and she was seriously alarmed. He obviously did not know that his daughter was no longer staying at Storm Winds but was now at Trannoch, staying under the same roof as her abductor. This could turn out to be an extremely explosive situation. She wished that Max were here. Then there was the additional upset for Olivia that her mother had apparently died. The girl was in a delicate state emotionally as it was, what would this new news bring? Miss Cochrane came in with a fresh whisky for the guest, which she handed to him with a snide sniff, and a glass of red wine for Ailsa. It gave Ailsa a chance to think about how she would approach her next comment.

'Olivia is no longer here, Mr Franelli. She has gone to live in a neighbouring estate, er... a big house, you know? With many more people to take care of her,' she said diplomatically.

The little man had bolted upright at this, his black eyes flashing, and his expression tragic and puzzled at the same time. 'But...but how she no here? Why she away? Is baby good? Who are peoples she with? Is she working for peoples?' The questions came faster than Ailsa could work them out and answer them.

'Mr Franelli, I assure you she is being well looked after. She is not working; they are the family...' and she suddenly stopped short. Should she be the one to tell this man Olivia's business? She had only just met him; he could be anyone. She quickly jumped up and became brisk and business-like. 'I am going to phone the family and tell them to send a car for you. You will go and meet with your daughter, and perhaps she will tell you everything you need to know.'

He lifted angry eyes to her, an expression that flitted and passed as soon as it appeared, and he shrugged non-committedly, sinking backwards with apparent weariness into the sofa.

In the seclusion of the hallway, Ailsa pulled out her mobile from her jeans pocket. 'Max, Olivia's father has turned up here at Storm Winds. She has told him about the baby and the way it was conceived, and also that she was working and living here. That's all he knows. He has threatened the 'father', although he doesn't know that it's Malcolm, and he's here to tell Olivia her mother has passed away and he wants to take her to a new home.'

'Good God, as if we don't have enough drama at Trannoch without this!' She could see him in her mind's eye rubbing his temples as he often did when he was stressed. 'I'll get George to come over for him, and I'll speak to Father. He can decide what to do.'

Georgina Dillon, or to give her everyday name, Hunter, sat at her ornate Italian marble dressing table preening herself: doing her hair, touching up her expertly applied make-up, and manicuring her immaculate nails. Her suite at Trannoch consisted of two huge rooms adjoined by a connecting door, a beautiful bathroom and a tiny but functional dressing room. Her rooms had been furnished expensively, and her wardrobes boasted the most alluring and dazzling collection of clothes, handbags and shoes. All of this was paid for by both the Colonel and Malcolm MacKenzie. She got up and left her room.

On his return from Switzerland, Malcolm had pursued Hunter with his usual salaciousness and determination. He was in his own sitting room, nursing a whisky and waiting for Hunter. He thought she might be cooling off him. Their relationship was a toboggan hurtling down a steep slope which didn't always manage the corners. He enjoyed her company, her fierce, determined nature, and her cunning ability to get exactly what she wanted. He knew they were alike in that respect, but he knew deep inside that he wasn't *who* she wanted. She was around twelve years older than Malcolm, but this didn't stop him from wanting her. He thought about the many women he had had in his life and how the one he had least liked or been attracted to was Belinda, his unfortunate wife, who had committed suicide the year before. He had hated her with a passion, but she had come from an aristocratic family with money, which was the only reason he had agreed to marry her. Now he had Hunter, who had little to offer him, but he wanted her with a possessive passion which threw him off-guard. He was worried though, that fickle as the woman was, she would soon tire of him; things had changed with him since his illness; his roughcasting was starting to crack.

'Well! You look positively gloomy!' She swept into the room with an admonishing smile, sitting on the armchair nearest him, despite his tapping the seat beside him on the sofa.

'Sorry, I was deep in thought!' He shook himself out of his low spirits, knowing she had no patience with anyone who was fed up. 'You look beautiful, darling. Sit here beside me,' he commanded.

Hunter put her head coquettishly on one side lifting wide the lids of her eyes so the inky blackness looked startlingly large and expressive in her almost lineless face, and in direct contrast to her short blonde hair. 'No, I want to sit here by the fire. Get me a drink, darling. I thought one would have been waiting for me!' She sounded petulant.

Malcolm went over to the drinks cabinet and took a bottle of chilled white wine from the bucket. He poured her a large glass and joined her again by the fire. Her eyes narrowed as she watched him, trying to work out what he was thinking. She felt a strange vibe from him.

'What are you doing here, Hunter?' he suddenly asked.

She hesitated for a long moment, gathering her thoughts. 'Doing here? You asked me to join you here after dinner!' She was more impatient than startled.

'I mean at Trannoch. What are you doing here, really?'

She felt tantalised by this question. She liked to be wrong-footed, it showed a bit of lively spark. A bit of *contretemps*. One of the things which had annoyed her about Malcolm since he became ill was that he had become much more stable and homely, and much less exciting in consequence. Malcolm wanted stability and companionship now. Hunter wanted those things like a hole in the head. 'Why, darling! What a perfectly amusing question! I am here obviously, because my daughter threw me out of Storm Winds, my rightful inheritance, through my son, Joshua.'

'Yes, I know what *brought* you here, but I really meant, what do you want out of this relationship with me?'

Again, she put her head on one side, quickly and carefully crafting her answer. 'I'm here because you and I are meant to be together, Malcolm.' There was the merest trace of irritation in her voice.

'And you are not really here for the Colonel? My Father?' He sat forward, as eager as a schoolboy on his first date.

She got up and walked over to the window, looking out to the perfect lawn and the mountains beyond. She was giving herself time to think. This line of questioning had momentarily thrown her, and was forcing her to think about her situation, which entirely bored her. Hunter was always in first gear, but now she was beginning to labour uphill. 'My darling Malcolm, your father and I have history, you know that, but it's you I want. You I need.'

He looked at her intently, taking a gulp of his drink before answering. 'Yes, I know you have said that before, but I have to look at my side of things. I probably don't have more than a year to live. I have my fortune to leave to my children, *three* of them, and I wonder what will happen to you when I am gone.'

41

Hunter purposefully misdirected the conversation. 'Oh, darling! Don't be so maudlin! I am sure you will live forever. I *need* you to live forever, so I will hear no more of this horrid talk of dying and morbid things like that. Pour me another drink and we shall talk about nice things like dinner parties and holidays abroad!'

Malcolm smiled weakly, and poured them each another drink. 'I do adore you, you know that, darling, don't you?' He sounded very slightly pleading.

Hunter's face shone with relief. She kissed him swiftly on the cheek, then smiled a humourless smile.

'Of course I know it.'

Denbeath had shown Mr Alberto Franelli into the library where the Colonel and Max were having a whisky together by the fire. The rest of the occupants of Trannoch were in the Great Room, gathered after dinner, as usual, except for Olivia who was ensconced in her suite watching TV on her own.

'Won't you sit, Mr Franelli?' Max asked quickly, as the Colonel towered above the little Italian in a threatening manner. 'May I get you something to drink?'

'I see Olivia.'

'Of course you will, we just need to talk with you first.' Max was at his most diplomatic.

'I see Olivia now!'

'Whisky?' Max ignored the man's plea and poured from the crystal decanter. Max handed it to him, and he immediately downed it in one, gasping at the strength. He was obviously not used to drinking much except beer, judging by his reaction and his extremely large belly.

'I see Olivia now!' he repeated, his eyes rolling in dramatic fashion.

'Look, I know you have trouble understanding the Queen's English, but we are trying to help you here, you stupid little man.' It was the Colonel, of course, but thankfully the 'stupid little man' didn't understand most of what he was saying.

'You see, we brought Olivia here to have her baby because she was quite unwell at the beginning, and, as I am a doctor, I was here to look after her.' Max and the Colonel had hurriedly concocted this story together after Ailsa had phoned.

'It was you!' Alberto Franelli put two and two together and made five. He spat at the floor in front of Max, and jumped up to face him.

'No, it certainly was not! No, please just listen...' But before he could say anything more Alberto had landed a punch on Max's jaw which sent him reeling back and as he tried mid-air to balance himself, he fell, hitting his head off a table. It was so sudden and unexpected that Max didn't even have a chance to put up his defences. He sat up, rubbing his chin, as the Colonel shouted obscenities at the Italian, who didn't understand a word the blustering giant said to him, which was probably just as well. Denbeath rushed into the room. Behind him came Olivia, white and ill-looking, who had been on the way downstairs when she had heard her father's unmistakeable voice.

'Papa! Papa!' she shouted, and rushed into his arms, oblivious of the fact that Max was being helped to his feet by Denbeath, and the Colonel was snorting and bellowing like a bull ready to rush at a red rag.

'Olivia!'

The two embraced with an exaggerated sentimentality which, had the Colonel not been helping his son, would have balked at this open show of affection. The two Italians began an energetic conversation, gesticulating and hugging throughout, while Max was helped to a chair by the fire amidst his protestations at being treated like someone half-dead. The third MacKenzie son felt the small lump on the side of his head where he had struck the table, and a cut at the corner of his mouth due to the punch. In truth, neither of these were serious. Max's pride was the thing hurting most.

'Papa says that Mamma has died suddenly,' and Olivia burst into tears. Denbeath rushed to fetch her a glass of water, but her father insisted she should have a glass of wine. Denbeath glanced at Max for his thoughts on the matter, and Max nodded.

'Won't do her or the baby any harm,' he said gruffly.

'Papa also says he has come to Scotland to build a new home for us. I told him I live here now, and he is not happy I am safe from man who attacked me.' The Colonel's face reddened with anger. 'I tell Papa that we not know where attacker is, and that you protect me. I say, I want to stay in Scotland, and I will not leave now. I say you protect me,' she said, with meaningful looks at both men, who in turn exchanged glances. So, Olivia had not named Malcolm as the man who had raped her, the father of her baby.

The relief dripped from the Colonel's face like jam from a spoon, leaving his countenance sagging and pasty-white. 'Hrumph... well, tell your Pa... er... your father... that we will pay for his flight back home to Italy, and that he can stay here at Trannoch for the night,' the Colonel finished with gruff kindness. Again there was a stream of words between the two, which, even if any of them had understood Italian it would have been virtually impossible to follow, as it was peppered with exclamations and tears. Eventually the young Italian looked up, with a decisive expression on her lovely face.

'I had Papa and Mamma only, and now just Papa and me.'

Max and his father looked astonished as the girl added, 'Papa say will stay here with me until I have baby. Papa will come to Trannoch.'

'Darling, what was the commotion yesterday evening?' Hunter delicately lifted her napkin onto her beautifully-cut pale green skirt. It was the day after Olivia's father had arrived at Storm Winds and had subsequently been transported to Trannoch to be met by the Colonel and Max.

'That is not a conversation for now, my dear.' The Colonel patted her hand as the family looked on.

Carys picked at her eggs and turned a superior gaze on Hunter. 'I heard Italian voices,' she said, much to the Colonel's annoyance in view of what he had said.

'Carys, I have just said the conversation stops here.'

'Yes, I know, but I wondered, as there was more than one Italian voice, if it was someone connected with Olivia? She doesn't appear to have made it to breakfast this morning. She surely can't be suffering from morning sickness *again*? I do think she is playing us all for fools the way the staff have to run after her and jump to her every whim.'

'Well, it takes one to know one,' Malcolm managed to say, through the enormous mouthfuls of bacon and egg he was throwing down his throat.

Carys reacted only with a supercilious arch of her left eyebrow. 'You seem to be feeling better Malcolm! The way you are hurtling that food down your gullet, you would think you hadn't eaten for days!'

'Shut up.'

Hunter was not to be outdone by an overly-superior, childish woman, whether or not she was the Colonel's daughter-in-law. 'Maxwell, *darling*,' whatever happened to your mouth? Did you cut it shaving? Or, God forbid, were you brawling last night? Was that what I heard? With your social standing and professional capacity in the community, I do think that is unworthy of you.' She smiled a humourless smile.

'What you may think of me is no concern of mine.' Max didn't lift his eyes from his paper.

Malcolm grunted under his breath, just before the Colonel erupted into one of his furious rages, and Aria burst into tears.

'Enough! All of you! There are children at the table, and I have already told you, I don't want to discuss what happened last night. Either refrain from this sniping or leave the room!'

None of them looked in the least upset by this, but the children looked shocked. The Colonel had every intention of letting the other adults know what had happened the previous evening, but not at table when his grandchildren were visibly upset. It failed to dawn on him that his outburst was the main cause of it.

Hunter rubbed her throat and cast her mind back over her post-breakfast conversation with Malcolm. She had bumped into Malcolm on the terrace. He pulled her around the side of the house, away from the windows or any prying eyes, and kissed her fiercely. He was still buoyed-up by the conversation previously, when she appeared to really want him, rather than his father. He couldn't have been more wrong. She pushed him away, and, hiding her disgust, said the first thing which she hoped would forestall him, 'I think we should get married!'

Malcolm had immediately looked delighted, then studying her cold face, his brow had careered into a deep frown. 'Why?'

She answered swiftly, 'Because we were meant to be together.'

He had laughed sardonically. 'So, do you think the same when you are in bed with my father?'

'Don't be crude, Malcolm.'

'You're not denying it!'

'I neither deny nor admit to anything, ever, darling. You should know that by now.'

'You know I am ill.' It was a statement rather than a question. 'You didn't want to talk about it before, but you need to accept the facts, Hunter!'

She nodded, trying to keep the distaste from her expression. 'Yes, of course I do. You lost no time in letting everyone know, and sympathy reigned. Unfortunately, I don't do sympathy.'

He looked at her incredulously, then it was as if everything suddenly rushed into place in his mind. Hunter didn't want him. When he had learned about his illness, it had affected a change in him. He still had hope that he would live much longer than the Doctors predicted, and, because of that, he felt he deserved some happiness and fulfilment in the time left to him. Hunter was the person he knew would fill that gap. But if he thought he had led a life of self-servitude, not caring deeply for anyone else but himself, he had reckoned without the competition posed by Hunter. He was nothing compared to her. In this particular pond, she was a shark, and he was a minnow.

He reached out and with one hand, grabbed her by the throat. 'You absolute bitch. Well, let me tell you something, *Georgina:* you will never get your grubby hands on my money, never, as long as I walk this earth.'

She could hardly speak his hand was so tight. She flung him off. 'Get off me! Well, judging by what you told us all, you won't walk this earth for very long anyway.'

'Exactly, and that is why I will never marry you. I want my children to get my money, not you.'

She turned to go, she was rubbing her neck as she threw at him, 'Suit yourself – it's your loss.'

'I'll see you as far away from Trannoch as possible!' he shouted, just as the Colonel strode through the French windows, onto the terrace, and watched Hunter as she stomped away. His son was pacing in anger.

Unfortunately for Malcolm, the Colonel assumed his son had made a play for Hunter and she had refused him, not realising it was the other way around. Malcolm had inadvertently thrown Hunter and the Colonel closer together. The Colonel bellowed at Malcolm that Hunter was part of the family (which she clearly was not) and would stay as long as he had anything to do with it. Malcolm was angrier than he had ever been, seeing for the first time in his miserable life another person who could be as mercenary as he. Hunter, however, was triumphant.

Later that day, Hunter was examining her marks which Malcolm had inflicted. She picked a stylish scarf from her dressing table drawer as she thought grimly how easily she could drop Malcolm like a stone. She would place herself figuratively and physically at the left-hand side of the Colonel: at table, at functions, and any other times when the he was performing a public duty or when he was with the family. After some time, she knew, the family would reluctantly accept this.

Chapter Four

Joyce Whitelaw had taken a holiday home in a small Italian town not far from Sienna. It suited her as it was quiet, and she could take the time to plan out where she would go from here. She was not a sociable person, and when the woman next door to her moved over to the fence to speak to her she felt irritated, wondering how she could avoid contact. The neighbour held a gardening fork, and began to wave it in the air in tandem to her spurge of Italian, of which Joyce understood nothing.

'Er...no Italiano, erm...me speak only English...er... Anglaise.'

She displayed the typical ignorance of other languages of many native English speakers.

The woman studied her for a minute before answering, 'Ah, so you are English?'

Joyce was surprised to find someone who could speak English in such a remote, rustic village. She brightened slightly.

'Where you come from in England?'

'Oh, not England, Scotland. A place called Fort William. You won't have heard...'

'I know it.' The woman's face had darkened with an expression Joyce could not make out. 'It is near Arnasaid, no?'

Again Joyce was knocked off-guard. 'But Arnasaid is such a small village! Do you know someone there?'

The woman looked to her left and right surreptitiously before replying, 'We know of a family – the MacKenzies. Come over to supper tonight, and my brother and husband tell you about it. She smiled a malevolent smile, as Joyce agreed.

'Max! What the hell happened to you?' Ailsa, clad in wellington boots and a pink spotted Mac was making her way along the main street in Arnasaid on her way to see Clem. She was going to help her friend with the cleaning and organisation of her new tea shop. Clem was moving into Storm Winds in the next few days, and her little apartment there was spick and span, all ready for her.

Max had popped out from the surgery to buy a cake for him and his receptionist, for their morning tea, and his jacket hood was pulled down as far as it would go to shield him from the torrential rain. 'Hiya,' he said, blushing slightly as if he was a teenager who had been embroiled in a playground fight. 'I can't explain now, but it isn't anything to worry about.'

'Oh, okay, well, are we still meeting in The Wee Dram tonight at six for some Dutch courage before we confront your wayward son?'

'Absolutely.'

'Hi! It's me!' Ailsa was thumping on the locked door of the gallery, as the rain poured down her hood and onto her face. Puzzled, she went back down the outside stone stairway to the little apartment underneath, and, finding it locked too, she pounded on that door. Just as she turned away, swearing under her breath as she had said she would be there sometime in the morning, the door opened to reveal Stephen Millburn, his face flushed, and his shirt unbuttoned down almost to his waist. As she stood staring at him uncomfortably, Clem appeared, looking slightly dishevelled, her belt on her jeans hanging open at either side. They both looked confused and embarrassed, and Ailsa in turn was as uncomfortable as they.

'I can come back if... if... it's inconvenient...' she trailed off.

'Ailsa! Don't be silly!' Clem admonished. 'Come in! We were just... just...'

'Just pulling the furniture about,' supplemented Stephen, with an amused look on his handsome face.

Ailsa went in and saw the tables all piled at one side, chairs on top, waiting to be cleaned and placed, paint pots piled against a wall, and what looked like a yoga mat in the middle of the floor. 'Doing stretches?' she enquired sweetly.

'No, just creating a space... somewhere to sit... and... and have a... a... cup of tea,' Clem finished lamely.

'Aren't you supposed to be managing the team felling the trees in the East forest?' Ailsa suddenly swung round on Stephen. He looked startled, then turned and picked up his jacket.

'Yes, Ma'am!' he said sarcastically, his eyes glinting with rage at the put-down, but he managed to pull back his dignity enough to lean into Clem and kiss her on the cheek, before walking past Ailsa and leaving the room with a slight bang of the door.

'Well, that wasn't very nice, was it?' Clem was righteously irritated. 'Why pick on Stephen like that, Ailsa?'

She had no answer to this. She could not explain the feeling of catching the two of them in what appeared to be more than a kiss and a cuddle.

'Sorry, I guess I was just a bit embarrassed landing upon you when you were, er...er...alone, and I was banging the door down. But I was a bit irritated that he left the team alone – they're all new casuals. He really should have been looking after them, Clem.'

'Yes, well, you're right of course, but you didn't need to be quite so heavy handed with him. We're both friends.'

'Yes, sorry Clem, and you're right too, I was heavy handed.'

'Let's just get to work on this place?' Clem relaxed a little.

'Okay, so, what furniture do you want moving?' Ailsa asked with a wicked glint in her eyes, and they both laughed as the mood lightened.

'It's not like you to be so stuffy!' Max said later, with a grin. 'Anyone would think you were jealous!'

Ailsa did all she could to stop the flush from rising, but The Wee Dram was so dark inside she doubted he would see it anyway.

'Don't be daft, Max... I was embarrassed to catch them like that – anyone would be.'

'Hmmm,' he answered, with a swig of his pint.

'I just think Stephen Millburn has been far too used to doing what he likes when he likes, with no accountability. It's time someone faced up to him.'

'I think you are right,' Max said, surprising Ailsa. 'Stephen has pretty much been given free rein. I mean even Dad treats him like another son. It will be good for him to know who's boss for a change.'

A small vase stood on the edge of Hunter's dressing table filled with fresh flowers she insisted was refilled every second day. She picked up a large daisy from the bunch and swung round to face the tall window overlooking the courtyard. The Colonel and Malcolm were walking across the cobbles, apparently deep in conversation. She felt strong emotions as she watched them. Anger, pity, disgust, and a strange smattering of an emotion she didn't recognise – fear. They all caught in her throat. She looked at the daisy she had just taken from the vase, and began to pick the petals, letting them drip from her fingers. She smiled to herself, and softly spoke.

'She loves him...she loves him not...she loves him...'

It was just before 7 o'clock, and Max and Ailsa headed up the hill to Mufty's barn. They went around a little winding back road first, so as to avoid being seen. They could hear voices as they approached, and Ailsa's heart started to beat rapidly. It was beginning to get dark, and the long shadows cast an eerie feel.

At a signal from Max, they crept around the corner to find the three boys passing round a bottle of single malt whisky and drinking straight from the bottle. At Michael's feet lay a bag and Max, coming forward quickly and diving in amidst various exclamations, picked it up and turned it upside down. Out tumbled – not packets of drugs of any sort, but a heap of what looked like games and films – pirate copies Ailsa assumed.

'Dad!' Ryan said, with more than a touch of panic in his voice. Ailsa stepped in and neatly took the whisky from John as he stood by with a sneer on his face. 'How did you... where did you...' Ryan stammered.

Max ignored his son's questions. 'Right, the three of you get down the brae. George is waiting with the car, get in and get home. I will be talking to both your parents – again.

'Aye, well much good it'll dae. My Mum and Dad are fine with me drinking, and anyway, I'm sixteen. I'm no a baby,' Michael slurred.

'Sixteen is still underage,' Max said shortly. He did not want to have to deal with the other two. His own son was enough to deal with at the moment. 'I could report you to the police.'

'Aye, but you're no gonnae, cos that would mean Ryan getting into bother too,' John laughed contemptuously.

'I don't want you to say another word. Get down the hill right this minute.' Max was seriously annoyed at this attitude, more so because the boy was correct in his assumptions, and he wouldn't dream of reporting his own son. After a long stare at the doctor, the boys decided to do as they were told, for once, and turned to go. Michael took the bag with him. Max decided it wasn't worth the aggravation, although he would mention it to their parents. Ryan looked beseechingly at his father, but Max just shook his head and turned away, and Ryan had no choice but to follow the others down the brae.

'At least it wasn't drugs,' Ailsa said, as they made their way down the hill together, watching the Trannoch car pull away.

'No, but I'm pretty sure that Ryan pinched that whisky from Dad's drinks cabinet again. It's a vintage you wouldn't be able to buy in the SPAR.'

'What will you do?' Ailsa asked, as Max's arm went around her shoulders. She still had the bottle of whisky clutched in front of her. 'Anyone seeing us would think we were the ones drinking behind the barn,' she giggled.

He grinned, then became serious. 'I have no idea what to do with him. Something that will hopefully bring him up short and make him really think about what he's done. I've no idea what punishment will have that effect on him. This parenting lark is really, really hard.'

'I wouldn't know. But hopefully I will, someday.'

Max stopped in his tracks and stared at her. 'You mean you want a baby?'

'Well, yes, at some point. Why, is that a problem?'

He tried to appear nonchalant. 'No, not really, I just hadn't thought about having another child that's all. It's a bit of a shock.'

'Well, not right now, obviously. Are you saying you don't *want* a baby? Don't *ever* want another baby?'

Max hesitated just a moment too long before saying, 'No, not really. I don't know.' This was not the response Ailsa was looking for and she fell silent.

Max filled the silence. 'It's a lovely sunset, let's walk back to Storm Winds and you can ask Jim to drive me home.'

The evening was beautiful. It was dark walking along the headland, but the blazing sunset lit up the western isles, flint clouds topped the Cuillin ridge on the Isle of Skye, and the water, mellow in its greyness, spilled gently on the shore. Ailsa knew almost every inch of this walk and loved it more every time she took it. She never failed to count her blessings at being able to live in such an amazingly beautiful part of the world – having Storm Winds, her friends and of course Max.

The discussion tonight, however, had taken a strange turn. She was not sure whether Max was telling her he absolutely did not want a baby in the future or not. Ailsa was nearly thirty five, and the maternal clock was ticking. She had never thought of having a baby before. Her full-on life in London was not the kind of environment she had considered suitable to bring up a child, and her previous marriage had been only three years long when she was much younger. But here, in the North West of Scotland, where her ancestors had roamed the mountains and fought in the glens, she felt she was truly home. She was settled for the first time in her life, and she wanted to put down her own roots, to continue the lineage, to make her own piece of history. She suddenly realised she wanted to leave her own estate, Storm Winds, to her own child.

True, she and Max were only months into their relationship; there had been no talk of engagement, marriage or children up until now. They both knew in their own minds that they were strong and that they had a solid future together, and that was all each of them had wanted. But Ailsa realised now she wanted more. She thought about the conversation as they walked under the peaceful night skies, her heart sinking as deeply as the sunset behind the mountains, as she realised that now she had a creeping doubt. He hadn't categorically said 'no' to a baby, they hadn't even discussed it properly, but what if that was really how he felt? What if Ryan and Aria were enough for him, if he felt he already had his family, where would that leave her? Would it be worth getting into a long lasting relationship with Max if he was determined never to have another child?

'What are you thinking?'

'Oh, just this and that,' she smiled, and shrugged.

'I'll just get going when we get to Storm Winds. I feel I need to see Ryan tonight and not leave it until the morning.'

'Okay.'

For the rest of that week Ailsa and Max did not see each other, chiefly because they were both busy. Max had to go on two separate evening home visits, and had been away for two nights at a medical conference in London. Ailsa was busy with the estate, preparing the East Wing, and overseeing the painters and decorators who were helping to do up the accommodation. The builder was adding another much needed bathroom. She was also throwing herself into her writing, hiding away in her library well into the early hours until Miss Cochrane shooed her out and to bed with exclamations at the time she was spending alone.

'It's one o'clock in the morning!' the housekeeper whispered, as if there were lots of people in the house she might waken. 'The fire's oot, and this place is like a fridge! Get away to bed with ye!'

Ailsa almost laughed at the vision of Miss Cochrane, her hair in little sponge rollers, with a net tied round her head which reminded her of the play *The Steamie* and a long garish green dressing gown over her pyjamas. Cocky was holding a cup of hot chocolate in her hand which she handed over. Ailsa sighed, saved her work, and shut her laptop, realising that her hands were like ice.

Hunter turned and prepared to go down to breakfast. She thought about Malcolm with contempt. She had only used the hateful man to ensure her place at Trannoch. When the Colonel wanted to bring her here, he had met with opposition from all of his sons except Malcolm who had stuck up for his father only because he wanted Hunter to himself. Now that she was there, and 'fitting in' (by her own account) with the household; finding her place as true mistress, by dint of age and nothing else, she wanted nothing more than to cast aside the second son of the Colonel, and concentrate on claiming her rightful place. She much preferred younger men, but she was willing to compromise if it meant she would be in a position of authority at Trannoch. When she found out Malcolm was ill, she knew that as far as she was concerned, his fate was sealed. She couldn't bear to be around ill people, the sour smell and feeling of contamination was too much for the feisty, beautiful Hunter, who had never known a day's illness in her life.

The Colonel was her real prize. She had led a furiously passionate affair with him when she was young, at the same time as she was seeing Sir Angus Hamilton-Dunbar, Ailsa's father. Hunter gave birth to Ailsa then immediately had her adopted, as she would not let a mere baby stand in the way of her ambitions. Hunter mesmerised and bewitched both men, but the Colonel, she admitted only to herself, was the only man she had ever felt any emotional attachment towards.

Hunter had come full circle. After having fled Scotland for Australia, where she met and married a rancher, Ricky, who at that time was a rich man. He had died a few years previously. By the time she had met Ricky her own son was two, but Hunter, in her typically selfish way, refused to either tell Ricky who the real father was or tell the real father about a son. Joshua grew up knowing that Ricky had adopted him, and not knowing or caring who his real father was. His only ambition was working the ranch with Ricky. Hunter made frequent visits to London over the years, meeting the Colonel both there, and in Australia. Then she had heard that Sir Angus was dying, and that he had found his blood daughter, Ailsa, who had been living and working in London. So, when Ricky died, Hunter had high-tailed it back to Scotland to try and use her son to oust her daughter. It was not to be. Ailsa had carried out DNA tests and established without doubt that she was Sir Angus's daughter, and Hunter was her mother. Ailsa had inherited the entire estate of Storm Winds, along with a huge fortune and land stock in the North West, many properties across the area, and a villa in Italy. Joshua had gone back to Australia at the end of last year, but before he went, he showed Ailsa a DNA test which Hunter had previously secreted away. Neither Joshua nor Ailsa had any idea if the Colonel knew Joshua was his son.

'The Colonel and I are arranging a dinner party and dance for Saturday.' Hunter in one fluid movement swung round elegantly from the sideboard, a plate in her hand filled with scrambled egg and mushrooms, and took her seat next to the Colonel as usual. He was buried in his broadsheet newspaper.

'Oh? It's the *Colonel and I* now, is it?' Carys said with her acerbic tongue. 'How things change quickly around here!'

'How are you feeling this morning, darling?' Thomas was already flapping about in a matronly fashion as he entered the breakfast room. He kissed Cary's cheek before she had a chance to turn away. She ignored him.

'I hope you will all manage it? We have invited some very influential people. It will be a most gracious affair,' Hunter twittered on.

'Who needs to be influenced?' Carys asked loftily, with an icy stare. 'We are socially well above any local dignitaries who may come along, unless you are looking for a local dignitary yourself, Hunter?'

'Carys, shut up and stop being so bloody snobbish.' Noel very rarely joined in any conversation, and Carys was not the only one who looked up in surprise.

'You can count me out – I'm meeting an old University friend on Saturday; it's been arranged for ages.' Malcolm was currently in remission, and was feeling almost back to his old self again. He was also feeling enraged by Hunter's attitude to his illness, and to himself. The fact she had quite openly dumped him, without actually admitting to it, left him feeling put-upon. He suspected she was back in his father's good graces, but he could only guess at the extent.

'Well, un-arrange it,' the Colonel barked at his second son. 'Hunter has gone to a lot of trouble arranging this, and I want you ALL to be there.'

'Also me and Papa?' Olivia had crept so quietly into the room that no one heard her arrive. She had only recently started to dine with the family, mainly because she did not want her father to think there was any bad feeling towards Malcolm, or anything which would make her father suspicious about her keeping to her suite and not joining the family who had 'rescued' her. Malcolm had never spoken to her since she came to live at Trannoch, and this made it easier for the young Italian. Alberto followed in her wake and noisily filled his plate from the warming dishes on the sideboard. Olivia helped herself to some toast and coffee.

'Er...erm...yes it does, Olivia,' the Colonel stammered, while Hunter's face turned pale.

'Darling, do you really think...' Hunter got no further.

'You heard me,' was the brusque response, and Hunter closed her mouth hurriedly.

'I thought you Italians ate a healthy Mediterranean diet?' Carys pointedly remarked to Alberto, as she surveyed the pile of sausage, eggs and bacon and four slices of toast on the one plate.

'Is good, no?' was all Alberto returned.

'Oh, it's good alright, you won't find anything but the highest quality at Trannoch, but it is obviously far too good for my own figure.' As Alberto seemed neither to understand nor worry about this remark, she ploughed on, 'You know, you remind me of someone.'

The Colonel and Max both groaned in anticipation.

'Eh?' Alberto looked enquiringly at Carys, a line of yolk oozing from the corner of his mouth.

'That's it! Hercule Poirot, the Agatha Christie detective!' She looked round the table triumphantly. 'Do you know him?'

'Non personalmente,' Alberto said, rudely pointing his eggy fork in her direction, and was gratified to hear the chuckles round the table at this.

'He understood *that* comment alright!' Max said in an undertone to Ryan next to him. Ryan smiled up at his father gratefully. It was the first time Max had spoken normally to his son in three days.

'Grandfather, Mum has asked me to help in her new tea shop while I'm home from Uni during the summer holidays,' Melody said, and received approving glances from Max and her father, Noel.

'Good, darling. That will give you a bit of insight to working life,' the Colonel said, as if he was some kind of authority on this, and he smiled warmly at his granddaughter.

'Are you going to let your granddaughter work in a *shop*?' Carys asked, as if the Colonel had suggested sending her down a coal mine.

The Colonel put his paper down carefully and slowly turned to his daughter-in-law for a long minute before he spoke.

'Oh...oh!' quipped Max.

'The day I take advice from you, Carys MacKenzie, is the day your husband takes over the running of Trannoch – thankfully neither event is ever likely to happen.' There were muted laughs around the table at this. Carys lifted her teacup and put it to her beautifully made up lips with no more than a tiny flicker of emotion in her eyes. Thomas merely shrugged.

'Dad, can I talk to you?' Ryan caught up with his father as he took the wide stairs two at a time. Max stopped and looked at his watch.

'Okay, come up to my study. I need to get my case for work.' Ryan followed him.

'Well?' Max did not do preambles.

'I just wanted to say, I'm sorry.' Ryan shifted from one foot to the other.

Max sat on the edge of his desk, with his arms folded in front of his chest. 'Okay, thank you for apologising. You go back to school in a few days, and I don't want you to leave when there is any atmosphere between us.'

'Neither do I.'

'You need to do better. You are only thirteen, and it would worry me if you were drinking if you were seventeen, never mind thirteen. It's not on.'

'Nearly fourteen.'

'Yes, nearly fourteen.' Max managed a half-smile. 'Still too young, and worrying.'

'I know.'

'So what are you going to do about it?' Max was starting to think that his son was saying only the things he wanted him to hear.

'Well, I'm not going to hang out with John and Michael any longer when I'm home for the holidays. They're older and gang up on me, and ask me to do things I really don't want to do.'

'Like stealing your grandfather's whisky,' Max said dryly.

'Yes, Sir.'

'You don't have to call me "Sir", Ryan. I'm your father, not your teacher.' Max sighed, the conversation a few weeks' ago with Ailsa ringing in his ears.

'Okay.'

'If they're bullying you, I want to know about it. Are they?'

'Kinda. But it's okay, I'm not going to do what they want me to do any more.'

'Okay. I have spoken with both their parents again, and I've said I'll talk to the police if I find them anywhere near either you or Trannoch again. It seems that they both told their parents that you were the instigator, that it was you who had decided to steal the whisky.'

'I knew they would say that.' Ryan looked straight into his father's eyes. 'But it's not true.'

'Hmmm, well, I do believe you. I will get your report in a few months' time from your Head at Criandornoch, and I will be reading it very carefully. Have you been behaving at school?'

'I had a Head's report last term.' Ryan was nothing if not honest.

'What for?'

'For messing about in science, and cheeking Mr Dunsmore.'

'No drinking or smoking?' Max's eyes were like a gimlet's, boring into his son's.

'No.'

'Well, keep it that way. I hope you owned up to Grandfather for stealing his whisky?'

'Yes, I did, and he has said he won't pay for my school trip to Paris. If I want to go, I need to get a holiday job and pay for it myself.'

'Seems a bit lenient for Grandfather! You'd better watch yourself Ryan, you have plenty of brains. Don't waste them away on dangerous people and things which could ruin your chances forever. Now, I need to go. I'll see you when I get home.'

'Dad?' Max stopped in the doorway and turned.

'I really am sorry, and... and... I love you.'

'I love you too, son.'

Chapter Five

The rain was virtually horizontal. It stabbed the cliffs as it came in from the direction of the sea, and the sting felt like icicles, cold and incessant like a winter's day rather than a spring one.

Ailsa's two best friends, Connie and Jan, were at Storm Winds for the weekend. Connie had been her adviser when she became the owner of the huge estate in Scotland, and as a lawyer, was able to offer her friend valuable advice. Jan owned a small business, a tiny cafe in central London which made more money than a large restaurant in the centre of Manchester would do. Both friends had spent many weekends with Ailsa since she moved to the North West.

'It will be exciting going to Trannoch for a dinner party!' Connie said, buttering her toast.

'Yes, the last time we were there was at the barbeque for the Highland Games, your first official public duty, Ailsa!' Jan said, 'by the way, this porridge is amazing!'

Ailsa remembered how terrified she had been, opening her first event. She had never even been to a Highland Games before.

'What are you two wearing? It's usually very formal, as I said in my email – I hope you have something lovely and sparkly? The Storm Winds contingent needs to measure up to Trannoch!'

'Don't worry. We won't let you down. Just wait till you see our dresses, they are absolutely beautiful.' Connie pointed her fork at her friend. 'Cost an absolute bloody fortune, but it's worth it to mix with the landed gentry!'

'I have a local girl coming in to do our hair and make-up about three o'clock, then we'll take our time and have a little drink while we dress! We have to be there at half six.'

'I can't wait!' Connie smiled.

'Ms Jan Holland and Ms Connie Stapleton,' Denbeath announced, in a huge voice which came from somewhere near his feet, and which most people did not realise he possessed. Jan and Connie walked nervously into the packed room.

'The Lady Ailsa Hamilton-Dunbar.' At this, the voices dropped significantly, and the occupants of Trannoch's ballroom looked appreciatively at Ailsa, looking resplendent in a long cobalt gown. She nodded very slightly in a friendly fashion and took Max's outstretched hand. He pulled her towards him and kissed her on both cheeks, he then kissed Jan and Connie who were outwardly nervous.

'You look beautiful, darling. Jan and Connie, you both look lovely!' he said warmly.

'Thanks, Max! You're not looking so bad yourself!' Connie said, smiling. 'In fact, if you weren't besotted with one of my best friends, I think I would just need to pin you down.' Both Ailsa's friends had met Max several times and agreed that he was definitely the nicest of the MacKenzie brothers, although maybe not quite as handsome as Malcolm. He did however look very dashing this evening, in his MacKenzie tartan kilt.

Max chuckled. 'Well I hope this won't be too gruesome for you tonight. Ailsa begged the Colonel not to make announcements when people arrived, but he very fondly told her that he wanted everyone to see how beautiful she is.'

Ailsa looked astonished at this public proclamation from Max, even if it was just to her two best friends. 'I, er... you know I don't like a fuss,' she said shortly, as Max took champagne flutes from a footman holding a silver tray, and passed them round.

'Ah, Ailsa, I see you have your two London friends with you!' The voice rang out confidently from behind her, and she turned to Malcolm; a much thinner Malcolm, but nonetheless looking reasonably well. He was looking straight at Connie, his eyes roving over her voluptuous figure packed into a silver grey satin.

'Nice to see you again, Malcolm,' Connie said lightly, but Jan could see that she was uncomfortable at his stare.

'I hear you have been unwell,' Jan said, matter-of-factly. 'I hope you are feeling better?'

Jan meant no malice, but Malcolm visibly bristled at this public reference to his illness. 'I am well, thank you.' He looked at Jan as if she were something the cat had just dragged in, and she flushed.

'Is Calum here yet?' Connie asked Max pointedly. Connie had been seeing Calum, a bright young lawyer from the Colonel's law firm, since the fateful Ghillie's Ball at Storm Winds. He had been to stay with her in London, and she had stayed with him in his modest flat in Fort William.

'Yes, I saw him a moment ago, Connie, with Gregory.' She smiled over to Jan at the mention of the man Jan had met at the Ghillie's Ball. Jan glowed with happiness.

'You mean that fisherman?' Malcolm said spitefully. 'I wonder at some of the people the Colonel chooses to invite. I mean, look at the state of him. His hair makes him look positively wild.'

'Malcolm, shut up, for God's sake. Don't be so rude,' Max said in disgust, as Jan turned white. 'You are in no position to judge anyone.'

'Well well! Speaking up for the hoi polloi now, are we? How commendable! May I remind you, little brother, that I am in *just* the position to judge. You should watch who your friends associate themselves with, Lady Hamilton-Dunbar,' he finished with a sneer, and, before Max could answer, turned his back and walked away.

'Looking for fresh meat no doubt,' Connie said, and got a sharp look from Max. Whatever he said about his brother, he didn't want anyone else disparaging either him or anyone else in his family. Ailsa noticed, and gave him an apologetic stare, gently squeezing his hand.

Connie and Jan moved away to seek their partners, and the Colonel and Hunter joined Ailsa and Max.

'Well, you'll never be as beautiful as Carys, but you do look lovely tonight, darling!' Hunter said, with a smile packed with sugar.

'If that's a compliment, I'll say thank you, Hunter,' was Ailsa's dignified response.

The Colonel was babbling, 'Ailsa, you are a perfect vision, my darling girl! Maxwell, you are the luckiest of all my sons. I do hope you look after her tonight and make sure she is treated like the belle of the ball that she is? After all, her subjects would expect it!' He laughed appreciatively at his own joke, which was said half-joking, wholly in earnest.

Malcolm had looked for Hunter a few times but each time she was with his father. He was beginning to feel seriously irked at her attitude towards him, which had led to his unaccountably crass dialogue with Ailsa's friends.

When Denbeath announced dinner was ready, they paraded down the long hall in traditional fashion, the men escorting the ladies. As they left the Great Room, Ailsa just happened to glance around and saw Malcolm watching Calum as he awkwardly put his arm out to Connie. There was an unfathomable expression on the face of the Colonel's second son, and Ailsa gave an involuntary shiver.

Ailsa took her place, with Connie to her left and Max to her right. Ailsa stood at the table, then, when everyone was present, the Colonel sat, and they all followed suit. Ailsa glanced around the huge table as the first of six courses was served. Carys looked pale, but beautiful as usual, her light pink strapless dress hid the smallest of baby bumps, and her turquoise eyes looked back at Ailsa with an expression of jealousy, superiority, or just plain hate. Ailsa couldn't work it out. She noticed Clem and Stephen Millburn at the other end of the table, too far from her to hold a conversation, which was a shame as she would have liked her friend near her. Malcolm was still eyeing Connie, his brows lowered in a dark stare, and Olivia, seated next to her father, looked frightened and alone. Hunter patted the Colonel's hand almost every time he spoke, with a hopeful glance at the strangers in the party to ensure they had noticed the intimacy. There were deep undercurrents in the gathering, and Ailsa, feeling a sense of morbid intent, lapsed into a gloomy silence.

'Are you alright, darling? You seem very quiet this evening. I hope it has nothing to do with my dissolute brother's little episode earlier?' Max was tucking into his Chicken Balmoral with relish.

'Well, yes, it is, partly. He's so spiteful, Max,' she answered, in an undertone. 'Why does he have to be like that? I know he has his own crosses to bear, but he was positively hitting on Connie.'

'Hardly hitting on her. Okay,' he hurriedly added as he saw she was ready to jump in, 'he did look her up and down quite openly, but that's just him. She is quite obviously head over heels with... what's his name? Oh yes, Calum, who looks as if he is at least ten years younger than her. Please just forget my brother, Ailsa, and don't let him ruin your night.'

Ailsa perked up after this, holding several conversations across the table with different people, most of whom she had met, and a few she had not. One was introduced as Sir Pierce Donald, a widower of some fifteen years, and a very quietly spoken, distinguished kind of man in his early seventies. He was tall and distinguished looking, and had a quirky way of nodding his head after everything he said as if, in a nice way, encouraging the other person to agree with him. Ailsa liked him almost immediately. As she spoke to him, she noticed that Hunter was gazing at her.

'Are you happy up here in Bonnie Scotland, Lady Ailsa?' Sir Pierce nodded politely, 'or may I call you Ailsa?'

'Of course, please do. I much prefer it,' she laughed lightly. 'I am really happy here. Storm Winds is a magnificent estate, and I feel at home there.'

'I knew your father, of course. He used to come across to Mhainaray occasionally for a change of scenery.'

'Mhainaray?'

'Oh yes, it's a small island, just off the coast of Skye. Been in the family for years, you know. Instead of your magnificent mountains here, we have rolling green hills, heather and shelter from the Isle of Skye which makes it warm and verdant.'

'It sounds lovely,' Ailsa said, smiling.

'I've known the MacKenzie boys since they were born. They used to come over from Arnasaid Bheag on the ferry and stay with us, myself and Lady Moira, when they were home from school. It was a pleasure to have them stay. We had no children of our own you see.' His voice was touched with sadness at this last statement. 'Young Maxwell here, was the serious, studious one, but he could be just as wicked as his other brothers on occasion!' and he laughed a gentle laugh. Max caught this as he turned from his conversation with his niece Melody, to his right, who was not due back at Uni for another few days. He grinned.

'Must you blot my copybook with Ailsa, Uncle Pierce?' Max grinned affectionately at the older man.

'Was Uncle Max naughty when he was young?' Melody quipped delightedly. 'Please tell us, Uncle Pierce!' Sir Pierce was not a real uncle, but all the MacKenzie boys and their children called him such.

'Oh, I couldn't possibly tell you now, and misrepresent him to Ailsa. But I will certainly tell you when we get a quiet moment together, Melody!' and Sir Pierce touched the side of his nose conspiratorially, and left it at that.

The dinner passed off with no incident, and afterwards the party congregated in the magnificent ballroom, where there was to be dancing to traditional Scottish music. Ailsa and Max sat in a small group in a corner with Connie, Jan and their two boyfriends, and Ailsa couldn't help noticing that Connie's eyes were flashing with excitement and she was red faced. She wondered if it was the wine, which had been very potent. When they were all supplied with more drinks, Calum looked round the little party nervously, and stammered a request that they should all be quiet because he had something to say. This was a promising beginning, and they all fell silent, looking at him expectantly.

'I... er... we... wanted you all to be the first to know,' he began. 'No, that's not right, you're not all actually first to know, because we've told our parents... anyway, I want you all to know...'

'Oh, get on with it!' Connie burst out, laughingly.

'Aye, okay Connie. I just wanted to say the right thing.' Calum looked wounded.

'And you have, darling, but I can't wait another minute,' she said. 'Calum has asked me to marry him.' And although through Calum's disjointed speech the friends had all guessed as much, nonetheless they were delighted, as Connie swung round her left hand with a beautiful sapphire engagement ring on it. They all made such a racket hugging and kissing and shouting congratulations that the people near them stopped dancing, then gradually the rest turned to look and the music came to a halt.

'Sorry for the hilarity, everyone,' Max said to the audience, who looked on expectantly. 'It's just that we have had a very happy announcement and, if I may?' He looked at Calum who nodded. 'I would like to announce the engagement of Calum and Connie. Can we raise our glasses, please?' He waited until everyone sought out their champagne flutes before he continued, 'May I wish Calum er...'

'Andrews and Stapleton!' Ailsa hissed in his ear.

'Calum Andrews and Connie Stapleton, a long and happy engagement... sorry, I mean life... together!' and as Ailsa rolled her eyes at his mistake, everyone laughed and raised their glasses.

That same day three people had landed at Glasgow airport and embarked from the Pisa, Italy flight. They collected their luggage and made their way out of the airport to a short stay car park where a car awaited them. One of the men took a key from the top of the tyre on the passenger side, and they loaded their bags in. The woman sat in front, keying in a post code. They were quiet as they drove through the mid-morning traffic. Once on the road north, they drove quickly, as the road was reasonably quiet. They were staying in Scotland for a few months at least. They had work to do, and these things take a long time in planning. None of them were meticulous in their planning. Quite chaotic in fact. In the meantime they were headed to their friend's house in Fort William where they would stay for a while to decide on their next course of action. She had arranged the stolen car with new plates, and had it placed in the car park.

Joyce Whitelaw would be waiting for them.

Melody was still chuckling over her conversation with Sir Pierce in the ballroom, when he told her of the scrapes Max had got into when he was a boy. He was never as adventurous as his two big brothers, Noel and Malcolm, nor as quiet as Thomas, his younger brother. Max nonetheless had a temper, which, when roused, could out-do anything his siblings could produce. Sir Pierce had told her of the day they all took one of the Mhainaray boats out, when the estate manager was not looking, despite the fact that they were all under the age of twelve, and Noel was the only one who had ever actually rowed a boat himself. Neither Max nor Thomas who, was only three, wanted to go, and Noel and Malcolm bullied Thomas until he cried himself almost into hysterics, before they gave up and told him to get lost. Max was just turning six, and he refused to let his older brothers bully him too, so he went. The boys soon got into difficulties, the boat ran aground on some rocks, and it was all the three could do to scramble out and onto the biggest rock, but the tide was coming in. It was only because of little Thomas, who had sat on the beach for an hour and a half waiting for them to come back, that they were saved. On the way to tell his uncle, he met the estate manager, a surly giant of a man called Frank and confessed. Frank then got out another boat and went to find them. He brought them back, bedraggled with sea spray and tired, but otherwise alright. Frank had taken them to his estate office and questioned them, really angrily, as one of the Mhainaray boats was damaged and he would need to fix it. Thomas was still bawling as if the world had come to an end, and Frank snapped in rage.

'That's enough!' he had shouted at Thomas. 'You're bawlin' yer eyes oot aboot these three laddies who are safe, and I have to worry about a boat that now needs mending! You stupid little boys! I should give you all a good hiding. Aye, an' I'll start with you because you won't stop that greetin' like a baby!'

'Don't you dare touch, Thomas. You horrid big bully!' Max hid his little brother behind him as he faced up to the man. His temper was starting to flare, and his only thought was of his little brother who was crying and anxious. 'He had nothing to do with it. He's too wee!'

'Oh, aye! And I suppose you're Mr Samson yersel', wee yin!' But, before he could say another word, Max had picked up the nearest thing to hand, a paperweight off the desk and threw it at the man. Frank, sitting behind his desk, caught the marble implement on his left temple; he saw it coming but did not have time to turn away. There was a yell, then a crash, and the redoubtable Frank fell backwards and onto the floor.

Silence! The four boys went white and Thomas burst out crying again.

'You've killed him!' Malcolm said, more in admiration than fear.

'Don't be stupid, he's just knocked out.' Max had heard this expression recently when the cook had hit her head off the table and collapsed at Trannoch. He ran around and put his ear to the man's mouth and nodded, affirming that Frank was still breathing.

'Will we run away?' Noel asked, seriously.

'You'll be put in prison, Max!' Malcolm said sneeringly. 'They'll put chains round your ankles, and you'll be in a dark cell with rats.'

'I'm going to get Uncle Pierce,' Max had said firmly, and the small boy had run up the hill to the imposing estate house of Mhainaray, burst straight into the library, where Sir Pierce was entertaining his friend, the local doctor, and announced: 'Uncle, I've just hit Frank with a big thing off his desk, and he's knocked out. I tried to kill him actually, but it didn't work, cos he's still breathing. He was going to smack wee Thomas!'

Dr Munro was out of his chair in a flash, and, followed by Sir Pierce, the two raced down to the office where the other three boys were now howling, and Frank was sitting up behind the desk wondering what had hit him. Dr Munro pronounced him slightly concussed, and he was sent to his cottage to go to bed, and await the doctor. The two grown-ups managed to get the tale from Noel and Malcolm. All four were sent to bed. Max was unusually resentful, as he was normally the most law-abiding little boy, and next day completely refused to say 'sorry' to Frank, who had been summoned to Sir Pierce's study in order that the boys might apologise. Max therefore stayed in bed for a further morning, until he eventually, and grudgingly, gave his apology.

Sir Pierce had related this as the best of the worst of her Uncle Max, and Melody had squealed with delight as he dished the dirt on her favourite uncle. It had been a fun evening for her, she was mature for her age, and she had enjoyed the time spent at home during a short break from Uni. She was making her way to the little cloakroom next to the Colonel's library when she heard voices from the room – the door was slightly ajar.

'Now listen here, if you say anything, *anything* about this... I'll... I'll...' came an angry male voice.

'Shut up. You know fine well you won't do a thing. The first born? Ha! You'd lose everything, especially your damned inheritance,' said a female voice.

'You know quite well that the Colonel has already said he would split the inheritance equally amongst the four brothers, so just shut up, you silly bitch.'

'Don't you dare talk to me like that! Anyway, all I want is another 10 per cent of the business, that will still leave you with a majority of 60/40.'

'I built the business up myself! You have no right...' There was a resounding slap, and Melody flinched and drew back from the door.

'You're nothing but a bastard. I don't want to set eyes on you ever again, and I want my 10 per cent by next week.'

There was the click of a lighter. 'Well that's going to be a bit difficult since we both live here,' he said. 'You'll get your 10 per cent, but just keep out of my way, and if you say anything about this, I swear I will kill you.'

Melody heard the sound of footsteps on the polished boards of the library coming towards the door. She backed into the cloakroom and took a few deep breaths. She didn't need to see who it was; they were both voices she recognised.

Noel and Carys.

Olivia was getting ready for bed. She pulled her nightgown over her bump, which was still neat for almost full term. She looked round her bedroom. It was dark now, the shadows from the tall sash windows cast around her like a group of sinister onlookers. Her bedroom led onto a new en suite bathroom, put in for her when she came to live at Trannoch. There was a door on the other side of the room which opened into her elegant sitting room, both rooms overlooking the courtyard and the mountains beyond. The suite had been decorated to her own taste and colours, and she spent most of her time here as far away from the family as she could. It helped to have her father here, although she was nervous in case, by some way, he would find out that it was Malcolm who was the father, and therefore her abductor.

She thought about the beautiful people at the dinner party as the quiet strains of music floated up the ornate stairway to her. She wondered what they had made of her and her father. Olivia was of good working class country stock. Her father was a builder's son, and he had taken over the business to provide his wife and daughter with a comfortable lifestyle in a large converted villa, where he had done all the work himself. This had set them apart from their friends who considered them to be punching above their weight and having ideas beyond their station in life. But it particularly suited Olivia and her mother, who always felt they were socially elevated from the working class lifestyle into which they had been born. Olivia's mother had insisted her daughter was brought up properly with manners and education.

She was a beautiful girl, with long thick dark hair and lovely dark eyes. Her olive skin and slight build were typically Italian. She loved her rooms at Trannoch but felt lonely and isolated. However, she was also clever. She knew the MacKenzies would do anything to protect their reputation, which was why she had insisted that her father come to live here. He had sold the house in Tuscany and the business, and had come to find her, but she also was certain that he wouldn't stay at Trannoch. He was a simple man with simple tastes, and he did not fit in to the social circles in which the MacKenzies moved. In fact, they were worlds apart. He had talked to Olivia about building a house in the small port of Arnasaid Bheag – where there was plenty of land to buy, but Alberto was reluctant to stay in Scotland. Similarly, he had now nothing in Italy to return to, so he felt he had to cut his losses and stay where his daughter and the expected baby were to settle. Olivia felt she could, in time, settle at Trannoch. The party line was that she was a long lost cousin of the Colonel's late wife, who had been half-Italian, and therefore the Colonel believed that this was a plausible explanation for her coming to stay at Trannoch. No one believed it of course, but no one could be certain, though there were a few good guesses. Malcolm's reputation went before him.

Only she and Malcolm really knew what happened that night, though even Malcolm was unsure of the exact nature of the 'attack' as he had been quite literally out of his mind drunk. Olivia had been attracted to him, and when he had led her to the little secluded Folly deep in the woods around Trannoch, during the barbeque, she had willingly participated. She had had quite a lot to drink herself. Suddenly she had sobered as she looked into Malcolm's eyes and heard him grunting like a wild animal, saliva flying everywhere. She had tried to shove him off her, shouting to stop, but Malcolm had held her down. She punched and kicked him, like a fiend, but he had held her wrists until they swelled. Punching her, he had cut her lip, sending her flying back before he staggered out of the Folly and away. He had little memory of any of this.

Not wishing to go to any of the family, she had made her way back to the house and found refuge in a bedroom, where she cried her eyes out, asking God's forgiveness and cursing the day she met Malcolm. She vowed he would pay, and with this thought fresh in her mind, Ailsa had found her. Instinctively, Olivia knew that this was the perfect person to tell.

Putting the past behind her, she thought back to earlier that evening. Her father had gone to his room shortly after dinner. His room was in a different part of the house to hers, one the MacKenzies kept for their less inspiring guests. She had taken a walk in the grounds as she normally did in the evening, and came upon Malcolm sitting by himself on a small wall in the courtyard. She hadn't spoken directly to him nor he to her since she came to live at Trannoch. She turned to walk away, but he had already seen her, and spoke.

'No, wait Olivia.' His voice was pleading, and she turned back.

'Why?'

'Because I want to talk to you.'

'Oh? Well I no want to talk to you.'

'Please. I won't touch you. I only want to talk.' He looked so dejected that she moved over towards him and sat on the wall.

'I'm sorry.'

'Sorry?'

'For what I did. It has haunted me. I feel I can't live with myself.'

'Okay, what you want me do about this?' she asked straightforwardly.

He caught his breath before he spoke. 'That is my child you're carrying. I want to be a father to it... he or she. I want to look after you and the baby.'

'And how long you feel like this?' Her voice was steady and without emotion.

'I suppose since my illness. I came to question my own mortality.'

'Really?' There was the slightest touch of sarcasm in her voice. 'Well, I tell you this, Mr Malcolm MacKenzie. I can no keep you away from my baby, but I keep you from me. I never want you touch me again. I hope you go to hell.'

He put his head in his hands, and she listened with satisfaction to him crying quietly before she walked away.

Chapter Six

The next day there was a celebratory breakfast at Storm Winds. The children were back at school, so Max had stayed over after the ball, as had her two friends and their partners. Miss Cochrane, was 'fair scunnered' at having to produce champagne for breakfast. She muttered away to Jean Morton, the fiercely religious cook who attended the 'Wee Free' church and abided by its strictures, and who was equally shocked at her mistress and friends having champagne on a Sunday morning. It was blasphemy, plain and simple, and she had never heard of such a thing. So, Jim Hutton, the not-so-fiercely religious handy man had been sent down to the cellar for three bottles for the table in the breakfast room.

'Here's tae ye, wha's like ye, gie few an' they're aw deid!' Max toasted, as he lifted his glass, and the boys nodded in satisfaction at this example of the Scots language, but the women had no idea what he was talking about.

'Here's to you,' Max translated.

'Whoever is like you,' Calum supplemented, 'very few and they're all dead!'

'Charming!' Jan laughed.

'Yeah, when I've worked that out, I will come up with a really brutal remark,' Connie said gulping her drink.

'Are we going to eat, or just sit here and get drunk?' Ailsa said, rising to get a plate and help herself to breakfast from the hotplates on the sideboard.

'Just sit here and get drunk, I think.'

'Connie, really!' said Calum affectionately.

Ailsa continued, 'Jean made all this specially, right before she condemned us all to hell in a hand cart for blasphemy, drinking champagne for breakfast on the Sabbath.'

'Great! Better have the last supper then!' Gregory said, with a wide grin.

Max was surreptitiously eyeing Ailsa. She had not been quite herself for a few days, and he felt she had been quieter than usual at Trannoch the evening before. She looked round and caught his eye, giving him a half-hearted watery smile, which made him think she was just emotional as her friend had got engaged.

The fifth bottle of champagne was emptied, and they had sat there through breakfast and lunch, frostily delivered by Miss Cochrane, in rebellious mood, as it was Eileen's day off. They all went up to bed afterwards to sleep it off.

A week later Ailsa was in her library. The fire was lit, as it was a cold and wet spring afternoon. Jan and Connie had left the previous Monday, Jan to stay with Gregory for a few days and Connie and Calum heading to London for what they called an engagement mid-week break.

She was struggling with the latest chapter in her book, in which she had discovered several mistakes which had to be corrected before she tackled the next. Consequently, she was not in the best of moods, needed to focus on her work, and was irritated when the library door opened and Miss Cochrane walked in followed by a bad-tempered looking Stephen Millburn.

'Mr Millburn is here to see you, Ma'am.' Ailsa and Stephen both looked at the housekeeper in surprise; she had dropped the title some time ago. Ailsa knew this did not bode well.

'Thank you, Miss Cochrane.' Ailsa sighed and rose from behind the enormous library table, stepping down two steps to the level beside the fire. The housekeeper shut the door behind her with a little protest bang.

Stephen had called the landline, which Miss Cochrane had answered as expected. He had asked her to remind Ailsa they had a meeting scheduled for three o'clock, and it was now half past three. Stephen told Cocky to tell Ailsa to come straight across to the estate office as Roddy was leaving early at four o'clock that day.

'And may I ask why you didn't call Lady Ailsa's mobile, instead of this phone?'

A deep sigh had followed. 'I tried it, and she's switched it off. Perhaps you should tell her to put it on again, so that people can contact her.'

'Is that so?' Miss Cochrane had been annoyed at the younger man's tone. She, like Max, thought that Stephen Millburn got away with far too much in his capacity as estate manager, and that the Colonel treated him much too leniently, however good a worker he was. She was irritated by his patronising manner.

'I need you to tell her to come over here now. We won't wait any longer.' Miss Cochrane suspected that Roddy must be listening to this conversation, and this had made her worse.

'Now, you look here, young man. Lady Ailsa is working in her library and has asked me *most particularly* not to disturb her today, which is probably why she has switched off her mobile. You will just need to come over tomorrow.'

'Don't be ridiculous!' His voice rose heatedly. 'Ailsa has obviously forgotten about the meeting, so I need you to go and tell her – NOW!'

Miss Cochrane held the handset away from her and looked at it as if she would like to hurl it over the cliff, but put it to her ear again. 'I've said all I'm going to say.' She hung up, and set it back on the cradle with a self-satisfied curse.

As Miss Cochrane expected, the front doorbell sounded a few minutes later, and a slightly contrite Stephen stood on the doorstep.

'Well?'

'Sorry, Miss Cochrane. I was out of order.' He tried a half-smile, but was disappointed if he thought he could win her over that easily.

'You were,' she said stridently.

'May I come in? I really need to talk to Ailsa.'

'Stephen! What can I do for you?' Ailsa felt her stress levels rising, between the problems with the book and now her estate manager descending upon her looking as handsome as ever in black jeans and jacket. He was the last person she wanted to see.

'May I sit down?'

'Of course, please do.'

'I'm sorry to remind you,' he said carefully, thinking about the ding-dong he had just had with the housekeeper, 'but we had our usual meeting in the estate office set for three o'clock today?'

'Oh God, I completely forgot,' she said wearily. 'Can we move it to tomorrow? I'm really sorry Stephen, but I am a bit behind on work.' She sank into the chair opposite him.

'Well, not really. Roddy has other things he needs to do tomorrow. The next time we could make it would be Friday.'

'Sorry, but I have things on myself, on Friday. Let's just leave it till next week?' It was more an instruction than a question, but Stephen was already aloft his high horse.

'Are you avoiding me?'

There was a startled silence. 'What? Why on earth would I be avoiding you?' She was genuinely surprised. 'I'm just busy on Friday, I do have things to do, you know!'

'You mean like writing stories?' he said sarcastically.

'What is that to do with you? And anyway, even if I was planning to go fly fishing from a canoe, that's no concern of yours!'

Stephen stood up suddenly, and Ailsa felt she had to stand too, so as not to be disadvantaged. He said, 'Very well, you just do what you have to do and I'll make all the decisions and run the estate. I don't know why I bothered to include you anyway, it's obvious you are reluctant to put the estate and its needs before yours. I am used to Sir Angus, and he always put the estate first.'

'How dare you! How *dare* you? Who the hell do you think you are talking to? I *pay you* to run the estate, and you don't, you *absolutely won't* dictate to me!' She was close to tears but managed to hide that little detail quite successfully.

'Yes, well, *Lady Ailsa*, I'm afraid I've just about had enough of your orders. I will be in my office at three o'clock tomorrow, and I will take Roddy off the job he's doing so that we can meet. In other words we will drop everything to accommodate you.' He headed for the door and turned back. 'Oh, and an apology to both Roddy and I wouldn't go amiss when you get there, for wasting our time,' and, before the speechless Ailsa could respond, he flung open the door and marched down the hallway and out the front door.

Ailsa was so angry and over-wrought that she slumped back down in the chair, and like any self-respecting heiress, burst into tears.

'Hi, where are you?'

'Out on the headland with the dogs, why?'

'Ailsa, it is torrential rain. Do you need to go out on the headland now?'

'Is that a rhetorical question?'

'No, it was a concerned one.' Max tried to keep the irritation out of his voice.

Ailsa sighed. 'Well you needn't concern yourself about a little rain. Did you phone for anything in particular?' Max fell silent at this.

'Olivia has had a baby boy,' he said, after a long pause.

'Oh? Well I suppose that's some mildly good news for a change.' She wiped the rain from her face with the back of her hand.

'What is wrong with you?'

'I hope he doesn't take his personality from Malcolm, poor little sod.'

'Well, who knows, but they're saying he looks like her.'

'Well that's a blessing anyway! What's she calling him, Mussolini?' And she erupted into sardonic laughter.

'Has something happened?' He tried another tack. This was so unlike her.

'Well, you've just told me Olivia has had her baby, so I guess, "yes" would be the answer.'

'I'm coming over after surgery,' he said firmly, and hung up.

Ailsa drove the jeep over to Trannoch about an hour later. She told herself it wasn't anything to do with the fact Max had said he was coming over in his 'controlling doctor' voice, or that he had rudely hung up on her, which she detested. She had a present for the baby which she was going to wait until Olivia was out of hospital to deliver, but on the spur of the moment decided to leave it with the Colonel.

'Ailsa!' Both the Colonel and Hunter jumped to their feet as she was shown into the drawing room. The fire was on and the little table which sat between them had on it a whisky and a white wine. The Colonel gave her a hug, but Hunter stood back, fearing that if she tried a hug, then her daughter might shove her away.

'Sit down, dear. Denbeath, a red wine for Lady Ailsa if you please! So you've come to congratulate me on becoming a Grandpapa again?' He was beaming from ear to ear.

'And I, a step-Grandmama!' Hunter said with a little laugh to hide the fact that she actually meant this.

Ailsa, as usual, ignored her mother. 'Yes, I just wanted to leave a gift for them... er... for Olivia, for the baby. I'm sure she'll have enough visitors already at the hospital without me adding to them!' The Colonel looked bewildered at this. Denbeath brought over her wine from the table at the other side of the room, and she took a large gulp. Her hand was shaking.

'Darling, Olivia is here at Trannoch!' Hunter jumped in, delighted that she was the one to break the news. 'Didn't you know? She had the baby here, in the middle of the night, and Max delivered it!'

'What?'

'Yes, it's true. There wasn't time to take her to Dunlivietor hospital, but Maxwell phoned a local midwife to come in.'

The Colonel nodded his head. 'She was too late. By the time she arrived, my Maxwell had delivered a healthy boy!' he finished proudly.

Ailsa felt her emotions rise like a tsunami, coursing up her body to her neck and face which turned bright red with anger. Max had phoned her about an hour ago, and he had known since the early hours of the morning. Why didn't he tell her? It was this lack of communication which maddened her so much. She was also suffering from a sense of desperation and sadness since talking to Max about having a baby. Olivia had just had a baby and she was beginning to wish that it had been her, but these were feelings she refused to recognise. In addition to this, Max – *her* Max, apparently delivered the baby, which he had failed to mention. It may not be a huge thing to him as a doctor, but on top of everything else it was the proverbial straw that broke the camel's back.

'Are you alright, darling?' Hunter saw the anger in her eyes and lost no time making reference to it. 'You look annoyed.'

'Of course I'm not annoyed! How could I be annoyed about such a wonderful thing as Max delivering a baby?'

But Hunter chose to press the point further. 'Well darling, it's just that you seem less cheery after I mentioned it, than before.' Her smile was a painted slash.

This time Ailsa had nothing to say, her emotions were through the roof, but she was not going to break down in front of them, so she ignored Hunter, but the Colonel noticed it. 'Ailsa, I think you know your mother is speaking to you.'

And there it was. Hunter had finally wormed her way back into the Colonel's life effectively enough that he was standing up for her against Ailsa, she who had been like a daughter to him since she came to Scotland. She felt disappointed and unsure of herself, but she managed a weak smile and spoke calmly.

'May I leave this for Olivia, Colonel? And, I really better be getting on my way. Maxwell said he would pop in after surgery.' She had no intention of telling them that there had been any friction between the two of them.

'Very well, leave it here, and I will ask your mother to give it to Olivia when she wakens from her sleep.' The Colonel was driving his point home referring again to Hunter as her mother.

Ailsa left the room hurriedly and literally bumped straight into Max in the hall.

Without a word he took her hand and led her up to his study. He motioned for her to sit on the chesterfield, and poured them both a drink. Then he lit the already laid fire and sat down beside her, studying her for a long few minutes before speaking. He could see that she was struggling with her emotions, she had already surreptitiously wiped a few tears away.

'Please, tell me what's wrong.'

She bit her lip at his gentle tone. She almost wished he was angry, as that would have been easier to deal with. 'I don't know,' she said finally. 'I just feel really up and down, and get upset easily. I seem to be angry all the time, and I seem to make other people angry too.'

He nodded. 'Yes, I've seen all of that in you. I also think that you are probably angry with me for not telling you that I delivered Olivia's baby. I presume that's why you are here?'

'Well, I came for two reasons. Firstly, to give the Colonel a gift for the baby, and secondly, because I was angry with you for hanging up on me. I didn't know until five minutes ago that you had delivered her baby, but I admit I was a bit upset you didn't tell me that on the phone. It would have been a lovely thing to share.'

He nodded. 'Yes, I know. I realise that now. It's just that I haven't been used to sharing with anyone for a long time.'

'Okay, look, it's forgotten.'

'Are you avoiding me?' He leaned forward, his elbows resting on his long legs, cradling his whisky in both hands.

She gave an exasperated laugh. 'That's the second time someone has asked me that today. I admit I didn't want to see you because I was angry with you at that point for hanging up on me, but, in general, then no, of course I am not avoiding you.'

He nodded. 'Good, I'm glad to hear it. But you said someone else had asked you that today?'

'Stephen Millburn asked me the same question. We had a bit of a row.'

'Stephen? Why did he say that?'

Ailsa told him. 'I am not going to be controlled by anyone. Not Stephen, not you, not anyone,' she flashed, the anger back.

'Okay,' he said evenly. 'So... do you still have feelings for him?' he asked quietly. Ailsa had told Max when they got together about how, at one time, she thought she and Stephen might have become an item. But things happened, things changed, and he already had a strong attraction to Clem. So, her own attraction to Stephen had long gone – but had it?

'No, of course not, he irritates me to death. He swans about my estate like he owns it, ordering my staff about, and ordering me about. He calls me *Lady Ailsa* in a sarcastic way, and you know how I dislike anyone using the title. I still can't get used to it myself. He even made fun of my writing today.'

'So why don't you get rid of him?' Max was listening to her intently, picking up little signals here and there as she talked. He could see she was suffering from stress; the signs were all there.

'Because then I would be left with only Roddy. There is too much work for one, and Roddy needs direction.'

'Do you want me to speak to him?' Max said quietly. But this was the last thing Ailsa wanted.

'Max, have you not been listening to a word I've said? He is very controlling, and if you talk to him – man to man – then he's going to have even less respect for me. No, I need to manage him myself.' She calmed down as quickly as she had flared up.

'Fine. But I won't let him bully you. I hate bullies.'

'Yes, I know.' Her eyes twinkled for the first time. 'Melody persuaded Sir Pierce to tell her about you and your brothers' adventures with the boat when you were all young, and you half-killing the estate manager at Mhainaray with a paperweight. She told me all about it.'

He chuckled, 'I'm afraid I might slip down the ranks of favourite uncles with Melody now.'

'Absolutely not. She told me she misjudged you, and that you weren't as boring as you made out to be!'

'Great. That makes me feel so special.' He turned to face her, sitting with one leg tucked under him on the sofa, looking straight at her. 'Anyway, I think there is something else wrong with you that you don't want to admit to.'

'Oh?'

'Yes, the baby.'

'Oh, I'm not bothered about that now. I know you were run off your feet at the surgery today and...'

'I don't mean Olivia's baby, Ailsa. I mean yours – ours.'

She fell silent again, hoping he wouldn't notice she was near to tears.

He did.

'I've been thinking about it a lot,' she owned quietly.

He put his glass down and held her hands in his. 'So have I.'

She slowly lifted her head. 'And?'

'And,' he took a deep breath, 'and I think I have been selfish. After l lost my wife, I have tried so hard to blot things out, to immerse myself in work, and then, when the kids come home, to immerse myself in them. It took a long time for me to let you in Ailsa, and, let's face it, you didn't make it easy.'

'Cheers.'

'But, when I did, I thought I was complete, happy. When you mentioned a baby, I suddenly thought that it would upset that careful little world where I am cocooned.'

'And now?'

'And now, I realise that there is you, who I need, who I want, to let in. I need to share everything with you, not just the things I decide I want to share. I need to communicate better with you, and I need to trust. I can't just make every decision and do everything that concerns us – myself. I *would* like a baby, but just not right now. I think we both need to get used to each other a lot more before that happens. We just need to live and love a wee bit longer.'

She laid her head on his shoulder, as he kissed away her tears.

It was dark when he woke. He carried Ailsa through to his bedroom next door and put her under the covers. He climbed in beside her and snuggled up.

'Damn the Colonel, she'll bloody well sleep with me tonight,' he said to himself, and he too, feeling exhausted, fell asleep.

Chapter Seven

Alberto Franelli was bursting with pride at the arrival of his baby grandson. As he strolled around Trannoch grounds, he smiled with contentment. More than a week previously, he had witnessed the scene between Olivia and Malcolm, hidden in the shadows. His daughter was to marry Malcolm, and it was all his doing.

He couldn't make out the words but the sentiment was plain. When his daughter threw her final comment at Malcolm and walked away, Alberto waited a few minutes then approached the man. He was sitting slumped on the wall of the terrace, his head in his hands, sobbing quietly. He did not hear the Italian approaching.

Instead of questioning Malcolm about what he now already believed, Alberto took him by the scruff of the neck and punched him, sending him sprawling over the terrace wall and onto the lawn.

Malcolm did not resist.

The Colonel and Hunter had gone out to dinner and Alberto had to contain himself until the morning to speak to him.

'I'm sorry, Sir, Mr Franelli has ensconced himself in your library and wants to speak with you and Mr Malcolm MacKenzie.' Denbeath turned to leave the breakfast room which by this time only held Hunter and Thomas, besides the Colonel.

'Do you want me to come too, darling?' Hunter was agog with curiosity at this announcement and wanted to be in on any action.

'No, I don't. Where the hell is Malcolm anyway?' boomed the Colonel. 'He didn't come down to breakfast.' His tone held a hint of surprise. He had just noticed his son was missing.

'I believe he had breakfast in his own quarters,' Denbeath replied.

'Well, get someone to bring him down to the library.' The Colonel threw back his chair in impatience and stalked out.

Malcolm was none the worse for the punch. Alberto was not a tall man though Malcolm was. It could have been much worse.

'So what's going on?' The Colonel feared the worst and was proved right as the Italian answered.

'I punch this man. I know this man attack my girl. I hear my girl and he talk. I know he did it.' Alberto was not an intelligent man, but had worked out the situation and wielding his considerable builder's fist, had hit the nail on the head.

The Colonel looked as if someone had punched him too. Surprisingly, he said, 'Well you didn't hit him hard enough, as he is still standing.'

'Look, I just want to make it plain, I didn't 'attack' Olivia, I didn't *hurt* her, I...I just didn't stop.'

'You restrained her, you bloody fool. It doesn't matter whether you hurt her or not. You held her down and didn't stop, and that's enough,' The Colonel raged at his son. Alberto couldn't follow all of this conversation.

Malcolm wondered momentarily where his father got the details of his detestable act, but thought it better to keep quiet. In his mind and drunken state, he had truly thought she wanted it, and she did at the beginning, he was sure, but when he got a bit rough as he had tried to do with Ailsa...' he emitted a groan.

'You marry my girl, my Olivia.'

'Marry? Don't be ridiculous, he can't marry her, if he does everyone will know that the baby is his.'

'Is that all you are worried about, Father? The reputation of this damned family?'

'Don't you dare...'

'If he no marry, then Polizia will know – I go!'

Malcolm got up and walked over to the window. His whole world was falling apart. At this point the tide was beginning to turn for Malcolm and instead of brushing his mistakes under his self-righteous MacKenzie cloak, he began to see himself clearly for the first time. He despised himself.

He looked out at the spring gardens. 'If she will have me, then of course I will marry her. I am sorry for what I did, but I cannot undo it.'

'Are you stark raving mad?' The Colonel's face was as red as the library upholstery.

'No Dad, that's you,' Malcolm shot sarcastically at his father and continued, 'Mr Franelli, I will marry your daughter. It is the least I can do for her.'

The little Italian stood, drawing himself up to his full height. 'She will marry. I make her. In my country we do right. I go her now, and say.'

As the door closed, Malcolm put his head in his hands again. The Colonel poured a whisky for each of them and they downed it in one gulp.

'You realise that, as your wife, she will be entitled to half your fortune?'

'Yes, and due to my illness, she may hope that comes sooner rather than later.'

All of this had happened over a week ago, and Alberto Franelli had stage-managed the MacKenzies, that illustrious family, to which his own grandson now firmly belonged.

The Colonel as usual had managed everything in his own inimitable way. Malcolm and Olivia were to be married as soon as she felt able, in a civil ceremony in Fort William.

Olivia was quite happily resigned to this arrangement, as she knew that their marriage would mean her baby was secure for life, buoyed-up by the vast MacKenzie fortune.

Malcolm was even more resigned. He knew that his rights and responsibilities had been taken away from him, because of the incident which had brought him to this point. His illness had made him think about how long he had on this earth, and for the sake of his child who seemed to shine like a little beacon of hope in his otherwise worthless life, he was surprisingly, mildly content.

There was no celebration, no party, no congratulations and no fuss. They were accompanied only by the Colonel and Noel as witnesses, and Olivia and Malcolm were driven straight home afterwards. Laura, a young nanny installed by the Colonel, looked after the baby until the sombre party arrived back at Trannoch.

Fredrico Alberto Mason MacKenzie was christened two days later, with the whole family attending the church in Arnasaid.

It was an understated event by MacKenzie standards, with moments of quiet joy; the new Mr and Mrs Malcolm MacKenzie distancing themselves in a painfully obvious way. They all congregated back at Trannoch with the usual ostentatious buffet meal and lots of champagne in evidence.

Olivia began to grow in confidence. She had always been beautiful but now, instead of hanging her head and avoiding people's eyes, she held her head aloft, set her shoulders back and carried herself with a grace borne out of her taking charge of her own destiny. She decided when she came to Trannoch that Malcolm would never touch her again. She had made it plain that their separate living arrangements would stay the same now that they were married. From the MacKenzies she learned that manners and decorum were not a thing of the past, but socially important to a family of which she was now part. Funnily enough, her father had been the one to point this out inadvertently as he interacted with the MacKenzies. He was rude, noisy, demanding and showed no respect in the least for the Colonel. The rest of the family may reel against injunctions and bouts of controlling rage from the Colonel, but they all held him in the utmost respect and would never publicly demean him, whatever they said in the comfort of their own quarters. The Colonel could not bear the Italian man for his undignified manner and lack of respect in his home.

Fortunately little Freddy was a beautiful baby and was duly passed amongst the guests for 'goo goo cuddles' as Hunter called them.

Malcolm enjoyed a softening of the bad feeling toward him, as, apart from the Colonel and himself, none of the others knew Alberto had been the one to instigate the wedding. 'At least he has done something right with his miserable little life,' Carys said disgustedly, referring to Malcolm.

The children were home as it was the beginning of the Easter break, and Melissa in particular fawned over her little half-brother. Ailsa watched her as she sat cradling him on a chair beside a set of French doors and was the only one to see her tears fall and splash onto Freddy's tiny face.

'Are you okay, Melissa?' Ailsa caught up with Malcolm's daughter later as she sat alone on the terrace.

'No, not really.' She gave a weak smile.

'Can I help?'

'I don't think anybody can help.'

'Well, I'm not promising, but you could always try me.'

The younger girl looked up. 'It's just everything that's happened. First Mum, then Dad, you know.'

'Yes, you've had a hard time, Melissa. Why don't we have a stroll and you can tell me about it?' They walked through the gardens and up into a forest path which wound its way up a hill that was so high it was almost classed as a mountain. They didn't go very far as it was a chilly day, and they were shaded from the weak March sun. It was spring, but they had no real warmth as yet.

'I said last year... something David and I had seen...I didn't say anything else...'

'Yes.'

'Do you remember?' Melissa was almost sixteen but at this point she was very childlike in her vulnerability.

'I remember,' Ailsa smiled encouragingly.

'I saw Dad. Several times. He...he was with other women.'

'At home?'

'Yes. My mother couldn't stand up to Daddy.' Again she exposed her own vulnerability by calling Malcolm the childish name. 'One time he threw Mum out of our suite so that he could take another woman in. After that happened, I heard her arguing with him – they argued and fought all the time, and she said she would go to Grandad if she didn't get her own suite of rooms, which she did.

'But didn't anyone else know what was going on?'

'No. He brought them in the door from the courtyard and up on one of the back stairs.'

Ailsa thought for a minute about the ubiquitous Denbeath and how he suddenly appeared no matter what time she herself arrived at Trannoch. He at least must have realised, but she doubted anyone else did. Max would have told her had he known or suspected. *Wouldn't he?*

'What age were you and David when that happened?'

'I was about ten. David was eleven.'

'My God, I am so sorry, darling. Is Olivia the reason this is all coming to the front of your mind now?'

'Yes. I am scared for her. She started off here in her own rooms. She was pregnant when she came here, and then suddenly she gets married to Dad. They are still in separate suites. I am not a child nor am I stupid. He either loves her because she's so beautiful and has taken the baby on as his own child – or Freddy is his own baby, and she wants nothing to do with him. Maybe he has got some hold over Olivia, I don't know...' She searched the older woman's face for answers.

'Melissa, you know your Dad is ill?' She nodded. 'Well, I think he wants to put things right. You need to talk to your Dad and ask him to explain what happened.' She shook her head furiously.

'No. I can't. I've never been able to talk to Dad. He won't tell me anything. He can't talk to women normally.' This comment was astonishingly shrewd, but as she was including herself in the 'women' it would have been funny in other circumstances. It was a complete contrast to the childish way she had spoken earlier. Melissa was at that terrifyingly unpredictable age between being a child and an adult.

'I am so sorry, Melissa. You should not have had to deal with this. Is there no one you can talk to?

'I'm talking to you.'

'Yes, you are, and I am very grateful for your trust. However, I cannot break another's trust. What I can promise you is that I will speak with your Dad. He can't just walk away from you and David.'

'Thanks, Ailsa. But Dad has never been there in the first place – to walk away.'

When Miss Cochrane brought Ailsa her mid-morning tea in the library, she found Ailsa almost dancing with excitement.

'Good news?'

'Oh Cocky, the best news! My book has been accepted by the publisher.'

'Ailsa, that is splendid news.' Miss Cochrane clasped her hands in delight, and to Ailsa's astonishment, she hugged her.

A tap came at the door and Stephen Millburn put his head round. 'Sorry to interrupt, just a quick reminder about our meeting this afternoon.'

Ailsa nodded. 'Yes, I did remember, this time, Stephen.'

'Ailsa was just celebrating the acceptance of her book. She's a true authoress now!' Miss Cochrane was still euphoric about the news, forgetting that Ailsa and Stephen were not the best of friends.

'Really? That's good news!' he said, looking like he had no idea why he just said what he did.

She came down to earth with a bump. 'Thanks, although I seem to remember you were not too complimentary about my writing...'

'No, and I'm sorry about that.'

He didn't look sorry.

'It's just that when there is so much real life work to do on the estate I find it hard to believe you sit in here all day and write fiction.'

'Get out.'

'Eh...sorry?'

'You heard me. Get out, Stephen. I can't even be bothered explaining. I just don't want you here right now.'

'And the meeting?'

'I think you should leave.' Miss Cochrane opened the library door, and Stephen took one look at the housekeeper's face and went.

Ailsa took Bluebell and Rosie out to the headland as usual that evening. The days were lengthening. The trees were getting greener and flowers were pushing through the icy land, determined to make a go of spring. Ailsa stood and looked across to the mountains on Skye. They were clear tonight, the jagged land pointing towards the westward sunset.

She had so much to think about. How could she help Melissa? How could she advise her when her father was such a womanising, lecherous predator? However, he had seemed to improve a bit since his illness, and she needed to speak to him about his daughter. She had no idea what her reception would be, but, thinking back to last year when twice he had made a pass at her, she had to think carefully about how to approach it.

'Well Ailsa, what can I do for you?' Malcolm had taken Ailsa into the library at Trannoch after Denbeath had quietly approached him after dinner with the news that she was here and wanted to talk to him. 'May I get you a drink? Red wine?'

'Thank you, yes.'

'So, to what do I owe this pleasure?' Malcolm still had a bit of his old self in him though a different, more fragile self, given his illness. His new duties as father to Freddy had done more to turn him around than anything else. He was still charming and very good looking, but now was less confident than before.

Ailsa gathered all her resolve and spoke directly. 'I need to talk to you about Melissa.'

He looked surprised. 'Why? What has she done? Has she been naughty?'

'Absolutely not. But she is growing up, and she has lost her mother.' Malcolm dropped his head, then took a gulp of his drink. 'She saw all the...er...relations between you and Belinda, the disagreements and the fights, and she wants to know about Olivia.'

'Wants to know? Wants to know what?' His gaze was slightly blurred and his eyes narrowed. He had taken quite a few glasses of wine at dinner and now was knocking back the whisky.

'She has been thinking about how you came to end up with Olivia, and a new baby, when you don't even live together here.'

'That's none of her bloody business. She's just a child, for God's sake.'

'She's *your* child Malcolm.'

It could have gone either way. He swung round with his glass re-filled and walked slowly to the sofa opposite her into which he slumped, his whole body seeming to sag and shrink into the fabric.

'You know, I hated boarding school.' He looked into the yellow liquid swilling in his glass. 'I hated it with a passion. I was sent away at five years old when all I wanted was to be at home with my parents. I begged the Colonel to let me leave, but he has always been very traditional and has old-fashioned ideas about bringing up children. My brothers seemed to get on alright, but I was the one who was always in trouble. I was suspended several times, and I was once sent home for a week to "think about my crimes" – stealing drink from the little shop on the corner. All I could think about was that I was so happy to be coming back to Trannoch. I guess I just wanted a bit of attention. The Colonel left the country for a week – avoiding me, I suppose, and I think that was when it all started. When we had David and Melissa, I had battles royal with Dad, because I didn't want to send them away. It was no use though. He did the whole "under my roof, you'll obey my rules" argument. In a way, I was happier and surer that they were getting a good upbringing at the school than they would here with my wife and me. I thought they were protected there.'

Ailsa glanced at him in surprise. 'Protected?' It was a strange word to use, and Ailsa began to feel a rising sense of alarm.

'Belinda and I were unsuited from the beginning. I met her and shortly afterwards she told me she was pregnant. The Colonel made me marry her, of course, and bring her here. David was born, then Melissa just over a year later. Our relationship deteriorated quickly after I found her with another man.'

'*Belinda* had an affair?'

Malcolm gave a sneering laugh. 'Ironic eh? Everyone believed it was I who had made everything collapse and here it was little insipid Belinda. I retaliated of course with a string of women I brought up the back stairs to our rooms. No one knew except your efficient Miss Cochrane.'

'Miss Cochrane knew?'

'Yes, she saw me one of the times I was round the side of the house seeing off...er...someone. It was dark and your housekeeper was apparently visiting Denbeath with some deep and meaningful household question. She hasn't told you? Well, well, seems that particular secret is safe, and now with you then, Ailsa!' He took a long gulp of his whisky.

'Unfortunately, Miss Cochrane is not the only one who saw you – your children did too.'

Chapter Eight

It was Easter Sunday and a blustery wind was accompanied by intermittent sunshine, seahorse waves and rapidly changing landscape. Ailsa had agreed to go with Max and the rest of the MacKenzies, to church. She had been brought up by Episcopalian adoptive parents and attended the Sunday school in the local church, but as an adult had only ever attended church for weddings, funerals and baptisms. She had never felt the need to practice any faith she might have.

The small historic church in Arnasaid was packed to the brim with locals as the MacKenzies trooped in, almost like Royalty descending upon them. As was tradition in the 'Kirk' certain pews were set aside for people whose ancestors had paid for this privilege in days gone by. Nowadays most people sat where they liked, but despite the Minister's pleas that it was 'good to mix' the Colonel insisted their own MacKenzie pew was kept vacant for them each Sunday. A large sum donated to the coffers helped secure the seating arrangements.

The Colonel and Hunter sat in the front with Noel, Malcolm and Olivia, accompanied by their children, Melody, David and Melissa. Baby Freddy was at Trannoch with Laura the nanny. Behind, in the next two pews sat the rest of the family. Carys was fuming that Olivia seemed to be the centre of attention, primarily because as a staunch Catholic she had bobbed to the altar and crossed herself before taking her seat. Some older members of the congregation balked visibly at this before she took her seat with a satisfied look on her face.

Olivia had openly rebelled at first when the Colonel had broached the subject of church on Easter Sunday. He insisted that those of the family who were home should attend church regularly. But, of course, since Ailsa was not part of the family this didn't apply to her. Max asked her as he wanted her company, not because he was trying to convert her. Once, Malcolm's son David had been learning about different religions at school and thought he would try a few alternatives before he settled on one, or none of them. The Colonel shut down that argument faster than a rat going up a drainpipe. At a recent evening meal, he had told Olivia that, now she was well, she would naturally attend Arnasaid parish church with the family. It wasn't a question, not even a rhetorical one. It was an order. Olivia had surveyed the head of the family with a flash of newly found confidence. Her father would have backed her up, had he been there, but Alberto Franelli was measuring up a plot in Arnasaid Bheag, with an eye to building a home there. He couldn't bear the thought of staying at Trannoch any longer, but refused to go back to Italy without his daughter and grandson, so he had decided to stay in the area and do bits and pieces of work when it came up.

'No, no.' Olivia gestured with her hands as she spoke. 'I am Catholic. Where is Catholic Church? I go to here.'

Carys was delighted at this, and hurriedly answered her before anyone else could 'The nearest one is in Dunlivietor, only a few miles away. Why don't you pop off to that one?'

The Colonel was angry, but the sardonic response from Carys apparently escaped the Italian woman, who merely smiled a reply.

'Freddy was christened in the Church of Scotland, Olivia,' Hunter patronisingly and slowly explained. You both took a vow that he should be brought up in our church.' She almost spelled it out to her.

Olivia held her head up high. Her beautiful black eyes darting from one to another around the table. 'That no mean I go. Bambino, he too young to go.'

'Oh, couldn't we get her English lessons?' Carys asked the Colonel in mock sincerity. 'It would help you so much, Olivia, and we would all have a better chance of working out what you are saying.'

'Shut up, Carys. That's unwarranted. Olivia is not stupid, please don't treat her as such.' The room went quiet as Malcolm threw down his cutlery and left the table. Had he known it, this simple defence began to affect a change in Olivia towards her new husband. She was grateful to him for sticking up for her towards these strong outspoken women around the table. Because of this one action, she had decided that she would go to the church with Malcolm and use the new-found power she had gained by marrying him, very much to her advantage.

On the run up to the Easter weekend, Olivia planned a spree, copiously spending her newly acquired money on herself by purchasing a new spring wardrobe. Melissa, in whom she had found an ally – it was too soon to call her a friend – helped her with the best fashion lines. Melissa even sat with her while she tapped her laptop and sent for thousands of pounds worth of dresses, shoes, bags and accessories. Most of them were sent over from Milan in Italy, the fashion capital of the world. Malcolm never blinked an eye.

Easter Sunday lunch was held at Trannoch after the service. It was a lively affair, as Sir Pierce had been invited to join them, and Alberto had declared, 'I no go to a no-good church.' By which everyone surmised he meant a protestant one was not good. But he invited himself to lunch, nonetheless. Stephen Millburn and Clem were also there. Surprisingly, the Colonel had assented when Melody asked if she could bring her new boyfriend. She had been madly in love with a boy for over a year, whom she had met at Uni, but had ditched him in favour of a local boy she had met in a pub in Arnasaid Bheag a few weeks ago. No one knew anything about him, and Ailsa and Clem were both itching to see him.

They were meeting in the Great Room as usual, for drinks and canapés, before they went into lunch. Ailsa was sitting with Max, Melody and Sir Pierce. Max was looking slightly distracted and kept glancing over his shoulder.

'Who's getting your attention over us?' Sir Pierce smiled, to chuckles from both Melody and Ailsa.

'Oh, er...sorry, it's Ryan. I have a sneaking suspicion he may be pinching the booze.' Max was apologetic.

'Of course, he is,' Sir Pierce laughed. 'He's what, fourteen now? I seem to remember you and your brothers began with a few beers at that age, Maxwell. The Colonel always gave you wine with your dinner around that age too.'

'Things have changed now, Uncle Pierce.' Max used the childish title without thinking. 'Ryan has been in trouble recently with the Colonel for taking his whisky – Ailsa and I rumbled him one night, him and two local toe-rags who were bullying him into it.'

To Max's surprise, his uncle laughed loudly at this, and so did Melody. 'Oh, Uncle Max, you are so funny. No one would think you ever got up to the high jinks you did when you were young, and now you are jumping up and down at Ryan having a drink at a family lunch.'

'Yes, well, that's what happens when you grow up, Melody. You realise you have responsibilities you didn't have when you were fourteen years old,' Max grinned, looking straight at his niece.

The door opened and Denbeath showed in a tall, handsome young man who looked decidedly nervous. He swiftly looked around, and his eyes settled on Melody. She jumped up. 'He's here!' she said happily. She went forward, taking his hand, and drew him into their little group.

Ailsa had been holding her glass out to have it re-filled and she swung round at Melody's voice.

'Dougie!'

'Hi, Ailsa, or should I say, Lady Ailsa? How are ye doin'?'

'I'm... er... yes... I'm fine. How are you?' The colour crept up her cheeks.

'Aye, I'm good thanks.'

'So how do you know Melody's boyfriend?' They had all settled at the long table in the dining room for lunch. Max looked at her calmly as he buttered his roll. He didn't realise that Melody, who was on his other side, heard her uncle and had started listening to this conversation.

'I... er... met him when I went to Skye last year, when things were getting too much for me. I booked into a small hotel with the two dogs, and he came into the lounge bar and started speaking to me.'

'You mean he chatted you up?' Max smiled.

'No... yes... a bit.'

'I see.'

'What does that mean?'

'It means, I see. You met him in Skye, I just wondered how you knew him.'

'Do you know he is twenty eight?'

'Bit young for you, eh? Did you know that when you met him?'

Ailsa flushed in anger. 'No, I didn't know, Max. It wasn't a blind date or anything, I just met him in the hotel bar. I didn't really care about wondering about age either. It didn't even get to that point where I was assessing things. I was making the point more for the difference in age between him and Melody. You and I were not together at that point, and I needed someone.' She thought that an age gap seemed larger when people were younger, though she didn't qualify this.

'Well, if he's twenty eight, there's actually only a few years between him and Melody, but I'm not judging you.'

'No? It seems as if you are.'

'I'm not, and I think you are being irrational. I don't really care that you got together, you've told me how you know him, which is really all I was asking.'

'Yeah, well maybe that's just it, Max. Maybe I thought you would have cared just a little.'

Max was alone in his study later on that night sitting at his old battered desk reading the British Medical Journal. Ailsa had gone home, giving a lame excuse, and he was disappointed that he had apparently said the wrong thing again. He knew that she had gone because she was upset with him. He had been planning a cosy night by the fire listening to some good music. A knock interrupted his thoughts and he looked up to see Melody.

'May I come in, Uncle Max?'

'Of course, you may. Come in and sit by the fire. Glass of wine?'

'Yes, thank you. Working on Easter Sunday, *really*?' She kicked off her shoes and curled up on the couch. He was delighted to have some company although he drew the line at socialising with the rest of the family. He poured two glasses of red wine and joined her on the chesterfield. The fire crackled, throwing a warming heat around the room, and shadows up the walls.

'Do you like Dougie?' she asked suddenly.

'He seems like a nice kid,' Max responded, with an awkward gulp of his wine.

'Kid? Max, he's in his late twenties!'

'Yes, but I'm in my forties, so he's just a kid to me.'

'You know of course, because she told you, that Ailsa met him in that hotel on Skye last year?'

'Yes, I know.' Max's tone was nonchalant, though his lips were tight.

'There was nothing in it. Dougie told me she was trying to escape Storm Winds for a few days – she actually gave him a false name! They kissed, Max, but that was it.'

'Oh? I didn't know that, but I am ambivalent about it.'

'Really? You don't look it. I think the problem is that you were upset when Ailsa said she knew him, especially since he is a bit younger than she is. It threw you. Now you are refusing to think about your feelings.'

'You should consider giving up medicine and going in for counselling. It's a pre-requisite of a doctor to be devoid of "feelings", to be bad tempered and mostly, socially inept. You'll never fit in.'

'Don't change the subject,' she giggled. 'You need to talk to her. She's the best thing that's happened to you since... er... for years.'

'I know.'

'Well, don't shut her out. I can't believe what Ailsa has achieved since she came to Scotland. She has turned that musty old mansion inside out, literally. She is a lovely, kind and giving person. Don't throw that away, Max. Talk to her. She needs you, and you most definitely need her.'

'Ok, I will. Incidentally, when did you grow up and become so cheeky?' He grinned.

She snuggled into the comfortable cushions and sipped her wine. 'Well, someone has to tell you, as you don't seem to see it yourself. You're such a bloody grouch.'

'And you're not too old to put over my knee, young lady,' he chuckled, and ruffled her hair affectionately.

'Oh, do shut up, Uncle Max. Oh, and... love you.'

'Love you, too.'

Noel was sitting in his office contemplating his life. He worked hard, he never complained or spoke out about what was happening in his life, but for the first time in his fifty one years he felt useless. When his wife Clem left, he hadn't batted an eye. His main thought was 'take it or leave it'. He really had no time for the emotional turmoil and drama women seemed to bring, but this time was quite obviously the worst.

Carys was pregnant.

Thomas apparently couldn't father a baby, but then Thomas was another story and he really didn't want to give his youngest brother thinking space. He knew that he himself was the dark horse of the family and he was happy with this label. His daughter was the most beautiful young woman he had ever seen, was intelligent beyond measure and the kindest, most thoughtful person. She was tentative in her relationship with him but that was fine by him, as long as she was still there or thereabouts and gave him a passing thought every now and again, that was all that he thought mattered. All that he wanted or needed.

The problem with Carys was that she was a bitch of the first order. Recently she had become partner in his company, and had helped to build up the art business. This had meant many times when they travelled abroad, staying in hotels. Loneliness pulled them together, and an unfortunate result of this was Carys had become pregnant. A baby was absolutely the last thing Noel wanted. He despised babies. Even children up to around the age of about twelve sickened him in the extreme. After that he could tolerate them, as they appeared to begin to be more self-sufficient. He had tried to talk her into a termination, but she refused. She was absolutely delighted she was pregnant. She was gloating. He had heard that Carys and Thomas couldn't have a baby. He had no idea if this was true, but the obvious gossip surrounding this would be that it was someone else's. He wished it were anyone else's but his. Carys was using him and insisting she get a greater share in the business, and he had no idea how to stop her – short of killing her, and he had thought about this. It amused him to think of several ways in which he could end her life. But he agreed to her 40 per cent demand, hoping, for her sake, that she wouldn't come back for more.

Malcolm had a difficult conversation with his two eldest children on Easter Monday, explaining everything which had happened with Olivia, giving some but not all of the fine detail of how Freddy had been conceived. He wept as he told them he was sorry for all the wrongs he had committed, including the treatment of their mother. He said that if it wasn't for their grandfather, he would probably be in jail, and Melissa uncontrollably broke down at this. He mentioned nothing about Belinda's own affair nor the fact that Olivia had made out his attack to be more brutal than it actually was, though he now accepted the fact that it had been an attack. This part could wait until they were fully adults. In fact, he laid himself bare to his children in a way that he had never done before. None of the Trannoch children knew about how Olivia had conceived, and the Colonel would, if he could help it, make sure that they never did.

Ailsa couldn't put her mind to her writing on Easter Monday. The MacKenzies had planned a family picnic if the weather was fine, and it was, but she wasn't going. Gennina had the day off and she decided to take a look at the East Wing and see how the decorating was progressing. Storm Winds had so many rooms and corridors; the East Wing was like another house entirely. This part of the house had not been used for a very long time by the family, apart from by the guests who attended the grouse shooting parties. Four separate parties had been arranged, three of which coming from the USA. There were around thirty people in each party, which meant a heck of a lot of catering, but here Gennina's organisational skills had been absolutely brilliant. She'd had a huge wipeable board installed in the estate office with the grand plan in glorious technicolour from eight different marker pens. One of the events which Ailsa was not too happy about was a grand dinner at the end of each of the weeks of shooting, as she was to be the guest of honour. She hadn't thought of having anything to do with the shoots, so as usual she was at daggers drawn with Stephen over this.

The work was coming along nicely, all the wood on the doors was original as was the bare wood on the high skirting boards or 'wainscoting', as Cocky called it. The rooms were being freshly painted, and the old oak floors re-varnished. Fresh bedding should arrive soon. The new bathrooms were finished and just had to be decorated. She nodded in satisfaction, then wandered slowly across the courtyard to the office.

'Not going to the picnic?' To her surprise Stephen was in the office kitchen, washing his arms and hands in the Belfast sink.

'No,' she said shortly.

'Clem is working today, in case you were looking for her.' Clem was now settled in the apartment at Storm Winds, but they hadn't seen very much of each other as yet. She was busy with her new tea room through the daytime, leaving early and coming home late and exhausted in the evenings.

Stephen was with her often anyway, and Ailsa had no wish to include him in an invitation to socialise.

'I thought she would be there. What are you doing here?'

'Nice to see you too!' His back was to her, so he didn't notice her mutinous expression. 'As it happens, I was rescuing one of your sheep which had a fight with some barbed wire on the fence.'

'I see. Is it okay?' she asked, in an unconcerned voice.

He flapped the water from his hands and turned around, reaching for a towel. 'Yes. I needed to call out the vet – she needed a bit of attention on a tear, but she's fine otherwise.'

'Okay, thanks.' She turned to her own office and banged the door behind her.

Stephen just shook his head.

Max was not at the picnic either. He'd had a house call to an elderly man who had fallen and broken his hip. The locum was on holiday and it was Max's turn. He had planned to join Ailsa at the picnic until he realised she had phoned the Colonel to tell him she couldn't make it. There was a note scribbled on Max's desk pad letting him know.

He looked at the note thoughtfully. This was about their row obviously. He thought about his conversation with Melody last night, and how, as a result of this, he was going to talk to Ailsa to ask if she wanted to go to Mhainaray next weekend. Sir Pierce had left them with an open invitation to come across anytime, and he thought it would be good to get some time to themselves without the warring MacKenzies suffocating them. However, this little plan would need to wait for another day.

The sea was indigo blue. The sun shone and there was a soft westerly breeze as Ailsa turned the headland towards Arnasaid. Bluebell and Rosie scampered happily along with her, and she enjoyed the sight of the boats bobbing in the gentle swell of the ocean. Arnasaid was busy due to the bank holiday's good weather, and she sauntered along the front and up the brae towards Clem's teashop. It was late afternoon, and she knew her friend would be shutting soon.

The jingle of the bell as she entered alerted the occupants, who were few. At one table sat an older couple, not local she thought, and the other table... her face grew hot as the young woman turned to look at her. It was Melody and Dougie.

Chapter Nine

'Ailsa!' cried Melody, and immediately jumped up, 'come and join us!'

'Well actually, I'm just here to see Clem and how things were doing, I didn't really want to eat,' she lied.

Dougie watched her with a questioning, almost pleading expression, like he was asking her not to feel awkward and to forget what happened before. She in turn looked at him, and it was as if she was looking at an entirely different person to the Dougie she had met on Skye. She saw his young years. She saw the light in his eyes as he looked at Clem's young, vibrant daughter. Brought up in a fiercely traditional way, Melody was conversely a very pragmatic and modern thinker, and she had no problem with the little dalliance between her boyfriend and her Uncle Max's partner. Dougie had told her exactly what had happened, a night in full view of everyone in the lounge bar, where they had drank and talked – and kissed. The second night cut short when Dougie discovered she was not 'Emily', and it had ended before anything had begun. Ailsa saw the mannerisms she remembered boys having from when she was young. No threat there, no warning. She had no feeling for Dougie whatsoever and now just felt annoyed that both Melody and Max knew about them. She had no thought of being a distraction to the couple, as that was what he had become to her. She felt like she was coming out in a cold sweat.

Clem appeared. 'Ailsa! How nice to see you! Would you like to have some tea and cake?' Ailsa greeted her friend, and the change in the room suddenly made her decision easy.

'Thank you, Clem, and yes I would like cake and a glass of Prosecco please.' She smiled and reluctantly took her seat beside Melody and Dougie.

She enjoyed one of the best afternoons she had had for ages. Dougie and Melody joined her in Prosecco, and they ate their way through several amazing homemade cakes as they talked. Ailsa felt there was little awkwardness, which was probably down to the Prosecco, but she really hoped Dougie felt the same. She needn't have worried, as Dougie only had eyes for the beautiful Melody, with her long auburn hair and perfect face. Melody had been working for her Aunt Clem waitressing, whenever she was home for the holidays, but this was her day off. They sat there until the evening. When the shop had closed, Clem, seeing her other two employees were busy in the kitchen tidying up and getting ready for the next day, joined them for a rare escape from the hard work of running her new venture.

Blackness descended outside as they sat, drinking, talking and laughing. At around eight thirty the doorbell went, and Clem rose to answer it.

It was Max.

'I hope you don't mind me interrupting,' he said starchily, as the others looked on. 'I was up at your house, Ailsa, and Miss Cochrane said you were here. So, I thought I would come and find you, but if you're busy...'

'Oh, shut up Max, and sit down and have a drink and some cake!' Clem laughed. He sat, and with cake and Prosecco, he began to relax. They all talked and laughed until 11 o'clock when Max phoned a car from Trannoch and got them all home. Despite all the chatter, Alisa and Max had not talked much. Ailsa had been distant, and Max had no idea how to approach her. He dropped her off first at Storm Winds hoping she would invite him to stay.

She didn't.

The next day was raining torrentially, so badly in fact that Ailsa couldn't take her dogs out for a walk. She slept until quarter to nine in the morning, almost unheard of for her, and begged a pot of tea in her room from the concerned Miss Cochrane who had come in to see if she was alright. The tray, laden with enough food for around four people, was brought to her by a sympathetic Eileen, who sat on the end of the bed and demanded to know what had happened last night.

'Eileen, get off my feet, you donkey.' The younger girl leaned forward picking bacon, bread and little sausages from Ailsa's plate.

'So, what happened, Ailsa?' she said, as she made a sandwich with some crusty bread and bacon.

'Well, I was out with the dogs to see Clem, and Melody and Dougie were there — right there in her tearoom, having cakes and tea!' Ailsa sat herself up a little on her pillows. She felt slightly queasy.

'Gosh! So how do you feel about Dougs now?' It was a habit of hers to shorten people's names. 'Did you feel old?'

'Right, okay Eileen, don't rub it in!' Ailsa said indignantly. 'If you must know, I am so over him, it is unbelievable!' It was easy for a hungover Ailsa to speak in the same vernacular as Eileen. She would cringe at this memory later on, however.

The footsteps in the hall indicated another visitor, so Eileen jumped up off the bed just in time to admit Miss Cochrane, with a stern expression on her face.

'Ailsa, Stephen Millburn is in the library awaiting a proposed meeting with you. Can I tell him you will be down in ten minutes?'

'You can tell him, but I won't... I... er... er... I think I'm going to be sick...' Ailsa bolted to her bathroom and Miss Cochrane turned on her heel to tell the visitor that he would have no meeting with Ailsa that day.

The rain was incessant in the week following Easter weekend. The land became saturated and the rivers and burns were high, spilling onto the fields and down the rocky cliffs onto main roads and paths. Ailsa had to turn back from her usual headland walk to Arnasaid as one part of the path, sheer to the sea and backing onto the cliff with no other way around, was heavily flooded. The water fell like a ribbon down the side of the slate-black rocky side and onto the path, making the path seriously slippery and dangerous. There was no railing here.

Ailsa was looking forward to some fresh company. Connie, Jan and their partners, Calum and Gregory, were coming to Storm Winds a few weeks later for a bit of a holiday. It was now May and the weather was starting to improve, although just when it had got better with bright sunshine and milder weather one day, the next was invariably back to winter with strong winds and heavy, cold rain. Ailsa was really looking forward to her friends' arrival, as things had been difficult lately. She had felt so relieved when Max had confirmed to her that he was open to the idea of them having a baby, at some point, but now this recent awkwardness with him, coupled with all that was going on a Trannoch, really had taken the wind from her sails.

Hunter was on the way to meet a friend. She had thrown together an overnight bag, just in case, and had dressed in jeans, white ankle boots and white shirt with a navy scarf. She spent lots of time on her make-up and hair and looked like a forty year old instead of a fifty seven year old. She took one of the Trannoch cars and drove to Arnasaid Bheag. Here, she pottered around the little shops, picking up a beautiful red sweater from an exclusive highland knitwear shop, some new perfume and a book which she would probably never read. She visited one of the more upmarket pubs to order a large glass of white wine while she waited for the ferry. She could feel eyes upon her as she delicately sipped her wine. She knew she radiated power and sexuality in abundance and she basked in the forward gazes of admiration.

When the ferry arrived, she made her way to the gangplank with her overnight bag in one hand, and her bags with her new purchases on the other. She faltered slightly as she began the ascent up to the passenger embarkation level, and a tall, dark haired man approached with a wide smile.

'Can I carry your bags for you?' he said in a warm highland accent. Hunter stopped and looked into inky blue eyes dancing with warmth and fun, the tiny creases on the edges of his eyes darting outwards towards a head of black longish hair with more than a bit of a curl in it. Stylish he most certainly was, with an air of a well brought up and educated man. His dress was decidedly modern with a white shirt, black jeans, boots and black straight leather jacket. He was young — around Max's age, she thought.

'Let's go into the lounge area, and I'll buy you a drink.' It was a statement rather than a question, and she found herself meekly following him into a small area with its salt-sprayed windows to a table bolted to the floor, looking out at the bouncing sea.

'I've got you a white wine.' It was in a large plastic glass and he had a pint of cider. He sat a packet of crisps between them, as he joined her, acting as if they had known each other for years.

'What's your name?' he grinned, lifting his drink to his mouth.

'Georgina.'

'Mine's Andy.

'I don't remember you asking me what I wanted to drink.' She sounded petulant.

'I didn't.' He grinned again. 'I saw you in the bar and it looked like a white wine you were drinking. Would you rather have my cider?'

'Absolutely not.' She looked as if he had offered her poison.

'Okay, so drink and enjoy. Where are you off to?'

'I... er... Mhainaray.'

'Mhainaray? Only one hotel there. I'm staying there too. I'll meet you tomorrow night at seven thirty.'

'Excuse me? You're very sure of yourself! I... I...'

'Are you married or going to meet someone?'

'Well actually...'

'That's a no then. So, I'll meet you tomorrow night.'

'I'm sorry, but I don't just get together with any Tom, Dick or Harry who happens to chat me up on the ferry...'

'Okay, don't then, your call,' and, annoyingly, he lifted his cider and moved to the far side of the cabin and to another table.

She was left almost gasping. 'Who does he think he is? How dare he talk to me like that and stomp off?' She looked around to see if anyone had noticed, but the tables with tourists seemed to be engrossed in their own particular day trips, and weren't looking in her direction. She sat tapping her fingers in annoyance until she decided to cut her losses, picked up her bags and moved over to his table. He looked up at her with a grin as she approached, and she felt her heart jump in anticipation.

'I couldn't carry my bags *and* my drink,' she said sweetly.

He leaned across the table, put his hand under her chin and brought her mouth to his, kissing her roughly. His hand was on her neck, and he slid it underneath her shirt collar until she drew away, embarrassed and gasping with excitement. She had pulled away reluctantly, more bothered about the occupants of the cabin. But, as she looked around hurriedly to see what attention they were arousing, the tourists had moved to the windows in the vain attempt to spot dolphins through the murk. He then stood up and looked down at her with a mixture of amusement and desire.

'I'll go get your drink.'

'Georgina, darling, I am so pleased to welcome you to Mhainaray!' Sir Pierce held her hand as she stepped daintily out of the car.

'Thank you,' she said flatly. Her journey had brought her to the beautiful gothic grey stone mansion house which dominated the landscape of the small island. Sir Pierce had spoken with her at Trannoch and extended the invitation to her to visit his house, which, like Storm Winds, had been in his family for centuries. She had accepted. He hadn't asked her to stay over, but the last ferry to the mainland left in an hour, so she had assumed she would be asked to stay.

'What a pretty little island!' she said, her eyes then turning to swoop over the vastness of the building into which she now stepped. The hall was dark and traditional, with suits of armour, paintings and tapestries adorning the wood-panelled walls.

'Leave your bag in the hall, and I will have it taken up to your room. Come into the front room, and I'll get you a drink.' He said 'front room' as if it were a two up two down, and as she walked into the splendour of said room, the line of sash windows and French doors on two sides overlooked a hundred and eighty degree angle across the Sound of Mhainaray and out to the sea beyond. The mountains, which on this misty evening could be seen on the mainland, looked beautiful with patches of snow still visible on top, and Hunter almost gasped at the view before her. Not a scenery person, by her own admission, she thought that no one in their right mind could dismiss this particular panorama.

She sat on a comfortable sofa looking straight at the view with a feeling of satisfaction. Pierce had assumed she would be staying, so that answered one question.

'What can I get you, Georgina?' he asked in warm tones.

'A white wine, please.' He took a bottle from a tall fridge in an alcove in one corner where she could also see a rack stacked with vintage bottles of red wine.

'Are there any hotels on Mhainaray?' she asked innocently.

'My dear Georgina, you must stay with me! I already have had your room made up.' He looked almost aghast at the prospect of her staying anywhere else.

'Oh no, I realised that when you said you would have my bag taken up.' She smiled as she took the fine Edinburgh crystal wine glass full almost to the brim. She thought she had better watch herself, as she had had one in Arnasaid Bheag, then two on the ferry before she arrived.

'Oh good. Yes, there is a small hotel on the other side of the island which has an excellent restaurant, and one or two B&Bs dotted around. I was going to suggest we eat at the hotel one evening, if you are happy with that?'

'Delighted!' she replied, with a smug smile.

Hunter was not easy work. The staff at Mhainaray were tearing their hair out within a few hours of her arrival with her insisting she move rooms to get a better view of the sea, and a four-poster bed amongst other demands. Sir Pierce just shook his head with a chuckle when he heard. He had a great affection for the exciting, beautiful woman everyone but he seemed to call Hunter. Pierce had no idea why she had landed at Trannoch, but he dearly hoped it was not that she and the Colonel, one of his oldest friends, were in some kind of relationship. He knew what he wanted. He wanted Hunter.

Chapter Ten

'Okay, so, I am currently in work, with patients to see to, but I'll be there around ten o'clock. Will you be able to put me up for the night?'

'Certainly, Dr MacKenzie, we have a separate lodge for visiting parents due to our rural location, and it is currently unoccupied.'

Max rang off and ran his fingers through his darkish fair hair in despair. His bright intelligent eyes looked unseeingly across his surgery desk.

Ryan was in trouble again, and Max had been summoned to his school, Criandornoch, deep in the mountains.

'Hi, where are you?'

'I'm fine thanks, Max. How are you?' It was easy to spot the irritation in her voice, and he groaned.

'Sorry Ailsa, I'm all over the place today. *How* are you?'

It was such an unusual admission that she drew in her breath in surprise. 'What's up? Oh, and I'm currently out with the dogs.'

He smiled down the phone. 'The Head from Criandornoch called a few minutes ago. Ryan is in trouble and the Head wants me to go and see him.'

'Shit.'

'Shit indeed. I need to leave after surgery, so I won't make dinner this evening.'

'How long will you be gone?'

'A night, two nights at most, but not sure until I know what he's done and how serious it is. Listen, I know we were going to go to Mhainaray tomorrow. Why don't you go on ahead as planned, and I'll join you as soon as I get back?'

'Okay, well I might just go today since I'll be at a loose end anyway.'

The Sound of Mhainaray was almost black with the gloom from the chopping sea and lowering sky. Ailsa hadn't rung ahead to Sir Pierce, as Max would have done this, but she had packed a small bag which would last her at least three days. She thought about her plans as she peered through the rain-soaked window into misty nothingness. She had been overseeing lots of renovation work on Storm Wind's Dower House and also the East Wing for the grouse shooting season. Her plan was to rent out the Dower House as a holiday let. It was right down at the foot of the road, about half a mile from the main house, and almost hidden by part of the forest. Gennina was going to take care of the advertising and the bookings and was going to employ some extra cleaners for both this enterprise and the changeovers in the East Wing. The Dower House was ready to be let this summer, as the work there had been going on longer than in the big house.

The first renters were due the following weekend for a week, and Gennina was very excited and feeling very important about her role in all this. The other venture Ailsa was developing was to begin a writers' retreat some weekends, now that she was a published author. She was very proud of this, and she was planning to contact some prominent Scottish authors to engage for guest appearances at her retreats. She would use the newly refurbished rooms in the East Wing for accommodation and some of the rooms in her own part of the house to work in. This couldn't be done until the autumn or even the beginning of winter, not that there was a discernible difference between the two. They had the shooting parties to host first.

The car from Mhainaray Manor met her at the pier. Ailsa had called earlier to let the housekeeper know she was on her way. It was a short half hour drive to the other side of the island and the house, and Sir Pierce was in the gaping doorway to meet her. Ailsa shook the fine rain from her blonde hair and discarded her coat on the hall stand. As he led her into the 'front room', she glanced over to the farthest away chair and stepped back in amazement. Hunter was there wearing a grin as wide as the Skye bridge.

'I... I... didn't realise you had... er... company.' Ailsa spoke falteringly, with a withering glance at her mother holding court so complacently.

'I know,' Sir Pierce said, apologetically, 'but I left you both an open invitation, and it wasn't until Mrs Monroe, my housekeeper, announced you were on your way that I knew you would be arriving. Where is Max?' he asked suddenly, as if he had just noticed his nephew was missing and looked behind her as if Max was hiding somewhere in the hall.

'Unfortunately, he couldn't make it today.' She was purposefully vague as she was damned if she was going to let Hunter know what was wrong with Ryan. The least she knew about her and Max's lives, the better. 'He told me to go on ahead and he'll join me either tomorrow or in a few days — I thought he would have called to let you know.' She began to feel the stress rising at this unfortunate mix-up.

'Oh darling, please don't worry on my account,' gushed Hunter. 'Piercey particularly asked me over for a little holiday, but he didn't know when you and Max would be coming over. I am over the moon to be spending some surprise time with my daughter,' she almost purred.

Piercey Ailsa thought disgustedly. She's lost it this time.

'Ailsa, I am delighted to welcome you, please don't be uneasy. Have a seat and I'll pour you a drink. Red wine?'

'Yes, a large one.' She smiled at him, giving a resigned sigh.

Max felt exhausted as he threw his bag on the chair in Criandornoch lodge house's small hall. After a particularly demanding afternoon surgery he had driven for two hours, the last part of which was a rumbling road with dips and loose stones, which pranged his 4x4 mercilessly, but kept him focussed on the drive. He wasn't thinking about Ryan as he drove, no point in getting really worried until he knew what was up. It was Ailsa who occupied his thoughts. Were they going wrong? If so, it was his fault. His life had been so insular since he had lost his wife Elaine, six years ago. He had thrown himself into his career, and had become surly and set in his own ways. He knew he was wallowing in self-pity; as a doctor he notoriously refused to diagnose or treat himself, but he was depressed. He recognised the symptoms, but wild horses wouldn't drag this thought from his subconscious.

Dr Graham had met him when he'd arrived and shown him into a formal sitting room. Max was offered a light supper, which he declined, and a large whisky, which he accepted. The situation with Ryan, who was currently in bed in the sanatorium so that the school nurse could ensure he didn't try to do anything foolish like run away, was that he was in serious trouble, serious enough for expulsion. Dr Graham skirted around the edges of his misdemeanours, almost apologetically, explaining that he had to follow due process and interview the parents. Ryan had been seen in a pub in the nearby village with a group of boys who were not at his school. He was not dressed in his uniform, which was good in that it did not bring the school into disrepute, and neither did he involve any other pupils. Ryan had taken a bottle from Dr Graham's own drinks cabinet — motioned to the corner where he had just replaced the decanter — and one of the school prefects had caught him smoking again, this time in the woodland path beside the school which the prefects dutifully monitored. When a prefect named Gordon had told Ryan to go with him to report to the Head, Ryan had punched him. It was only due to Dr Graham's intervention and the decency and understanding shown by Gordon that the police hadn't been called.

Max nodded gloomily. 'What do you suggest I do?'

'I think we'll talk to him tomorrow together. He's obviously in bed now, but we need to stress the seriousness of this. Had it been drugs he had brought into school then I would have had no option but to expel him immediately.' Max said nothing about the double standard. As a doctor, he had seen more cases of ill health and early death due to alcohol than drugs, but he was not about to lecture the Head around this. 'He is sitting his national 5s next year and he is a very bright boy,' Dr Graham continued. 'He's almost a year younger than the others in his class, so I could put him back a year, but he's also top of the lists most weeks. He does get a certain amount of freedom going into fourth year in the autumn, but, if I do keep him here, I think we need to take away all those privileges and drive it home to him that for the next year he will not be allowed to go out of the immediate school grounds without either a teacher present, which he'll hate, or a prefect, which he'll detest.'

'Well that's just tough. Does David know?' Max referred to Malcolm's son, who was a prefect at the school.

'Not to my knowledge.'

'Okay, well, with your permission, I will speak to my nephew tomorrow, after we have dealt with Ryan. I would like him to take a bit more notice of his cousin.'

The next day saw Max heading home to Trannoch, not quite settled in his mind about Ryan but feeling that they had made some headway in getting through to his son about the seriousness of his crimes and that they *were* crimes, in the shape of theft, underage drinking and assault. Put starkly before him, he seemed to waken up to the fact that he may be getting expelled, and he appeared to be righteously sorry. He was indignant at the restrictions placed upon him for the coming year but became much more contrite when he caught his father's eye. Max had left him on slightly better terms than those on which he had arrived. He was not convinced however that Ryan would still be at Criandornoch this time next year. He left the next day, picked up fresh clothes at Trannoch, and was soon on his way to Mhainaray.

Hunter was not amused. Sir Pierce, or Piercey as she insisted on calling him, had taken them out for a long exploratory walk around the extensive estate of Mhainaray Manor, and up into the hills. Ailsa, ever enthusiastic about her surroundings in Scotland, was delighted with the quietly rolling pastures and the bright yellow gorse which surrounded the house, so different from the rugged rocky landscape around Storm Winds. He pointed out all the areas of interest, which they were to Ailsa but not to Hunter, who had tottered behind tripping on the rough land, and turning up her nose at the sheep and deer droppings she had to endure along the way. When she paid any attention to Hunter, Ailsa could hardly contain her laughter at Hunter's difficulty in walking with her heels on the stony paths. Nowadays she didn't possess a pair of walking boots. It wasn't that the older woman was unused to the outdoor life — she had been the best markswoman for miles around when she was in her youth, hence the name Hunter — but gone were the days when she would walk for miles across the rugged landscape of the North West stalking deer and shooting rabbits for sport. Most of it had been done just to impress her bevy of boyfriends, who thought she was wonderful. She was angry as she wasn't getting enough attention, and enraged at Ailsa speaking animatedly with Sir Pierce about the hills, woodland paths and her own plans for Storm Winds. He listened, talked and advised enthusiastically.

'Excuse me! I seem to be stuck!' Ailsa turned to see an elegant figure, dressed in cream jeans, cream designer jacket and red high-heeled boots, one leg deep in a muddy ditch off the track they were following.

'What are you doing off the track?' Ailsa said, in amusement. 'Can't you follow the path behind us?'

Hunter ignored her. 'Piercey, darling, do please help me out of this mud,' she pleaded, with a hint of weariness in her voice. He instantly jumped to attention.

'Hunter, for God's sake, just pull your leg out. You aren't a complete imbecile, are you?' It was Ailsa, of course, her rage at everything which had happened in the last few days coming to the fore.

Hunter looked furiously at her daughter. She held on to Sir Pierce while she gave a huge pull and fell backwards into his arms. She then made a huge play of hugging him and wiping imaginary tears from her eyes. The boot was still embedded in the mud and she turned and looked at Ailsa who was laughing sarcastically at this. She half-hopped towards her. 'Well, thank you, for nothing.'

'The problem with you is you're jealous, as Pierce and I were having a conversation together about my plans for Storm Winds.'

Hunter had her hands on hips. 'Really? And why do you think I would have any interest in that cold wreck of a place?' The smile was malicious.

'Because you can't get your hands on it. Do you think I have forgotten how you forced your son to travel to Scotland to pose as my brother so that he would inherit the place?'

'He *is* your brother.'

'My *half-brother*. It's okay, I *know* he is the Colonel's son, Joshua told me himself before he left in disgust at your little game.' Her voice was raised several decibels now. Sir Pierce was watching this tirade, at first highly amused and becoming astonished at Ailsa's revelation.

'How *dare* you shout my business all over the island!' she screamed, though her words were now faltering.

Ailsa was beginning to lose it. 'Your business? That's a laugh, your *scheming* more like it. You came back here only because Sir Angus had died, and you wanted Storm Winds. Don't try to deny it. You don't care for *people*, you just care for *things,* so just shut up, you spoiled bitch.'

'Please, ladies, there are people over there in the hills who can hear you, please...'

'You little...' The slap resounded as Hunter drew her hand across Ailsa's face with a crack.

Ailsa reeled from the shock. 'How dare you?' Ailsa sized up to the older woman and lifted her hand to give as good as she got, then lowered it, with a shake of her head. Caught unaware, and thinking her daughter wasn't going to retaliate, Hunter relaxed and laughed a laugh devoid of humour. Ailsa took a step towards her, and with a push sent Hunter sprawling backwards into the mud. Even her head hit the mud, and she was covered from her feet up to her beautifully-cut short blonde hair.

'Hey, is everything okay?' A tall dark figure was running through the bracken towards them, another walking a good bit behind. 'Are you having problems here?' He grinned widely at the older man who smiled back. 'Don't worry, I'll help you get her out.'

Ailsa saw that the other man who was behind and coming nearer, was Max. She felt a whole load of emotions explode within her and tears started to run like a burn down her face. He came towards her, seeing only her, and held her, kissing her face and hair and her finger-marked cheek.

'Max, I'm so glad... I... I...'

He kissed her lips through the ever increasing rain, her body encircled in his arms.

Hunter couldn't move. She was wedged deep in the pile of mud which she thought was slightly moving underneath her, pulling her down inch by inch.

'Eh... Max, mate, gonnae put her down and gie a hand here?' The other man grinned and knelt on the path beside Hunter. She recognised that voice; the man she had met on the ferry.

It was Andy.

'I think it would be better if you left tomorrow as planned.' Max sat on one of the sofas at Mhainaray, looking at a sparkling clean and unrepentant Hunter.

'I don't remember asking for your opinion,' Hunter snapped coldly.

'You didn't, but I'm giving you it anyway,' he said, with a sip of excellent brandy which their host had just opened for them all after their little escapade. By the time they had arrived back they were all drenched. The teeming rain had added insult to injury, especially in the case of the already mud-caked woman. Hunter was incensed, as Pierce had stood back while Andy, the man she had met on the ferry, and Max, had wrenched her from the ground. Between them they had half-carried her over a mile back to the house, where she indignantly and roughly threw them off and stomped up the stairs, much to their amusement. Her other boot was now buried deep in the mud of Mhainaray's hills.

Andy left for the hotel, and Max told Ailsa later that he had arrived at the pier only to find his old friend there, having just dropped off some people for the return ferry. Andy had taken him to Mhainaray Manor, then they had both gone for a walk to find its occupants.

An hour later, Mrs Monroe had been sent to ask Mrs Dillon to come down to the front room, as Sir Pierce and the others would like to speak with her.

It was 'the others' that did it.

'I'm not quite ready yet. I'll be down as soon as I am.' She inwardly fumed at being summoned in this cursory way. Mrs Monroe looked like she would quite cheerfully slap *her* face for her. She had heard about the fight between the two women — these stories have a habit of spreading faster than the lighted heather on the hillside.

'Well, they're all in the front room.' Mrs Monroe turned on her heel and slammed the door behind her.

'Hunter, we just think it would be better if you stick to the original plan, as you and Ailsa don't seem to be... er... clicking at this point in time,' Sir Pierce said, his lips twitching as he thought about the scrimmage.

'Well, that's an understatement! My daughter, as you have witnessed, is rude, foul-mouthed and behaves like a hooligan. I can't believe she holds the title "Lady" when she is anything but.'

'Well, you've got a bloody nerve! You slapped me! You call me your daughter? You abandoned me! Remember that? You're nasty and malicious and have the sheer audacity to say that about me!' Ailsa threw up her hands in disbelief.

'At least I didn't punch you, like a guttersnipe, and shove you in a quagmire!'

'I certainly did NOT punch you! But you deserved it anyway, you stupid, self-centred...'

'All right, all right!' Sir Pierce intervened, 'I really think you have *both* behaved badly and should just settle this by apologising.' They both looked scornfully at the owner of Mhainaray.

'Absolutely not.'

'Over my dead body.'

'Well, at least you both agree on something,' Max said, with a laugh. 'I would give up if I were you, Pierce. They're just not going to admit it and play nice.'

'Where did that man Andy go anyway? He was very chivalrous at helping me from the mud after my daughter punched me and I fell in...' Hunter said innocently.

Ailsa looked at her contemptuously. 'Why, have you had a fling with him, too?'

'You really need to speak more respectfully, darling. Your turn of phrase is vulgar in the extreme.' Hunter's eyebrows were higher than the arches on the Forth Rail bridge. She ignored her daughter's fuming expression as she continued, 'I think he said he was staying at the hotel?'

The temperature in the air amongst them very slowly decreased. Sir Pierce who had been quietly studying her face asked suspiciously, 'When did you have that particular conversation?'

'Oh, on the ferry over here,' she answered airily. 'He said he was staying there.'

Max re-filled the glasses then sat down again. 'Yes, actually, he does stay at the hotel every time he comes back to Mhainaray,' he chuckled.

'Yes? Sorry, you said when he comes back? Does he work here?' Hunter was too eager for her own good, and Sir Pierce cast a disappointed eye at her.

It was Max who perceived the look between them. He pondered what this meant for a few minutes before saying, 'Andy is Uncle Pierce's nephew, and he just happens to own the hotel on Mhainaray.'

It was shaping up to be a wet start to the summer. Nothing unremarkable if you live on the west coast of Scotland, but the damp and dismal quality of the days seemed to seep into people, making them feel dull, cold and wet. The land around Storm Winds was sodden, the drenched trees seemed to inconsolably droop and the flowers and shrubbery lifted rain-trodden heads through an uncompromising gloom. And this was July.

Ailsa was writing in her library. Her book was not working out the way she envisaged, and she felt headachy and upset. She was also thinking about Max. She felt they had made a bit of headway when they were on Mhainaray, but she was worried that this could not be sustained now they were back and into a routine again. She didn't want a baby at the moment either, she had so much to think about and plan, but it still worried her that Max was a bit sceptical about having another child, despite his vigorous protestations. All this was hanging over her.

Gennina joined her at eleven o'clock to talk about the plans.

'Right, so the new bedding has all arrived for the East Wing — the extra bathroom is finished and there are only one or two tiny little touches to finish it. The first people are coming tomorrow to the Dower House, and everything is okie dokie there too.' Gennina enthusiastically ticked off her list on her clip board.

'That's fantastic, Gennina, but why didn't you wait until this afternoon to have our usual estate meeting before you said all this?'

Gennina looked shamefaced. 'I don't want to start anything, but...'

The door opened and Miss Cochrane showed in Stephen Millburn. His face was painted with animosity and hurt, as he took a chair opposite Ailsa.

'I hope you don't mind me intruding...'

Ailsa felt almost sorry for him. 'Not at all, Stephen. We were just going to talk about the first holiday occupants for the Dower House.'

'And you thought you would discuss estate business with Gennina and not me?'

Ailsa could see how this looked, and she glanced at Gennina.

'I came to see Ailsa, because I was fed up with you ordering me about!'

'Oh, I see, clyping on me, were you?'

Ailsa, being a Londoner, was unfamiliar with the term but guessed it was something to do with talking about Stephen behind his back. She saw the hurt in his eyes.

'Well, I can't talk to you about anything. You treat me like a kid and...'

Ailsa felt she knew just what Gennina meant. 'Listen, can't we just...'

'Well, you are just a kid. You have no idea about running an estate.' Stephen was getting heated now.

'I don't WANT to run the estate! No one could get past you anyway, even if I DID want to!'

'That's because I am the estate manager. I'm YOUR manager.'

'I report directly to Ailsa! I am a professional PA!'

Ailsa nearly laughed at this. 'Right okay, let me put it plainly. Firstly, if you can't just discuss your issues in a grown-up way without shouting at each other, then we will end this discussion here.' She conveniently forgot her little episode with Hunter on Mhainaray. 'Secondly, Gennina, you do report directly to me, but have almost a dotted line to Stephen. He is, as he says, the estate manager, and oversees everything. Thirdly, I agree with Stephen on how this meeting looked, and we'll discuss our points at our weekly estate meeting together. Lastly, Stephen, it would be really good if you gave Gennina some room on the Dower House project — her ideas are important, and she is a brilliant organiser.'

Silence.

'Okay, I agree to that, Ailsa,' Stephen said, and she almost fell off her seat.

'Yeah, okay, sorry Stephen. Didn't mean to leave you out.' And that was that.

Chapter Eleven

The breakfast table at Trannoch was buzzing with chatter, clanking of plates and scraping of knives and forks as the MacKenzies ate together. The children were all home from school — the summer holiday started in mid-July at Criandornoch school, and they were all, except of course for the disgraced Ryan, having a good break.

'When do you go to France?' the Colonel shouted down the table to Malcolm, as if his second son was in the next door sitting room.

'Tuesday. We're all packed and ready to go — almost! Aren't we darling?' He smiled at Melissa, who nodded and nibbled at her scrambled egg quietly. He was not there yet with his children. He had almost seventeen years, David's age, to try and make up, and he was finding the task daunting, but in a martyrish way he accepted it gladly. He was going to take David and Melissa to Carcassonne himself for a week, and he was actually looking forward to getting to know them again.

'Morning everyone!' Hunter sashayed into the room, her tight black cut-off jeans and white, long, open necked Gucci shirt showing off her 'California tan' which was the name of the sun bed company who had supplied her with the new sun bed currently residing in a small room next to her dressing room. There were a few grunts of acknowledgement round the room, mostly they ignored her. She took her place beside the Colonel who beamed at her enthusiastically.

'How did Mhainaray go?' the Colonel bellowed from his vantage point, inches away from her.

'A distant memory! But now that you mention it, it was perfectly foul.' My daughter, "The Lady Ailsa", as she likes to call herself, really is the limit. She ruined everything.'

Max lowered his paper and his brow. 'I don't think that's fair. She doesn't call herself that, and she goes out of her way to remind people she wants to be just Ailsa.'

'Why Max, I didn't see you behind that paper. Don't you know it is rude to read at the table?'

'Yes.'

Hunter looked at the Colonel for support. When she got none, she steam-rollered on. 'I wonder at you allowing your son to read at breakfast?' she whined. The Colonel then ignored her too. She looked round the table to find someone to pick on, and she settled on Ryan, trying to look inconspicuous, with head down eating some bacon and fried eggs.

'It's so nice to have all the children home from school. Ryan, unless I am mistaken, you must be very bored at Trannoch after Crian... whatever its name is. No scope for starting mischief! What will you get up to in your spare time these holidays, I wonder?'

'I... I... er...' Ryan looked upset and sent pleading eyes over to his father, whose temper was heating significantly during this, but it was David who came to his aid.

'Please don't speak to my cousin like that, Mrs Dillon. He's been through enough, and anyway, it has nothing to do with you.'

Melissa looked across at her big brother with nothing short of hero-worship. Melody gave a little laugh, and Malcolm a loud guffaw.

Hunter opened her mouth to take a slice off David, but Max was there before her. 'Hunter, I don't think that is in any way helpful. Ryan has done wrong, and is being punished, and more than you need to know.' He put down his paper and buttered some toast. His son looked at him gratefully. Ryan caught David's eye and the older boy gave him a conciliatory nod. Ryan, looked up to his cousin more than any of his uncles, and second only to his father, and was mildly happy.

'Sorry, but must we listen to little childish squabbles around the breakfast table?' Carys had picked up some toast and was sitting back down at her place.

'Well, it's a change from listening to you.' Noel, who spoke little, usually had an interesting point to make when he did.

Thomas, who also spoke little and never had an interesting point to make, piped up, 'That's not very nice, Noel, my wife is pregnant and shouldn't be upset...'

Carys looked at him in disgust. 'Oh, do shut up, Thomas. I am perfectly capable of speaking for myself. I don't need you bleating away trying to back me up and failing miserably.' There were chuckles round the table at this, but Thomas only smiled weakly and continued to eat.

Olivia appeared at that moment. A much more confident, beautiful Olivia, who looked as far removed from how a new mother usually looks as is possible. She said good morning gracefully, then picked some toast and fruit from the sideboard, sitting herself down beside them. The Colonel smiled at her. He was becoming fond of Olivia, chiefly because she had given him a beautiful baby boy to play with. He had never played with any of his own children, or other grandchildren for that matter.

'How is Freddy?' he asked.

'He fine, thank you. Laura has him out in the pram for a little walk.' Her English was improving as fast as her confidence, much to the chagrin of Carys who had now lost that particular line of bullying, but it didn't stop her looking for other avenues. She was very jealous of Olivia who was 'back to normal' in terms of her shape, and who more than matched her in looks — Carys being an ice maiden of blondness, while Olivia was a dark, sensual beauty.

'I meant to tell you, Olivia,' Carys paused for effect, and they all sensed that something rude was coming. Noel clicked his tongue in exasperation, and Max groaned loudly. The Colonel began to go a deep shade of red, but Carys mowed on in there. 'There's a new gym with lots of exercise classes opened in Arnasaid Bheag. It is brilliant, lots of weight machines and other equipment. Of course, I only ever need our own little gym here at Trannoch, but you may wish to try something a bit more... er... challenging, to get back into shape?'

Olivia looked at her questioningly. 'Hmmm. I try and go,' she nodded with a delicate sip of her coffee. 'Then when you have baby we go together? You will have big, big belly to get rid of, no?'

Max spat out his tea, and Noel tittered in amusement. Malcolm threw back his head with a huge guffaw, and the children all sniggered cautiously. Only Thomas looked surprised, and the Colonel looked severe.

'Now, now, Olivia, no need to be rude.' His voice was gently admonishing, and Olivia opened her black oval eyes widely in mock surprise.

'Oh, so sorry, no rude Colonel, just try to help.' The glint in her eye as she looked at the other woman sent a warning. Olivia was not going to be messed with.

'Like Carys help me.'

'She said *what*?' Ailsa was laughing hysterically, so much so that Max gave her a nudge.

'Okay, you don't need to let the whole pub know!'

'I'll tell you,' she said, wiping her eyes of running mascara, 'Olivia will be a force to be reckoned with at Trannoch when she gets a bit older, if she stays that long.'

'What do you mean?'

'Well, she is in her, what, early twenties? And already she has a baby and a fortune. She's gorgeous and can get the best that money can buy. Why would she want to stay with Malcolm?'

'Well, for one thing, Dad would never let her leave with Freddy. He's his grandchild, and I've never seen him so besotted with any of us as he is with Freddy. Dad would be absolutely heartbroken if she left.'

'I know, heartbroken enough to let her go without a penny if she decided to,' Ailsa said drily, 'but she has the world at her feet, so to speak, and I hope for the Colonel's sake she will stick around, and Melissa's actually.'

'Melissa?'

'Yes, she's developed a bit of an allegiance with Olivia, which is great.'

'Well as long as she doesn't lead her astray. I hope she doesn't forget Mel is only a child.'

Ailsa looked at him with a mixture of impatience and affection. 'I thought I had washed that old stuffed shirt out...'

He laughed, and drew her in for a kiss, just as two figures passed by. The light was behind them, and it was difficult to see who they were. Then Ailsa's mouth opened wide.

It was Hunter and Andy Donald, the man who pulled her from the mud on Mhainaray.

'Max! How's it going?' The affable Andy spotted them, and Max stood and shook hands. 'I... er... just met the lovely Hunter in Arnasaid and we thought we would get some lunch, or a drink, or something...' he tailed off.

'Yeah, right,' Ailsa thought to herself.

'Come and join us?' Both Ailsa and Hunter looked rankled at this, but she sat down and Andy went for drinks, nonetheless.

Hunter was frosty. 'How are you, Max?'

'I'm very well, thank you. How are you?' He only just managed to stifle a laugh. She spoke as if she hadn't seen him for weeks. Hunter took out a nail file and began to file her nails. Ailsa and Max looked at each other with a 'what's she all about' look.

'Here we are, pint for you, white wine for you, and for the beautiful, er... Ailsa, isn't it? A red wine.' Ailsa had to admit to herself he was very good looking, but arrogance sometimes follows good looks — it was so in Andy's case. Hunter's face clouded over.

'So, when did you two get together?' Andy hadn't seen them since he helped Max pull Hunter from the mud.

'Six, months ago,' Max said doubtfully, counting up in his mind.

'Seven,' Ailsa said, and Andy burst out laughing.

'God, Max, that's the longest time ever...'

'Yeah, okay Andy, thanks for that,' Max chuckled, lifting his pint.

'What about you?' Ailsa asked sweetly. 'How long have you two been together?' Max put a warning hand under the table and on her knee. Hunter looked at her venomously, and Andy grinned.

'Don't be ridiculous, Ailsa,' she spat. 'I met Andy first on the ferry to Mhainaray. We've only just bumped into each other. Do grow up.'

'Give her about ten minutes.' Ailsa ignored her mother and directed the comment to Andy.

He gave a huge belly laugh. 'Sorry, can you tell me how *you two* know each other?' The penny suddenly dropped for Andy as he pointed to Ailsa and Hunter.

Ailsa and Hunter both looked away. Max grinned 'Oh sorry, Andy, let me introduce you...'

Ailsa and Max walked from Arnasaid across the headland towards Storm Winds. It was a beautiful evening, after the continuous rain, the colours of the sunset deeply red and orange, the sun drifting slowly downwards behind the Cuillin ridge. They walked hand in hand, enjoying the breeze salting their hair and lips, and hearing the gentle lap of water on the shore. As they neared the part of the pathway which turned slightly round the cliff, they saw Storm Winds, beautiful in its grey stone, clinging to the headland, the forest rising up into the mountains behind.

'It's yours,' Max breathed, his arms around her, pulling her close.

'I know. I still can't quite believe it. It's beautiful and bold and angry like the Storm Winds of its name.'

'An apt description of its owner too!'

'Cheers.'

'It is very poetic though.' He turned and cupped her cold face in his hands, kissing her. He took her hand and they walked slowly on.

'That's why I hate Hunter. She tried to take it away from me.'

'But, Ailsa, she can't. No one can. It is yours now — rightfully yours. You were both so funny in the pub, both in a right strop, but not willing to give in or talk to the other civilly. I know you will hate me for this, but you not only look alike...'

'Don't even begin...' She chased him down the path which led to home, both laughing and shouting like kids.

Malcolm drove through a small quaint village full of yellow light shining on houses of grey stone and window boxes bursting with flowers. The river could be seen through the gaps in the houses, and, at the very end of the village road stood a cottage, two stories high, with a powder blue door in the middle and shutters open wide to the day.

'Here we are!' Malcolm said cheerfully, as he looked in dismay at the size of the place. He had never lived in a house smaller than Trannoch, nor had he stayed in a hotel unless it was opulent and had at least four stars, so this place looked like something one of the estate workers would live in.

'It's so cute and pretty with all the flowers and stone,' David said, surprisingly, as he took in the little stream which ran down the hillside at the side of the house, and the chickens which had found a hole in next door's fence through to their cobbled courtyard. His father expected that it would be Melissa who would appreciate the rustic charm of the place, after all, he had picked the cottage solely for his daughter.

'You said it had wi-fi Dad, didn't you?' was all she said. But Malcolm understood. Melissa was on a mission.

'Er...yes, I'm sure the agency said so.' Malcolm looked around the kitchen doubtfully as if he expected to see a notice saying 'wi-fi here' or something. 'Anyway, good job I got someone to come in and cook and clean for us.' He threw one of the cases on the flagstone floor in the enormous farmhouse kitchen. 'There didn't seem to be too many restaurants in the village as we passed through, and I doubt we could get a cab to take us to Carcassonne, five miles away.'

'We've got a car, Dad.' David had heard this last comment as he brought in two smaller cases and flung them down. 'I can drive. I brought my licence with me, as I knew you would want a drink.' His tone had an edge to it, which made his father stiffen his shoulders, but say nothing. All the Trannoch children were used to driving around the estate when they were in their teens, and passing a test when they were old enough was par for the course. It was the drink comment which had annoyed Malcolm, but he was determined to keep the atmosphere light.

'Talking of which, I spy a wine rack...' Malcolm plucked a bottle, found an opener and three glasses, pouring sizeable amounts into each glass and handing one to each of them in a toast, in order to hide his discomfort.

Melissa had been on her phone since the wi-fi comment, but managed to take the glass, toast the other two and repeat the inane words, 'happy holidays!' in response to her father, while texting with her left thumb.

'Why do we need a cleaner, Dad?' David asked, as they pulled out seats around an ancient pine table and sat down. 'Mel and I have to make our own beds and tidy round our rooms at school, plus we all get cooking classes up to fourth year. We could have fended for ourselves. It would've been fun.'

Melissa looked at her brother in disgust. 'I'm here on holiday, David, and I am not going to cook or clean anything!'

'Nor will you have to, darling.' Malcolm re-filled his glass and threw his jacket over the back of the chair. 'Gosh, it's hot. We'll find amazing little restaurants and eat out most evenings.' He was warming to his subject, 'I'm sure there will be information somewhere around on taxis. I appreciate your offer, David, but you are on holiday too, not here to drive us around.'

David opened his mouth to say something about not needing a drink like his father, then thought better of it, and went to have a look around.

There was a pool at the back of the house which looked suspiciously green, and was obviously full of algae. The woman who came to do the work arrived early next morning. After providing a hearty breakfast for them, she threw up her hands in theatrical despair at the state of the pool, saying in a loud voice that they would all die from bacterial poisoning should they decide to swim in it. Luckily, David was proficient in French, and caught the gist of this. Though he looked respectfully serious at Madame Berger's comments, he chuckled behind her back, and spoke fluently to the owner later that morning about the urgent need to have the pool cleaned.

David hired a bike and went off on his own exploring the region. He was a sporty boy, and was already deciding he would like to do sports science at Uni, though he knew his grandfather would have something to say about that.

'Enjoying it, darling?' Malcolm was stretched out on a sunbed near his daughter, beside the newly cleaned and de-bugged pool.

'It's okay,' she shrugged, her mobile phone her main focus of attention.

Malcolm tried again. 'There's a play on in an open-air amphitheatre in Carcasonne this evening. I've bought us tickets. I think you'll enjoy it,' he grinned hopefully.

'I hate open-air theatres,' she said, not lifting her eyes from her phone.

Malcolm was at a loss how to handle this behaviour. At Trannoch, his father was always there to take control, and he let him. He took a deep breath, and a sip of his late afternoon gin and tonic. 'Really? Have you been to one before?'

She hesitated, 'No, but the thought of sitting on those stone steps instead of proper chairs, just leaves me cold.'

Malcolm gave his daughter a sideways glance. 'Is it because it's a religious play?'

Melissa hadn't known this. 'Absolutely. Had it been Shakespeare or something, that would have been mildly bearable. Not going. You go with David, I'll be all right here.'

'Well, you know, I am really pleased you said that darling, as I momentarily forgot. It's Macbeth we're going to see. So glad you like Shakespeare,' and he got up to go and get changed. 'Be down for six thirty; I've ordered the one and only taxi.'

Melissa stared after him in anger, and mild admiration. 'He tricked me!' she said out loud, as her father disappeared inside.

The following few days Malcolm and Melissa spent by the pool, while David went off on his mountain bike. Gradually the air between them defrosted enough to allow occasional unrehearsed comments. On the fourth day, Malcolm had just poured his gin and tonic, when Melissa looked up from her phone.

'Any cider, Dad?'

Malcolm knew he drank far too much, and he didn't want that lifestyle for either of his children, but he was choosing his battles. 'Yes, there's some in the fridge.'

She brought back a cider and began drinking straight from the bottle. He balked at this, but said nothing as she eyed him with a look that dared him to question her.

The question came straight out of the blue. 'Do you love us? Me and David?' She had only had two mouthfuls of cider so he could hardly blame that on her abrupt question.

'Yes, very much.' He was blown away and didn't know how to dress it up. He didn't need to.

She nodded slowly. 'How could you have treated Mum the way you did?' Again, that frankness threw him to the point of gasping for breath before he spoke.

'Your Mum and I didn't love each other,' he said finally. 'I have done many, many terrible things in my life, but...'

'You hit her,' she said, simply and calmly.

'Yes. Only once...although, once is definitely too many times,' he hastened to add. 'She made me get help, anger management classes, or she would have told Grandfather.'

'Why?'

'Because we had got to the point where we both wanted to hurt each other. Nothing worked between us anymore. We had a hate which nothing could shift. I snapped.'

Again that calm nodding acceptance. 'She took her life because of you.'

Malcolm felt like she had reached in and pulled out his heart. The pain was intense, the burning feeling of an empty soul, and the sensation that he was under water.

'I believe she was paying me back, she knew I couldn't reach her again, I couldn't win again. The last word was hers,' he said, as his face melted in pain. 'I am not walking away from my guilt, I shall feel that a part of me has gone, and that it was my fault, for the rest of my life. If ever I was sorry for anything, *really* sorry... then your mother leaving us all because...because of me...'

Melissa never moved as the tears coursed down her tanned cheeks. They sat like that for a long while, not speaking, each of them clutched their own grief.

'Oh, Dad!' She jumped up from her seat and fell into his arms as they cried together.

The Arnasaid Round Table, of which Ailsa was part, had decided to move the date of the Highland Games this year to the middle of July. The reason for this was that there were lots of English tourists who came to the area when their own children were off school, which was much later than the Scottish school holidays. This meant, hopefully, that they would have more income from the tents selling local produce and all the games, competitions and other associated activities.

Ailsa was once again opening the event, and she was excited about this year, as there was to be a book festival attended by two eminent Scottish authors who would give talks. She was also going to give a talk on her own newly published novel, which she was nervous about.

The after-Games barbeque was at Storm Winds this year, and, with everything going on with the Dower House, preparations for the grouse shoot and all the renovations and work, she wondered how it would ever come to fruition. She had decided, along with Stephen and Gennina, that they would put up huge tents on the lawns as the weather had been very wet recently.

On the Thursday, Connie and Jan arrived, and the three friends danced with excitement at seeing each other again. Their bags were taken up to their rooms by Jim Hutton; and they congregated in the blue sitting room, Ailsa's favourite room, with nibbles and wine.

'I have so much to tell you! I can't believe its July already, so many things have happened in this last year it is absolutely frightening.' Ailsa reached for some crisps.

'Well, I have some news for you, too.' Connie flicked back her wild red hair, her eyes flashing with excitement.' The other two looked on expectantly.

'Oh, don't say anything else until Clem arrives!' Ailsa begged. 'She's just finishing up at her tearoom, and she said she would come right in here when she finished. You know she lives here at Storm Winds now? I never see her though, she is so busy with the shop which has been a brilliant success.' A knock came at the door, and, Miss Cochrane, on her way to her own quarters, showed in Clem who dived at Connie and Jan and they all jumped up and down again making Miss Cochrane tut-tut in disapproval and leave the room hastily.

'Oh, it's so great to see you both! And you too, Ailsa, cos I haven't seen you for ages either with all that's going on!' Clem laughed as she accepted a glass of red wine.

'Your hair is different!' Connie said, her head on one side surveying her friend.

'You know what? I haven't had time to get it cut, so I let it grow,' the owner of the sleek brown bob announced. 'Anyway, what's the hanes?'

'Hanes?' Jan asked enquiringly.

'News... goss...' Clem rolled her eyes.

'Well, Connie has some earth-shattering news, but we were waiting until you arrived so that she can tell us!' Jan said, sipping her wine. 'You'd better shout on Jim and ask for another bottle Ailsa, this one hasn't lasted us long!'

'Oh, he's away off now. It was a long drive from the airport with you two drunkards,' Ailsa said laughing.

'Cheek! We only had two little bottles each on the flight,' Jan said.

'And the one in Heathrow, as we were early,' supplemented Connie. 'Oh yeah, and the one at Glasgow airport, as Jim got caught in traffic.'

'Okay, okay, never mind all that now, just tell us your news, Con,' Ailsa said impatiently.

'Well, Calum and I have set a date to get married.' She beamed.

'Aw, brilliant!'

'Great!'

'Congratulations!'

Their comments came thick and fast.

'It will be in London, as that's where my relatives live, and I have hundreds more than Calum,' Connie said. 'You three are bridesmaids! I know we just got engaged recently at the Trannoch Ball, but we decided to just bloody go for it!'

There were hugs and tears, and Ailsa popped down to the cellar for more wine for them to toast (so they told themselves).

Connie told them the biggest news was that after they were married they were coming up to live in Scotland. Connie was a lawyer and could practice English Law, but realised she would need to take a conversion course in Scottish Law before being able to become a full-blown partner to Calum.

Calum's father owned the firm, and they would live in Calum's flat until they could find a house in or around the town.

Ailsa was over the moon with this piece of news. 'That's brilliant, honey,' she said. 'Now all we need is you, Jan, to move here too, and we will all be together.'

The Games were a great success. Ailsa was taken to the opening ceremony amongst the usual pomp and circumstance in the customary limousine, made a short speech, and then the Games began. A different Ailsa it was from the shy timid one who had opened the Games the year before. Max was standing in the crowd, with the rest of the MacKenzie clan, and looked on proudly at her standing poised at the mic, up on the dais in front of a crowd of around three hundred people, welcoming them to Arnasaid Highland Games.

Then the talk on her book was to be got through, which she did with ease and charm once she got started. She answered some questions from the audience. One woman caught her eye as she asked her question. She was probably in her mid to late seventies, Ailsa guessed, and was dressed elegantly and expensively in direct contrast to most of the audience who wore typical outdoor garb of jeans, shorts and waterproof mountain jackets.

There was something about her...

One man, of around forty, standing near the elegant older lady, began an obtuse line of questioning. 'You hold a title, is this why you have "Lady Annabel" as the main protagonist? Is she autobiographical?' he asked, in a slightly confrontational way, which got heads turning to see who had spoken. Then, 'What makes you think this book is good enough to be made into a historical costume drama?' And finally, 'I found your characters quite stilted. Do you think they act and speak like real people?' All innocent enough questions but laced with a certain animosity which surprised Ailsa, and Max, who was also in the audience to support her.

Ailsa signed a pile of books for the queue which had formed, which took her a few hours, after which she flopped back in her seat exhausted.

'Did you see the older woman at the book reading, the one near that awkward man? She looked familiar, but I don't think I've ever seen her before,' Ailsa mentioned, as Max appeared with a welcome cup of tea.

'I couldn't see her from where I was sitting. There's bound to be some difficult people who like to put others on the spot.'

Neither she, nor the contentious man who had been asking all the questions, had waited for a book to be signed.

The barbeque was in full swing. Ailsa had changed into jeans and a white shirt and sandals which looked fresh and summery, although the weather was anything but. Max had on jeans and a black shirt, and although not the most handsome MacKenzie, as no one could beat Malcolm for looks, he was tall and muscular. His face was good to look at, with his clear eyes and well-cut lips. Ailsa looked at him standing on the lawn talking to some locals, his bottle of beer in his hand, and talking animatedly, for him. His kind, caring face lighting up as he laughed. She hoped that they would be alright. It had been a rollercoaster year for them, but hopefully they would come out the other side unscathed.

A woman came sidling up to Max, put her hand around his waist, and when he turned to see who it was, he kissed her once on both cheeks. They stood looking at each other, then Max leaned over to a passing waiter and picked up two drinks, one for himself and one for her. Ailsa felt her blood run cold. Andy seemed to know her too, he kissed her on the cheek, but she stood by Max's side. They laughed and talked amongst the three of them like old friends — or lovers? She turned away to find Connie, Jan and Clem. She didn't see Max for most of the evening after that.

When everyone left, and Connie, Clem and Jan had met their partners and gone to the blue sitting room, Max found her in the library on her own.

'Where did you go?' Ailsa demanded, in a low cool voice which made Max raise his eyebrows.

'I was just catching up with Angie,' he said cautiously.

'Catching up? I haven't seen you for hours. Who is she?'

'An old Uni friend of mine and Andy's. I haven't seen her for years. She just turned up.'

'Oh yeah? Just happened to materialise out of thin air? You looked very thick with her.'

'What are you trying to say, Ailsa?'

'That you looked very thick with her. That you looked at her as if you're in love with her.'

'Don't be ridiculous. I just haven't seen her for years and she happened to be in the area on holiday...'

'Are you?'

'Am I what?'

'In love with her?'

Max sighed, and looked into her eyes. 'I was, once.'

The next morning Ailsa didn't want to get out of bed. She thought about Angie: very thin, good looking, intelligent, with long dark hair, long legs, a dress far too short for a woman in her forties, if she was the same age as Max, with her bare arms round his waist. He hadn't even mentioned her! She felt as though this was the last straw for them. He hadn't wanted to admit to it, but he was *once* in love with her, *once*. It looked as if it were the case when he met up with her again yesterday. And to actually admit it too! Why hadn't he mentioned her? Why hadn't he introduced Angie to her? They had had a big argument — huge — and they had both said some regrettable, unforgiveable things, but Ailsa felt that failing to mention her to Angie was the worst thing she could imagine. Was he ashamed of her? But at the Games he had seemed so proud of her. He told her so. Why had he avoided telling this woman that he was already in a relationship? Max had said she was nothing to him now but an 'old friend'. Well, it didn't seem like Angie was just an old friend to her! She had cried and shouted and eventually stormed away up to her room where she locked the door and refused to speak to anybody. In fact Miss Cochrane was the only one who had approached, knocking the door and asking if she was okay, no one else.

Not even Max.

Gennina was biting the end of her pencil, presumably to stop her biting Stephen's head off as the four of them, Ailsa, Stephen, Gennina and Roddy were having their estate meeting as usual the following Friday.

'I just think there's something suspicious about them,' Gennina said petulantly.

'But what have you to base this on?' Ailsa said wearily. Her fuse was short, and her head was aching with strain.

'She has nothing to base this on. We've been through all this already.' Stephen turned the page in his notebook. 'Okay, I think we should talk about the projected revenue stream from the Dower House and how we can utilise this in investment...'

Gennina, not to be shoved aside like this, fumed. 'There is something suspicious about these two men and that woman. I absolutely deffo know it.'

'Aren't they the ones who booked for a week, then extended it as they liked it here so much?' Ailsa asked.

'Yeah, they extended for a month. That month is up at the end of the week.'

Stephen shut his book with a snap and tried to keep his temper intact.

'Why don't you tell us what you think you saw?' Roddy rarely spoke at these meetings, but was a good arbitrator between the two.

'Well, they are always skulking about the grounds,' she began haughtily, 'I've seen them round the back of the house looking in the windows when you were all out.'

'Wait a minute, if you saw them acting suspiciously, why did you agree to extend?' Stephen butted in.

Ailsa ignored Stephen. 'You mean the Dower House?' Ailsa was beginning to look worried.

'No, I mean this house. Also, I saw them coming out of the side door, the one that goes to Cocky's and Clem's rooms.'

'*What*?' Alarm bells were beginning to ring for Ailsa, and Gennina looked pleased only for the fact that they were listening to her now.

'Why didn't you say so before?' Stephen was now annoyed that he had brushed this aside.

'Because you wouldn't listen to me. You *never* listen to me. I'm sick of it.'

'Okay, okay. Listen, if this group of people think they are going to spy on us, they're sadly mistaken. Anything else, Gennina?'

The PA looked around the group conspiratorially before she dropped the bombshell. 'Well, I saw them one evening, when I was going home late. It was in Arnasaid, near where I live, you know?' They all nodded with get on with it expressions. 'And I saw the three of them behind the hotel. The path I take home winds behind the hotel, and I thought they were just there smoking, but they weren't. They were talking to another man, a man who isn't part of the Dower House group, and he handed them something.'

'What?' all three asked in unified desperation for her to continue.

'It looked like a gun.'

Chapter Twelve

There was a shocked silence. The three others looked at each other in dismay, Ailsa got up and began pacing the floor.

'A gun? Do you mean a rifle or revolver?' Stephen asked.

'They were quite wee guns. Not guns like you use in the grouse shooting.' She sat back quite pleased with herself at being able to create this sensation.

'I think we should report this to the police,' Roddy said uncertainly, and Ailsa nodded in agreement.

'Yes, Roddy, this is no job for us. I agree we should report it,' Ailsa nodded.

'What have you been reading lately?' Stephen suddenly asked.

Gennina looked at him quizzically, moving the chewing gum around her mouth, cracking it before answering, 'Well, I have been reading a good thriller. I can't remember the name, and now I'm reading Ailsa's book.'

'What about Enid Blyton?'

'Eh who?'

'Enid Blyton? The famous children's author? I hear her adventure stories are full of people who meet in dark alley ways and talk about secret things like gun running...'

'Stephen...' Ailsa gave a warning look.

'I have no idea...' The penny suddenly dropped, and Gennina looked at him with dislike. 'You know what?' She got up and gathered her papers together.

'Gennina, please sit down,' pleaded Ailsa.

'What?' Stephen grinned.

'You can just piss off, Stephen Millburn. I'm not going to answer to you any longer,' and she took her papers, her bag and her tears out of the office and headed home.

'Stephen, I really think you should have listened to Gennina. She is not one to have a great imagination, and I really think she did see something,' Ailsa said in annoyance.

'Oh, come on Ailsa. You don't think she actually saw the folk from the Dower House conspiring with another guy who had a gun, a revolver at that? Ailsa, *seriously*?' He was incredulous.

'It's not unheard of to have guns these days. Look what happened last year when Olivia got hold of one! Maybe in this part of the world they're only usually for shooting game but I think you should go after her,' she said firmly. Both Stephen and Roddy looked at her enquiringly.

'I'll go,' Roddy said, and started to get up.

'No, I want Stephen to go.'

'I'm sorry, no. Ailsa, I will not go after her, I really think she has lost the plot. All this self-importance with seeing to the Dower House is going to her head.'

'Stephen you are such a jumped-up egotistical bastard at times. Just get out.' It was beginning to be a habit, ordering her estate manager to leave.

Roddy smiled to himself, as Stephen threw his chair to the side and left.

Connie and Jan left at the end of the week to return to their jobs and lives in London. They were worried about Ailsa. They had not been able to work out what had gone wrong at the barbeque following the Games, and Ailsa had failed to enlighten them.

'I think they've had a row,' Jan said, pushing her blonde hair out of her eyes. They were on the flight back home to Heathrow.

'I think they're both finding it very hard. I wouldn't be surprised if they decided to go on a break, as they say,' said Connie.

'It's such a shame. They don't know how suited they are to each other, but they just can't seem to see it.'

'That's exactly it. They're so good together, but part of the problem is they're so different and they've lived in different worlds. Ailsa has been brought up by great adoptive parents who had regular jobs and an ordinary life. She is a modern day heiress, so to speak. She's just so fresh in outlook on how to run an estate and is making Storm Winds all modern. She's had a positive effect on Trannoch too for that matter. Max though, has been brought up in an elite society, where money is no object, all the boys sent off to Eton or similar schools then Oxbridge, and coming back to one of the oldest and most respected estates in Scotland is all that he really knows. Although I must say, out of all the MacKenzie boys, he is the one who has carved his own path for himself, and has worked damned hard. I really like Max, and I want him for Ailsa, end of.'

The cabin crew came round with drinks. 'Okay, you two look like Prosecco girls, and I'm doing two for twelve pounds which means you can have two each for only twelve pounds each!' His sense of humour and camp manner was infectious after the seriousness of the conversation. Connie looked at Jan.

'Two Proseccos each?'

'Yeah, why not.'

Ailsa took Bluebell and Rosie out on to the headland that night. The air was soft and the sound of bells from the boats in Arnasaid harbour could be heard in the stillness. She loved that sound. It reminded her of the cow bells she heard as a child on a holiday in Austria. The tops of the Cuillins peaked upwards towards the redness of the sunset, and the rain, for the first time in the last few days, had subsided.

'Hello!' The voice interrupted her thoughts and the dogs began to bark uncontrollably.

'I'm so sorry,' Ailsa said. 'Hello, I can't think what is making the dogs bark.'

'I presume you are Lady Ailsa Hamilton-Dunbar?' The man came nearer in the twilight and she could see that he was one of the three people from the Dower House.

'Yes, I am,' she admitted nervously. 'You are on holiday here, in the Dower House?'

'Oh yes.' There was something off with the way he was looking at her and speaking, and she felt a sudden urge to run back home. His Italian accent was strong, and dripped smarm.

''I hope you are having a good time? I need to get the dogs back...'

'No need to rush,' he said in a quiet, almost threatening voice. 'I just wanted to ask you, if I may, would it be possible to stay another few weeks?'

'Oh, actually, I think I need to check the book.' She was already walking backwards away from him.

'Okay, but if you could let us know, I would be grateful,' he said with a smile through the dusk, his voice slowly dripping like treacle from a spoon.

'I will get back to you. Good night!' And she turned towards home, walking quickly away from the danger she had felt creep into her bones.

'Did we do any checks before we let them in?' Stephen was sitting behind his desk in the estate office looking every bit the competent manager and making Ailsa feel like an office junior.

'Checks? What kind of checks do you do, can you do, for a holiday home? Talk sense, Stephen. He's not taking out a mortgage, he's only staying for a holiday.'

'Well, with Gennina in charge, God knows who they might be.'

'You need to apologise to her.' Stephen, like Ailsa, had his own little office within the bigger estate office where Gennina presided. They were in there now with the door shut as they had heard the PA just come in and she was making a cup of tea in the tiny kitchen.

'No way.'

'Stephen...'

'No, I won't do any such thing. If she can't take a joke then that's her affair.'

Ailsa didn't know how she kept her temper. 'But it wasn't a joke, was it? You don't think much of her, that's for sure.

You can't see her good points for her young daftish way of talking and acting. But she is very good at organising and thinking up ideas once she has a project to look after. She needs to be helped — nurtured — not bullied.'

'So, you think I bully her?'

Ailsa smiled. 'Yes. You bully everyone Stephen. It's your way. You even tried to bully me at the beginning, and that's why we fight, because I won't let you.'

He smiled up at her. 'You're right I suppose. I've never been good at taking orders from anyone, least of all...' he came to an awkward stop.

'Least of all a woman? Yes, I'm sorry to put it bluntly, Stephen, but I think you are a bit of a chauvinist. Not that I blame you entirely, as you've spent most of your life with the MacKenzies and their old-fashioned ways, where the Colonel is definitely a chauvinistic patriarch. He's head of the family and the sons all fall in line, then come their partners some way after that. No bloody wonder.' She got no further as she noticed that Stephen was looking at her keenly.

'Are you including Max in that?'

'I don't want to talk about Max, thank you.'

He nodded understandingly. 'Okay, get her in,' he said, with a wave of his hand at the door, displaying the very chauvinism Ailsa had just talked about. She gave a sigh and opened the door.

'Gennina, could you come in here a minute please?' She came, with her head held high.

'Well?'

Ailsa bit her lip in amusement. She wasn't going to let them off with anything.

'Gennina, I am sorry I upset you,' Stephen said grudgingly.

'Oh?'

'What do you mean, "oh"?'

'Is that what you call an apology?'

'Yes, it's all you're going to get.'

'Really? Well you have really wounded me with your bullying and sarcasm.' It was as if she had practised this sentence, it came out so fluidly.

'Okay, sorry and sorry again, will that do?' He was starting to get irritated.

'I don't think you mean it.' She was driving the point dangerously home.

'Well, I'm not prepared to say any more.'

Ailsa's intentions were slowly being unravelled. 'Okay, Gennina, Stephen has just apologised. Can you please just accept it and we can move on?'

'Not until I know he really means it.'

'What d'you want, blood? Ailsa, I'm out of here.' He rose up, took his jacket and phone and left.

'The best made plans of mice and men...' Ailsa quoted softly and returned to her own office in despair.

The new Malcolm was back from France. He had just been for a hospital check-up and was so well that he didn't need to go back for another six months. He was feeling fit and he was embracing his new perspective on his sordid, unhappy life. He had talked a lot with his children about his previous behaviour, and David, the very grown-up young man that he was, accepted that his father wanted to change and was trying to make a new and better life for them. Melissa had come full circle with him, from the time she told Ailsa she hated him to that talk they had, prompted by Ailsa. It was as if this talk had slowly sunk in and she was seeing her Dad in a different light altogether. He had fallen off the pedestal, and she was finding it hard to put him back on.

He walked the five miles from Trannoch most days into Arnasaid as part of his new fitness regime, then called for a car to take him home. It was on one of these journeys that he bumped into Angie.

'Well, well, well, and how are you?' She hugged him and held him back to look at him. She noticed the frailness of a thinner Malcolm before her, though he was tanned and healthy looking. 'I didn't see you at the Games, though Max introduced me to all the others.'

'I was on holiday with my children,' he smiled. 'Do you want a coffee or a drink or something?' She looked at him again, wonderingly. In the past Malcolm would just have pulled her into the nearest pub without asking. She nodded, and they walked towards The Wee Dram.

Malcolm had been a few years above Max and Angie at Uni, and when they all met at regular student meetings and drinking sessions, their paths had crossed. 'How long have you been here?' Malcolm asked, as he handed her a glass of cider. 'Have you seen Max yet?'

Her eyes narrowed. 'Not long, a week and a half, although I am here for a month. I heard the Arnasaid practice was looking for a GP, although I had no idea Max worked here. I happened to go to the Arnasaid Games, and Andy Donald asked me to the barbeque at Storm Winds. I saw Max there.'

'Oh, having you here would be great!' Malcolm said sincerely. 'May I ask, do you have family or...'

'No, I'm divorced, no children. You?'

'Two children by my first marriage, and er... one baby from my second.' Malcolm still had trouble saying this out loud, due to the fact he felt now that he didn't deserve little Freddy or Olivia.

'How nice!' she said sincerely. 'And Max, he said there was "someone" but didn't say who it was. We were in a crowd of friends. Do you remember Andy? He was in our year at school. You were older, but I remember you mixed in the same crowd.'

'Yes, I know Andy, he lives around here and has his hotel business and other fingers in other pies,' he touched the side of his nose conspiratorially, 'And yes, Max has "someone" like you say, Ailsa, or should I say Lady Ailsa Hamilton-Dunbar, no less.'

'Well! How exciting!' Her face had fallen almost imperceptibly when he broke this news, but she kept her voice even and tinged with enthusiasm. 'And does Lady Ailsa live in the area?'

'Yes, she opened the Games. She lives almost equidistant from Arnasaid and Trannoch. She owns Storm Winds, where the barbeque was held. I'm surprised no one mentioned that!

The two families go back centuries together, and Ailsa has only in the last year known that she was to inherit Storm Winds from her blood father.' Malcolm said this with a slight hint of resentment, as he had pursued Ailsa himself, to be shot down in flames, and hadn't quite got over that particular pain yet.

'Well let's drink to old feuding families!' She lifted her glass and chinked it against his.

They knew it was the middle of the night, and that the house was full of sleep. They did hear noises, however, and they tried to tell Ailsa, but she was sleeping too. Then Bluebell suddenly began to growl. Ailsa had left open her doors to her little stone balcony, as it was warm that night. She shushed the excited dog, who settled down on the chaise longue next to her bed, beside Rosie, and all was quiet for a further half an hour until both dogs began to growl, and Rosie to give little apologetic barks. They could hear something, and once they started, they meant to go on.

'What on earth is the matter?' She walked over to her doors where the soft wind was blowing, and the room was breathing in the voile curtains, and blowing them out into the fresh westerly night, in out, in out. She could see nothing.

'Ailsa, are you okay?' The housekeeper's urgent knock alerted her and she went to the door with a mystified expression on her face, as the dogs would not shut up.

'Hi Cocky. Yes, I'm fine, I've no idea what's wrong with them. They just started growling and barking and...'

'Ailsa, are you okay?' It felt like a dream, with echoes of everyone asking if she was okay, Stephen materialising at the top of the stair in shorts and a T-shirt. He had quite obviously stayed overnight with Clem, who followed him up the stair. Miss Cochrane looked at him in distaste at his 'half-nakit' state as she would have put it. She knew of course that he stayed occasionally with Clem, she was the housekeeper and she had one ear to the ground, but that didn't mean her staunch Presbyterian soul had to like it. Clem and Stephen were now in a long-term relationship, and even if they weren't, Ailsa wouldn't have batted an eye. It was the twenty first century for God's sake! She told herself, unconvincingly, that seeing him like that, in her house, had no effect on her.

'The alarms in the front and sides of the house have tripped,' Clem said. 'We looked at the box when we heard the dogs barking.'

'Why didn't we hear the alarm?' Ailsa was flustered.

'Because it is always set to silent in case a deer or other animal knocks against one of the doors,' Stephen said. 'I just wanted to check you were alright, but I'll go over all the rooms downstairs now, just to make sure.'

'What's the point in it being set to silent...?' But he was already on his way back downstairs.

Miss Cochrane brought Ailsa and Clem hot tea in the blue sitting room while they checked the other rooms; Jim Hutton, who stayed in a cottage on the estate was phoned, and he jumped on his quad bike and rode up to the big house. He noticed when passing that, at the bottom of the drive, the Dower House had all its lights on.

'Right, so the window was forced open in the study, but, although there was a bit of a mess, nothing seems to have been taken. I've been round the outside too, with Jim.' Stephen was all estate manager now, as he stood in his hastily put on jeans and ski-jacket. 'You need to check everything Ailsa, but I suggest in the morning, not right now.'

'Yes, I'll check, but I never use the study. I've only been in there once, I think. I never liked the room.'

'Well, as we're amongst friends, and we all probably know anyway, there are antiques and paintings all over Storm Winds, worth a fortune. Maybe they thought they would find a safe in there, but, as we know, it's in your library.'

Ailsa had for the moment completely forgotten this, and was annoyed, firstly at Stephen's patronising attitude, and secondly that Stephen was the one to point it out. 'Yes, it is,' she admitted reluctantly. 'I will see to it, but right now Cocky's bringing us a brandy, if you'd care to join us?'

He looked at her and Clem sitting on the sofa, Jim in the background, the clock ticking round to three o'clock and shook his head. 'No thanks. I'm off back to bed.'

Sir Pierce Donald had made up his mind. He would never have a woman in his life again, as they were too much bloody trouble, and he, in his early seventies, could not be bothered with trouble. The thing was, he had thought that the uncontrollable, beautiful Georgina Dillon, who looked around twenty years younger than her age, would actually be the one he wanted to settle down with. He wanted her. He had invited her to Mhainaray more than once over the summer, and she had made his life a chaotic, argumentative fairground of mixed emotions. She was bright, spontaneous and funny, and he wanted her to be Lady Donald.

The problem was that Hunter wanted to be Lady Donald too, but not necessarily to marry Sir Pierce Donald to get there.

On the weekend of the Games she was in Mhainaray with Pierce, enjoying being wined and dined. She had not wanted to attend the Games, as Ailsa would be the centre of attention, and she couldn't bear that. So, she took her overnight bag and made her way to the island. There were no dashing Andys on the ferry across this time, she noted, and, as far as Andy was concerned, she was no more than a bit of fun to him. But then again, he was no more than a bit of fun to her too. On the first visit to the island when the fateful fight with Ailsa had taken place, she had gone over to the hotel at seven thirty in the evening, the time Andy said he would meet her, though at that point she had no idea he was Sir Pierce's nephew or that he owned the hotel. He wasn't there. She had a drink and had gone back to Mhainaray Manor seething that he had made a fool of her. On the day that she had fallen in the mud, and Andy had rescued her, she waited until everyone was getting ready for the evening meal, then told Mrs Monroe that she had a bad headache and that she wouldn't be down. She had slipped out one of the back doors and got the gardener to drive her over to the hotel, slipping him £20 — she originally tried to give him £10, but he was having none of it — and telling him to keep this a secret from Sir Pierce and the rest. He gave her his mobile number as she said there would be another £20 for him when he returned for her.

Andy, who was a good bit younger than herself, was there this time. Grabbing a bottle from the bar, he had led her upstairs to a huge room which could only be described as a penthouse apartment, with circular bed and claw foot bath all in one room. The tall windows looked across the Sound of Mhainaray, and she stood as he tore off her clothes leaving her there, unashamedly naked in the moonlight. She pushed him down on his knees and he kissed every inch of her, as she stood apparently indifferent, sipping champagne. Her attitude infuriated him and delighted him, in equal measure. Their lovemaking was fierce and feral, interspersed with shoves and slaps and groans as each vied for control over the other. Afterwards she dressed, sipped the last of her drink, and with a blown kiss, walked out without a backward glance.

Sir Pierce, who was a good bit older, was a different matter. When he led her to his four-poster bed he was much too gentlemanly like for her liking. The fumblings beneath the sheets as he slowly slid off her clothes made her want to slap his hand away and pull them off, herself. Then, his slow rhythmic movements were so gentle and soft that she felt she was drifting on the slow boat to Mingalay. He almost lulled her to sleep. She felt about as excited as when at eight years of age, her parents told her she had to join the girl guides.

Colonel Mason Smith MacKenzie, age wise, wasn't far behind Sir Pierce. There the similarities ended. He was unpredictable, sometimes exciting, sometimes couldn't care less, but always kept her on her toes, wondering. One evening they were both on top of the library table, books and inkstands and pens sent like flying missiles across the floor. The fear of being rumbled revved up their duel pistons considerably. Footsteps in the corridor outside the unlocked door helped them both to the summit quicker than a cable car going up Ben Nevis. Conversely, another time, the Colonel had drank so much whisky his boat chugged softly back into harbour half-way through; Hunter discovered, disgustedly, that he had fallen asleep on her.

It was, however, very satisfactory to have three stupid men at her disposal.

Chapter Thirteen

It was now unseasonably warm, hot in fact for the North West, and the scenery looked spectacularly lit up and seemed to come alive in the warm rays. Tourists were arriving in their hoards, and the B&Bs and hotel were booked solid in Arnasaid Bheag, and in Arnasaid itself it was the same story. Ailsa was outside a lot, walking her land and soaking up the sunshine with its health-giving vitamins. She was sitting on the terrace when Malcolm arrived.

'Hi!' he said with a grin. 'May I join you?'

'Yes, of course,' she said warily, caught off guard. 'How are you feeling after your holiday?'

'Seems like weeks ago now, but it was only a fortnight since I got back. Yes, I'm fine thank you, and good for another six months at least!'

'That's great news,' she said, and ran to a stop. She was unsure of this new Malcolm, but she did sense he was genuine enough.

'Can I get you a drink, Mr MacKenzie?' The icy tones from the housekeeper floated through the waves of heat.

'You can, and you may!' he said, with a laugh. Cocky's expression did not falter. 'Er... are you having one, Ailsa?'

'Yes, I'll have a glass of wine with ice, please.'

'Ice in your wine! How extraordinary! I'll have a whisky and soda, if you please.'

'Certainly.' Miss Cochrane spun round leaving frozen footsteps in her wake.

'She never changes, does she?'

Ailsa laughed, 'No, but I think you have, Malcolm.'

He looked thinner and smaller without his veneer of bombastic arrogance. 'Yes, I would like to think I have changed. I want my kids to like me, and I want to help them and be a father to them before it's er... before it's too late.'

She noticed that his kids liking him seemed to be his first priority, but at least it was a start. Miss Cochrane brought out a tray and sat it on the wrought iron terrace table between them, then left quickly.

'What's happened to you and wee brother Max?' The question was direct and took her breath away as she grappled with an answer.

'I really don't think that's any of your business, Malcolm.'

He took a swig of his whisky. 'I bumped into Angie recently.'

Ailsa's face clouded over in direct contrast to the huge expanse of brilliant blue sky above. 'Well? What's your point Malcolm?'

'My point is I think you and Max are great for each other, and I have no idea what you discussed, or what he alluded to in terms of Angie, but I know he told her he was in a relationship.'

'Not that it is any of your business. I don't think he did.'

'He didn't say who you are but he said there was "someone".'

'Well, whoopee do.'

'Ailsa, listen...'

'No, you listen, Malcolm. Max and I have been struggling for a while, and this was the straw that broke the camel's back. If he did say there was "someone", as you say, why did he spend almost the whole afternoon and evening with her? Why did he not categorically deny that he was in any way interested in her?'

'Because he's just not good at that sort of thing.'

'You mean, telling the truth?'

'Don't be facetious, Ailsa. You know what I mean.'

'Well, I'm not good at being an estate manager and managing this house and grounds, and everything which goes with it, but that is because I haven't worked at it long enough yet. In the end it is down to me to get it right.'

'Okay, point taken, but just as a subtle warning between friends. Angie is staying in the area. She has applied to the Health Board to be accepted as a locum GP for the North

West. That's why she arrived here in the first place. Max will have been informed a few days ago, long after the Games. She is still interested in him, Ailsa. It was written all over her face.'

'Well, good luck to them both.'

Ailsa was returning from Fort William where she was on a shopping trip for a few oddments for the rooms in the East Wing, ready for the first shooting party which would arrive the next week. She was thinking about Max. Did she love him? She had no idea how to answer her own question. Did she miss him? Definitely. Did she want him physically? Yes. Did she want him to be the father of her children? At this point she stopped questioning herself as the tears rolled down her face, blinding her.

Of course she did.

The road was quiet, with the white heat shimmering just above the tarmac. She was on the A830, just past Glenfinnan with its monument of a soldier everyone thinks is Bonnie Prince Charlie. This was the place where he arrived on the Scottish mainland after his journey from France, via the island of Eriskay, and this was where he waited for his troops to gather in order to lead them into battle. The famous viaduct used in the Harry Potter films also dominated this most beautiful of glens, and today, on the hottest day of the year so far, it was thronging with tourists of every nationality.

She was climbing up the road out of Glenfinnan, when she became aware of a huge gold pickup truck, one of the ones she thought was called Animal and animal it seemed to be. It was inordinately close to her tail. Wiping the tears away, she swore into the mirror, but the car didn't pull back. It looked like there were at least two people in it, and it began to rev and swerve as if overtaking, then pulling back at the last minute when it was faced with a car coming in the opposite direction. She began to feel her skin prickle and the anxiety rise. Her window in the Land Rover was right down, due to the heat, and she stuck her hand out and waved the 'animal' past, just to get rid of it. It was frightening her. At the same time she drove as far into the left as she could to make it easier to pass. They didn't pass, despite the fact there were no cars approaching on a long empty strip of road.

'Bloody hell!' she shouted, 'Get past!' But the car continued to sit alarming close to her. A parking place sign said a space was coming up in half a mile, so she put on her indicator to pull in left. To her amazement, the car pulled in behind her. She was beginning to shake with fear. What was this all about? She searched her mind for anyone who might have a similar truck, but no one she knew would drive aggressively close to her just for the fun of it. She checked her mirror and the driver was getting out to come towards her. She knew that smile. Where had she seen it before? A threatening smile, dripping with malice. She crunched her gears into first and took off back onto the road leaving a trail of dust, the pickup and its occupants behind her. It was the man she met on the headland at Storm Winds a few weeks ago who wanted to stay an extra few weeks at the Dower House. He had scared her then, and he was scaring her now.

Her heart was beating uncontrollably, and she was in a cold sweat. She looked in the rear view mirror again and saw the car leaving the parking space with a shriek of rubber on road. She didn't have hands free so grappled desperately on the passenger seat to feel for her bag, then fished for her phone. She tapped in the unlocking code and dialled 999.

'I'm on the A830 heading towards Arnasaid, just five minutes from Glenfinnan.'

'Which emergency service, please?' Came the voice calmly. *Irritatingly* calmly.

'There's a car chasing me, it's trying to – oh my GOD! Okay, it's just bumped into me – I'm going at seventy miles an hour and it won't overtake. It's crashing me!'

'Maybe you should slow down a bit? Sorry, I picked up that you were on the A830, where exactly are you? Glenfinnan did you say? What exactly is happening? Hello, are you there? Hello...?'

She had dropped the phone. She had to grip the steering wheel with two hands to try and get straight, but it was no good. With another huge crack, the cars made contact again, and she lost control.

Her Land Rover veered to the left, careered across a small strip of land and rammed straight into the loch.

Max and the current locum, Dr Antoni Kowalski were meeting with Angie Hughes and the surgery manager about the soon to be vacant locum GP role. They were discussing rotas and all manner of things medical, as well as welcoming her to the practice. Antoni was looking to reduce his hours, and the Health Board had recommended a new locum, but the fact that it was Angie didn't only come as a big surprise – it was hugely disconcerting.

She had called him a few days after the Games, asking if she could see him and he had refused. She had called again, a week later, asking him out for a drink and again he had refused. The third time she called was the same day the Health Board informed him they had a new locum who could assist the practice. She had pleaded him to join her for a drink so they could discuss the job. He agreed, thinking it was a professional matter, and they met in The Wee Dram.

'Well, you look very official!' Angie said, as he joined her, kissed her briefly on the cheek and sat opposite her.

Max said seriously, 'Well, I thought I was here in a professional capacity.' He put his folder down on the table beside them. She had bought the drinks already, and Max was pleased to note that there were only a few tourists in the pub, no one he knew.

She laughed. 'Max, you always were a bit dense.' She sipped her wine, her eyes twinkling.

He looked annoyed. 'Yes, okay, thank you for that, Angie.'

'Dense, but loveable,' she said, gulping down another mouthful of wine. She looked and acted quite tipsy and he wondered if she had had one or even two before he arrived. He was beginning to think this had been a really bad idea.

'So, you don't want to talk about the practice?' he asked flatly.

'No, I wanted to see you.'

'Angie, I told you I am seeing someone.' He rubbed his eyes wearily. 'This is not going to work, if you persist in this. I can't work alongside you if this is how it's going to be.'

'What? What do you think you see here?' Her mood suddenly changed from flirtatious to annoyed.

'This. Whatever this is supposed to be.'

'Don't flatter yourself Max. I wanted to see you as I knew you here, where I knew no one else. I had no idea you worked here. I just wanted a friendly drink with an old friend, or old lover, or whatever you want to call yourself.'

'I am glad you are coming to work with us. We really need another GP, and Arnasaid isn't the most glamorous of places to work. It's hard to get good doctors. I thought that was the only reason you wanted to meet.'

'Are you being deliberately naive?'

'No, I am being honest. What went on between us is now all in the past.'

'Is it? Someone said you and, what's her name, Isla, were on a break?'

Max fumed. 'I'm sorry, but that's none of your business, and her name is Ailsa. Look, let's just be happy we caught up again after all this time. I've moved on, you've moved on. Let's just leave it at that.'

She stood up and leaned across the table, kissing him full on the lips. 'That's just it, Max. I don't believe we have.' As she moved up to the bar to get more drinks, Malcolm came in.

'Malcolm!' Max hissed. 'Come and join us. Angie is here, she's starting at the practice, and I really need you to join us right now.'

Malcolm was amused at his brother's discomfort. 'Okay, let me go and get this, and I'll come over.'

Angie looked around and saw Malcolm coming to pay for the drinks. She accompanied him back to the seat then made a lame excuse, downed her drink almost in one, and left.

On this particular early August day, the hottest in the year, Max was on a call out to an accident on the notorious A830.

The surgery was quiet, and as the emergency services were on another shout at this point, asked for all who could attend. Angie came too, while Antoni was left in charge in Arnasaid.

Ailsa had hit the loch head on. The freezing water invaded every inch of her, as her car sank, as if in a dream, to the bottom. Following the initial impact the world went quiet. There was no noise, apart from a soft gurgle, as the air rose to the top. Items in her car which were not bolted down started to float like an underwater ballet, in front of her. Her bag, her purse, her spare shoes, like water babies as they danced in her eyes. Her brain tried to process what was happening. When it did, reaction set in, and she panicked. All her thoughts were subliminal. Things running through her mind like the objects she could see in front of her, like stuff on a macabre conveyor belt. Her hand reached to release the seatbelt. It was stuck. Parts of thoughts ran through her mind then were gone, 'crash...can't breathe...DON'T breathe... Max... Mum... Dad...Bluebell...Rosie...Max...Storm...Winds...baby...Max...' Her conscious mind reached out to grab and stabilise the thoughts, but before she could reach them, they tripped away on the crest of a gentle loch wave.

Arms thrust through the open window, tried to release the seatbelt, then pulled at the strap until there was enough room to get her through. Just as her trunk was freed her legs which were still a dead weight, caught. He put both feet on the door to give him purchase, and pulled with every sinew, his muscles clenching and going into spasm as he did so. Then, the belt gave and the loch heaved a huge wave of a sigh, its surge helping to pull her through the window.

Max and Angie arrived at the scene twenty minutes later, just as she was being covered while she lay on the stretcher and being taken into the ambulance which had come from Dunlivietor. The blonde hair spilling over the side, the shape, the build, the black jeans and red, loch soaked cardigan disappearing under the blanket...

'Oh my God, Ailsa!' He tore out of his car without even pulling on the brake.

'She's unconscious, Max, but breathing,' the paramedic explained to him.

'But what happened, Davy? How did...what...'

'No idea, Max. Until the police get the car out and they can have a look at it, we won't know.' He nodded over to three police cars, the officers standing about talking and taking notes from someone sitting on the grass.

'Your guy over there pulled her from the bottom of the loch. The cops want to talk to him properly. They've had an initial chat, but we're taking him in for observation too, as once he saved her, he collapsed too. He's a real hero. He just happened to be coming down the road from Arnasaid and saw her car hit the loch.'

'*My* guy?' Max was confused. 'What do you mean...'

There, on the grass verge, clad in a silver blanket, sat his brother Thomas.

Hunter was a risk taker. She loved the idea of having affairs with three men at the same time. The reason she carried on with these affairs however was more than just fun, she genuinely didn't know which one to settle with, and 'settle' wasn't a word that filled Hunter with much enthusiasm.

Andy was around fifteen years younger than her, exciting, fit and had the body which can only be honed in a gym. The Colonel was her first love, though much had changed since then, he was older for a start, less fit and definitely did not have the body of one who works out. He was tall and muscular though, with broad shoulders and a soldierly gait, borne out of his training in his army days. Sir Pierce, too was older, and neither did he have a particularly good body, although he too was tall, of slimmer build than the Colonel. He was fitter in that he walked every day, sometimes for miles across his estate and island hills of Mhainaray. But, being Hunter, she had to think about what she would gain from a proper relationship with each of them. She was, to all intents and purposes, already there with the Colonel. People thought and accepted that they were together. He was a billionaire, with huge amounts of land and Trannoch.

She didn't want Trannoch as much as Storm Winds, but as this was never going to happen, and Trannoch was worth far more, was statelier and more opulent, she might just have to settle for this. Sir Pierce was also hugely wealthy, his estate was surely worth millions, and she knew he had properties elsewhere dotted around the world. What she would gain from Sir Pierce was a much coveted title. Lady Georgina Donald sounded about right to her, and she would be able to stick one in the eye to that daughter of hers, and serve her right for cutting her out of a fortune and Storm Winds, her true inheritance, or so she continued to tell herself.

The problem with Sir Pierce was that he bored her. He was a gentle man, with elegance and poise, and liked the finer things in moderation; Hunter liked them every day and definitely not in moderation. He talked eloquently about art, history, politics and current affairs, everything in fact which Hunter hated and steered away from.

The problem with the Colonel was that he was a comfortable known entity. The thought of a comfortable existence really didn't set Hunter's heather on fire. Admittedly he had a mildly exciting streak of unpredictability. He also brought all the complications of a large family, all in line for the throne as it were, and Hunter would get shunted down the list, should the inevitable happen sooner rather than later. She did feel at home with him, and she enjoyed his company. During the infrequent times when her softer self came to the fore, she knew that he was the only man she had ever loved.

The problem with Andy was that he didn't want her long-term, or even in any shape of relationship. He wanted children one day. He wanted someone nearer to his own age to settle down with and enjoy the fruits of his labour, and time was ticking by for all that blatherskite, as he said to his pals. She knew she would never be the person he was looking for, that it would never be her. She didn't know this because she had worked it all out herself. She knew because he told her.

She thought about all three as she lay in bed with Andy, the afternoon sunshine streaming in the window, and her empty wine glass lying un-replenished on the bedside table. He was sleeping beside her.

The door crashed open and two figures tumbled into the room, one was the hotel manager, a young fair man in his twenties, and the other was Sir Pierce, looking angrier than either of the two love birds had ever seen him.

'Get up you...you...slut!' He said through gritted teeth, his refined voice making the horrible word sound almost pleasant.

'Hey, wait a minute Uncle Pierce, there's no need to...'

'And you can just shut up too Andy, you're a disgrace!' The manager left at this point thinking his usefulness had ended when he was unable to prevent the man entering his boss's bedroom, despite his protestations. He had actually stood in front of the door barring the way to the older man.

'Why, Piercey!' For the first time Hunter was flummoxed, not because she had been caught, but because 'Piercey' was obviously now off her list of suitors.

'Don't *Piercey* me!' he exploded. There was nothing tame about him now. 'Get up, and get your sorry backside back to the mainland. Ailsa has been in an accident, and she is currently unconscious in Dunlivietor General.' And he left in a more dignified manner than that in which he had arrived.

Chapter Fourteen

It had been a traumatic time for all of them, but most especially Max and Miss Cochrane. She had been tidying out the linen cupboard when Ian MacFarlane, the local policeman who lived and worked in the ancient police house in Arnasaid, had come with the news of the incident. She dropped a pile of sheets as white as her face, and held onto the handle of the door to steady herself.

'She's alive, Miss Cochrane, that's a' I know.' He was respectful of the lady who was his old Sunday school teacher, and whom his family had known all his life.

Her voice trembled. 'But what happened?'

'We won't know until we get the car oot the loch and we've questioned the witness properly, but it seems she was hit from behind by another car, and she lost control of her vehicle.'

Miss Cochrane swore under her breath. 'You said a witness?'

'Aye, but I canny tell you who it is...' Her steely expression made him add hurriedly, 'But I dinae see that it can do any harm – it was one of the MacKenzie lads.'

'Oh my God, not Max?'

'No, Thomas.'

Miss Cochrane had fled down the A830 to Dunlivietor as quickly as Jim Hutton could drive her.

Ailsa was in a coma. Max was pacing, asking questions and trying to make sense of it all when the consultant, Stuart McGregor, who was a few years younger than Max, came in. He knew him, the medical people in the area all knew each other. They shook hands.

'Sorry, Max, if I may ask, are you here in a medical capacity?'

'Er...no...I...er...' Max didn't know how to approach the whole, we're-in-a-relationship but currently-on-a-break, explanation. Stuart eyed him attentively, waiting for an answer. 'She's my...er...my neighb...' he got no further, as an exasperated Cocky butted in.

'Ailsa is Dr McKenzie's partner,' she said firmly, and Max looked at her in surprise.

'Okay, well, her brain has been starved of oxygen, but her vital signs are all good. She is obviously comatose, but we have hope that she will regain consciousness soon. We wouldn't say this to anyone, Max, but you know how it is. We can't say anything until she is awake.'

'Yes, I know how it is,' Max answered wearily. He felt he was to blame. He should have been there for her. He should have insisted that she listen to him and his explanation about Angie. He felt he was back to square one again, but like in the beginning, he had no idea how to reach her. He had stayed in a chair by her side, Miss Cochrane on the other side, his head in his hands as he watched and waited for signs of recovery. She had bought sandwiches and coffee for Max from the shop, but ate nothing herself and had not slept other than a few hours during the three days since the accident. They were both exhausted.

On the third day, Max was dozing in one chair, Miss Cochrane in the other. It was six o'clock in the morning and the hospital was waking. He saw a movement on the bed beside him and he woke slowly, with a crick in his neck. He looked over to Ailsa. Her head was moving almost imperceptibly, and her lashes were flickering. Her eye lids slowly slid upward, and a dazed look, which was replaced with a questioning one, searched around and found Max's own eyes. She tried to turn her head to him and called out in agony at the movement. Miss Cochrane woke with a start and sat up.

He jumped up and gripped her hand which was flapping at her side. 'I'm here Ailsa,' he said simply. Her eyes closed again. A single tear escaped from her right eye.

She was moved to a more secluded room as her nightmares began. Max moved too, but after many protestations from Miss Cochrane that she wanted to stay he got on the phone to Jim Hutton to come and take her home. 'Ailsa is out of the coma, but is still in a lot of pain, due to the extensive bruising and cracked ribs. Can you please come and pick up Miss Cochrane, Jim? Make sure she goes straight to bed.' He then rang off and called the Colonel. His father was overjoyed at the news and spread the word to the family who were all at the breakfast table.

That night Denbeath took one of the Trannoch cars and made his way to Storm Winds. It was a warm, windy evening, just gone seven o'clock, and he hoped that Miss Cochrane would be awake after he supposed sleeping all day on her return from hospital. She was.

'Come in, James,' Miss Cochrane smiled, as she opened the side door to her rooms. He sat down and she poured them both a whisky. She lifted the remote and turned off the TV.

'It's been a terrible time for you, Miss Cochrane.' Denbeath's face was sombre.

'Yes. At least Ailsa is now awake from the coma, and we will get her back. Oh, and James, can you call me Charlotte? I've known you all my life, and I use your Christian name. Why won't you use mine? It's quite a nice one. Ailsa calls me 'Cocky' now.'

He looked outraged at this. 'Very well, Charlotte. I will.'

Two men emerged from the forest and, keeping to the back of the house, walked silently towards Trannoch. It was a cloudy night, the blackness blotting out the light from the moon and keeping the stars hidden behind. The courtyard in the middle of the buildings was lit, so they skirted around this and through the kitchen gardens to the darkened back door. The first man tried the door.

On the way back, Denbeath drove the car round to the courtyard, his lights picking up the open back door. 'Strange,' he thought as he took the unusual path through the kitchen garden to the back door. He shut and locked the door behind him and made his way along the back corridor to his own rooms, switching on the light as he came in. He got into his pyjamas and made himself a hot drink.

It was then he heard the sound of footsteps in the corridor.

The Colonel was in his library. He was usually last to go to bed. He had been having a few whiskies and thought he had better go up before he drank any more. He debated with himself about Hunter. He couldn't make her out. Was she in love with Pierce? She had been over to Mhainary a few times recently, but this last time she had arrived following the news about Ailsa, looking quite depressed and less sure of herself than she was normally. But there was no Pierce with her. The news had quite obviously shaken her to the core, but he was pleased she had reacted like that, as he had thought she had grown even colder and more uncaring than she was years ago. 'Well, if she wants Pierce there's not a lot I can do about it,' he thought to himself, 'but I'll be damned if I'll give her up without a fight!'

It was then that he heard the scuffle, sharp bangs and muffled shouts coming from the kitchen.

'What the hell...?' He picked up a walking stick from the holder in the hall, and gingerly stepped towards the back of the house.

The kitchen was in darkness. He switched on the light and saw the back door was lying open. He made his way through the room and out the door, switching on the outside light.

Denbeath was lying on his face amongst the cabbages.

'What was all the commotion last night?' Hunter swept into the dining room with a less than concerned look on her face.

'Someone tried to murder Denbeath!' Aria said, with a look at her big brother Ryan who had supplied her with this tasty piece of information.

'What?' The older woman put down her plate and poured some coffee from the sideboard.

Noel looked at his niece sternly. 'That's enough of that kind of sensationalism, Aria.' He continued to read the paper while Aria looked like she was ready to burst into tears. Her uncle hardly ever spoke to her, but in Max's absence had decided to squash anything of this sort from any of the children.

'You missed all the discussion, coming in late to breakfast,' Malcolm piped up.

Hunter looked at him coldly. 'Where is the Colonel?'

Malcolm didn't even notice Hunter's look. 'At the police station,' he said. 'First someone runs Ailsa off the road and into the loch, there's an attempted burglary recently at Storm Winds, and now we have two men trying to get into Trannoch.'

Carys was almost full term now, but she managed still to look about six months pregnant, so neat was her figure. She said, 'its all very Agatha Christie.'

'Why is the Colonel at the police station?' Hunter asked, picking slowly at her eggs.

'Because he found the butler, of course.' Carys outwardly sighed at having to impart this information twice in the last few minutes, but inwardly enjoying herself. 'He heard a noise from the kitchen and went to investigate. He found Denbeath in the garden, on top of the courgettes.'

'Cabbages,' Noel said, from behind his paper. 'Now, can we just get on with breakfast and stop talking about butlers and cabbages?'

The Colonel gave his statement to Ian MacFarlane in his tiny office at the police house. The policeman had turned up at Trannoch shortly before midnight the evening before with Antoni Kowalski, to check Denbeath over. They had helped him to bed, and the doctor had insisted Denbeath stay there until he had called in to see the butler the next day. The doctor thought he may have mild concussion. Denbeath certainly had a lump on the back of his head where he had been struck, and scrapes and bruises from his landing. The Colonel had asked the policeman to check the house, which was so large that he could only manage the main downstairs rooms, even this took him twenty minutes, and then the Colonel had flatly refused to give any more information to Ian until the next day when he would come to the police house and give a statement.

The Colonel was not one to brook refusal, so Ian meekly left, saying he would see him tomorrow and visit Denbeath after he had been checked out and was fit enough to give him a statement too.

Eileen was checking her clipboard. 'Right, so if Maddy, Eilidh and Cheryl take rooms 1-3, Leanne and Karen can take 4-6 and the common sitting room.'

'Did Gennina show you where the linen cupboard is? On you go then, and mind I'll be in to inspect it all afterwards!' They all nodded, as did Gennina herself. The cleaners set to work to make up the beds and do a general dust round to get the East Wing rooms ready for the bus full of grouse shooters, which was due at three o'clock that afternoon. Eileen was in her element, ordering around her little merry band of cleaners. Maddy and Karen were new to her, both were in their forties or early fifties, and the other girls were young. It was a lucrative job for them though, even although it wasn't regular, as Ailsa paid more than Sir Angus had done for the extra help.

Stephen and Roddy came strolling into the estate office. When he saw the two, Stephen creased his forehead into a gully deeper than Glen Etive.

'Any news of Ailsa?' Eileen asked eagerly.

'It's Lady Ailsa to you, Eileen!' Stephen had had just about enough of the 'maid' and 'the secretary' as he called her and Gennina. They had met almost every day for the last week in the estate office, giggling and making plans for the 'grand clean-up', which was now complete, but the little team would be there doing changeovers until all the shoots had ended.

'Oh, sorry, Sir.' Eileen, who saw Stephen as being as important as a MacKenzie, blushed furiously. 'I...I didn't mean...'

Stephen looked slightly appeased. 'Okay, well you can get Roddy and I a cup of tea, then clear out!'

'Never mind, Eileen. I'll go and ask Miss Cochrane if there is any news from the hospital,' Gennina said loudly, with a poisonous look at her boss, as she and Eileen gathered their things up to leave the office. She wasn't going to stand for any nonsense from Stephen.

He turned and glared at her, but it was Roddy who answered, 'Lady Ailsa has regained consciousness.'

'Thank you, Roddy,' Gennina smiled sweetly.

Ailsa was suffering. She had been back at Storm Winds for a few days now, but did not have the strength or energy to move about much, due to the intense bruising and her two cracked ribs. She had left the hospital with enough painkillers to 'put down a horse' to quote her, and although the pain was being controlled properly, she couldn't escape the nightmares. The medication kept her from reading or doing her writing, as she felt lightheaded and fuzzy, and she found she couldn't concentrate. Jim Hutton moved a TV into the library, as she insisted in spending her time in here, but she was tired of watching daytime programmes – she had never watched very much TV anyway, preferring to go out, or to stay in and read.

Ian MacFarlane had interviewed her in the hospital once she was up and sitting on the chair, although she couldn't remember anything much about the actual car which had run her off the road. Thomas had visited her in hospital, and she had cried when she saw the MacKenzie she knew so little of, who had saved her from the loch. The police from Fort William had also visited her, to tell her that they spotted a car of that description from camera footage of the A830 round about the time of the accident, then discovered it was stolen, but they hadn't been able to locate it since. They thought that questioning her in this way would jog her memory and help her to remember information, but Ailsa was deliberately shutting down her mind to the accident, trying to convince herself that it had all been a horrible dream. Thomas had given quite a patchy description of the car, but apart from noticing there were two men in it, he could tell them nothing more. He had been pre-occupied with watching the car in front, which he recognised as Ailsa's. What Thomas could be absolutely clear about however, was the fact that the bump was no accident. That part of the road is long and straight, and he had seen Ailsa's car being chased at speed before the car accelerated and bumped it, then as the Storm Winds Land Rover had careered into the loch, the car had sped up and raced away as if there was a pack of Kelpies chasing it.

Ailsa had woken up to see Max by her side, as he had been all day, every day until she was let home. Her emotions were on high alert, as she had no idea where she was with him. He just wouldn't talk about them, or Angie, or anything that she really wanted him to. When she got discharged, he came with her in the car, holding her hand, especially at the point where they would need to go past the loch to get home. She broke down at that point and cried all the way to Arnasaid. Following this, she saw very little of him. Unhappily for Ailsa, he was back to his old aloof unreachable self, and in being such, his controlling, irascible side was to the fore. For Max, this was because he thought Ailsa had grown apart from him, given him up, and in a slightly warped way, felt that he deserved all he got. He thought she was too good for him so, he reverted back to his old ways.

A week after she got home, Ailsa was able to go for short walks with Bluebell and Rosie. She felt better for the fresh air and exercise, but she only walked around the grounds. She had almost got to the stage where she was going to take a hammer to the TV, she was so fed up with it. The evening before, she had asked Miss Cochrane for a glass of red wine, the first since the accident, and the housekeeper looked at her askance, fearing that she would make herself ill by mixing it with the strong painkillers she was taking.

'It's alright, Cocky, don't worry,' she said, with a sigh. 'I've not been taking them for a few days now – just ordinary paracetamol.'

'Does Dr MacKenzie know?' It was the wrong thing to say. Cocky was worried and didn't know how to handle this new development.

'No, he doesn't know, and he won't know from either you or me.' Ailsa flew into a temper. Her changes of mood had been a feature of her trauma, not helped by her confinement to the house. Her flying off the handle was a bit of a daily occurrence which both Miss Cochrane and Eileen were getting used to.

The next day when Max came in to see her, the housekeeper met him at the door. She had been waiting for him to arrive.

'Everything alright, Miss Cochrane?'

'Well, actually, I'm not supposed to tell you, but Ailsa had some wine last night and...'

'What? With those strong tablets? I told her not to think of it!' He flared up as quickly as Ailsa had done.

'I know, and I did tell her so. She was adamant that she was okay taking ordinary paracetamol, but please don't let her know I've told you.'

He smiled grimly. 'Okay, Cocky I won't, but thank you for telling me. I'm just going back out to the car for a tick,' he said, over his shoulder, 'is she in the library?'

Miss Cochrane nodded.

Ailsa looked up as Max came in, and gave a resigned sigh. 'I heard voices. I thought it was just you,' she said ungraciously.

'Nice to see you too,' he said with a grin.

She suddenly noticed the stethoscope around his neck and her face darkened. 'I promised Stuart MaGreggor I would keep an eye on your lungs,' he lied, without a flinch. 'Can you just turn around so I can listen?' He popped the stethoscope on his ears, before she could protest, and slipped it up under the back of her chunky knitted jumper. 'Yes, okay, you're fine.' He sat on the chair opposite her as she looked at him suspiciously.

'Lungs? Why would you need to check my lungs?'

'Because cracked ribs can stop you breathing properly, and you can develop lung problems. You are therefore more susceptible to infection. You've already had pneumonia this year, and I'm taking no chances. But, as long as you are taking the strong painkillers, it shouldn't be a problem, and you should be able to breathe easily.'

'She told you. Cocky told you that I hadn't been taking them.'

'Yes.'

'Well, okay, but I'm sick to death of the house, and I'm fed up with the telly, and I'm fed up being pushed around and told what I may and may not do.' The tears were not very far away.

'I know.' He waited until she calmed down a little before he spoke again. 'The hospital have come back to me with a Psychologist to talk to you about PTSD.'

'Well, that's just hunkie dorie,' she said sarcastically, 'and I hope you told them where to stick their Psychologist? I don't need to talk to anyone.'

'I think you do, Ailsa.'

'Really? Well maybe you should just talk to them yourself and say what an arrogant, annoying, self-righteous, controlling doctor you are, and see if they can possibly cure you?' Her eyes flashed angrily.

Max looked at her for a long minute. 'I'm going,' he said, in a quiet voice unlike his own. 'Let me know when you want to see me again, otherwise I won't bother you.'

Chapter Fifteen

The first few grouse parties had gone like a treat. The only thing the Americans were annoyed about was that Lady Ailsa Hamilton-Dunbar had not put in an appearance, but when Stephen explained to them what had happened, they had been very sympathetic. Ailsa's part of the house was now off limits to the guests as she recovered, which meant that the caterers had to transport the food from the Storm Winds kitchen, out the back door and across the courtyard to the East Wing and into a hastily set up dining room next to the common sitting room. None of the Americans seemed to notice that it was not the 'main house'.

When the early autumn sunshine turned the land gold and red and drew the shooting groups out over the hills, Ailsa chose to pick those times to go for a walk. She would sit out on a tiny terrace at the side of the house which had a half-view of the sea, and part of the mountains too. The good thing about sitting here was that it was fenced-in from the other outdoor parts of the house, so she met no one. She read lots of books in the sunshine, a fleece thrown across her legs, the dogs at her feet. When her body began to heal, her painful memories of the accident forced their way back into her mind and the tears flowed. It felt like a knife shoving its way into her heart. She thought she would never be back to normal.

The MacKenzies dutifully came to visit her. The Colonel, every second day. One of the days he brought Sir Pierce, who had become very fond of her, and even po-faced Noel managed a quick visit with his father. Carys sent her good wishes, but 'couldn't manage' as she was in the last few days of her pregnancy. 'You would think it was the middle ages and she was in confinement!' Ailsa laughed when she read the card and note delivered by the Colonel.

He surprised her by saying, 'I think she probably can't bear the competition to see her looking so bloated.' At which Ailsa managed a giggle through her damaged ribs.

Thomas came on his own, and she could see that he too, was suffering the after-effects of the accident. He was seeing a PTSD Specialist. Max had previously told Ailsa this, in a futile attempt to get her to do the same. Thomas was quiet and withdrawn, and had lost his puppy dog expression and childlike willingness to please everybody. A new Thomas had emerged from the depths of the loch, and Ailsa thought it was no bad thing. Hunter too, had sent a card but had not come to see her daughter. Ailsa told herself she had no wish to see the woman she would never call 'Mother'.

Max had not come back, and secretly her heart sang in pain.

Connie and Jan had both been in touch, they were shocked and saddened over Ailsa's accident. Connie was completely overwhelmed with dismay over the fact that her friend and Max were not back together, despite Ailsa's account of him being there at the hospital, and visiting her every day when she got out. What's more, Connie's wedding was in less than six weeks' time, and Ailsa was insisting she was coming to London herself. Her 'plus one' was now out of the picture.

When she began to feel almost back to her old self, physically at least, she boarded a plane and set off for her villa in Italy. She touched down at the airport mid-afternoon and was at her house by early evening. It was October, and the sun was still shining warmly, in comparison to the colder and wetter autumn she had left in Scotland.

She arrived to find her villa had been refreshed with a bright decoration which she had ordered following her holiday last year. She went to the little taverna and ordered pizza, feeling like a local as they greeted her, and sat reading her Kindle as she nibbled her food. Her appetite was still not quite as good as it should be. She awoke the next morning to the gentle Italian sun on her terrace overlooking the sea.

Hunter took the only taxi on Mhainaray to the manor house, not knowing what her reception would be. She was not one to be nervous or put out, though when Mrs Monroe the housekeeper opened the door, she did feel a certain apprehension. She managed to blag her way in, not exactly lying, but not really telling the truth either. She was reluctantly shown into the front room, and at her own firm request, the housekeeper brought her a glass of wine. Then she sat back and waited. After she finished the glass, she got up and found a bottle in the drinks cabinet and re-filled her glass, sitting by the huge windows opening out onto the sunset.

Sir Pierce arrived back after an evening attending the island's community project meeting. He was met at the door by Mrs Monroe who explained his visitor. He was not, by nature, an emotional man, not used to flying off the handle. although he could on occasion, like during the recent fracas, when he found her with his nephew.

He chose to hear what she had to say.

When he came into the front room, she jumped up to greet him and he stood, with his palm raised, silencing her. She meekly sat back down. He poured himself a drink and sat opposite her. After a long silence he looked at her directly. 'Well?'

'Piercey, I am so, so ashamed and upset by my behaviour and...'

'Oh, don't give me that shit,' he said surprisingly, 'and don't ever again call me that inane and ridiculous name.'

She drew in her breath, and rearranged her tactics. 'Okay, I was swept off my feet by Andy.' She whimpered almost as if she was saying it was Andy's fault. 'I fancied him, and we er... came together. I can't change that, but I am so sorry.'

'Sorry you got caught, or sorry you entered into it?'

She knew Pierce would not be fooled so she hesitated before she spoke. 'At first, sorry I got caught. But I am sorry now that I ever met Andy.'

Many minutes ticked by. 'Very well, I shall give you another chance,' he said eventually. 'You will have to gain my trust again, but I think we may just give it another try.'

He spoke not unkindly, and although Hunter smiled winningly, she had no thought of taking on any of his advice. Inwardly she was scornful. 'Pigs might fly...' came into her mind at that point. She was prepared to act out the part, because at the end of the day, Hunter needed Sir Pierce. Not for him, for his personality or body or life on this dismal little island, but for the title he could offer her.

She was determined to be Lady Georgina Donald.

'Ailsa, I'm sorry to interrupt you.' Max's opening line pushed a few of Ailsa's buttons which she definitely did not want pushed. Firstly, she was irritated at him phoning her in the first place, and secondly, that he actually *was* interrupting her.

Giovanni sat opposite her looking dreamily at her with his black eyes. He had bought her dinner and lots of red wine which was dulling her senses, and blotting out all notion of Max from her mind. She had eaten here three evenings in a row, in the little tavern, and each time, Giovanni, the guy who owned the bar opposite, had noticed her go in and come out alone. He had then actively pursued her.

'Max, what do you want? I'm actually quite busy.'

Max, the master of bad-timing said, 'I'm sorry Ailsa, I just wanted tell you because some time ago you asked me to let you know, that Carys had a baby girl this morning.'

Her mood fell like an elevator with broken machinery, plummeting down several stories.

'Oh.'

'She's not sure what she will be called, but I hope you will be back for her naming party at Trannoch next Friday.'

'I'm not sure, Max. I must go, I'll see you later.' And she rung off.

He stood up. His white linen shirt flapped against a darkly tanned and toned chest. He took her hands. 'We walk on the beach, come,' he said, as he led her out on the soft and warm night air.

The rest of the week was a blur. She met Giovanni every day. They walked on the beach, he took her to a winery, and they ate pasta in the glorious restaurants. He wrapped her up in his arms in an all-too familiar way, and Max crept into her thoughts. He kissed her until she felt the strange feeling in her gut which left her feeling empty and wanting more at the same time. Why were British guys not more like this? A gorgeous man in a romantically strong and commanding way sweeping her off her feet without mentally trying to control her? At the end of the week she invited him back to her villa and they ate tomatoes with an indescribably amazing aroma, buffalo mozzarella and green olive oil, with freshly baked bread from the bakery two doors down, and drank aromatic red wine which made the wine at home seem like vinegar. They sat on the terrace overlooking the sea and eating and drinking in the warm buzz of the evening.

She would not let him stay. She did not want to go into the whole 'it's not you it's me' explanation, but she knew that lovely though the time they had spent together was, she had no notion to enter into any kind of relationship with him. He was theatrically upset, but left nonetheless.

She didn't see him again.

Olivia was going to see her father in Arnasaid Bheag. She had little Freddy strapped into the back seat of the car and sat alongside him. One of the gardeners drove her, an older man who had worked at Trannoch all his life. She had not yet got her licence. She had been used to her parents driving on the right hand side of the road, and she hadn't bothered when she came to Britain. Anyway, as a student, she had not possessed the kind of income which would allow such a thing. She had begun to get into a pattern of visiting her father every Friday. Alberto was overjoyed with his grandson, a beautiful strapping boy, and held him and played on the wooden floor with him almost the whole time they were there.

'How are things at Trannoch?' Alberto asked. They were speaking in their native Italian.

'Yes, okay,' she smiled. 'I'm beginning to find my way around the house, and find my feet with the MacKenzies. That took a lot of pretence on my side, that I was more confident than I am, but they are starting to accept me, I think.'

'Accept you? I should think they should accept you!' His voice rose in irritation. 'It's that man Malcolm who they should no longer accept, not you.'

'Yes, I know Papa,' she spoke wearily which told of many repeats of this particular conversation. 'But what is done is done, and cannot be undone. He is trying to be a good father to Freddy. I believe he loves him, and that is all that matters.'

'Well okay, but that man will get his comeuppance one of these days, and I hope I will be there to see it.'

Hunter was ecstatic. She had managed to get back into Sir Pierce's clutches and she was very much gloating and patting herself on the back. Unfortunately, her night with him, and his promise of 'sealing their relationship and getting back on track' was a non-event. He had consumed too much whisky and fallen asleep almost as soon as his head hit the pillow.

'So much for the *Lion Rampant*,' she thought bitterly, and with the moonlight on her nakedness, she got up pulled on her silk dressing gown, slipped out the room and made her way downstairs. Hunter did not turn in early, and half nine was definitely too early for her. The house was darkly quiet as she padded to the kitchen in her bare feet to get a hot drink, but after searching fruitlessly for coffee, cocoa or even Ovaltine (for God's sake, what was her world now coming to?), she decided to go back to the front room and get a real drink. There was no TV in this room, and Hunter was most definitely not a reader, so she went on the search, opening doors until she found a small sitting room with a few comfy couches, and a 50 inch television. French doors led onto the terrace which wrapped around the front and sides of the house. She popped on a lamp and looked for something interesting to watch. Half-way through a rather boring film which she at first had thought quite promising, she was disturbed by the wind rising around the house and the doors beginning to rattle. It was also quite cold and draughty in the room. She got up to pull the curtains and caught a scream in her throat when she saw a tall figure standing on the terrace just outside the door, looking in, and grinning like an up-turned half-moon.

Andy.

She opened the door. 'Andy! What the hell are you doing here? You absolutely can't come in...' she said, as he stepped over the threshold into the room.

'Is Uncle sleeping?' She nodded before he caught the back of her neck and pulled her into him. His hands were on her hair and his lips on hers.

She pushed him away. 'Yes, but Andy, I can't do this, I've only just come from his bed!'

'Eeeyuch!' he laughed and pushed her gently away from him.

She spoke too quickly. 'Oh, nothing er...nothing happened...it's just that...well...'

He folded one arm across his chest, the other hand on his chin as if he was listening intently to her garbled words. 'So, would you like me to leave?' His highland lilt spoke the words deeply and softly.

The amusement on his face irritated her. 'Well...I...er... after the last time...'

He moved to the door leading to the corridor and with a gentle clank turned the old-fashioned key in the lock and threw off his jacket. He walked to her and picked up the end of the silk waist tie on her dressing gown. Backing off, he slowly pulled it until the silkiness rippled in one fluid movement down her body onto the floor. She stood, shivering with feelings unrelated to the cold, her defiant chin tilted upwards.

He lifted her and carried her to the sofa.

Ailsa felt time hanging heavily on her hands, now that Giovanni was out of the picture. She was due to leave in two days' time, but just as she was wondering if her flight could be changed to later that day, there came a knock at the door. She started to sweat. 'If it's him, then I'll just tell him I'm leaving today,' she thought.

It was Clem.

The coastline was rugged in most parts near to Ailsa's villa, there was a long man-made beach they walked along, though at this time of the year most of the occupants were dog-walkers instead of sun-bathers. When Ailsa got over the shock of seeing her friend there without any warning, she showed Clem to a bedroom overlooking the sea. Clem threw down her small holdall, and they walked out into the bright late October sunshine.

'Well, this is a nice surprise, seeing you here!' Ailsa said too brightly, and for the third time since her friend's arrival. 'You do know though; I am going home on Wednesday?'

'Okay, that's no problem, if I wanted a holiday you would be the first one to tell me to stay on,' Clem smiled. 'That's how I got your address in the first place!'

'So, if you don't want a holiday, why are you here?'

Clem said nothing, but gestured over to a coffee shop on the boardwalk. 'Fancy a coffee? My treat?'

They got a table in the window overlooking the violet waves rolling onto the sand, ordered cappuccinos and luscious looking cakes, then Ailsa turned and looked at the other woman enquiringly. 'Has something happened back home?'

Clem shook her head. 'No, not apart from the usual dramas.'

'Well? What?'

'It's Max – no, as I said, nothing has happened. It's just, he talked to me, and I said I would talk to you.'

'Oh yeah? Come on, Clem, just tell me what all the mystery is about. You didn't come out to Italy just to tell me Max and you had a conversation!'

'He's worried about you.'

'*Kerchang*! So there it is! He's worried about me! Hallelujah! So why didn't he come himself?' She shoved away her cake and folded her hands on her lap.

'Well, for a start I don't think he would have met with a great reception, do you, Ailsa?'

Ailsa looked at her friend coldly. 'No, really? Well, Clem, in case you hadn't realised Max and I haven't really been much of an item for a while.'

Clem smiled. 'As a matter of fact I did notice. And as to why I am here, I had planned a two-night break from the teashop anyway. I was going to go and see some friends in Wales, but after talking to Max decided to get a cheap flight and come out here.' All the time she had been talking, Ailsa had been sitting wringing her hands in her lap, shifting from one side to the other on her chair.

'Why didn't he come? Why didn't Max just come?' went through and through Ailsa's thoughts as she desperately tried to make sense of what was happening to her.

Clem was starting to worry. Ailsa did not look well. Her hands shook as she lifted the cup. She had deep shadows under her eyes and had lost more than a stone in weight since her accident. She had a faint tan, which hid the bags to a certain extent, but there was a frailness and a certain lost look in her eyes which Clem had never seen before.

'Ailsa, Max loves you,' Clem said quietly, but this did more to upset Ailsa than anything.

'Well, he's got a funny bloody way of showing it. We've been "together",' she said, making speech marks with her fingers, 'for almost ten months and he has never once told me that. *Never once*! Not that I would want any man to just tell me that if they didn't feel it, but what am I expected to do? Where am I supposed to go with all this?'

'Why didn't Max come?' repeated in her mind.

Clem was getting alarmed at the way Ailsa was acting. She looked almost wild. Her voice was raised to a high pitch, and the few occupants of the coffee shop were looking over. 'Okay, okay, I really didn't want to upset you, Ailsa. I'm sorry.' Then she proceeded to put the other foot in it. 'It's just that Max isn't very good at that kind of thing...'

'You know what?' Ailsa leaned in close to her friend, her eyes almost manic. 'You're right there, he's no good at it, but I'm sick to death of people telling me that and me telling Max that, and nothing ever changes. Did he send you Clem?'

She hesitated. 'He didn't exactly send...'

'You see? You see what I mean? Why didn't Max come, Clem?' And she pushed aside her coffee cup and walked out of the shop and onto the sand.

'I think you were right to ask me to talk to Ailsa.' Clem was sitting in a tiny bar in the main street of Orbatello. Ailsa had been in her room at the villa since she walked out of the coffee shop and flatly refused to talk. She had come out periodically for food and drinks, and taken them back to her bedroom. She had remained there all the next day. Clem was on the evening flight on the Tuesday, and she had left the villa shouting through the door that she had to go out and buy a few things before she headed to the airport. They had not had another conversation. Clem had gone out and bought her a card and written a heartfelt note inside, apologising for her clumsiness, and saying she hoped they could get together when Ailsa came back home.

'Is she okay? What symptoms is she displaying?'

'Max,' Clem almost laughed, 'no wonder Ailsa thinks you are distant and uncaring, you treat her like a bloody patient rather than a partner.'

'Is that what she said?' He was like a teenager asking his pal's advice about his first date.

'Not in so many words, Max, but I'm going to give it to you straight. I'm no expert, but I think Ailsa is heading for a breakdown.'

Chapter Sixteen

Carys was holding her naming party for her baby. They were in one of the medium sized sitting rooms at Trannoch, with the whole family there, including lots of local people who knew the MacKenzies and were considered fit company, by Carys, for the occasion.

Exhibit A, otherwise known as Baby, was brought in by the nanny. Not Laura, the lovely young woman the Colonel had hired to look after Freddy, but someone Carys had picked herself from an agency in Dunlievitor. This woman, although older than Laura by many years, had been privately educated and had gone to a proper nanny education establishment which Carys foolishly thought made her a better person than Laura. The baby was what Cocky termed 'crabbit'. She was cranky and cried most of the time she was awake, and usually most of the night too. Not that either Carys or Thomas knew anything about this, as the nursery was far enough away to deaden that delightful racket from their spoilt, rich ears. Malcolm delighted in telling everyone the baby was just like her mother.

When she had been dutifully passed around to everyone to have a hug, whether they liked it or not, Nanny Black, as the new nanny insisted on being called, took her away to the nursery, presumably to be fed and tucked in for the night. In actual fact no one, including Carys, really cared as long as the incessant bawling stopped.

The idea of the party was for everyone to come up with a name for Carys and Thomas' baby, which would be considered and announced at the end with a prize for the best suggestion. The occasion was fuelled by lots of champagne, and any other drink anyone cared to mention, as well as a buffet in the usual MacKenzie style.

What the guests didn't know, and probably wouldn't have cared less, was that the name was already chosen. Amalie Marya MacKenzie was the name Carys wanted, and that is the name she would be given at the end of the evening, whether she Carys, walked away with the naming prize or not.

As the evening progressed, everyone was getting merrily drunk and coming up with ridiculous names which were engineered to provide a laugh rather than actually be considered, the sitting room door opened and Denbeath appeared. He walked across to the Colonel and whispered in his ear something that startled him so much he dropped his crystal whisky glass. Getting up, he motioned to Hunter, who was on the opposite couch with Sir Pierce and a few others. She looked bored out of her skin, and happy to escape. She followed him out to the library.

There sat a woman who had lost the first flush of youth, but at mid-seventy, was still a very good looking woman. Her dark eyes were pools of blackness in contrast to her white hair, which had once been a rich auburn, dressed up in an elegant chignon. Her high forehead was paying refuge to beautifully plucked and dark eyebrows. Her lips were a faint pink tinge on her otherwise colourless face, features disparaged by a dark and cold look.

She stood to her full height when they entered, which was around five feet eight inches, but somehow seemed much taller. Her expensive well-cut cream suit hurried into place over her ample hips and waist.

The Colonel and Hunter looked on disbelievingly, as the woman said briskly, 'Well, Mason, aren't you going to offer me a drink?' The Colonel jumped to attention at once.

Hunter's lip quivered slightly when she cried, 'Miss MacKenzie!'

Florence Jane MacKenzie was the Colonel's sister. She was a few years older than her brother and was the only person still alive who could control him.

'Wine please, Denbeath,' The Colonel said hurriedly to the butler; this was his first day back in service.

'I don't want bloody wine. Pour me a large whisky,' Florence said, in a stentorian voice. 'Oh, and Denbeath, I hope you are recovered now from your misfortunate mugging, or whatever they chose to call it. Your face still looks a bit bruised, and you, a bit bedraggled. You should be away to the sun instead of running after these reprobates.'

'Yes, Ma'am,' He gave a rare smile, and left in search of the drinks.

'Er...how did you know about Denbeath?'

'Oh, I have my ways, Mason, and I am certainly not going to divulge those to you. So, Georgina, what have you been up to? No good by all accounts?' Her searching eyes sought out the redness and forced it flooding up Hunter's face.

'I...er...I...nothing much...I...' Hunter for once was completely lost for words.

'Hmmm, if that wasn't a guilt-ridden answer then I don't know what was! Now, we'll get our drinks and I want to meet that silly, mendacious woman Thomas married, and also the Italian child.' The drinks had arrived and she took a swig large enough to fill Loch Linnhe. She swiftly re-filled from the bottle Denbeath had left.

'Oh, you mean little Freddy.' The Colonel's face was consumed with joy. 'You should see him, Florence, he's...'

Florence looked at him scornfully. 'Don't be absurd. You know I hate babies. Of course I didn't mean him. I meant Olivia.'

The Colonel didn't know what to say to this.

'I also want to meet that girl Ailsa soon – I hear she is having a bad time.'

'Yes, you'll meet her soon,' the Colonel nodded. 'Unfortunately, she is not here this evening.'

'Oh, that's my darling daughter...' Hunter began to gush, but was cut off unceremoniously.

'I know she's your daughter, and Saints preserve her for that, but I can't imagine her or anyone else being your 'darling' anything. At least we may hope that Maxwell can measure up to her. Sounds like he is quite taken with her, so she must be made of reasonably good stuff.' She got up, carrying her glass and the other two rose in tandem. They stood eyeing each other for a few minutes then the inimitable Florence said, 'Well, come on, don't just stand there with your mouths open! Show me where the scoundrels are!' and strode out of the room not waiting for them to follow.

But follow they did.

The police hadn't been able to trace the perpetrators of the crime, who they had managed to establish were the same people who had recently vacated Ailsa's Dower House. They hadn't found the car. The official line was that they were 'following up on their enquiries', but the unofficial one was that they thought they were just opportunistic tourists who thought they would try their hand at criminality. Where they got this from was anyone's guess and Max and Stephen Millburn, not to mention the other MacKenzie brothers, were raging that the case had been apparently put on hold as any leads were insufficient to keep the case going.

'Hi Max? Are you busy?'

'Cocky, what's wrong?' There was a slight tremor to Max's voice as he answered his mobile knowing that Ailsa's housekeeper never normally called him directly, unless there was a problem.

'Ailsa's gone missing.'

Two people stood on the hill above Trannoch looking down into the back courtyard. They knew that the estate managers seldom came near this spot. It was too steep for animals, and too overgrown for walkers. Deep within the bushes was a cave-like area which was just big enough for a place to overlook the estate house. The house was very busy this evening. There was some kind of party going on, and no entrance could be made tonight at least. The woman, who was the boss, was none too happy with them. Initially, they rented the Dower House with a view to burglary of both Storm Winds and Trannoch. This area had less than a one per cent crime rate. They left their doors unlocked for God's sake! What could be difficult about that? Then, the two bungled burglaries at Storm Winds and Trannoch had reaped no reward, leaving the old butler unconscious, and the plan scuppered.

Two mistakes.

One of the men had a very bad temper. Driving that woman off the road and into the water had been a huge mistake, and put them all in danger. The driver had only meant to scare her, furious that she hadn't let them rent the place for a few weeks more until they could manage their task. He had lost the plot completely when she seemed to recognise him in the lay by, and in an enraged state rammed her car.

Three mistakes. Now the woman had decided on a higher prize.

She had changed the plan.

Max had never considered himself a good driver, but to course the winding road from Trannoch to Storm Winds on a torrentially wet night like this at sixty miles an hour required a certain skill he didn't know he possessed. It was a feat in itself, even if it was incredibly dangerous and stupid. He skidded up to Storm Winds and saw Miss Cochrane in the doorway.

He shouted above the wind and rain, 'Did you call Stephen?'

'Yes, he's on his way.' Cocky was harassed.

'What about the police?'

'No, Stephen told me not to. They wouldn't listen, it's only been a few hours. If you don't come back in an hour, I will call Ian MacFarlane.'

'Okay, did you get the torches and rope and stuff?'

A voice came from behind him. 'Hi Max, I've got them here.' It was Stephen, and looking beyond him, Max could see and hear Jim Hutton coming up the drive in the quad to meet them.

'Okay, let's go.'

Florence was immediately surrounded by people of her own generation who had lived in the area when she and the

Colonel were growing up. One woman in particular came forward and kissed her on the cheek, then settled down beside her. 'Isabella, it's good to see you.'

'And you, Florence, glad you made it home successfully.' The Colonel, who was flitting about like a wasp round a jam jar, listened intently to this.

'Well, good of you to help with the flights and removal. I don't know how you manage, Isabella, I think these computers are the curse of the Devil himself. A drink, here, for Miss Woodhouse!' She snapped her fingers, and one raced through the gaggle of people to land in her friend's outstretched hand.

The other woman smiled. 'It was no problem, Florence, I am so glad you are back. I've missed your company.'

'Er...back? So have you actually left the South of France?' The Colonel interrupted in his carrying voice, laced with obvious panic.

'Of course! I have been planning this for the twenty years since I left Arnasaid.' Her face glowed with self-satisfaction. 'This was my home too, Mason, and I'm sure you have a few rooms to spare.' It was not a question. 'My old Ben Eldhi suite, for instance, will do nicely. Now, where is that Karen... Carrie, whatever her name is?'

Carys, who had been listening to this exchange while carrying on her own conversation, swung round. She eyed up the older woman with a look of galvanised steel.

'And *you* are?'

You could almost see the ice uttered from her lips sweep the room, freezing the occupants and rendering them motionless.

Noel and Malcolm, standing together, now exchanged looks of anticipated enjoyment. They said as one, 'Uh oh!'

Florence took a long time to answer, but the room-in-waiting was not unimpressed by the result. 'I am Aunt to your husband and his brothers. I have heard a lot about you, and I wished to see for myself if the information was true, which I am sorry to say it seems to be. This is why I asked to meet you personally. Will that do?'

'Aunt, who?' Carys held her head aloft, feeling she had just been thrust into a boxing ring with an audience of expectant onlookers.

'I am Miss MacKenzie, to you. I am the Colonel's sister. And, just for the record, I am not in the habit of answering people's questions, Carrie.'

'My name is Carys.' She was suddenly a little unsure of herself.

'Well, at last! You manage to introduce yourself.' And, at that, the gallant lady turned away from the outraged look, with a loud comment to her friend, 'Well, we can pick our friends, but unfortunately not our families.'

Carys flounced from the room to seek the bathroom. She had finally found someone who could bring her close to tears.

The headland was so dark that the three men found it difficult to walk without falling over the cliff, never mind look for Ailsa. There was no visible moon, and the light was practically non-existent.

'Whit aboot the beach, Sir?'

'Yes, good shout, Jim,' Max said. 'I'll go down the cliff path, and you and Stephen check the rest of the shrubbery up here.'

'I think we should stay together. We will need each other to pull her up if she's down there,' Stephen shouted through the rain.

They tentatively made their way down the rain-soaked and slippery pathway to the beach, torches ahead, searching, the beams casting narrow head lights across the little beach, with the sound of the waves crashing ominously in the background. They flashed the light across the rocks at the far end. Just as they were beginning to give up, Max gave a shrill cry.

'She's over there!' He started running before he got the words out. She was half-sitting, half lying on the rocks, her light jacket not preventing her being soaked to the skin, and staring with unseeing eyes out into the blackness.

'Ailsa darling, I'm here!' Max gripped her tightly, and with difficulty the three men pulled her from the rocks even as a wave tumbled and slapped over their legs.

'It's okay, Stephen and Jim are here too...'

They stood her on the beach and wrapped her in the tinfoil space blanket as Max took her erratic pulse.

'We'll get you home and warm soon...'

Her face was whiter than the frills on the waves, and her whole body was in a perpetual tremor. He put his arms around her, mainly to get some heat into her body. She slowly pushed him away. Her fevered look searched his body until her eyes found his, her face crumpled, and the tears fused with the pouring rain.

'You didn't come.' It was almost a whisper. 'You sent Clem, but you didn't come.' And Stephen caught her just in time as her legs folded.

The storm winds blew over Trannoch. Autumn docked in the North West, while the sea and rain lashed the rocky coastline. The ferries were off for three days due to the high tides, and the boats in the bay roller-coastered the waves as the chains that tethered them strained like dogs on a lead. If at all possible, people stayed indoors. Winds reached 85 miles an hour, and there was some damage to quite a few properties in the surrounding villages. Storm Winds clung to the cliff like a child hanging on to its mother.

Florence was marooned on Mhainaray. She had decided to look up her old friend Pierce, and had packed a bag and taken the ferry across to the island.

She knew about Hunter.

She knew that Hunter had been having an affair with three different men at the same time: Sir Pierce, his nephew and her own brother the Colonel. This was while under the roof of the Colonel and Florence's ancestral home. Florence had always kept up with her friends. Isabella, her staunchest ally, had written to her regularly for years, then when paper became a computer, she had emailed her. Florence's determination to keep up with the news saw her buy, reluctantly, her own PC, where she learned how to work one of the 'vile things' and successfully switched from pen to keyboard. Emails and some internet shopping were really all she could cope with, but she was still young enough to learn a new skill.

Isabella was a very astute woman who had her finger in more pies than the chip shop in Fort William. News travelled to her. She was interested, as opposed to gossipy. She was kind and considerate of the people in the community in which she lived, and they in turn, sought out her ear, when they wanted someone to listen. So, she had a database of knowledge stored in her over-active mind.

But on this occasion, it wasn't Isabella who had supplied Florence with the information which had brought her storming back to Trannoch.

It was Sir Pierce himself.

Ailsa had been hospitalised for two nights following her rescue from the beach at Storm Winds. She had awakened to a room where the whiteness of the immediate surrounding area merged the walls and the ceiling together. There were medical appliances surrounding her bed, and seeing these, a rising panic led her to scream out, bringing a nurse running to her side. She had lots of people talking to her about how they could help her overcome her PTSD symptoms, and one woman in particular really got under her skin to the extent that she agreed to go through the Psychotherapy sessions. She had two sessions before she was discharged, with lots more booked in to help her, going forward.

Miss Cochrane was there every inch of the way for Ailsa. She was there by her bedside, knitting as her patient slept, and running errands for magazines which were never read, and crisps and chocolate which were never eaten. It was like a replay of the situation when she had her accident.

Ailsa never once mentioned Max. Cocky was distraught about the situation. She had thought it was a mistake for Ailsa to go to Italy at the time she chose to do so, but who was she to throw a spanner into the works? And now this situation where she was getting better one minute and back to square one the next, was a difficult situation to deal with for both the patient, and her housekeeper. Ailsa had no recollection of that night, other than the fact she felt a huge desire to 'escape', despite the fact it was raining torrentially, and the temperature had plummeted to around 2 degrees. As to what had happened when Max, Stephen and Jim found her, that was fuzzy, floating in and out of her mind like the objects she had seen in front of her in the loch.

Cocky had decided to tackle Max one day shortly after Ailsa had been discharged from hospital, with the 'sound' advice that he should keep away.

Max had lost weight. He had never been in the least overweight but he now appeared to be quite thin, his cheeks hollow and his clothes beginning to sag. This seemed to be the only visible effect of the whole sordid episode. Miss Cochrane had called him directly on his mobile and invited him over to Storm Winds one evening. Ailsa was in her sitting room at the front of the house, and she was in her own suite.

'Would you like some tea, or a glass of wine, perhaps?' Miss Cochrane's hospitable nature came easily to the fore, as her guest looked at her with distraught eyes, filled with a hopelessness which touched her heart.

'I'll have wine, if I may,' he said, in an unnaturally robotic voice. He was twitching and shuffling in a way she hadn't seen before. Her eyebrows raised at his tone, but she said nothing, not even when she offered him a tray of sandwiches, which he politely but firmly declined. 'Is there something I can help you with, Cocky?'

'I am worried about you, Max, and I am also worried about Ailsa,' her voice quavered unnaturally. Max poured her some wine, which she would normally have resisted, but she accepted gratefully.

He looked at her with mourning eyes. 'I don't know how to reach her. I feel helpless.'

'I know you do, but I think it best if you leave her to recover.'

'Leave her? Cocky, I love her.' The words hung in the air like fog coming up from the sea. He glanced upwards as if he was looking for the words to catch and take back. He gasped as he tried to get his emotions in check. He realised that he had said out loud what he was actually feeling.

'I know, but you need to let her be treated by other doctors who are neutral to her. She has so much going on in her mind that she couldn't cope with the worries surrounding your relationship.'

'Did she tell you that?'

'Max, she has hardly talked in the last few days since it happened far less talked about her feelings for you. If you could leave her to other doctors to help her recovery, I hope and pray that things will get back to normal.'

Max nodded, as he sipped his wine. 'Okay, I will keep away, but please can you let me know immediately if you think she needs me, or if, she asks for me?'

'I will definitely do that.'

Ailsa sat in her library, the tears coursing down her face, wishing that Max would visit her. She felt so hurt, but it hurt more to even think, so she pushed it from her mind. She kept seeing the floating objects in the water, felt the panic rise as she wanted to breathe, breathe, and yet no air would come. The water had pushed away the air. She continually processed the series of events from the time the other car bounced her off the road, re-living the moment of impact, the water rising around her, the cold like fingers playing a keyboard, climbing up her body. Everything dancing in front of her, the pain, the dark, the panic and then the silence. It was the silence which scared her most. As the water rushed through her ears it deadened all sound. She watched as her body moved upwards, up, up – was this what happened? Was this how it would be when she died? When she woke up there was a loch full of faces standing around her.

They had helped her breathe again. They had made her live again. But she wasn't really living. She couldn't – wouldn't remember the pain and the cold and the fear.

Then her mind kept going back to that fateful short holiday in Italy, when everything had fallen into place. In her mind she was forever floating upwards, up, up, and on the way up she had realised it was Max. But her feelings had been couched in fear, anger and despair. She didn't know how to go to him, but wanted him with her.

But Max never came.

Thomas had taken time to recover too. He had been kept in hospital that night for observation, then had gone home to a hero's welcome at Trannoch. Or rather, the Colonel, Noel and Malcolm had emptied a few of the Colonel's best whiskies. Carys was ambivalent, thinking it couldn't have been as bad as the police and Max had made out. Hunter, other than a sugary smile and a gentle pat on the back, said nothing.

It was Olivia who amazed them all with her comments, spoken openly at dinner the night he returned. 'You have done a great, great thing, Thomas,' she said, quietly and kindly. 'You are not a brave man all the time, I think? But that is when people are really brave, when they feel such fear, but do it anyway. The Lady Ailsa thanks you, I think, for her life.'

Carys had smiled sneeringly, 'That loch is actually not as deep as some around here, otherwise Thomas would never have been able to stomach it. He doesn't swim very well.'

'Is easy to make fun.' Olivia had looked her straight in the eye. 'But you would not do it Carys, not even for your bambina,' She dabbed the corners of her mouth daintily, and with a dignified nod, left the table.

No one rose to Carys' defence.

There were frequent storm winds over Trannoch as the MacKenzies sat down at the dinner table, which was bursting at the seams. The children were home from school, as it was the October half-term holiday. Alberto had been invited, Stephen and Clem were there, and of course, Hunter. Melody was home from Uni. She had pleaded with her grandfather to invite Dougie, and he had assented.

'It's beginning to feel a bit like a school dining hall in here!' Hunter smiled grimly at the Colonel.

'Well there's only four of us, there's much more adults.' Ryan detested Hunter, and his words were laced with something not far short of venom.

'Many,' corrected Max, in a weary voice.

Hunter stared at the boy, whom she thought was nothing more than a trouble-maker and a nuisance. She proceeded to swat him like a fly. 'I was speaking to your grandfather, if your remark was addressed to me.'

'Wha' she say?' Alberto asked, and was ignored.

Ryan looked Hunter straight in the eye. 'Yeah, it was, actually.'

'Enough, Ryan,' the Colonel spoke, mildly for him.

'At least there aren't any screaming babies here. Thank goodness for nannies and nurseries! I'm afraid listening to them gives me indigestion.'

'Well, Hunter, you haven't been used to that in the past. Not with Ailsa, at least.' Carys was put out by the older woman. She actually felt the same about the way her baby seemed to scream constantly, but she wasn't going to tolerate anyone else complaining.

'Wee Freddy doesn't scream or cry very much,' Melissa smiled consolingly at Olivia, with whom she was beginning to have a real bond. Olivia returned the grin.

'Wha' she say?' Alberto asked again, and was ignored again.

'Well I happen to know that Ailsa was a very well-behaved baby,' Hunter lied.

'Really? Did you fly over from Australia to see her then?'

'I won't have Ailsa's business talked about,' Max snapped.

'Hear hear!' Clem said with a smile.

'Max, darling, Ailsa is my daughter.'

'I am fully aware of that tragic fact, but I won't have her talked about when she is not here, especially when she is ill.'

'Lady Ailsa seems to have been ill quite a bit this year.' Carys assumed a thoughtful expression. 'Perhaps she should go back to London, maybe Scotland just doesn't suit her.'

Max glared at her angrily. 'Are you deaf? I won't ask if there's something wrong with you as it is quite evident there is. Ailsa has been through a horrendous incident, and I WON'T have you discussing her when she's not here.'

Carys looked at him in surprise. Max didn't normally react so vociferously, and she was impressed. Unfortunately, his reaction was fuel to the fire. 'I don't know why you're getting upset, Max. You're doing a sterling job of defending Ailsa, despite being on a break!'

Ryan and Aria both looked stricken. Ryan had not been best friends with Ailsa since she got into a relationship with his Dad, but he had grown to like her, chiefly because he loved his Dad dearly and wanted him to be happy. In recent weeks his father had been far from happy.

'Well, that is my own personal business as well as Ailsa's. Don't you dare openly talk about either Ailsa or I, in anything resembling personal terms again.' Max got up from the table. 'Sorry Dad, excuse me, I've suddenly lost my appetite.' And he left the room with a crash of the door.

'Touchy!' said Carys, then gave a false falsetto laugh.

'It's no wonder he's getting so thin, when he keeps storming out of meals!' Hunter's voice dripped with disdain.

'Wha' she say?' Alberto asked for a third time, and gave it up.

'Yes, and it's no wonder my sister can't bear to be around us for very long. Having to listen to this family squabbling every meal time is really getting too much.' The Colonel banged his fist on the table, sending all the crockery around him jumping.

'Where is Aunt Florence anyway?' Thomas asked. He had just noticed she wasn't there.

Everyone looked in the Colonel's direction enquiringly. 'She's gone to stay with Pierce for a few days. It may be longer if this weather keeps up, as the ferries are off.' He was watching Hunter's expression as he said it. Her face fell as quickly as her fork, and his aching doubt over Hunter's relationship with Sir Pierce was confirmed. 'Perhaps you would like to pay one of your little visits once the ferry is back on, Hunter?'

Hunter looked aghast, then began in a simpering voice. 'Me? Darling, I have no idea what you mean! I didn't have anything very much to do with your sister. In fact, I believe I only met her a few times in the past.'

'Perhaps you should join me in the library after dinner, and I will explain it to you then.' His face was red with anger as he made an agitated but dignified exit from the room.

'Why they all leave?' It was Alberto again. Nobody answered him.

Hunter's face was fearful as she rose to follow him.

There was a silence which could be felt. The children gradually began talking to each other. Clem and Stephen looked at each other questioningly, then the others gradually picked up their own conversations.

Melody's boyfriend took a gulp of his red wine. 'Wow! Is it always like this?' He asked her cheerfully.

'Pretty much.'

'Hmm, good gig.'

The Colonel and Hunter had met in the library.

'You and Pierce are having an affair.'

'Darling, whatever are you talking about?' Hunter used her most persuasive voice.

'You know exactly what I mean, so please don't deny it.' The Colonel's nostrils were flaring, his face red and his voice could be heard down the hall.

'Listen, I...'

'I don't want to have a conversation about this.' He poured himself a whisky, but didn't offer her one. 'I just want to let you know what is going to happen. I want you out of here tonight. For good. You have made a fool of me once too often, and I have no wish to hear your excuses or lies. I will never *ever* trust you again. You are a disgrace. I'll give you one hour, and the car will be out the front waiting for you. If you don't have time to pack the extensive wardrobe bought with *my* money, then you will lose whatever you leave.'

'But Mason...'

'Furthermore, don't ever utter my name in public again. Now OUT!' He held open the library door, and Hunter, far from looking distraught, was like a raging bull herself.

'Very well, I will go. You will rue the day you had the audacity to do this.' She flounced past him and up the stairs, her head held high.

Colonel Mason Smith MacKenzie sat at the desk and poured himself another drink, while a stray tear escaped from his eye. He swiped it angrily away.

Chapter Seventeen

Eileen had a day off. Her boyfriend was working, and she had decided she wanted to get healthy, so she had taken up walking. Her friend Mhairi was up for a long walk, taking sandwiches and drinks with them. The loch sides are practically uninhabited, and there are no shops or pubs to pop in for lunch. Eileen had only done this particular walk she was planning once before, with her local guide pack when she was in her teens.

'Do you think we're daft attempting this?' Mhairi said to her friend, in a doubtful voice, as they sat on the pier in Arnasaid Bheag waiting for the boat to take them up Loch Nevis to the start of the arduous walk which would take them four hours to complete. It was really quite misty on the water, although the sea was very calm after the storm. The late October sun was trying to add warmth through the gloom, although it was early, and they had high hopes it would shift in an hour or two. The path was mountainous and sheer in some parts, down to Loch Morar, the deepest loch in Europe. Eileen looked at her friend with a mixture of fear and excitement.

'Och, we'll do it no probs!' Eileen's upbeat sunny nature was infectious, as was her laugh. The boat glided across the glass-like surface of Loch Nevis. Mhairi had been brought up in the area, the same as her friend, and knew this sea loch well. She had never attempted this particular walk though.

'Oh, we don't do daft walks like that roon the mountains, that's for tourists!' Mhairi's Dad had said to her time and again as she was growing up. It had put her off.

They couldn't see the tops of the mountains. It was as if the clouds had fallen. The guy steering the boat looked at them with a mystified expression. 'You two lassies doin' the walk back to Morar?' he asked incredulously.

'Yep! Want to come?' Eileen, the irrepressible, giggled.

'No way! You're both aff yer heids! It's no' half misty. I hope you know the way!' He shook his head, and walked away leaving them wondering if they should turn back. But Eileen was resolute and bullied her friend into submission. Mhairi looked like she was going to burst into tears.

The boat went to Knoydart first, to drop off supplies to the few houses there, and to the 'Most remote pub in Britain', before going on towards Tarbet, to the landing place on the beach. From here, the path rose steeply upwards, so steeply, you could only clearly see the start of it. It was rocky and wet with mist, until they got to the top and the start of what is surely the most beautiful walk in the country, around the shores of the loch. At this point, they only glimpsed a tiny part of the loch. The mist came and went. At some stages they could only see around 50 yards in front of them, but their chatter and laughter kept them warm and in high spirits as they made their way forward.

After around an hour of walking, as if on ice, the mist changed quite definitely to fog. Mhairi was getting very fretful, but Eileen the ever-enthusiastic, tried to calm her down. Even Eileen, however, had to admit defeat, when at one point she tripped on the rocky path and sent a large stone flying to her left which landed with a distant 'plop' a moment later. They were high up. They were very high up, and there wasn't much between the path and the edge. Mhairi was getting hysterical.

'Eileen, I don't like this!' she said, with tears in her eyes. 'What'll we do? I can't call anybody, cos I have no signal here. My Dad is working away. What'll we do? You heard that stone. The path is slippy and...and...'

'Let's just find a place to sit and we'll eat our sandwiches and we'll feel a bit better.' The resourceful Eileen pulled her friend back from the left, where the loch was, and over to the right, found a rocky shelf with a kind of overhang, and sat down there. They were dressed for the weather, that was one thing in their favour, and they were quite sheltered and dry under the rock.

They felt a bit more cheerful when they had eaten, and decided to stay where they were until the fog lifted. It was still only eleven o'clock, and there would be plenty of light for the next few hours. They played 'rock, paper, scissors' to pass the time, and all of a sudden, without warning, the fog lifted like a curtain going up in the theatre, and the beauty of the landscape almost took their breath away. It was as if they had been dropped into another land. The loch looked immense, blue and completely different from the shadowy mass of water they had seen at the start of their walk. Mhairi again nearly panicked when she saw how high they were and how far they would fall if they dropped, but Eileen again cheered her up with her bubbly chatter,

'Gee, are we in Kansas?' she said, in an American accent. The relief of knowing they were safe set them off into hysterical giggles.

Two hours later they were only an hour from the road which wound from Morar village. There was still no sign at this point of any habitation. They shared some chocolate and took photos with their phones of the magnificent scenery, and plenty of selfies with the loch in the background. They filled their lungs with pure mountain air.

'Oh, my phone's working!' Mhairi was ecstatic. 'Shame we don't need rescuing now!'

Eileen laughed, 'Yes, pity there aren't any gorgeous hunks coming to save us! Mine's working too. Not far to go now, then we can phone Archie, and he'll come for us to the road end.' She referred to her boyfriend. They had a spring in their step as they rounded a steep bend to see the last part of their pathway laid before them, around six miles of winding cliff paths.

'Hey, what's that?' Eileen stopped and stared.

'What?'

'That! Down there on the rocks beneath that high cliff bit about a mile down that way,' Eileen said urgently.

'Is it a sheep?'

Eileen looked at her friend scornfully. 'Don't be daft, it's solid, not woolly.'

'How can you tell that from here?' Mhairi retorted.

They started to walk quicker. 'I just can. Plus, you don't get 20 feet long sheep – that looks enormous!'

'D'you think it's Morag?'

'The Monster? No. As I said, it looks solid,' Eileen answered, as if it was a feasible question.

As they got nearer, the lie of the land meant that the cliff hid the object from their view. The cliff itself was reasonably smooth, so they walked to the edge to have a look. As they peered down, they saw what it was, and without speaking, they turned to each other. Eileen, as usual, was the first to speak.

'How the hell did a car get up here?'

Ailsa had developed a few different habits since she got out of hospital. She took to sleeping downstairs in her favourite blue sitting room rather than going up to her bedroom. She had no idea why she did this, but with her two dogs cuddled in on the couch with her, she did feel safer. Following the attempted break-in a few months ago, Jim Hutton had been tasked with a security project which had meant the ground floor and all its entrances, of which there were several, were alarmed. It was then Jim's task to set the alarm before he finished work in the evening.

Also, Ailsa insisted that she would eat when she felt like eating, rather than having regular mealtimes. Jean Morton, that kitchen doyenne, was initially upset, but thought in a roundabout way, that she understood. So, Jean had taken to making up meals and keeping them in the huge fridge until Ailsa felt like eating. If it was when Jean had gone home, she made her own food, or heated the food up. This was no hardship to Ailsa, as she had made her own meals since she left her parent's house to live in her flat in London, and she missed cooking. It actually seemed to give her a purpose. She had also started taking the dogs their walks down the driveway, then around the open areas of the lawns, skirting the woods, but staying away from the beach and the headland – her special place. She didn't think about why she did this, but at the moment, it just felt right.

On this particular day, she had just come in from a walk around the grounds, and took a sandwich into her library. She could not concentrate on her writing and had done none since her 'accident'. It was a grey and windy day, and the fire, one of Ailsa's favourite things, was crackling happily, raising her mood. She took a book and curled up by the fire.

Max arrived. He came in the kitchen garden door, nearly scaring Jean Morton out of her wits, as she had been dozing by the range. Miss Cochrane took him into her own sitting room and gave him a cup of tea.

'They've found the car that crashed her off the road.' He didn't need to explain which car, Miss Cochrane knew what he meant. She noticed a frailty in his voice.

'Oh God.'

'It gets worse. It was Eileen and her friend who were walking the shores of Loch Morar who found it. No one in the car...' he hastened to add, 'but it was definitely the same car. The police think it was driven up onto the cliff, then something jammed on the pedals to ensure it went forward while they, whoever "they" are, got out and left it to tumble over the edge. It didn't quite make it into the depths, it's really rocky at that part, and it crashed there.'

'But why did the police not spot it?' she asked, not unreasonably.

'No idea. Had she not survived they would've made more effort, I imagine. They would search the coast, but the loch is pretty much inaccessible to vehicles. They must have been good drivers to get the car up there, it is no more than a rocky path.'

Miss Cochrane nodded. Max was struggling. She knew that although it was important information, he didn't come for that only. 'She's in the library.'

'Cocky, I don't know if I...I can't...'

'Max, just be strong. Ailsa loves your strength. Go and talk to her, and if she throws you out, you go away – and then come back. I think Ailsa has been pining for you, and that is making her worse. Just be strong.'

Sir Pierce looked across to his visitor with a feeling of affection and warmth. Florence was looking back at him with feelings of anger and pent-up frustration.

'I can't believe you are back!' He was like a parent talking to a long lost child. 'I am so, so glad to...'

'Oh, save it, Pierce.' She drank her whisky faster than a horse at the trough. He topped it up.

'Is there something you wish to discuss, Florence?' He looked anxious and upset.

'You know why I am here, Pierce. One word – Georgina. What in hell's fire do you think you are doing? Have you completely lost your mind?'

'I...er...don't...'

'And please don't insult my intelligence by saying you don't know what I mean by that. You are having an affair with her while she is sleeping under the same roof as my brother, who, I may add, loves the "bones" of her as they say. He is an idiot. As you are,' she finished, with a sweeping hand as if she was swatting midges out of the way.

Sir Pierce sat back, clasping his drink, his look reflective. 'Georgina is the most exciting, interesting person to come into my life for a long time.'

'Oh, I am well aware of her attributes, you don't have to spell them out for me.'

'I had no idea she was in a relationship with the Colonel, she didn't admit to that. What she did say was that the Colonel took her in when her daughter threw her out of Storm Winds.'

'Of course she did! Ailsa threw her out because Georgina tried to lie and cheat her way into illegally inheriting Storm Winds – *that's* why she threw her out. Hunter even wheeled in her trick card, Ailsa's half-brother Joshua all the way from Australia.'

'You know, when Ailsa and Georgina were here a few months back, they had a ferocious argument, and I don't think Ailsa thought I had picked her up on it, but she did say that Joshua was not Sir Angus' son, but Georgina and...and...'

'Oh, spit it out, Pierce. Are you trying to tell me Joshua, or whatever his name is, is the Colonel's son?' She sat back again with a satisfied smile on her face.

'Er...yes, I am afraid that is what I heard.'

'Well, I would prefer you kept this to yourself for the meantime. The Colonel at one time thought the baby Georgina had given away for adoption was his baby, so you can imagine how he felt when Ailsa was found and brought back.'

'Does the Colonel know about his other son?'

'That I do not know, but I trust you will not disclose this, Pierce.'

'I wouldn't dream of it.'

Sir Pierce filled both their glasses again. 'I fear I have made a bit of a mistake.'

'You mean about Georgina?' A bit of a mistake?' She threw back her head with a huge laugh. 'How can you be so bloody stupid, Pierce? I am sorry to be blunt, but what exactly do you think she sees in you?'

'Well, that's a bit harsh...'

'I know it is.' She sobered for a moment. 'Someone needs to invade your little world here where you are King and set a few things straight. One word, Pierce, *title*. That is what her crummy hands are reaching out for. She wants to be Lady Donald.'

'I know.'

'You know, but you are not willing to let her go.'

He looked thoughtful. He smiled at her. They had been lovers once. A long time ago, before Lady Moira came on the scene. Florence had been, was still in his eyes, a beautiful woman, and Lady Moira, well, she was a very nice, well brought up woman, who moved in the same circles as he did. She could never measure up to his first love.

'I would give up Georgina, you know, if...if...'

'If what?' She took delight in pushing him.

'If someone else would take her place.'

'May I come in?' Max put his head round the door. Ailsa looked up from her book. 'I just wondered how you are.'

'I'm fine,' she said flatly. She looked neither pleased nor surprised to see him. Max thought there was no evidence of Ailsa 'pining' for him, in the look.

He came in and sat opposite her on the other wing-backed chair at the fire, without invitation. 'Cocky's bringing us some wine, if you fancy it.'

'Hmmm, I suppose.' She shut her book with a snap, as if she was annoyed at the interruption. The dogs danced round his ankles. He picked up Bluebell and cuddled her.

'So, how are you feeling?' Max searched for words to say to her.

'Max, I think you know that I am okay. I have done what you and Cocky wanted me to do. I have had some PTSD counselling, and I am feeling much better.'

'Good. I'm just...er...'

'Here we are then!' Cocky's voice was overly cheerful as she brought in the wine. She put it on the little table between them and left with a backward glance.

Ailsa picked up her glass and took a sip. She looked across to Max, who had done the same. 'I don't know how to do this,' she said.

He didn't ask the obvious, he just nodded. 'I don't either.'

The fire crackled in the grate, the room grew dark, and their faces were lit by the dancing lights of the fire.

'Everything that has gone on, I can't...I don't feel I can cope with it.' Her eyes were mutinous, as if it was all his fault.

'You don't need to cope. Just let's get through it.'

'Is that not the same thing? You make it sound so easy.'

'It's not. It's hard. It's hard and horrible.'

'It is horrible.'

He stood and put logs on the fire. The room suddenly lit up as if someone had turned on the light. He sat again.

'You didn't come. You sent Clem, but you didn't come.' She uttered almost the same words as the night on the beach.

Max leaned forward in his chair and ran his fingers through his hair, struggling with his emotions. He remembered Cocky's words a few minutes ago.

Ailsa loves your strength. Be strong.

'I know, and that was a mistake. I thought you wouldn't want to see me, so I decided not to go to Italy. It was the wrong thing to do. I'm sorry.' Although his words were remorseful, he kept as stoic as he could.

'I thought I hated you.' She looked at him with eyes wide with pain.

'And?'

'I...I... don't hate you. I...I...'

He reached out and took her hand.

The Ghillies' Ball was in full swing. It was a few weeks since Ailsa and Max had talked, and they had seen each other almost every day. They were both taking things very slowly, as their relationship was still fragile, but they each believed, with time, they would get there.

Connie and Jan, accompanied by Calum and Gregory, had arrived and surrounded Ailsa and Max. They all planned to go south together, Ailsa and Max included, after the Ball, in preparation for Connie's wedding. Jan and Ailsa were both Maids of Honour. Calum's best friend from school, Scott, was the best man. It would be the first time Ailsa and Max had been away together, except for their stay on Mhainaray.

A much thinner Ailsa and Max greeted their friends and prepared to have a good night. Dougie and his band were playing in the ballroom which was a veritable bank vault full of gold leaf decoration, the splendour and opulence out-doing anything Ailsa had, or would wish to have, at Storm Winds. The bottles of champagne were being pulled, corks loudly popping, and waiters flitting in and out between the groups of people, handing out the flutes. Ailsa wore a turquoise blue tartan dress, full skirted, and tied at the back. Most people wore some sort of tartan. Max had a waist coat in the MacKenzie tartan with a matching bow tie. He was looking happier than he had been for many months now.

'Hello everyone!' A confident voice broke into their conversation, and Ailsa just had time to see Max's thunderous expression before she swung round.

It was Hunter.

'What the hell are you doing here?' Max had taken her to the side away from Ailsa.

'Well, Maxwell, your father very kindly asked me to come for Ailsa's sake. Of course, I very much doubted that he had meant what he said about my not coming back, so I called him and said Ailsa would be really upset if I wasn't invited.'

'You mean you used your daughter to get back into the Colonel's good books? It won't work.'

'How dare you accuse me of being conniving!'

'Just stating a fact.' He didn't believe a word of what Hunter said, and his eyes searched the room and found his father watching them. He stomped over to ask what was going on.

'Son, I did say she could come,' he said with a grin, 'Hunter needs teaching a lesson, and we are going to do just that tonight.'

'Dad, what are you up to? Don't lower yourself to her level. Please.'

'Oh, it's not necessarily me who is going to do the "teaching".' He swung round as the doors opened, and Sir Pierce and Florence walked into the room arm in arm. Hunter's jaw fell faster than a stone dropped from the top of Ben Nevis.

Ailsa took in the woman's figure as the new arrivals moved towards her. Every line on the face was light, though she must be around the age of the Colonel. Her stately gait carried her across the room as her clothes folded gracefully over her tall, elegant frame. Her eyes were bright with life and vitality, and a spark of something which Ailsa, on this first meeting, could not work out. But, when she spoke, strident and low, it was the voice she recognised. A questioning voice, a demanding voice. Where had she heard that voice before? A vision of her own book came into Ailsa's mind, then an audience, and a few difficult questions came running towards her with the explanation. Her own book signing. This woman had been there.

Pierce and Florence sallied up to the Colonel. 'Mason, your Ghillies' Ball is absolutely wonderful!' Florence eyed Hunter as she spoke. 'Georgina, won't you be the first to congratulate us? Pierce and I are *seeing each other.*' She emphasised the phrase with a little chuckle.

Hunter was very white. 'Really? Pierce, I would have thought your preference was for a much younger partner?'

'Like yours you mean?' Florence knew all about Andy.

Hunter looked enraged. 'How very strange you two have got together so quickly.' Her voice was laden with sarcasm.

'Oh, we're not in the least worried about how that will look to others, if that is what you are insinuating. Florence has a very good reputation, and is held in very high esteem in these parts, unlike some I could mention.'

Hunter fumed.

'And to answer your question about age, we are closer in age than most folk.' Pierce gave Florence a little hug. 'I always think that the best thing in life is having friends and family we can trust, who speak the truth, and are true to each other. Don't you think so Florence?'

Ailsa looked quite distraught about this whole little scene. Not that anyone else except she, Max and the Colonel had been privy to the dialogue – the party had gone on around them. It was just that with everything which had gone on between them since Hunter had descended on Storm Winds over a year ago, she felt sad that they still had no connection.

'Absolutely. Now, Sir Pierce may have had a soft spot for you, Georgina, but thank the Lord he came to his senses. Now, can you please get me a drink, Mason?'

Hunter, ashen-faced, faded mutely into the background.

Max put his arm around Ailsa.

'Try not to let her get to you.'

'Well, it's pretty hard when she's in my face all the time, spouting venom.'

'I know, but Dad said she was carrying on with three of them at the same time. Andy always was a bit of a womaniser when I knew him at Uni.'

'So, Andy is the guy who was with you in Mhainaray? When Hunter fell in the mud?'

'Yes.'

'Well, I can definitely see the attraction,' and for the first time since he found her on the beach, her eyes glinted.

Food was served out, buffet-style in the room next to the ballroom, and the dancing continued. Ailsa looked around her. She had loved her own Ghillies' Ball last year, until it had been unceremoniously interrupted by Hunter coming back from the dead and taking over. It had been the first time Ailsa had met her birth mother, and since then, she had been trying to forget it.

'Ailsa, darling, may I talk to you for a minute?' Ailsa looked up to see the slightly stricken face of Hunter, with what looked like streaks in her make-up where tears had fallen. She felt a little sorry for her, and agreed to find a quiet room to chat.

Hunter was pacing. 'Do you mind if I...?' She took a cigarette out of her packet. Ailsa shook her head. She was choosing her battles.

'What is it? Why do you want to talk to me? Haven't you done enough damage for one night, or one year for that matter?' Ailsa was quietly scornful.

'I have made mistakes, Ailsa. Some I am not happy with, and some – I couldn't give a damn about.' Hunter threw her daintily defiant chin in the air, blowing little circles of smoke above.

'So?'

'Darling, you are so crass at times, I can't believe it. Here am I, trying to bare my soul to you, and you throw words at me in a hard voice. I can't bear it.' There was still that insincerity in Hunter's voice which made Ailsa angry.

'Why don't you just stop play acting, and tell me what you want to tell me.' Ailsa was weary of all this.

'I want you to take me back. Back to Storm Winds.'

'Max, I need a drink.' Ailsa took his arm and they found a reasonably quiet corner. She told him what had happened with Hunter, and he just shook his head. A young guy brought a tray with two drinks, and they sat together, watching the people go by, talking about Hunter, the Colonel, and Sir Pierce and Florence.

Across the room a woman appeared on her own, carrying a champagne flute. She was looking around for someone, her thin figure turning in a green dress, seeking someone out. Her eyes fixed on Max, then moved to Ailsa, then back to Max again. She gave a sultry smile, and held her glass aloft in a salute.

It was Angie.

'What's she doing here?' Ailsa felt that she didn't have any energy left for more drama this evening.

'Nothing to do with me, Ailsa.' Max was swift and strident in his reply. The last thing he wanted to do was send mixed messages to Ailsa. 'Dad invites everyone from around here, it is tradition. Anyway, I think you'll find Angie is already taken.'

'Really? Anyone I know?'

'You remember our earlier conversation?'

'Which conversation would that be?'

'The one about Andy.'

Dougie handed the microphone to the Colonel with a smile, then remembering suddenly about his notoriously loud voice, took it back with a word in the Colonel's ear.

The Colonel stepped onto the small dais and began to speak.

'Ladies and Gentlemen, I wanted you all to join in a little celebration. Two of our very good friends, Calum, from our family law firm, and his beautiful partner Connie, will be married in a few days, and I thought we could give a little pre-wedding toast to them.' There was a cheer, and a distant 'pop!' The Colonel beamed. 'That'll be the champagne!' Which was duly brought in and poured.

Everyone started to cheer and celebrate. The main door to the ballroom opened, a woman ran in on legs seeming to go in different directions, screaming at the top of her lungs. People screamed when they saw her. They clutched each other, they gasped, then the room suddenly drowned in silence. She was covered in blood.

The woman came up to the Colonel, her screams ripping through the room.

'What the hell?'

'What's happening?'

'What's she doing, for God's sake?' and sundry other exclamations abounded.

It was Miss Black, the nanny.

'You need to call the police!' she shouted in consternation. 'She's dead! She's dead!'

Carys had moved forward as if in a dream. 'Amalie...?'

'She's dead, and he's gone. He's *gone*!'

'Amalie...?' Carys shouted.

It was then that the Colonel noticed the blood covering her navy dress, and all over her hands.

'Who's dead? Who's gone?' he shouted desperately. 'Max! Max, come here!'

Max, Noel and Ailsa all ran over.

'Freddy! Freddy's gone, and Laura is dead!'

Chapter Eighteen

Fredrico Alberto Mason MacKenzie had been kidnapped. He was taken from his nursery. When Ian McFarlane, the only police officer in Arnasaid, arrived, everyone except the family and their partners and friends had left. The shock waves slowly reverberated throughout Trannoch, Storm Winds and the communities of Arnasaid, Arnasaig Bheag and Dunlivietor.

When Ian arrived he took a statement from Miss Black. It transpired that Laura, Amalie's nanny, had been out for the evening, and Miss Black was watching both babies. Her own rooms opened off the nursery, where she was watching TV with the door slightly ajar. She said she heard a noise and went through to see two men standing in the darkened room; a woman lifting the sleeping Freddy from his cot. She had screamed, and one of the men produced a gun. Freddy and Amalie both woke, crying. She reported that they had shouted at her to *shut up*, and *move away from the cot, then the baby won't get hurt*, which she had done, shaking from head to foot. As the three began to back off towards the door, it opened behind them, and Laura, coming home from her night out bumped into them in the darkness. Then she too had begun to scream. She flung herself at Freddy trying to wrestle him from his captor's hands when one of the men punched her, chiefly to silence her. She staggered unseeingly and the man with the gun fired at her on the way down. She crumpled to the ground, her face hitting the floor. The woman put her hand over little Freddy's mouth and they swiftly left. Miss Black switched on the light and ran across to Laura turning her over, but the beige carpet was spewing with blood moving like lava from a volcano. Laura's eyes were lifeless.

He had put a bullet through her back and into her heart.

By the time Miss Black gathered herself together and got her arthritic knees down the staircase, they had escaped out one of the back doors, the noise of their departure deadened by the music and revelling from the Ball.

A specialist Major Incident Team (MIT) were on their way. Ian had also managed to get a very sketchy description of the three suspects, though Nanny Black was so upset that she wasn't able to give very much. It had been pitch black, she had insisted in a wailing voice. Ailsa and Stephen couldn't corroborate the fact that this fitted with the description of the people who had rented the Dower House. Even the men who had forced Ailsa off the road couldn't be verified as the same people. Ailsa asked if Nanny Black heard an accent as the three from the Dower House had been Italian, but, apart from being 'foreign sounding', she didn't know.

Ian had no experience of a kidnapping case, but he knew enough that an incident room would need to be set up at Trannoch. There were certainly plenty of rooms to choose from. He phoned his assistant at the police house to bring down some equipment they may need. The suspects might make contact soon, and he wanted his colleagues to be ready.

Olivia was inconsolable. Alberto, her father, had been called. The Ghillies' Ball was not his thing, but he needed to be with his daughter now. Ailsa tried to help her, but she threw back her head and howled. It was a piercing, feral sound like an animal caught in a trap. It resonated through the library, eerie and sinister. Malcolm had lifted her slight figure up the stairs to bed, followed by Max, who sedated her by jabbing her as she thrashed about the bed, half-screaming and half-crying. It was Malcolm who pleaded with his brother, 'Give her something,' and Olivia herself didn't even know where she was, far less that she had been given a sedative. Alberto stayed with her, while Malcolm went with the Colonel to the ballroom.

Carys wasn't much better, she whimpered as she cradled her own sleeping Amalie; who had been brought downstairs.

No one was allowed in the nursery now, as it was a crime scene.

The Colonel was almost as bad as his Italian daughter-in-law. His face seemed to have collapsed in pain, and his shoulders slumped forward in defeat. There were not many situations the Colonel couldn't control, but this was one of them.

Malcolm was distraught. He had sat with his arm around Olivia as though they were a happily married couple, but had said nothing as she rocked back and forth, tearing at her hair. She was silent now; the medicine had begun to work. Thomas and Noel were equally shocked and upset, though no one could fathom why the eldest brother should be so. No one knew that he was thinking that it could as easily have been Amalie who had been taken. Through the crisis, Noel suddenly found he possessed a modicum of parental feelings for his secret child. Max was the only brother who held it together, and Ailsa, watching him taking charge of the situation, helping the others, and rousing the staff to provide hot drinks, felt a wave of love wash over her. Surrounded by grief and despair, in the midst of tragedy, she couldn't help thinking how lucky she was to have Max.

With surprising practicality and focus, Hunter assisted the family by handing out drinks and trying to be useful. Ailsa thought fleetingly that her apparent sadness lent more to a claw-back of her own pitiful situation than anything else.

Florence announced that she and Pierce would stay at Trannoch until. 'Things get back to normal,' as she put it, as if they ever could. Ian advised that everyone should stay anyway; it was after eleven o'clock, and the police teams were on their way. No one argued with these arrangements, least of all Hunter, as she scurried about getting the staff to make up fresh beds as far away from the nursery as possible.

No one slept very much. The Colonel never moved from his position in his armchair by the fire, where he fitfully dozed. Max went up to bed then came back down a few hours later. Ian MacFarlane paced the library floor, speaking to the teams en route, giving as many facts as he could. The adrenalin was rushing through his veins like water escaping from a cracked dam. He had never worked on a case as serious as this one. He had done a stint in Fort William where the most serious crimes he had faced was a small drugs haul from a boat, for some fishermen's personal use, and a few car thefts from a group of teenagers known to the police for their other petty crimes. He had then returned to his roots in Arnasaid Bheag. But this was something else. He was worried that he didn't have the experience or aptitude to step up to the plate, and he hoped he would be good enough in the Boss's eyes to be included in some small way with the investigation on his doorstep.

At around one thirty in the morning, a snake-like fleet of cars and vans drew up at the front door of Trannoch, the professional looking men and women spilling onto the gravel. Ian MacFarlane took a deep breath and opened the front door.

He was a tall fair man of around fifty five, with a navy trench coat over an impeccable suit, pristine white shirt and neat tie. He had a handsome, but unsymmetrical face, with hooded blue eyes, and a narrow nose which was slightly off-centre, and looked as if it had been broken with a punch and never re-set. His hair was thick and cropped around the neck and sides, and was swept back from his brow, which was strangely without lines. He came forward to his subordinate with a smile which looked like it often slept.

He took in Ian's nervous appearance with an intelligent swoop of his bright eyes. 'Sergeant MacFarlane?'

'Yes, Sir. Would you please come in? I have tried to set up a room for you.' Ian's eager, respectful tone put Detective Superintendent Robbie Burnside in a better mood. The line of cops followed them in through the hall and to the library. There was a long table in the centre which had been set up, flip-charts had been strategically placed, and best of all, a table held fresh coffee, soft drinks and sandwiches which had just been brought in by the Trannoch night shift staff. None of the necessary equipment was present – this had been brought by the team and would be taken from a van and set up.

The Colonel and Max were the only family members now present. They both came forward to meet the influx of police, the Colonel with a bewildered expression.

'Sir, I am Detective Superintendent Robbie Burnside, and I am the Senior Investigating Officer in charge of this case. I won't introduce all my team tonight, but these two are Detective Inspector Julie Cooper and Detective Sergeant Alec Smith.'

'I am Colonel Mason MacKenzie, and this is my son, Maxwell. We both live here at Trannoch. My son Malcolm and my daughter-in-law Olivia MacKenzie have gone to try and get some sleep. They are the parents of the baby who was...who has...'

Max, seeing his father struggling with the words stepped in. 'I gave Olivia a sedative. She is distraught, as you can imagine. She's the baby's mother. I'm a doctor.'

The Superintendent knew who everyone was by this time – they had briefed him on the way up in the car. He smiled gratefully.

'Thank you, Sir. Now, may I suggest you both try and get some sleep while we unload all our equipment and settle down here? I presume you are happy for us to use this room for our work? Good. Is there a hotel or two in the area we can use? As you can see, we're a large team.'

'There a few B&Bs and a small hotel in the area, but we have set up rooms in an unused wing of the house, which have been made up and are ready. Ian advised how many roughly, there would be, and we have lots of space, so please make yourself at home.' Again, it was Max who took charge.

'Thank you, Sir. Is the wing away from the murder scene, the nursery?'

'Yes, it is completely separate from the main house. The suites where the family sleep are all in the main house on the first floor, but quite far away from the nursery, except Olivia and Malcolm's rooms. They have been moved to other bedrooms. The extended family members who will now stay with us have been put in the North Wing, where we house all our guests.

'Thank you.' Robbie turned to his team.

'PC MacFarlane, you will work with DI Cooper and DS Smith. Your knowledge of the area will be invaluable to us.' He spoke to Ian swiftly and crisply.

Ian bristled with pride. 'Thank you, Sir.'

Julie pulled him away to the side. 'Ian, you can use yer fantastic knowledge of the area now an' show me where the nearest bog is.' Her Glasgow accent was thick, with hard edges, nothing like the soft highland accent in which he spoke. She grinned. He grinned back.

'Well, there are lots to choose from...'

They had got in some supplies for the baby. He was now probably just over six months, they guessed, and they had previously bought baby food, nappies, and changes of clothes. The woman had children of her own who were now grown-up, so she understood what was required. Her children had found out what their mother was really like, and moved away, but she knew how to deal with babies, and Freddy was a wonderful baby. The place they were in was damp and cold, but she dressed him accordingly. They needed him well and alive in order to get a good price for him.

Ailsa and Max entered the breakfast room at around ten thirty the next morning. Noel, Hunter, Florence and Pierce were there, the others having either come and gone, or had not yet surfaced.

'Melody called me this morning. She's on her way home,' Max said, as he picked at his bacon.

'Well, that's good, Max.' Ailsa knew how fond Max was of his niece.

'I can't believe this is happening to us!' Hunter whined, as she spooned her porridge.

'Us?...Us?' Florence pulled her eyebrows together in a condescending frown. 'You include yourself in our family, despite what you've done?' her voice rose in annoyance. Pierce patted her arm comfortingly.

'Florence, just ignore her, our focus is obviously on the baby and poor Olivia and Malcolm,' Pierce said gently.

Hunter was put out. 'I went out of my way to help this family last night. I am as upset as anyone!'

Ailsa smiled grimly at the falseness. 'You did, Hunter. You helped the staff prepare for the visitors, and we are grateful.' She was genuinely trying to praise Hunter, and not get pulled into anything.

'We are grateful? *We* are grateful? Well, Ailsa, that is very generous of you to say so, but may I remind you, I have been accustomed to being at Trannoch long before you were even born,' Hunter spat.

Ailsa looked at her with a mixture of pity and anger, suddenly losing it. 'The difference is I was invited here, as a friend, while you crept up the back stairs...'

'Just shut up, all of you!' The strangled voice came from across the table where Noel was wrestling with his feelings.

Max looked at him in undisguised amazement. 'You okay, Noel?'

'Of course I'm not okay. My nephew has just been kidnapped and all that odious woman can think about is the part she played last night. It's bloody disgusting.' He put his head in his hands, then rubbed his eyes.

'Mel is on her way home, Noel,' Max said quietly. Noel nodded, then got up slowly and left the room. Max looked after him in wonder. His eldest brother was always the calm one in a predicament, but he was quite obviously struggling with this particular crisis.

While the family had been trying to sleep, the police teams had been hard at work. Forensics had been sent in a helicopter to Loch Morar, to secure the scene around the car. A mobile van had been set up in both Arnasaid and Arnasaid Bheag to encourage people to drop in with any information they may have on the trio. CCTV had been collected to be examined from the only two small supermarkets, there were no other cameras. No need to have this type of security in an area which enjoyed less than a one per cent crime rate. The uncomplicated nature of the surveillance meant that the team would get some kind of results sooner rather than later.

On day 2 (as the police called the next morning), when daylight broke, the real police work began. Helicopters dropped the team on the shores of Loch Morar to take their samples from the actual car at the bottom of the cliff, and the immediate area at the top of the cliff, where the perpetrators had jammed the accelerator of the car and jumped out. Joanne Cummings, the Crime Scene Manager, very quickly discovered that these were not terrorists or even very sophisticated criminals, in fact they seemed to be acting irrationally and without a plan. They would get them soon.

The incident room, formerly the library, was now off limits to the family. The Colonel objected strongly to this. He wanted to be in the thick of things in case any news or calls came through, but Robbie Burnside gently informed him that they had to be allowed to do their jobs for the benefit of the family, and that he would arrange to sit down with the Colonel and his sons each day and explain where they had got to in the investigation.

That morning the library was buzzing with activity. The four MacKenzies sat down in unison, the exhaustion seeping from their bones seeming to dampen the air which was frazzled with excitement and anticipation. The police slept in rotas, just in case the suspects called them at an unorthodox time. Robbie, Julie and Alec, as the top team, were up front. The room was full of scattered police, and the four MacKenzies eyed them expectantly.

'Okay, so before we get ready for the contact, we need to discuss our media strategy. I will shortly be speaking to the press at Trannoch gates this morning to issue a statement, as you all know. Now, Julie and Alec, take it from here, please.'

Julie stepped forward almost before Robbie stopped speaking. 'Colonel, we are looking at a media strategy, and we would advise involvement from the family, an appeal to the public...' the Colonel jumped to his feet.

'TV? I will not have our family paraded on the screen like a mini circus!' His face was rapidly reddening.

'Dad, just listen to what they have to say before we decide,' Max interjected, putting a hand on his father's arm to get him to sit back down. Noel nodded in agreement with Max.

'I know it is difficult, but we should gather lots of evidence from the crime scenes, and are in a good place with the investigation...' Julie was interrupted again by the Colonel.

'Young lady,' he began patronisingly, 'I don't see that you have moved forward at all! What good will a conference do, other than provide early evening entertainment for the masses?'

'Sir, these strategies work hand in hand with the leg-work we have carried out already, and have been extremely successful in the past. The public respond to a plea from the families, and it might just jog someone's memory to a sighting or a nugget of information which would help us.' Alec was out of breath, but satisfied to see an approving nod from Robbie.

'Exactly,' the Superintendent agreed. 'We need your help to do this right, Colonel. As the head of this family, and thinking about your role in these communities in the North West, we need you to talk to the people.' He was at his most diplomatic.

'*I'll* do it.' All eyes moved to Malcolm. 'I understand where father is coming from, but Freddy is my son, and I will speak out for him.'

'Great, thank you, Sir.' Julie was forceful, silently competing. 'We don't want the whole family there, but if you and the Colonel...?'

'Very well, very well,' The Colonel said, grudgingly, 'I shall attend if it helps Freddy.' Max patted his father encouragingly on the back.

Julie was swift to answer. 'Brilliant, thank you both.' She turned to Robbie, 'Shall we move forward to our own briefing discussion?'

'Absolutely. Thank you, Sir.' Robbie dismissed the MacKenzies with a nod.

The chairs had been set out in rows in the ballroom. A long table had been positioned at the top, dressed in white cloths and with mics pointing towards the five chairs. Police boards with 'Grampian Police' had been set behind like a backdrop for a stage play, and the reporters and camera crews were all in place.

The shutters on the cameras sounded like an audience clapping the entrance of actors in a show, as the Colonel and Malcolm filed in with Det. Supt. Burnside, DI Cooper and DS Smith.

The baby was playing his own part famously. The woman smiled down at him. He was so beautiful, with his huge black Italian eyes, his gorgeous smile, and his innocently trusting arms around her neck. It almost made her give up the ghost.

But he cried at night. He missed his mother, and he knew he was in a different environment. He sensed it. He smelled the dampness and he knew he was in a different place. So, he cried. His arms flew out for Olivia, but she wasn't there.

Robbie was having a briefing with his team. They were scattered around the library, facing the wall of books over which had been hung a set of white boards, with various photos and pieces of information written in different handwriting, depending on who had recorded it.

'Julie?'

She jumped to her feet, springing into action. 'The two scenes have been secured. Forensics have been at the Morar site since we came up last night, and we're expecting a report in the next few hours. The cliffside there is practically useless to climb down, unless you are a proper climber, it's almost sheer down to the rocks. The guys are abseiling down, under the instruction of the mountain rescue team, to collect their samples.'

Robbie nodded. 'Okay, what about here? The nursery and the back utility rooms, boot rooms etc., and vegetable garden where the previous assault took place?'

'All secured too, Sir. Reports due in an hour.'

'Good. And everything set up for a call coming in to any of the MacKenzie's phones, or the landline here?'

'Yes, we've got the phones on the table over by the window, and the family are all on standby in the dining room and one of the larger sitting rooms, to get here quickly when the call comes through.'

'DS Smith?' Robbie sat on the end of the antique library table, and looked questioningly at Alec.

'We've set up two portable incident caravans, in the car park in Arnasaid, and the harbour in Arnasaid Bheag. We're hoping we can get the locals to come in and have a chat and see if they have heard of, or seen, any of the three suspects.'

'Thanks. What about the press?'

Julie piped up, 'They're congregating at the gates down the drive. The Colonel has his estate managers patrolling the estate grounds, which are huge, and we have uniforms guarding too, both here, and up at Storm Winds, the other estate house. Only two guys there, as the staff have been moved over here to Trannoch.' She was not letting Alec get too much airtime. There was a love-hate relationship between the two. Both were young, ambitious, and very competitive.

'Okay, thanks. Julie?' Robbie said again as he motioned her over to the boards.

Julie was very business-like. Her short dark hair was sleek, her eyes bright, even after virtually no sleep, and her slim, tall figure in black trousers and white shirt moved up to the boards to explain where they had got to. 'We are looking for three people: two men and a woman. From the descriptions we have of them from Storm Winds' staff, they are probably between thirty five and fifty. They stayed at the Dower House at Storm Winds, on a self-catering basis for a few weeks. It's a holiday let. They were seen around the town, in the general store, and in and around the harbour area. Gennina, who works in the estate office says that they had non-British accents but couldn't be more specific. All three are white – characteristic descriptions here,' she pointed to narrative on the boards. Miss Black, the other nanny, couldn't corroborate these descriptions. She said it was too dark in the nursery, when the incident took place, although she described their accent as "foreign".'

'Everything all set up for a call?' Robbie had asked this question at least three times in the last few hours, but no one picked him up on it, no one who valued their skin, that is.

'Yes, Sir, all okay,' a few of them chanted in unison.

'Okay, great. Now, someone get me a sandwich.'

Chapter Nineteen

'Move! Move! Move! Call coming in, get the family!' Julie practically screamed out the code words, as she got the signal from the guys manning the phones.

Things began to happen very quickly as the carefully rehearsed scene came to life.

'Who the hell do you think you are talking to? Do you know who I am?' It was the Colonel of course, talking to the kidnappers on the line. 'Six million? You must be stark raving mad!'

They had already prepped him about how to communicate with the perpetrators, but it hadn't seemed to sink in with the Colonel.

'Six million!' one of the cops said in a low voice to his mate. 'There's no way that's ever going to happen!' Alec had heard, and responded.

'For your information, that would be a pebble on the beach to the MacKenzies. Now shut up or I take it to the Boss. Understand?'

One of the cops was the same grade as Alec, but he knew they had stepped out of line. They resented his intrusion, but merely nodded, with an eye on Robbie, hoping no one else had heard.

Julie put her hand on the Colonel's arm as a calming gesture, holding up notes of instruction to him to remind him what they had agreed.

'Okay, bring the baby back to Trannoch, and I'll give you the money.' The Colonel's voice lowered several decibels, as the silent room heard a cackle of laughter faintly emanate from the phone. This wasn't the tactic Robbie had advised, but he had reckoned without the Colonel, his position and status in the North West, and his never-ending desire to get exactly what he wanted. Julie gesticulated to the Colonel

229

with a 'rolling' gesture, meaning, as the Colonel very well knew, to try and keep them talking in order for the trace to be successful. Her next note she put in front of the Colonel's nose said, 'Ask for PROOF OF LIFE.'

But the Colonel was agitated and was listening to the kidnappers. He suddenly said, 'Tomorrow? I'll not bloody well wait until tomorrow! Wait a minute, wait...' he ended desperately, as the line went dead, and he collapsed in defeat onto the chair.

Robbie looked at the team, frantically trying to get a trace, then he gave a sigh and shook his head in anger.

They had been so close.

The mist, damp and cloying, moved in from the sea, deadening all sound and obscuring everything in sight. The deer crept down the mountain slopes, using the screen to pick their way through the vegetation of the vast estate of Trannoch. The crunch of gravel underfoot alerted the deer, and they swiftly and gracefully danced back to the mountainside under cover of the trees. The police were doing their bit to guard the massive estate, as they patrolled round the perimeter.

'Get me a drink, Malcolm,' the Colonel ordered, as his six-foot-three frame sank deeper into the chair. The drinks were poured, and the three MacKenzies lifted their glasses to their lips. The sound of a robotic voice pervaded the air, followed by the Colonel's strident tones, as the conversation was played-back.

'We can put this through the software, Boss, and the voice will be clearer,' One of the cops said to Robbie, who was pacing again.

'Okay, well, do it.'

Olivia awoke the next morning to a fresh hell. She had slept a black sleep of nothingness through the night, due to the sedative. But, the next day, lying in bed, a wave engulfed her, bringing her to her senses, and new shocks pierced every part of her. She screamed out in uncontrolled agony.

Malcolm had slept in the adjoining dressing room, with the door opened so that he could be there when she woke. He ran through and lifted her into a sitting position, putting arms around her. His face contorted in sadness as she screamed into his neck.

There was a flurry of activity in Arnasaid. TV cameras were to be seen on the main road, cars rolling by with cameras stuck out of windows, and several people visiting the mobile incident room parked at the harbour. Reporters were stopping people in the street asking what they made of the kidnapping, and tourists wandered around looking bewildered about the recent developments.

Gennina was in the main grocery shop, a mini-mart which sold just about everything imaginable. She was living at home with her parents, mainly because she didn't want to be part of the unfolding drama at Trannoch. She had told them all she knew, and she just wanted to stay out of it.

As she turned in the small aisle she bumped into a man. He dropped what he was holding, and she hastened to apologise. He stooped to pick it up, and hurriedly made his way to the counter. The girl behind the counter was the shop owner's daughter, who worked there, part time, after school. She was making small talk with the man. Gennina came up behind him, she was the only other person in the shop. The man paid, and swung round to face her. He was tall and dark, with a beard that hid half his face. But it was his eyes. They drew her in and mocked her in one glance. She knew those eyes, she had seen them several times before, but it didn't hit her until she realised what he had dropped, and was now buying.

Baby milk.

Robbie was in a stew. 'What the hell?!' he shouted to no one in particular. In all the years Julie had known him, she had never seen him lose his temper. There was a line of uniformed police in a row in front of him. 'What were you doing out there, other than sitting on your arses? A stranger goes into the shop in Arnasaid and buys BABY MILK for God's sake, and you lot are what, sitting on the beach enjoying the scenery?'

'Sir, we were in the van, interviewing the locals.'

'Great.' The sarcasm was dripping from his tongue. 'So, while you were having cosy wee chats with villagers and tourists, one of the suspects dons a beard – brilliant disguise! – and walks into the shop in full daylight to buy milk for the kidnapped baby. Fantastic!' The four men and three women looked as if they wished they were anywhere but here as they listened to the tirade. 'Now get out there, and try and do some real police work for a change. Find the bastard. He can't have got far. Simmonds, have you interviewed the girl in the shop?'

'Yes, Sir,' Simmonds said nervously, shifting from one boot to another. His fair hair and bright blue eyes made him look ten years younger than his twenty five years.

'*And*?' Robbie was getting seriously nettled.

'And...and...she's a grade A student at Dunlivietor High, majoring in languages,' he read, word for word from his notebook.

Robbie squashed him with a look of steel. 'I don't bloody want to know about her. I want to know about the man, you idiot!'

'No...I know, but...it was that, which helped.'

Robbie looked as if he would like to swat him like a fly. 'Helped?'

'Yes, helped. Her, the girl in the shop, her study of languages...to recognise the accent...he's Italian.'

Max handed Ailsa a coffee. She looked worn-out, as did the rest of them. They were in a corner of the sitting room. Max hadn't been at work for two days, although it seemed like a lifetime. Cocky was in the vast kitchens with Jean Morton and the Trannoch staff, helping to keep meals and drinks supplied to the family and police.

'Olivia is in a bad way,' Ailsa said, sipping her coffee.

Max glanced at her. 'Yes. But I think she is a bit better than last night. I slipped up to give her another sedative and she threw a lamp at me.'

'That's *better*? God! Did it hit you? Was Malcolm still there?'

He managed a weak smile. 'It did, on the back of my head, and he was. I'm glad she fought back. Even if she did nearly knock me out.'

'I could almost say Malcolm is turning over a new leaf!'

Max hesitated, 'Yes, strange the way tragedies like this bring people together. I think he is really gutted at what has happened.'

'Well, yes, who wouldn't be? I mean kidnapping a baby isn't an everyday occurrence.'

'I don't mean that, although of course they are distraught about that. I meant...'

Ailsa studied his intelligent face. 'Yes, I see. I think you're right. Malcolm has been trying to make amends since Olivia came to Trannoch.'

'At least now she's letting him in, a bit, and I'm glad he's there for her.'

Ailsa changed the subject. 'What are they saying? The cops, I mean?'

'Well, they are looking at the CCTV in the shop, although the disc needed changing and they don't know if there's enough left to have captured him. But Gennina was able to describe him to a tee.'

'I can't believe the guy's brass neck, just to walk into the shop and buy milk in plain daylight.'

Max grinned. 'Did you just say, "brass neck"?'

'Yes.'

'Don't ever say that again.'

'That's my line.'

'I know, but it works just as well for me,' he winked.

She suddenly felt a rush of emotion, as she looked at his face smiling at her. 'I couldn't resist lowering myself to use the vernacular...' she smiled back.

Carys slowly sipped her tea. 'Thankfully, it wasn't Amalie.'

'Shut up. Why do you have to be such a bitch, Carys?' Noel folded up his newspaper and threw it down on the breakfast table. They were the last two to leave, Miss Black having just left with Amalie in her arms to take her back to the little sitting room next to the one occupied by the rest of the family. Here she was looked after and played with by nanny; Carys going between the two rooms. Miss Black took the baby out for fresh air round the walled garden in her pram, with a police escort.

'I'm only stating a fact. I saw it in your face, Noel.'

'What? What on earth are you talking about?'

'I saw it in your face when you saw that she was safe, and that it was Freddy who was taken. You were relieved, happy even.'

'That has nothing to do with anything.'

'Maybe, but knowing you are her father and you can't, and never will have a relationship with her, must eat into you,' she said snidely, putting down her own napkin, and standing up. 'It's up to you whether you want to own up and be a father to her. Thomas never will.'

'Thomas loves her,' Noel almost shouted.

'Really? Well, maybe he wouldn't love her quite so much if he knew big brother was the daddy and not him.'

'Shut your stupid mouth. Someone might hear. Are you threatening me?' He rose and stood in front of her. She tilted her chin upwards in defiance. 'At this time, of all times, when we are going through all of this?' he snarled and swept his hand outwards.

'You know what I want. I don't care if it's not the right time, I want a further share of the business. I want to be a full partner with fifty per cent of the shares.'

He walked right up to her until his face was almost touching hers. 'I'll tell Thomas myself first.'

As he left the room, the person who had been listening at the door stole away into the cloakroom opposite, out of sight.

The short afternoon slipped into darkness. The sky was streaked with black and blue as night rushed in to follow day. There was a tension in the incident room which was like an electric charge – fizzing in the air. There was a feeling that events were moving quickly, with several updates from Robbie. They had gathered DNA and lots of other clues from the cliff side where the car had gone over, and also some valuable evidence from inside the car, which they didn't disclose. They had established that at least one of the three was Italian, and the upside was, they didn't seem to be particularly intelligent criminals, hence the rather bungled attempt to buy baby food, and the apparent lack of planning. All of this information gave them hope, balanced out with an overriding feeling that things weren't going to end well. Day two was drawing to a close, but it felt like a lifetime had passed since the Ghillies' Ball.

The MacKenzies continued their routine, and afternoon tea was brought into the sitting room. Miss Cochrane helped to serve out the tea, although the cakes were untouched. Stephen Millburn joined them, he had been out on the estate, and now came in with a grim expression and sat beside Clem.

The Colonel ordered a large whisky, and this was everyone's cue to have something a little stronger. Ailsa and Max had the obligatory red wine. The fire had been made up and it hissed ominously in the grate, throwing a threatening light into the dismal room. The door opened again and Det. Supt. Burnside came in. Everyone looked at him expectantly, and the Colonel jumped to his feet.

'Colonel, Mr MacKenzie, Dr MacKenzie, could you please come through now?'

'Has there been...' the Colonel barked, as if it was all the Superintendent's fault. He cut him short.

'No, Sir, there has been nothing, but they said they would ring in the evening, and it is 5.30 p.m. now. We want to talk about the format of the discussion again.' Robbie's brows rushed together, meeting in a deep furrow, which split his forehead in two.

Noel sprang up. 'I'd like to be present too, I am the eldest brother, and I want to be there to support father.' This was accompanied by a loud sneering laugh from Carys at the other end of the room.

'Of course, Sir.' Robbie strode forward through the doorway, and it felt to Max at least, that they were being led to the gallows.

Thomas, who had been sitting quietly for hours on a window seat, looked at his wife in consternation. 'Carys, I am surprised at your reaction!' He never quite seemed to choose the right words.

She turned and looked at him coldly. 'Really?' her voice was septic. 'He wasn't there last night, why is he bothering to go now? It's not as if he can do anything. I'm not sure why Maxwell has been asked through either. The baby is nothing to him.'

Ailsa had moved to sit beside Clem, Stephen and Melody, who had been by her father Noel's side since she returned from Uni. Ailsa looked shocked what she heard from Carys. Hunter had kept mostly silent for the last few days, realising if she was to be accepted by the family again, she would need to keep her nose clean. She sat alone, nursing a drink, slyly taking in the proceedings.

Florence unexpectedly cut in, before Ailsa had a chance to respond. 'You are quite the little witch, aren't you?' Her cutting voice was laced with undisguised scorn and disgust. 'I am sure *Lady Ailsa* would tell you that Maxwell was asked to attend as firstly, he was there in the beginning when Nanny Black came rushing into the Ball, and secondly, the Colonel asked him.'

'Really? Well, that explains it then,' Carys retorted sarcastically. 'Anyway, I don't know what it is to do with you, Florence.'

'Miss MacKenzie, if you please!' She drew herself up to her full height as Pierce came forward and put a steadying hand on her shoulder. 'I don't have to explain myself to the likes of you. Thomas!' she raised her voice to her nephew, who got up and moved over to the little group. 'You really need to ask yourself why this woman is still at Trannoch. If you were half the man the Colonel or your brothers are, you would have chucked her out years ago.'

Thomas looked stricken at this, and opened his mouth to answer, but his Aunt was there before him. 'I know what you're up to, you...little...schemer.' Florence's last three words were accompanied by three pokes in Carys' chest. 'Thomas, what she needs is a good slap on that false face of hers. I know what you are plotting, and you will never get away with it. Don't ever underestimate a MacKenzie – don't *ever* underestimate *me*.' And Florence Jane MacKenzie took Pierce's arm and turned away in triumph. 'Pierce, a little wine, if you please!'

Carys watched her in undisguised horror. All sorts of things snowballed through her mind as she took in this last speech. 'What did she know? Was this about her and Noel? How did she know...?' but as no one heard her thoughts or could answer her questions, she sat lamely down on the window seat, allowing Thomas to bring her a drink.

Ailsa and Clem eyed each other surreptitiously with a, *what the hell was that*? expression, as the room again trickled into silence.

Freddy had developed a cough. He was up half the night, and the woman was irritable and cross as she had to be up half the night too. He was fretting and wrestling with the woman almost as if he was trying to tell her he wanted to go home. She was getting impatient with him. She couldn't stand this much longer. She told the two men they had to arrange a time and place now to drop the baby, and pick up the money. They had already decided on a place, and they would tell the family tonight.

Olivia came down the stairs. She knew another call was coming in this evening, and she meant to be there. Freddy was her baby, her flesh and blood, and no one would keep her away from the incident room tonight. Yesterday, she was so wracked with grief she could do nothing; today, anger had taken over, and she meant to get her baby back.

At six o'clock the call came through. 'Move! Move! Move!' the Sergeant with the earphones busily began the equipment start-up process to begin recording and attempting to trace the call. The room shifted into place. Olivia, who had come in and was sitting beside Malcolm, began to shake. He put his arm around her. She looked bedraggled and ill. Her hair hung limply, and her face was devoid of make-up. She had gone from superstar to victim in a world where she knew nothing but pain. 'There but for the grace of God go I.' Was on the lips of more than one of the people in the room.

'Yes, this is Colonel MacKenzie, as you very well know, since you asked for me, and I spoke to you yesterday.' The top team groaned as one. Julie thought, 'You can lead a horse to water...'

The robotic voice disguising sounds of the perpetrator came over the line, filling the library. 'We meet tomorrow.'

'Wait a minute!' The Colonel tried to talk slowly and deliberately as he had been instructed. 'I want to see my grandson. I am not meeting anyone until I know that you have Freddy in your possession.' Alec nodded encouragingly.

'No cameras on our phones,' the voice came again.

'Then I am not handing over *any* money, far less six million pounds.'

'Wait, wait!' It was almost a scream, and Olivia jumped to her feet. 'Let me talk to my baby, I no have to see Freddy to know he my baby!' Robbie hesitated, then nodded, and she took the microphone from the Colonel, who gave it up without a word.

'This is Olivia, the baby's mother,' she said, and there was a long pause before they answered, almost as if they were taken aback.

'So? What you want?'

'I want to hear my baby. I know my baby. Put the phone to his ear. I will talk,' she said, in a strong, controlled, voice.

'Okay.'

'Hello, darling!' The tears streamed down Olivia's face, but she kept her voice steady. 'How is my little Freddy? How are you, *caro bambino*?'

'Ooaah! Ooaah!' the sound bounced off the walls, and was followed by a racking cough. Olivia and Malcolm's faces both drained of colour.

'Freddy!' Olivia suddenly lost it and dropped the mic. Malcolm picked it up and began the negotiations as directed.

'There is a flat field in the place, Dunlivietor.'

'Yes, we know where the flat field in Dunlivietor is,' Malcolm said. It was used for various events like horse trials, was pretty isolated, and with nowhere for the police to hide.

'It has to be only you, and the Colonel. No police, or you do not get your baby back.'

'There will be no police,' Malcolm said flatly.

'Stand in the middle of the field, and sit the bag of money open, so we can see the notes. Seven o'clock tomorrow.' They rang off.

The guy in charge of the equipment stood up with two thumbs in the air. 'Boss, we've got them.'

There was a muted cheer, slapping of backs and shaking of hands, as Olivia hit the floor.

Chapter Twenty

The next day brought freezing fog so thick you could not see the lawns from the windows of Trannoch. The family were advised to stay in the house as security became more of an issue. Previously they had walked around the grounds to get some fresh air. More uniformed officers were drafted in to augment the ones already there. Robbie was concerned about the many ways Trannoch could be accessed: from the mountainside, which was often used by walkers, and the fields which stretched for miles across the land and were delineated only by three feet high drystone dykes.

The family trooped downstairs in the morning for more of the same. It was a torturous waiting game in a fraught, tense atmosphere. Alberto had his arm through Olivia's arm, and Malcolm walked solemnly behind as they entered the breakfast room. Max and Ailsa followed, and then Noel, Carys and Thomas, with Nanny Black carrying Amalie. Connie, Jan, Calum and Gregory had been given permission to leave and fly to London for their wedding.

Florence and Pierce were already at the table, Clem and Stephen had been and gone, and the Colonel was reading his usual broadsheet which had been handed over to the police at the gates with other deliveries. He was shaking salt on his porridge.

'Ye Gods!' The Colonel looked up from his paper. 'This is absolute codswallop! He hit the paper with the back of one hand. 'They've been interviewing the locals and they are coming out with all sorts of drivel!'

'What sort of drivel?' Sir Pierce asked.

'Well, about how friendly these villains were when they met them in the street and said they were here on holiday in Storm Winds' Dower House, and all sorts of stupid, inane things just to get their names in the bloody paper!'

'Dad, forget them, they probably said nothing of the sort.' Max buttered some toast. 'You know what the press can be like.'

'Who cares what they say?' asked Olivia. She had had a shower and put on some make-up and looked forlorn and fragile, but with a glint of inner strength which hadn't been there the day before.

'Quite right, my darling,' Malcolm said quietly, and though everyone present turned surprised eyes upon him, no one spoke. 'My darling' was not something any of them had witnessed Malcolm say before. 'Would you like me to get you something to eat?'

Olivia shook her head.

'Better try something,' Max said. 'Keep your strength up, Olivia.' So, she assented and nibbled on a piece of toast and marmalade.

'What time is the "drop" tonight?' Thomas asked, almost brightly, as if he were referring to a film coming on TV, and not a major incident.

Olivia threw down her toast and sank back in the chair.

'This is not to be discussed at the table!' shouted the Colonel. 'Olivia, I apologise for my youngest's clumsiness.'

'I want to be there,' she said, her eyes straight at the head of the family. 'I go too, and get my baby.'

'Absolutely not! Don't be ridiculous!' If Thomas was clumsy, then he had obviously learned from the master. 'You will stay here and make preparations for his return.' The Colonel's bombastic voice shook them all to attention.

'I go.' Olivia firmly pulled back her chair and stood, her head aloft. 'And no one here, not *one* of you! will stop me.' And she left the room.

'Okay, so we've pinpointed the area as here.' Julie was pointing to the map, with Alec on one side of her and Ian on the other. Robbie was opposite, staring intently.

'Any ideas, Ian?'

'Yes,' Ian couldn't keep the excitement out of his voice. 'It seems to be right on the Black Loch, which is not really a loch but a kind of sea inlet down the coast. It was called this as it's shaded by the high cliff and always looks black. You can't get there, other than by boat.'

'So, it looks about ten, fifteen miles down the coast from here,' Alec said, determined to get his tuppence worth into the discussion.

Robbie got up and paced. 'Do you think it has anywhere there, where they could hide?'

'I'm not sure, but if I could ring my Grandad, he knows every inch of this coastline...' his voice dropped off and he looked embarrassed. It was almost like he was phoning for permission to stay out late...

'Good idea, son. Get on with it!'

'Sir, I have some information,' Ian said five minutes later. 'There is a fisherman's shack there, right on the wee beach. It belonged to an old guy who lived there until he died a few years ago – Long Black Joe, the "black" being a reference to the loch. He used his boat to go up the coast and into the tiny pier at Dunlivietor to go to the mobile bank when it came, and to pick up provisions.'

'Oh aye, and what was the "Long" in reference to?' Alec asked and got a few titters in response.

'He was really tall.'

'Right.'

'Anyway, let's not spend the day talking about how the old guy got his name,' Robbie spoke impatiently. 'Ian, that's good work.' Ian glowed.

A surveillance team was briefed later, and it was decided to put them on a boat to go down the coast to the Black Loch. The guy who took Gennina and her friend up Loch Nevis that fateful day when they found the suspects' car, was going to navigate his own fishing boat, as he too, knew the coastline like other people knew roads. The fog was nothing to him, in fact it would shield them from view. There were other fishing boats who were to be seen frequently, in the area, so they would be as safe as they could be. They would need to wait until the fog lifted, however, or it would be futile in this weather.

Two people stood at the perimeter of Trannoch, one on each side, screened by the fog.

'What they say about tonight?' The one on the outside spoke urgently in a thick Italian voice.

'Look, I don't want to do this anymore,' came the voice from inside the perimeter.

'You no do it? Okay, I kill you.' The shining metal of the gun could be seen through the fog.

'You never said you were going to murder her!' The voice was whining.

'It happened. What about tonight?'

'Malcolm...and...'

'And who, Polizia?'

'No.'

He lifted the gun and brought it up to their eyes. 'Polizia?' he asked again.

'They're going down the coast in a boat.' The panic was palpable.

'When?'

'I think this afternoon, they have to wait for the fog to clear.'

'And tonight?'

'Just Malcolm.' The voice was firm.

James Denbeath was pouring coffee for Miss Cochrane, as the two sat in his sitting room. Of the staff, the two were the most affected by the situation, and Cocky was feeling ill with anxiety and stress.

'Here you go, Charlotte,' he said, stiffly, still struggling with the break in old tradition which meant he called her by her first name.

She smiled. 'Thank you, James.'

'An update, they have arranged a place in Dunlivietor. You know the huge field there? To meet tonight and hand over Freddy.'

'Oh, James, I am so afraid! What if something goes wrong, and one of them is hurt, shot-at even? How did it ever come to this?'

He broke tradition again, and sat beside her on the sofa. 'Charlotte, we have to be brave. The Colonel has been in war zones, this will be nothing to him. Besides, he will not go in the car going right into the field, I believe he and Olivia will be safe in another car on the perimeter.'

'I know, but it's his family who might get hurt, not the enemy! Will he take instruction from that nice Det. Supt. Burnside? You know what the Colonel is like.'

'I've known him all my life, so yes.'

'I just hope and pray he doesn't do anything stupid.'

James put down his coffee cup, and took Cocky's hand. She was startled into silence by the gesture.

'Charlotte, this kind of thing makes one think of one's own mortality,' he said quietly, and Cocky almost smiled at his formality.

'I know.'

'After this...after this is all over...' He cleared his throat. 'I want...I would like, to...er...be with you.'

She was stupefied. They had been friends since youth, but she had never thought they would end up together, and she wanted to be clear. 'In what way, be with me?'

His voice was shaking slightly as he took her hand again. 'I would like to spend what life I have left, with you, Charlotte. I would very much like to marry you.'

The surveillance team rolled down the long drive of Trannoch at around half past three. The fog had cleared slightly, although the local guy assured them that he knew the water like the back of his hand.

'They should have gone earlier! This is a complete waste of time.' The Colonel was pacing the library where he, his sons and Oliva had been summoned, for another update.

'Sorry, Colonel,' Robbie eyed the man who was bellowing in a voice designed to quell the spirits of anyone, least of all a mere Detective Superintendent. 'We couldn't risk sending them out in that thick fog. This is the earliest possible time they could go.'

But the Colonel was not to be pacified. He was extremely distraught with the whole situation, and his own lack of control around proceedings made him feel angry. He thought he could do a better job than the police, and he wasn't slow in voicing his opinion.

'We are now in the third day, and you haven't got them yet! Who is calling the shots, you or the bloody kidnappers? My grandson is in a shack down the coast, why can't you just go and get them, you bloody fool? In my days in the army I led troops...'

But Robbie didn't want to hear how the Colonel led his troops, and swiftly interrupted his flow. 'Okay, everyone but Julie, Alec and the family – OUT!' Robbie ran his fingers around his collar as the cops all dispersed. He was not about to undergo a further dressing-down by Colonel MacKenzie in front of the whole squad.

'Please, sit down, Sir.' Robbie said firmly. 'Let's all talk rationally.'

'Sit down, Dad!' Noel was unusually forceful, as his father angrily took a seat.

'Now, first of all, we are in a reasonably good place with the investigation. We have collected lots of evidence from the crime scenes, have had a sighting in the store, and now know where the suspects are. I admit it may seem that we are not going quickly enough, but if we don't have evidence, we can't convict the criminals when we get them. The fog is the main problem today, and it hampered the surveillance team getting going, but they are on their way now, to do their job.' Robbie was at his most patient, although he felt he could cheerfully strangle this pompous, domineering man, especially since his team was working flat-out to produce a result.

'Why can't you just go in the boat and get them now then?' The Colonel was hardly less vocal than he had been a minute ago.

'Because of the risk. The main reason for our surveillance to be there is to check we have the right people. They'll need to leave the shack with the baby to do the drop.' Your grandson could be shot.' Robbie said finally, as the Colonel started to fume again.

Malcolm jumped up and moved over to the window. His second son was trying to hide his own emotions.

'Let's all just calm down,' Again Julie was trying to make her mark, but this was rubbing salt into the wound.

The Colonel stood and banged his fist on the table. 'Don't you dare tell me to calm down! Who the hell do you think you are talking to? I want her to leave.' He had had a problem with Julie since the first moment he met her. Bad enough that a Detective Superintendent should tell him what to do, far less a slip of a girl like her, he thought.

Robbie looked at his subordinate, whose face had gone red in anger. 'Julie, please leave.' And she left. Alec could not help but give her a tiny smile of 'encouragement' as she went.

'Now, we are going to keep *calm*,' Robbie defiantly emphasised, 'and we are going to talk about how we approach the drop tonight. We have done a recce of the place, and we can have the armed units hidden in the trees in case it becomes nasty.' He knew in his heart of hearts that it probably would, but he played this part down to the family. We have agreed that Mr MacKenzie can go seemingly alone, in the car, although we will have another car just on the roadside with you, Colonel, and Mrs MacKenzie in the back. There will be another two cars in the carpark on the front, hidden amongst the other parked cars, with others from my team in them. The car we will give you is bullet-proof, so you will be safe. Malcolm, you will stop the car and as instructed by the suspects, you will take the money and lay it down. You will pick up the baby and return to the car. I will be in one of the cars on the roadside where we can see what is going on in the field.

'Won't they be suspicious of lots of cars in the car park at that time in the evening in the dark?' Malcolm asked.

'Shouldn't be. There's a restaurant at the front, I'm told people use the car park while they go to eat there. Okay, I think that's it. Is everyone clear?'

'I can't bear it!' Ailsa muttered to Max, as they sat with the rest of the family in the sitting room. It was just after five o'clock, and the Colonel, Malcolm and Olivia were being fitted with bullet-proof vests in the library. Robbie had spoken to the District Commander on the phone, giving him his regular update, and endured another volley of abuse for agreeing to allow three of the family to be involved in such a high-risk incident. The Commander said he was on his way from Headquarters, and Robbie put his head in his hands in frustration. That was all he bloody needed.

There was a deep feeling of excitement and fear which seemed to seep from the ancient wood panelling and permeate around the rooms of Trannoch. Every breath they took was filled with trepidation. The police in the library felt it too, but they were used to this, it was a bread-and-butter detail to the MIT team.

A young cop held open the back door of an unmarked police car, and Olivia got in, the Colonel beside her. Julie was driving, and Robbie was passenger. The family watched from the front sitting room window as Malcolm got in behind the wheel of another car. An armed unit got in the other two cars, and Robbie, Julie and Alec were all armed. Four cars took off down the long drive, with a slight skid on the gravel, which crunched under the tyres. Now that the fog had lifted, they were visible right down to the opulent gates.

'Well, I hope and pray everything goes well,' Florence said, as she and Pierce sat at the fire.

Ailsa sighed. 'As long as Freddy is brought back alive, that's the main thing.'

'And my girl come back alive!' Alberto was pouring himself an enormous whisky. Hunter eyed him distastefully.

'You may wish to leave some for the rest of us!' She said with a disparaging half-smile. But Alberto's English was not sufficiently cultivated to understand the sarcasm beneath this comment.

'Plenty there,' he responded and plunked himself down on a chair by the window.

Carys was sitting filing her nails, distancing herself from the rest. She was probably the least affected with the kidnapping and the drama surrounding the family. When she discovered that her own child, whom she had barely spent any time with, had not been taken, she thanked her lucky stars, and moved on. 'How long do you think it'll take?' She asked no one in particular.

'Are you asking about the rescue of a kidnapped baby, or finishing your manicure?' Florence's tongue was as caustic as Carys'. 'Hate to think we were keeping you from something.'

Carys withered her with a glance, or at least she felt it was suitably withering – Florence remained unconcerned, sipping her whisky, talking quietly to Pierce.

Max got up and poured himself a whisky, and a red wine for Ailsa. He was amazed at how she had coped with the whole situation, especially since she was still going through the effects of PTSD. He hoped she wouldn't crumble when this was all over. Clem and Stephen came in and sat near Ailsa and Max.

'I think we should all just stop sniping at each other,' Max said. 'I can't imagine how terrible it must be for Malcolm and Olivia, to say nothing of Dad.'

'I agree.' Sir Pierce spoke up surprisingly. 'Florence, can you please just remember the family, who are now in the thick of it and stop bitching at each other?'

Florence looked at him, mildly surprised. 'My word, you do have a pair then darling, do you? You are right of course, I shall subside!'

Carys gave a smug smile of satisfaction at her enemy being told off.

'And, that goes for you, too, Carys,' Max said, catching the smile.

'Thomas, are you going to let your brother talk to me like that?'

'Yes, please just shut up for once,' Thomas said, getting up to get himself a drink, as his back was almost bored-through with a look from his wife.

Max had his mobile on a little table in front of him, so that he could be contacted immediately after it was all over. He said a silent prayer to anyone who may be listening that there were no casualties, and Freddy would be brought back safely.

Unfortunately, his prayers would not be answered.

It took them half an hour to drive to Dunlivietor and get into position. The armed unit was positioned in the trees at the nearest point to the middle of the huge flat field, and the car with Olivia and the Colonel was parked between two other parked cars, which Robbie had arranged to be there so they would be less noticeable. The third car was in the car park, facing the sea, with long range cameras placed in the back window facing the field. The fourth car was driven by Malcolm, and sat just further down the road, so that the police could let him know when a car was heading into the field. It was only six o'clock. Right now, it was a waiting game.

It was very dark. The fog had lifted to be replaced by a freezing sleet which turned the field white, glowing in the darkness. One or two cars entered the car park, and people got out, making their way to the restaurant under hoods and brollies, shielding themselves from the harsh weather.

The street was quiet at five minutes to seven, when a dark green car came speeding along and turned sharply through the gap in the trees and onto the field.

'Malcolm,' Julie's voice came through the earpiece. 'Take your time, drive slowly and steadily into the field. Do exactly what we have told you to do.'

'They're here.'

Chapter Twenty One

He could see the car the minute he drove in through the gap in the trees. He felt sick with anxiety, and his brow was beaded with sweat.

'Let us know when you're in,' Julie said in his ear.

'Okay, yes, I'm here.'

'What do you see?'

'There's a man and a woman in the front, and I can just make out a head in the back. I can't see the baby car seat.'

'Okay, wait until they make contact. We'll hear the message come through, and when they hang up, we'll talk. Okay?'

Malcolm didn't answer. He took out the earpiece, and threw it on the passenger seat. He opened his door and got out. He held his hands up high so the kidnappers could see he wasn't armed, and took the holdall from the boot. *He was going to do it his way.*

'Malcolm, wait until instructed!' Julie shouted down the earpiece. 'Malcolm!'

'Malcolm has left the vehicle,' came the voice of the surveillance team contact.

'I bloody know he has,' Julie said angrily. 'He's taken out the earpiece.'

'Armed unit, stay where you are for the minute,' came Robbie's voice.

'Okay, Boss.'

Malcolm held the holdall in one hand, and the other hand aloft, as he walked slowly to the mid-distance between the two cars. They were around 200 yards apart. He didn't need to ask if the baby was in the car now. They had rolled down the driver's window, and he could hear him screaming in the back.

Malcolm, his gut wrenching, put the bag down and opened it. There was a layer of £100 notes on top of plain paper, not visible beneath the money. It was all the Colonel had in his safe at Trannoch – around £5,000. He would need to get Freddy away before they discovered it.

Slowly the doors opened. The driver and passenger got out – the woman and a man.

'What's happening?' Robbie's voice came over the phone.

'Boss, the two suspects in the front have got out.'

Robbie ran his hands through his hair. 'Don't wait for me to ask! I want to know what's going on!'

'Sorry, Sir. The man has opened the back door. Another man is still in the back seat, he's picked up the baby. The baby is alive and screaming in the car seat. He's walking towards Malcolm. He's putting the car seat down. Picking up the holdall...'

'He's picking up the bag?' Julie could just about make out the figures in the field.

'Yes, he's...Sir! He's lifting out some of the money!'

'Okay, armed unit, be ready to deploy on my word!' Robbie swore under his breath.

The armed surveillance guy kept talking, 'Sir he's picked up a bundle of the plain notes. Malcolm needs to get out of there, NOW!'

But Malcolm had other ideas.

'He's moved forward, he's picking up the car seat!'

'Armed unit, stand by!'

'He's turning his back! He's running with the car seat towards the car, suspect has his weapon out!'

'Deploy armed unit! Repeat, deploy!' Robbie shouted, as they started up the car and screeched off the road and on to the field. The armed unit came out of the trees like a swarm of ants, and ran towards the cars.

The man fired at Malcolm, then he and the woman ran to the car, leaving the bag sitting forlornly in the sodden grass.

'Man down, man down!'

It played before their eyes in slow motion. Malcolm was racing back to the car holding the car seat with little Freddy out in front of him to shield him in case they fired. The gun was pointed, then a shot rang out, and Malcolm tripped two or three times, staggered, and fell on top of the car seat.

The baby stopped screaming.

Olivia screamed. She could see a rough outline of figures, and also heard the commentary as it flooded the vehicle. She could see the cops and the Colonel were distracted, and before anyone could see what she was doing she slowly pulled the handle on the back door and jumped out.

She ran towards the field.

'Olivia is out! Running towards the suspects!'

'What the hell?' Robbie's voice had risen several decibels. 'Get her back!'

Julie was already out of the car, with Alec coming out of the other car and running after her. They reached for their weapons.

Olivia was hysterical. 'My baby! Freddy! Bambino, bambino!' She screamed as she ran stumbling towards the scene. She came upon Malcolm lying in a heap over the car seat, and slumped down on her knees, just as another shot rang out, and she collapsed beside him.

'Olivia down! Suspects back in car and driving away!' Julie screamed as the headlights came hurtling towards her. 'Alec! Watch out!' The car flew straight at her partner, and she watched his body hit the windscreen and fall onto the field before it sped away.

'Alec down! Repeat Alec down! Malcolm and Olivia and Alec all down! Suspect's car on the move out the field!' She ran over to her partner and took the pulse in his neck. He was alive. She left him there, she knew they would have already called for an ambulance. She ran back to the car and got in beside Robbie. The Colonel had got out when he saw the suspects' car drive off.

Julie dug her foot into the accelerator.

The armed guys sent a volley of bullets into the car as it sped away, and it skidded, the back window shattering. It bumped out of the field. As it flew around the corner, a man's head could be seen stuck to the window with blood.

'Got one of them at least!' a sergeant reported with satisfaction.

'Get the bastards!' Robbie screamed as the two parked cars chased the suspects down a narrow track away from the town.

'That's a dead end,' Ian MacFarlane's voice sounded, just as the car screamed to a halt at the gate which led directly onto a cliff walk.

The woman sprang out and lifted her gun.

'Put your weapon down!'

A strange smile crossed her face just as the man got out of the car, holding up his hands.

'Weapon, down!'

She slowly lifted the gun and fired three shots before they took her out.

'Why haven't we heard anything? It's nearly eight o'clock! I really can't stand this any longer!' Hunter whined, as the phone on the little table rang.

'Max here.'

'Sir, we have got the baby, and he's alive,' Robbie said.

'Oh, thank God!' Max said in a shaky voice, as he looked round the room at the expectant faces. They all visibly relaxed.

'But both Malcolm and Olivia have been shot. The ambulances are here, and are taking them on to Dunlivietor hospital.'

'Are they...are they alive?' The silence could be felt.

'They are, but Malcolm is in a critical condition.'

'I'll be right over.'

Jim Hutton drove them as they had all had a few drinks. Ailsa, Noel and Alberto went with Max, as they ran out to the car. They sped down the road towards Dunlivietor as fast as the Land Rover would go on the icy roads.

Florence paced the sitting room. She was clutching her mobile which Max had said he would call immediately with any news. A knock came at the door, and one of the staff, a young twenty something came in.

'Well, Molly, what is it?' Carys said impatiently. 'Can't you go to Denbeath for anything you need?'

'No, Madam,' Molly said firmly.

'Well what is it then?'

'Your baby was heard crying and...'

'Crying? Where is she?' Carys couldn't keep the panic from her voice.

'She was in your room, in her cot, but...'

'Well, what is Nanny Black doing then?' Carys was moving quickly towards the door. 'Get up there at once and tell her to go to the study, I'll see her there when I've got Amalie.'

'Well, that's the problem, Madam. Nanny Black is gone.'

'Gone? What do you mean *gone*, you stupid girl?'

Thomas rose at this last, and Florence got up too, rallying round the stricken woman.

'Where has she gone?' Florence demanded.

'I...I... don't know, but the other staff have been complaining about the baby crying for a few hours. We thought she was just not settling, then I went up to see if everything was alright, and she was still in her cot, crying. I took her down to Cook, who is looking after her.'

'And Nanny?' Florence snapped the question.

'Nanny Black has left, all her clothes seem to have gone, but... I found this...just sticking out from under the valance sheet on her bed.'

'Well, what is it?' Florence asked, as Carys snatched a piece of paper from the young woman's hand.

Molly looked directly at Florence. 'It looks like a page out of a diary, and it has writing on it, and...'

'And I suppose you haven't read it?' Carys snapped. Molly said nothing but averted her eyes.

'Yes, well thank you, Molly. You can go, and don't mention a word of this to anyone!' Florence said majestically.

'Yes, and the police will want to question you!' Carys was acrimonious, and as she turned her back, Molly burst into tears.

'Oh, leave the girl alone, Carys. It's not her fault.' Florence sat heavily, her bulk spreading into the corners of the upholstered Queen Anne chair. The door shut on Molly's sobs.

'It looks like a flight number.' Thomas was looking over Cary's shoulder.'

Carys looked at him in disdain. 'Don't be so rude. I will read out what it says!' Her haughty voice was high-pitched, and Thomas looked deflated.

'It looks like it could be a flight number,' Carys said, ignoring the slight chuckle from Florence and Sir Pierce. 'The writing is terrible, but it looks like...yes... flight from Inverness to Pisa, I think it says, hard to make out...'

Thomas looked mystified. 'But, why would she leave so suddenly?'

Florence looked at him almost pitifully, and said, 'we'd better let the police know.'

'Malcolm has been moved to Fort William.' The doctor spoke directly to Max, whom he knew. 'He needs specialised care, which we can't provide here.'

'And Olivia?' Max asked.

'She's doing okay. Shot wound to the side of her neck, just missed her right carotid artery, but she has had heavy blood loss. She's still unconscious, I'm afraid.'

'Okay, thanks, Dan. What about the baby?'

'Well, he's stable, but very ill. He has a severe chest infection, and two broken legs, due to being crushed, but he is beginning to respond to treatment.'

'Thanks again, Dan. Oh, and, you have my number to update me? I need to get to Fort William.'

'Of course.'

The Colonel, who had arrived at Dunlivietor hospital with the police, got in the car with Max, and Jim drove them to

Fort William. Dunlivietor hospital only had a few wards, and was not used to managing critical care patients. Fort William hospital was only forty five minutes down the road. In this instance, however, time was of the essence, and they travelled by helicopter used to lift people from the islands to the hospital.

Ailsa returned to Trannoch, her very bones weary and her head pounding with the whole episode. The police brought her back, and she went to the sitting room to give everyone the details. Max had phoned and updated them immediately after he spoke to Dan, but didn't expand. It was after eleven at night when she returned, and she was almost fainting with exhaustion. Florence sat her down and got a plate of food and a glass of wine, and forbade anyone to question her until she had eaten.

'Better?' Florence asked her kindly.

'Yes, thank you.' She told them about Malcolm being in a critical condition and moved to Fort William. The latest she had heard from Max, around ten minutes before, was that he was 'not doing too well'. Whatever that really meant, she did not know. Olivia had regained consciousness, and was reasonably stable. Little Freddy was very unwell, but was in good hands. She relayed the information almost word for word.

Carys came in at that point, went to the table and poured herself a glass of white wine. Ailsa looked at her in surprise. She was slightly bedraggled, her blonde sleek hair escaping from the 'roll' at the back of her head, and her usually impeccable make-up, a bit smeared.

'Where's Amalie?' Florence questioned.

'The assistant cook, Mrs Wilson, has her, in the room adjoining mine.' Carys took a swig of her wine, relaxed her shoulders, and sat down. 'She has agreed to step in. She has children of her own, who are grown-up now, but she soon settled Amalie.'

'What's happened?' Ailsa was confused.

Florence looked at her, with a perturbed expression. 'Ailsa, as though the day could not get any worse...'

'Oh my God, what now?' Ailsa sighed.

'Nanny Black has disappeared.'

'Disappeared?' Ailsa repeated confusedly.

'Well, it appears that around five o'clock, she took one of the Trannoch cars and left. She took all her belongings, and placidly passed the police at the gate, who recognised her as the Nanny, and didn't make a move to stop her. She was on the passenger list at Inverness airport, on a plane to Italy.'

'What the hell? What are the police saying?'

'Well the information is sketchy at the moment – so much is going on with the rescue of Freddy and everything, that Nanny Black is definitely not a priority.'

'But Italy? What is going on?' Ailsa took a gulp of her wine to try and calm herself down.

'Robbie Burnside is not saying too much. They are all back here, as you know. The one guy alive from the shoot-out is now in the only cell in Arnasaid Bheag police house. But Pierce, Thomas and I have been talking about it, and we have come to a conclusion, based on what we know.'

'And that is?'

'Nanny Black is in on it.'

A woman was drinking champagne on a flight leaving Heathrow, where flights from Inverness changed for Pisa. She smiled cynically to herself as she flicked unseeing, through an in-flight magazine.

They thought they were something, those MacKenzies, but she and her sister had shown them. She cast her mind back to the scene in the service station on the main road from Fort William. She had been waiting patiently for her sister, drinking tea like tar and watching the entrance, before making her way to the toilets. They had meticulously planned this escape, and it had come off like a dream.

'All clear, no one here!' her sister Joyce had called out, with a laugh, as she finished trying the last cubicle door in the toilets to find it empty. 'I've parked the car round the back of an empty building across the road. They won't find it for a few days, hopefully. Here's the stuff: tickets, some money, bag with a few changes of clothes.'

'Okay, thanks. And I'm being met at the airport?'

Joyce nodded. 'Yes, Mateo's friend will get you. I've got the flight number and times jotted down – where is that piece of paper?' She searched her bag and pockets, to no avail. 'Oh well, you won't need it. His name is Reano, and the flight info is on the tickets. I'll join you in a week or two, with enough money to set us up for life.' She was not an emotional woman, nor was her sister. They didn't hug or kiss in their parting, just nodded and went their separate ways.

Joyce bought a roll and bacon, and a cup of tea, before making her way to the bus stop across the road. She was on her way to Fort William ten minutes later, and sat quietly in a window seat, smiling triumphantly.

Sir Pierce, Florence and Ailsa slept in the sitting room. The others managed to go to their beds about two o'clock in the morning. Miss Cochrane came in looking for them and covered them with blankets as they lay on the sofas. She was distraught. Nothing like this had ever happened in any of their lives. Cocky made her way back to Denbeath's sitting room, where they each took a chair with a footstool, and pulled throws over themselves. They felt they needed to be together. They all slept with one ear open for the phone.

Max spoke in a voice that hardly sounded like his own. He came into the sitting room at around half past eight, just as the western sky was beginning to rise in a glory of red and orange. It had snowed during the night, and the freshness of the day seemed in direct contrast to the occupants of Trannoch, who had got through the night in a tumult of emotions.

The tide was turning.

Max went straight over to Ailsa and clung to her. His face was distorted with anguish and pain.

Malcolm was dead.

Chapter Twenty Two

The month of November blew in on a desperately cruel wind which blasted the land and tore ferociously through the pine-wooded mountains. The whole world felt wrong. The headland Ailsa walked each day was full of dark shadows. People were different. Everyone had been affected by the tragic events, not just the MacKenzies, but the wider community seemed to go about their daily business with a heavy heart and a look over their shoulders. There was a sense of change. There seemed to be a palpable lack of trust in visitors on whom the area depended. Increased security at both Trannoch and Storm Winds turned the historical homes into fortresses, casting a foreboding eye of scrutiny on everyone who passed through their three hundred-year-old gates. Freedom was talked about in the past tense.

The tide was turning. Malcolm was dead.

As death's dark veil shrouded Trannoch, each one of the MacKenzies struggled to comprehend the horror which was the culmination of the last few days. Malcolm dying was an unimagined tragedy none of them had foreseen. Each day that dawned would not contain Malcolm, the most flawed, charming, sinful, immoral, handsome man any of them had known. At each meal there would be an empty place, and in David, Melissa and Freddy's lives, there would no longer be a father. Whatever they all thought of the second son of Colonel MacKenzie, he had been a huge presence in all their lives. So far as was in his capacity to love, he had loved his children. He had latterly tried to show respect and contrition to his new wife. Malcolm had been very far from perfect, but each one of the MacKenzies felt deeply their loss.

Olivia was getting better by the day. She had come home from the hospital and was recuperating at Trannoch. DS Alec Smith had broken a bone in his neck, besides other injuries, and lay in hospital with a frame screwed into his skull and shoulders, keeping him steadfast while he slowly recovered. The Colonel was bearing up admirably with a calm acceptance. He thought it was largely because he had thought he would lose Malcolm to cancer, and had geared himself up to this fact sufficiently enough that he was able to cope with losing him now. He thanked God every day that his grandson had been saved, and he was immensely proud of Malcolm giving his life to save his own son. The Colonel was a soldier through and through, his mantra was being prepared to die for his country. To die saving your own son was the ultimate glory sacrifice. He just wished he had been able to do that for Malcolm.

Ailsa had cried with Max that night. She had taken a step back in her own recovery. The last few days – it seemed like weeks – had been so traumatic, but she knew that if Max was with her, they would get through it together. Florence and Pierce went back to Mhainaray, and Clem returned to Storm Winds to her own little apartment; Ailsa went back home too. This was after the police had concluded their investigation – the post-op had gone on for three weeks. During which time the children had been brought back from school to attend the funeral of their father and uncle. All the MacKenzie children were at Criandornoch, but for security reasons it was thought best to leave them there, away from the publicity and events at Trannoch. Two family liaison officers had been posted at the school, one to help David and Ryan, and the other, Melissa and Aria. They met with them each day, and supported them, updating them where necessary on events as they unfolded.

David and Melissa were fraught and distressed, David more so than Melissa. When he was young, he had practically worshipped his father, but sadly Malcolm's lifestyle had eroded much of the respect David had for him. Although the Colonel hadn't told them about the way in which their stepmother had conceived, they were both old enough to put two and two together. They knew that their father had been trying to reach out to them in the last year, this was largely down to Ailsa who had rammed the point home. David had forgiven his father a long time ago, but Melissa was less forgiving. She had grown close to Olivia since she came to Trannoch, and little Freddy too. She was not as mature as her brother, but she was highly perceptive, and she saw that Malcolm was genuinely trying to make amends with his new wife. Olivia had told the girl herself, he was really trying hard to be a good father to the baby, and was considerate and caring towards his wife. She had begun to change towards her father, although with her being away at school for most of the time, she didn't have much time to try and build bridges.

And now there was no time left.

The Colonel had been too preoccupied to notice Hunter was still under his roof. She had slowly slipped into the role of Lady of the House again, taking charge of the staff, ordering them about. She managed the hospitality of the police too, simply because she had designs on Det. Supt. Burnside. She found out he was a widower, and that was all she needed to begin what she considered to be a gentle flirtation with Robbie. He would have said it was blatantly obvious. Not that she would have minded if he had been married. Frustratingly, for her, he came across as a very moral man, and she had to tread carefully. He was immersed in the investigation, acting in the most professional and courteous manner. Hunter's meaningful glances weren't lost on him nor on the few police who had stayed for the post-investigation, though they wouldn't have dared even tease him about it. When Hunter handed him a cup of tea, she would delicately touch his hand. When she sat beside him, she crossed her legs so that her Gucci skirt rode high up her thigh, and when she wore a low cut blouse, she thrust back her shoulders as she walked past him. He knew exactly what she was up to, but acted oblivious to her charms. 'Stupid idiot doesn't know what he's missing,' she thought, as she picked up the tray and slammed the library door.

Nanny Black was not a nanny at all. Robbie soon got the low-down on her; Mateo De Luca, from his cell in the police house in Arnasaid Bheag, was only too pleased to tell them everything he knew about her. He knew it was too late for him now, the evidence was stacked against him and he was keen to trade information for some reduction in prison time. Her name was Joyce Whitelaw, and she had lived in Fort William most of her life. Her experience, which prompted the agency to take her on, was 'vast', and her character 'impeccable'. It was an easy trace for the cops. They found, in a matter of hours, the agency's due diligence on the new recruit had been nil. The nanny school she had apparently graduated from didn't exist. In truth, owning a small private nursery from her home for less than a year was her only background in working with children. She had no children of her own. On a recent holiday to Italy, Joyce Whitelaw had met with a woman who was Olivia's second cousin, living in the same town where the Franelli family had lived. The woman was Mateo's sister. He had said his family was ostracised by Alberto and his late wife. The truth was, they had been cast aside because they were petty criminals. The woman killed in the shoot-out, her husband shot through the head, and the only one of the three who survived was Mateo.

By coincidence, Joyce had taken a house next door to the De Luca family home, where all three lived with their elderly parents and mostly grown-up children, as was the custom still in Italy. Mateo found out from some guys he knew that Alberto Franelli's daughter, his second cousin, was now very rich and living in Scotland. Alberto couldn't resist telling his old pals how his beautiful daughter had captured a rich man. Mateo's sister had asked Joyce over one evening to join the family dinner after talking over the fence to their temporary neighbour. Joyce knew of the MacKenzies and had heard of the new Italian bride. Joyce had said they were so well known, practically ran the whole area of Strathkinnieford, that they were the talk of the whole of the North West. The De Lucas initially made plans to break into Trannoch, and also to see Olivia and forge some kind of relationship again. They did not know when they arrived in Scotland that Olivia had a baby. By this time Alberto had broken ties with his old pals.

The De Lucas had plotted with Joyce as they sat on the decking in the Scottish evening sunshine. It was Joyce who had suggested she apply to Trannoch to be a nanny. She knew how to handle babies and young children, and the De Lucas knew how to forge the necessary documents. Her nursery had been shut down. She was desperate for money. This seemed an easy way to get some.

Gennina had spotted them out the back of the hotel in Arnasaid, handling what she thought were guns, but Stephen Millburn had scoffed at this to the extent that she had dropped it, convincing herself she must have imagined it. Stephen had thought quite a lot about this too since the shootings, and he blamed himself in part, for the deaths. Roddy had suggested getting the police at that point, but Stephen had thought it had all been a figment of Gennina's normally over-active imagination. Nothing had been done.

But the De Lucas had made mistakes too. Their pent-up frustration with the bungled burglary attempts at Storm Winds, then Trannoch, and their anger at not being allowed to rent the Dower House for a longer period, led the two men to drive Ailsa off the road and into the loch. As time passed, their rage and sense of injustice grew. If the De Lucas hadn't been shunned by the Franellis, they might have a share in some of the money Olivia had sent abroad to her other relatives.

Joyce had furnished the De Lucas with information necessary to enable the kidnapping. The time of the Ghillies' Ball was chosen so they could come and take baby Freddy with relative ease, making sure the staff were all engaged in hospitality, and away from the back stair leading to the nursery. But she had reckoned without the firearm. She was genuinely distraught that Laura had been killed. They had acted on impulse. Joyce had told them Laura wasn't usually home before midnight on her nights off, and she had fully expected this to be the case. When she had met Mateo at the dry stone wall in the fog, she had told him she wanted out, and he knew he should have shot her then, but he wanted nothing to stand in the way of their £6M. At that point he decided 'Nanny Black' would get nothing.

The Colonel arranged to host a dinner for the police team before they departed. He was eminently grateful to them. He could see Robbie was a very good Detective Superintendent and wanted to give something back for the service they had done to the family.

Robbie was astounded. When he told Julie she immediately said, 'Count me out,' then changed her tune when Robbie told the others that he wanted everyone there, or he would, as he said, 'Kick their backsides.'

It was the evening before the police departed. They were in their respective rooms getting ready. Robbie was thinking about Hunter. She certainly was a beautiful woman. She was slim and tall, and her blonde hair and dark eyes were a stark contrast. He knew she had been coming on to him. He had enjoyed the flirtation, but was too professional to have any kind of dalliance while the investigation was on-going.

But now the investigation was over.

They gathered in the Great Room. It was over three weeks since the incident, and Malcolm's death. The whole family who had been through the kidnapping was there, including Florence and Sir Pierce, who had come back over from Mhainaray. Trannoch and Storm Winds each had security installed at their main gates, and two new nannies had been vetted and installed in the nursery to look after the MacKenzie babies.

Hunter managed to sit herself down beside Robbie. The cops were all sticking together, but the Superintendent moved over to let her sit down. 'How are you managing?' he asked, as she pulled the split in her silver full-length gown further up her leg. He felt his neck under his bow tie grow hot.

'Oh, I'm fine thank you, Superintendent, although it has been a very difficult three weeks as you can imagine.' Her voice was sultry and lent nothing to grief.

Carys was seated across from Florence, and next to Robbie and Hunter.

'So, what will you do with your time now, Superintendent?' Carys asked, with an eye to Hunter.

He hesitated before he answered. 'I will go back to my usual routine, I expect.' He smiled cautiously.

'So, what does that mean, where will you be drafted?' Hunter asked coquettishly.

'Well drafted isn't really the right expression,' he smiled at her, 'and to answer your question, Mrs MacKenzie, I will go back to Headquarters.'

Carys' beautiful turquoise eyes met his. 'Well, you have done a brilliant job for us, Robbie.'

'Thank you,' he said. He felt baited between the two women.

'Are you okay, Ailsa?' Max asked, as he looked at her frail appearance and limpid smile.

'Yes, don't fuss,' she said shortly.

'Okay, I just thought you looked a bit...fazed.'

'Fazed?' she repeated. 'What does that mean?'

'Well, just a bit out of sorts.' He fumbled for the words.

'I'm okay, Max.'

'Here if you need me,' he said shortly, and started a conversation with Noel.

Ailsa looked across at the interplay between Hunter, Carys and the Detective Superintendent. Had they no shame? Malcolm's funeral was only days ago, and yet they were acting as if nothing had happened, flirting openly with the cops. Now was not the time. She excused herself and left the room to visit the cloakroom. It was dark and eerie in the hallway, and she got the distinct impression someone was watching her. 'All these pictures of MacKenzie ancestors!' She shuddered. Just as she put her hand on the cloakroom door, she looked quickly down the long corridor and saw a silent black figure slip up the stair.

Robbie excused himself a few moments later and pressed the green button on his phone, even as his long legs strode across the room and out into the hallway. He switched on the light and walked slowly into the library as he talked.

'What do you mean, it's not her?' His voice came loudly through the open library door. As she left the cloakroom, Ailsa heard the voice and stopped in her tracks.

'Her sister? So, you're telling me she gave her sister her own passport, and she went to Italy on the flight instead of her? Shit, okay, I've only got a handful of officers here. Yes, we still have our arms...okay, so she may be on her way here?'

Ailsa went into the library, shutting the door behind her, as Robbie swung round. She spoke in a low, fearful voice.

'I...I think she's already here.'

Julie's phone buzzed and she looked at the screen with astonishment – a call from the Boss who had just left the room five minutes before. She stood up and walked to the side away from the table. She guessed something was up. 'Hi!' she said, too brightly, under the Colonel's frowning gaze. 'Okay, will do.' She signalled to the others, and they immediately left the table. 'Sorry Colonel, Det. Supt. Burnside wants to see us quickly about something, please excuse us?' She tapped Max on the shoulder. 'Dr MacKenzie, Ailsa wants to see you for something, nothing urgent!' Again, too brightly. 'Be back very soon!'

Max mumbled something about knowing Ailsa wasn't feeling too well, which was a well-timed coincidence, and they all left at the same time. The Colonel shook his head in annoyance, but went on with his meal, as did the rest.

'Who else is in the house apart from the nannies and babies in the nursery?' Julie asked, as they all stood around the ancient library table.

'What about the babies? Won't she be heading for them?' Max said, in an urgent voice.

'Robbie called them on one of the nanny's mobiles,' Ailsa said, 'and they've locked the nursery and adjoining bedroom doors.'

'Just the staff then.' Max thought carefully. 'Most of them are helping with the dinner and drinks.'

'Except Cocky!' Ailsa put her hand over her mouth.

'I thought she had gone back to Storm Winds?'

'She had, but Clem and I are here, and she didn't want to stay in the house herself after what happened, so I told her to come here! God! *I told her to come here!*'

'That's not your fault, Ailsa...' began Max, but Robbie needed the facts, and now was not the time for comforting conversations.

'Is her room downstairs?' Robbie asked quickly. Ailsa had told him about the silent figure she'd seen going up the stair.

'No, her room hadn't been cleared out properly since we were all here. It's on the first floor, beside...beside...'

'Beside the nursery,' Max finished, a look of strained anxiety on his face.

'Right, team, get armed, and we'll get up there.

'Sir?' Julie called out as she looked at the sign-in sheet for the guns. 'There's one missing.'

It was dark in the hallway, though a silent moon shone through the cathedral-like window on the main stairway. Robbie and Simmonds, the youngest cop, quickly made their way to the dining room to tell the family and staff in attendance, to stay where they were. Robbie would listen to no questions about what was going on, other than to say there was an incident at Trannoch, and they had to stay put, with Simmonds in charge. Max and Ailsa were fine and had stayed in the library. Max phoned the kitchen on the internal phone to tell the rest of the staff to stay there and lock the door until further notice. Robbie hoped his young officer could stand up to the Colonel, if he decided to take matters into his own hands.

They made their way up the silent stair in a well-practised formation, firearms held in two hands outstretched. Julie in front, three officers following and Robbie holding up the rear.

A tiny speck of light shone through the keyhole of the door. Julie gave a signal to Robbie, and he nodded. She knocked on the door. They all pressed their backs into the wall, just in time, as a bullet came flying through the ancient wood. Julie counted a silent 'three' with her hand out in front, and they sprang.

'Police! Put your weapon down! Put your weapon down!' The adrenalin was pumping through Julie's veins as they fanned into the room, first to the left, then right, until Julie and two of the officers were in front of her. Robbie and the other officer stayed either side of the open door, unseen.

Miss Cochrane was sitting on a wooden chair, her hands tied behind her, and a length of duct tape across her mouth. Joyce Whitelaw, otherwise known as Nanny Black, was standing behind her, holding a revolver to the older woman's temple. She was still and calm.

'Well, you took your time!' she said, almost cheerfully, her eyes wild with excitement. 'Now, why don't you three just put down your guns, and we can talk sensibly?'

'Put your weapon down!' Julie repeated.

Joyce laughed a manic laugh. 'I don't think so. If you don't put your guns down in the next few seconds, I am going to have to shoot this nice lady.' She smiled apologetically.

Julie gave a nod. 'Okay, okay, we'll put them down and you can tell us what you want.' The three very slowly put their guns down on the floor in front.

'I used to stay on a farm when I was young...' Joyce said conversationally. 'I used to shoot the rats in the barn for my Dad. I am a very good shot,' she added warningly.

'Okay, guns are down. Just tell us what you want us to do.' Julie spoke calmly.

'I want you to let Mateo go.'

Whatever they had expected her to say, it was not this.

Julie was playing for time. 'You mean Mateo De Luca?'

'Of course, Mateo De Luca!' she bit back with force, her temper rising. 'How many other Mateos do you have in custody?'

Julie tried to defuse her anger. 'Sorry, yes, okay, it was just...'

'Unexpected? That a mere nanny could have feelings for a man ten years younger than her?' The voice was rising again.

'Okay, okay, how do you want to do this?'

'You will all go in front of me, and I'll take her in front of me, just in case you decide to try and shoot me.' She smiled. 'Go, with your hands up high.'

'Okay guys, come on.' The two officers went first out the doorway, turned right, then Julie did the same. Joyce pulled Miss Cochrane to her feet and holding the back of her tied wrists, pushed her ahead of her, the gun pointing in front. She was concentrating on the officers in front of her, making sure that if any of them turned on her, she would be there first.

'You need to lower your weapon.' Robbie was calmly standing in the corridor in front of her.

She jumped, and fired directly at him, while Miss Cochrane was unceremoniously yanked to the ground by Julie.

The shot hit him square in the chest, the force knocking him back. Joyce turned her gun on Miss Cochrane. The other officer who had stayed in the corridor with Robbie was behind her. She did not know he was there. He fired, and Joyce fell to the floor.

Nanny Black was no more.

Robbie had been wearing a vest the same as his officers, and he got to his feet, unharmed. Miss Cochrane was helped to her feet, and the tape across her mouth removed. She looked ill with fear and exhaustion.

There came a distant rumble accompanied by shouts and screams, as the prisoners from the dining room ran out, much to the dismay of Simmonds, and up the stair. When Max heard them go, he headed them off, and ran up the stair in front. He took in the scene, then checked Joyce, and stood back up, relief flooding his face.

'She's dead.'

Chapter Twenty Three

Robbie Burnside and his team had moved out a week after Joyce Whitelaw died. Now that there had been another murder, he had another post-op to do, and that meant reports to be done and evidence to be gathered all over again. He was patting himself on the back for a successful double operation. His only casualty was Alec who would be a long time in recovery. He was a good lad, and definitely one of his top team.

He had briefed the Colonel the next day in the library, with Max, Noel, Thomas, Carys and Ailsa present.

'Her sister was practically identical to Joyce, although they were 19 months apart in age,' he began. 'She too, was unmarried, and latterly lived with Joyce, who we found out "had form".'

'Form?' Carys' supercilious voice raked Robbie's nerves.

'Sorry, she had been previously involved in crime.' Shocked eyes from round the table reached his own. 'There was an abduction of a child about ten years ago, from Fort William. They held him for days in a basement before he was found, and, although she was implicated, there was no evidence to prove she was part of it. The child's father was a rich Saudi businessman, who had several business dealings in the area. They wanted the boy for ransom. We managed to find him before the deal went ahead.'

'Oh my God.' Ailsa voiced what the others were thinking.

'Joyce's sister was apparently involved too, though neither of them could be charged. Joyce had persuaded her sister to go to Italy instead of her, lying low so that they could share the money which Joyce had promised would come after she returned to Trannoch and managed to kidnap whoever was available as a hostage, getting thousands of pounds she knew was in the safe at Trannoch.'

Then there was Mateo. Joyce had fallen hook, line and sinker for the Italian man who had taken her into their home and colluded with the Scotswoman over the initial plan to rob both Storm Winds and Trannoch, which snowballed very quickly into a kidnapping and murder charge laid straight at their door. When she came back to Trannoch, she had eluded the sophisticated security installed at the main gateway to the estate, and inserted the old code for the service entrance gate, easily making her way back into the house. Her sister hadn't exactly been difficult to trace in Italy – in fact it took the Italian police team hours rather than days.'

In the week that he and the team carried out the post-op for the latest murder, he had been with Hunter twice. The first time was the day after Joyce had been shot, when Robbie was feeling a bit low after the episode – it usually hit him the next day. He had analysed his every move, trying to see ways in which he might have prevented her death. He was alone in the library at one in the morning when she had brought him in a large whisky, and wearing a silk dressing gown which left very little to the imagination. He had always scorned men who said they had been 'handed it on a plate', which Robbie always found to be completely sexist and distasteful. Hunter hadn't so much 'handed it on a plate', but 'took it for herself', which he didn't resist as it was the best fun he had in years. They lay on the hearth rug in front of the roaring fire afterwards, drinking whisky and laughing like teenagers. She was so good looking, with the light of the fire on her face and dark sultry eyes.

The next day she ignored him. She even went so far, the following evening at dinner, to talk to him as if he were one of the staff. Robbie began to think she was devoid of emotion. He then pulled himself back from looking inwardly; he himself was unattached, and as he dissected his own part in their clandestine meeting, he began to feel very uncomfortable. He knew Hunter no longer had a connection with the Colonel, as she had been open about the fact she too, was single. Also, she had been about as secretive as the front page of a broadsheet about the Colonel's shortcomings. At this juncture, he didn't know what to believe.

The Colonel had insisted that the police team should join them for meals in the dining room, rather than the previous arrangements.

'So, Chief Superintendent, I hear you are leaving in a few days' time?' Hunter asked surreptitiously.

Robbie searched her face trying to find where she was with this conversation. This was not the face of the woman he had been intimate with the evening before. 'You've promoted me! It's *Detective* Superintendent,' he answered, taken unawares as she already knew his title, she had used it often enough, 'and yes, we will be out of here by Friday.

'May I ask a teensy weensy favour?' She saw him start at this and was satisfied with his reaction. 'Will you *try* and leave the library in the state in which you found it?'

'There is no need for that!' Came the megaphone tones of the Colonel. 'I am really grateful to Robbie and his team for looking after us for the time they spent here!' He was at a loss to wonder what Hunter thought she was doing.

'Of course, darling.' Hunter patted the Colonel's hand, as she eyed Robbie. 'It's just that I've been looking after them whilst they've been here, and they do tend to be rather messy.'

Robbie eyed her with a mixture of bewilderment and annoyance. Was she trying to cover up what had happened? If so, she was doing a damn good job of it.

He waited for her that night in the library, and she arrived just after eleven o'clock. This was Robbie's personal space in the evenings after his team had either gone to bed or gone out. This time she was fully clothed, and Robbie was seriously annoyed.

'What the hell do you think you are you doing?' he said, as she took her wine and sat by the fire. He joined her, pouring out a glass.

'I'm having a glass of wine. Why? What are you doing?' she said innocently.

'You know damn well what I mean. Are you playing me?'

'Like a fiddle...' she agreed, and she pulled him up from the chair, his mouth on hers as his wine glass crashed in the grate.

Robbie smiled when he thought of those two nights. She was beautiful, exciting and made his blood boil, in more ways than one, but she was not for him. Right now, he wasn't looking for a woman, but if he had been, she would be nothing like Hunter.

Robbie wanted substance over style.

Florence and Sir Pierce sat overlooking the Sound of Mhainaray as they sipped their wine. Like the rest of the family, they had been seriously affected by events of recent weeks, and now they were back at Mhainaray recovering after the latest episode.

'So, when do you want to do it?' Florence asked directly.

Sir Pierce arched his questioning eyebrow. 'Sorry? Do what?'

'Get married of course.' Her voice was full of impatience.

'Oh yes, that.' He smiled and nodded in his quirky fashion. 'What about New Year's Day?'

'No, later. Spring, perhaps?' she answered without reason.

'Yes, that would be very nice.'

'Nice? I don't want it to be *nice,* Pierce. I want it to be bloody fabulous!'

The family were on the gravel driveway at the front door to say goodbye to the police. Hunter was conspicuous by her absence. Robbie shook hands with the Colonel, then the sons and finally Carys and Ailsa, who had been summoned by the Colonel to come and say cheerio. She had gladly driven over that morning.

As they got into their car, Hunter ran out of the doorway and straight to Robbie's vehicle, thrusting her hand in his window to shake. He took her hand and felt the post-it stick to his palm. A mobile number was scrawled upon it. He smiled to himself.

'Sorry, Colonel, I was busy and didn't realise the time.' She turned her dark eyes on him.

'Hrrrumph. Well, very well,' he conceded, completely oblivious to her action, or her 'little affair' as she herself called it, with Robbie. She was determined to see him again.

Robbie was determined to forget all about her.

The children's Christmas party went ahead much later this year, and it was again hosted at Storm Winds. The Colonel felt he couldn't have it at Trannoch as a mark of respect to his son, and the nanny, Laura, who had been the first victim. The Colonel had Laura's family visit Trannoch and gave them afternoon tea and an undisclosed sum of money, to cushion the terrible blow. She was their only child. They told the Colonel in no uncertain terms that they didn't want or need his money; none of the MacKenzies were responsible for the crimes which had taken their beloved daughter from them.

The Colonel had insisted in his own inimitable way, and they eventually accepted, saying they would set up a little garden of remembrance for Laura, near the shore in Arnasaid.

Malcolm lay in the crypt in the grounds of Trannoch, with his first wife Belinda and the MacKenzie ancestors. It was a beautiful little building, with a magnificent stained glass window depicting St. Andrew. It was attached to the tiny chapel which was no longer used for worship by the family, but where Malcolm and some of the family used to go occasionally to reflect. Little had Malcolm known on his last visit, just after Belinda died, that he would be interned quite so quickly inside its ancient walls.

Max and Ailsa walked the headland together, for the first time since the murders, and continued the path all the way round to Arnasaid. Clem stuck her head out the door of her tiny cafe as they approached, and pulled them inside.

'Look who I have here!' she smiled, and moved aside to show Connie and Calum, Jan and Gregory sitting at a table loaded with sandwiches, cakes and Prosecco.

'Ailsa, darling!' Connie jumped up. Ailsa burst into tears.

'God, honey, what's wrong?' Jan asked in concern. There was only one other table occupied in the cafe, and they got up to leave when they grasped with a smile what appeared to be an emotional reunion. Clem immediately locked the door and turned the 'closed' sign.

Max pulled over a chair for her, as they all rallied round.

'Get her a drink.'

'Here's a plate too.'

'Like a hanky?'

'Come on, out with it, what's wrong?' wound up Connie.

'Sorry.' Ailsa looked shamefaced. 'I'm just a bit emotional, and it's really good to see you.'

'Well, if that's good, can't wait to see what great looks like!' Jan said, and they all laughed, pulling over another table so they could all sit down.

'How was the honeymoon?' Ailsa asked, as she sipped her Prosecco.

'It was good thanks, but we thought about you all the time. It was so good of you to lend us your villa...' Calum answered for Connie as she had just stuffed a cake into her mouth. She swallowed, and looked at her friend.

'What about you two?' Connie spluttered through sponge. 'Max, I am so, so sorry about Malcolm.' They all rushed to offer their condolences while Max thanked them with a quiet dignity.

'But what about the murders!' Jan couldn't wait to say. 'We followed it on TV and the press. It must have been absolutely horrendous!'

'It was, and now the police have all gone, their investigation complete, and we're carrying on with our lives,' Ailsa said, very firmly drawing a line under the conversation. They all looked a little deflated at this. 'Maybe we could discuss it another time when I'm not such an emotional wreck?'

'Of course, we will, Ailsa,' Clem answered, with an eye to Connie and Jan who were just itching to get 'all the goss'. 'I asked the four of them here for Christmas, Ailsa, I thought you could do with a nice surprise.'

'Where are you staying?' Max asked with a smile, and Ailsa pounced on him immediately as he knew she would.

'They're staying with me! They always do! Don't be an idiot, Max! You'll all come back home with me.' Ailsa gave a watery smile.

'Home to Storm Winds.'

Chapter Twenty-Four

It was Christmas Eve at Storm Winds. Ailsa and Max were in the library. Connie and Jan had gone to Calum's parent's house for a party, which was to last all afternoon and evening. They had invited Ailsa and Max, but they preferred to spend a quiet evening at home. The fire was roaring and they were both reading. It was about four o'clock, and the open windows showed a white glow of hard frost outside. The wind was howling down the chimney. It was a comfortable companionable silence between the two, the elements taking centre stage.

Max yawned. His crossword fell from his knee to the floor, and he made no attempt to pick it up. Ailsa turned her book upside down on her knee, to keep the page, and studied his face. He smiled at her and said, 'Fed up with the book?'

'No, not really, just thinking about things.'

He nodded. 'Me too. You know, this has been a terrible year, and a wonderful year.'

'The best of times and the worst of times,' she softly quoted.

'You know, the whole thing with the kidnapping, and little Freddy?'

Ailsa answered sarcastically, 'Yes, I do remember that...'

'Very funny. Well, I think it really puts the whole baby question on a different footing.'

Panic flushed her face. 'You don't mean you don't want a baby? You're not going to make me go through all that again...' her brows were knitted in anxiety.

'Absolutely not. It's just that it puts things into perspective, life and love, and babies and stuff like that.'

'Stuff like that?' she laughed scornfully. 'Dr MacKenzie, your vocabulary and sentence construction are appalling.'

Max grinned. 'I know, sometimes I just can't find the right words. But I actually think I was right to be honest in the beginning and say that I was unsure, about having a baby I mean. Because, after what has happened, I am absolutely sure now that I want to have a baby with you, Ailsa.'

Tears filled her eyes, and she scrubbed them away. 'Well, gee, thanks!' she said, in a mock American accent, and ducked as he threw a cushion at her.

'That's what I get for trying to be nice and romantic.'

She chuckled. 'You are nice and romantic. You're the nicest and most romantic MacKenzie I know.'

'Thanks for nothing,' he grinned, as he picked up his crossword.

A little knock came at the door, then Cocky came in with a tray, upon which was a plate of cakes, a pot of tea, and a bottle of red wine with three glasses. Ailsa had persuaded her to join them. She no longer thought of the housekeeper as such, after the events which had tainted the last few months. She knew that Cocky was a very firm member of the Storm Winds family, and more of a mother to Ailsa than Hunter had ever been or would be.

It was obvious that it would be easier for Ailsa to accept this new arrangement, than Miss Cochrane, as she stood filling two plates for them, pouring out tea and filling the glasses with a very nice Merlot. Only then did she sit and help herself.

Cocky was eyeing the two of them quietly before she garnered her courage to speak.

'I...I...er wondered...if I could...'

Ailsa and Max stopped eating and looked at her agog.

'Whatever it is, of course you could!' Ailsa said, with a wide smile. Max chuckled.

'Ailsa, let Cocky speak!'

Miss Cochrane drew in her breath. 'Well, I have invited someone over to have tea with us...with me...with you and me.' Ailsa had never seen her blush, but she was pink now.

'*Really?* Who is it? I'm seriously intrigued!'

'Ailsa...' Max sounded as if he was talking to one of his children. She ignored him.

'Well?' Ailsa prodded.

Another knock came at the library door, and Eileen came in. 'Hi Ailsa!' she said cheerily. 'A visitor for Co...er... Miss Cochrane!' and she motioned him into the room.

'Denbeath!' Max said, as he stood and shook hands with the man he had known all his life. Ailsa got him a chair and he joined them by the fire, as Eileen left with a smile, pulling the library door closed behind them.

Thoughts were tumbling furiously through Ailsa and Max's minds as Denbeath sat there, looking as uncomfortable as he could be, wishing that he was anywhere else but here. The silence lasted, until Eileen clattered into the room again, with another teacup and glass, then winking at Cocky conspiratorially, clattered back out again.

Ailsa studied the two carefully. *What was going on here?* she wondered.

'Thank you for allowing James...er...Denbeath, to join us,' Cocky said nervously, and uncharacteristically filled herself another glass of wine and took a huge gulp.

Max was amused. He knew what was happening, and he sat comfortably prepared to let them have their moment. 'Very nice to have you here, Denbeath.'

'Thank you, Sir,' the butler said automatically.

'Oh, don't call him Sir!' Ailsa laughed. 'Anyway, is there something you want to tell us?'

'Yes.' Miss Cochrane drew herself up as she said, 'James and I are going to get married.'

'I knew it!' Ailsa spilled her wine all over the sandwiches in her excitement as she leapt up and hugged her beloved Cocky. James looked mortified, as she hugged him too.

'Ailsa, look what you've done!' Cocky had on her housekeeper hat.

'Oh, to hell with that! I'm so excited!'

Max laughed at her, glad to see her in high spirits once again.

They all settled down. 'Where? When? Where are you going to live?' It was Ailsa, of course, bombarding Cocky with questions.

'Well, we have discussed this and decided that we will both live here, if that's alright with you, Ailsa? I have my apartment here.'

Ailsa looked at Max, and they smiled at each other. 'I guess the Colonel will just have to find another butler then!' Max said firmly.

'No, Sir. If the Colonel will still have me, I will still retain my position at Trannoch.'

'And I mine, here,' Miss Cochrane said, smiling at Ailsa, whom she loved as her own.

'But Denbeath! er...James! How much longer do you want to work there? I mean you've been there all your life, now is *your* time! You're not getting any younger, you must be about...'

'Ahem, well, we'll not talk about that now,' Max interrupted Ailsa.

'And you, Cocky,' she said affectionately. 'You don't need to be housekeeper to me anymore, just enjoy your retirement!' She was persuasive, but Cocky was having none of it.

'Absolutely not, Ailsa. We both have jobs we love, and it keeps us young. We will still have a good life.' A gentle tear slipped from her eye as Denbeath reached out and clutched her hand in his.

Christmas Day was a celebration of two lives well lived. Ailsa had thrown a party for all the staff at Storm Winds and Trannoch. Ailsa's friends were all invited, and of course no party at Storm Winds would be complete without the MacKenzies, so they had been invited too. Max's kids and the other children were there, and Melody and Dougie. Florence and Sir Pierce were staying at Trannoch for Christmas, and they had also come along, with Hunter at the Colonel's heels. Olivia was there, and both Freddy and Amalie were brought in by the two new nannies. Freddy's casts were now off, and he was beginning to find his feet.

They made quite a crowd. The biggest sitting room, which was only occasionally used, had been set with a magnificent Christmas tree and decorations, a garland over the fireplace which Eileen had made that morning. The room smelled of musk and mulled wine.

The evening began with a speech, and Ailsa took centre stage. She told them how happy she was for Miss Cochrane and Denbeath and of how she wanted everyone to share in the celebration of their engagement. She talked briefly about them both, then surprised them by saying,

'And just before our happy evening begins, I want to give an early wedding present to the happy couple! To you, Cocky, and to you, James, I would like to gift you the Dower House as your own.' The older couple looked stricken, amazed and delighted all at once, and more than one tear was shed as the applause rang out.

As they all turned to start the party, Max gave her a hug and an affectionate kiss. 'Well done, Ailsa,' he said simply.

Hunter's face was a picture at this announcement. 'Well, that's you lost a house if I decide to kick you out again!' The Colonel said to her, as she stood by his side. She wasn't sure if this meant she could stay at Trannoch, or not. She thought she had better lie low for a while.

Jean Morton had been in the kitchen cooking most of the day with Cocky, Ailsa and Jan's help. Connie got off with doing anything in the kitchen as she protested she couldn't cook. Luckily for her, Jan agreed this was the case.

'These are awfy guid wee cakes,' Jean said, looking at Jan.

Jan smiled. 'Well, I can give you the recipes if you like, and you can make them for Ailsa's tea!'

'Great idea!' Ailsa said as she munched. She loved Jan's cakes. Then as she saw Jean's expression, she hastened to add, 'Of course, your baking is always scrumptious Jean, but these are nice for a change!' She winked at her friend.

'Aye, well, write a few of them doon, and I can hae a wee look,' Jean conceded.

The buffet was fit for a King, or even a MacKenzie. Lots of champagne was drunk, and lots of party games, singing and dancing filled the room as they all had a brilliant time. About half past nine, presents were given out, and the babies toddled and crawled about the floor, playing with Christmas paper and boxes. Max took Ailsa's hand, and led her out to the hall.

'Get your coat,' he said, with a grin.

Ailsa, looked at him in surprise. 'Coat? Max, what are you up to? I can't just walk out on my guests,' but she put on her red coat anyway. He picked up a bag from the hall floor.

'Why the bag? Where are we going? Max, its freezing! Are we going in the car somewhere?'

Max turned and kissed her on the cheek, and took her hand again, as they walked out.

'What have you got in the bag?'

'A picnic,' he said with a smile, walking in the direction of the headland.

'A picnic? Max are you off your head? Its freezing. Its Christmas, and I couldn't eat another thing!'

'It's more of a drinks picnic.'

There was nothing for her to say to that.

They came to the headland, to the spot where they had first kissed.

'Aha! You think it's our anniversary of getting together, don't you?' Ailsa smiled triumphantly. 'Well, sorry to burst your bubble, Doc, but you're a week early! It was Hogmanay!'

'I know.'

He moved over to a big boulder, stooped down to the bag and took out a tartan shawl. He spread it on the rock. He gave a little funny bow, and pointed to the rock. 'May I have the pleasure of your company?'

She laughed, and he looked out to sea. 'Oh, what's that?' he suddenly said, and Ailsa, completely taken in, turned to look. When she wheeled back round he was down on his knees.

'Max! Are you okay? Did you fall...?'

He reached into the inside pocket of his Parka, and took out a small box. He took her hands. She now understood, and a whole wave of emotions swept through her.

'Will you marry me, Ailsa?'

She laughed and cried at the same time as he took out a ring with a square diamond which was probably worth more than Max's yearly wage. But Max didn't work as a GP for the money. He slipped it onto her finger.

'Of course I will, you idiot!' she said in a shaky voice. 'Now get up off that ice, and kiss me.'

He did.

Max poured out the champagne into glasses he had taken from the bag, his own eyes glistening with what looked suspiciously like tears.

'What an old romantic you turned out to be, Max!'

'Me? I've always been a romantic, deep, deep, inside. Listen, you won't know what's hit you now. You've only scratched the surface on the romance front.'

She burst out laughing and slapped him on the arm. 'Shut up!' she chuckled.

'We'll keep this to ourselves until after Christmas,' he said, suddenly serious, 'I don't want to steal Cocky and Denbeath's thunder.'

'James's thunder,' she corrected.

They sat there looking across to Skye, and the Cuillin range which could be seen with its jagged ridge, framed by a navy blue, star filled sky.

The tide was turning.

'Rest in peace, Malcolm.' Ailsa and Max raised their glasses. So much had happened that year that they could hardly keep up with events as they unfolded. Their heads were close together as Max spoke their thoughts out loud.

'So many changes, so many tragedies.'

'And so many things to celebrate.' Ailsa glanced at her new ring. They heard the gentle lap of the water below. 'The tide's turning. You know, it's almost a metaphor for how all our lives have changed in the last year.'

'You know, you can be quite poetic when you like,' he laughed. 'Come on, let's get back to the party!' He helped her up, and they kissed under the stars.

So many changes. So many had gone before. So many were still to come. Ailsa and Max walked back hand in hand to Storm Winds, as the tide turned.

The End

Acknowledgements

I would like to thank my lovely Mum, who is sadly not with us now, but who has been and has meant everything to me, in terms of my writing, and throughout my life. The rest of my family for their support of my work, especially Emma and Ian.

Margaret and Dan Miller.

My lovely friends, especially Myra.

Chris Bryce of Spotlight Editorial.

A senior detective; an amazing, knowledgeable friend. He has steered me through the police scenes, and has helped me understand the brilliant work the police force carry out in Scotland. Thank you.

Leila Green from I_AM publishing for her true professionalism, help and support.

Michelle Fairbanks of Fresh Design, my wonderful cover designer, for her talent and continued patience.

About the Author

Fiona H. Preston was born and brought up in South Lanarkshire in Scotland, and still lives there now. Having worked for most of her life in a large corporate organisation, she decided to leave that world and concentrate on her writing. She has a BA Hons in Humanities. Her interests are many and varied, including music, amateur dramatics and collecting childrens' books and she has travelled extensively in the UK and Europe. Her favourite place is the North West of Scotland where this story is set. She shares her life with her close family and friends and her two Yorkie dogs.

To find out more about the author visit her website: fionahpreston.co.uk

Printed in Great Britain
by Amazon